AN OLIVE GROVE IN ENDS

AN OLIVE GROVE IN ENDS

MOSES McKENZIE

LB

Little, Brown and Company
New York   Boston   London

Copyright © 2022 Moses McKenzie
Hughes family tree copyright © 2022 Femi McKenzie

Little, Brown and Company
Hachette Book Group
1290 Avenue of the Americas, New York, NY 10104
littlebrown.com

First North American Edition: May 2022
Published in the United Kingdom by Wildfire, an imprint of Headline Publishing Group, an Hachette UK Company, April 2022

Little, Brown and Company is a division of Hachette Book Group, Inc. The Little, Brown name and logo are trademarks of Hachette Book Group, Inc.

The publisher is not responsible for websites (or their content) that are not owned by the publisher.

The Hachette Speakers Bureau provides a wide range of authors for speaking events. To find out more, go to hachettespeakersbureau.com or call (866) 376-6591.

ISBN 978-0-316-42014-3
Library of Congress Control Number: 2021950351

10 9 8 7 6 5 4 3 2 1

MRQ-T

Printed in Canada

*For Ty, my little man. I wrote this for you
so I pray you feel this. I thought we had years left.*

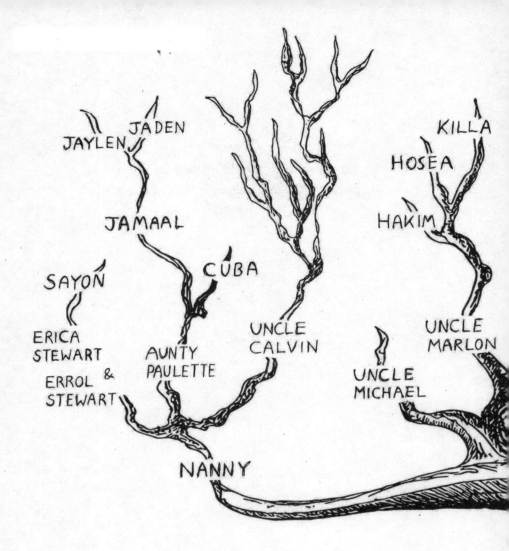

JAYLEN   JADEN

KILLA

HOSEA

JAMAAL   HAKIM

SAYON   CUBA

ERICA
STEWART   UNCLE
CALVIN   UNCLE
MARLON

ERROL &   AUNTY
STEWART   PAULETTE   UNCLE
MICHAEL

NANNY

HUGHES FAMILY TREE

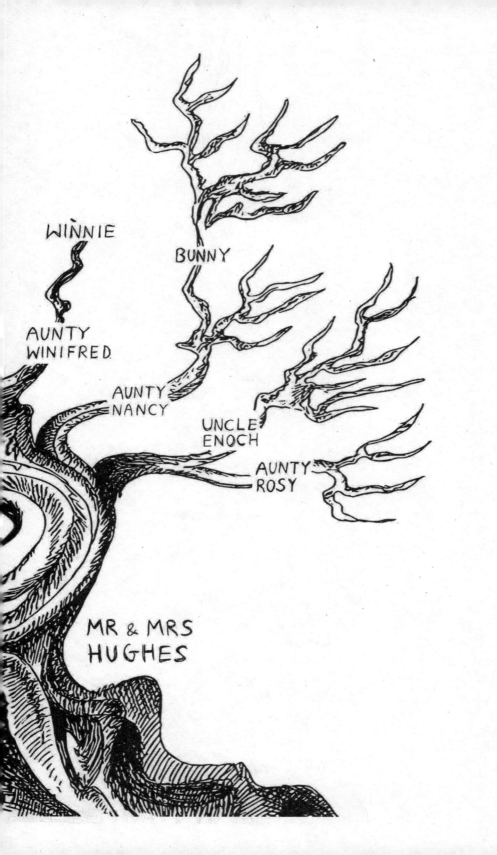

1

Look at the birds of the air, for they neither sow nor reap nor gather into barns; yet your heavenly Father feeds them. Are you not of more value than they?

– Matthew 6:26

This is a story, much like any other, of ends and beginnings. Like any story, it is hard to know where to begin. But I think it makes sense to start at home, or a home. Actually, it might be more accurate to call it a house; one that stood alone atop Mount Zion, overlooking Leigh Woods, the Avon Valley and the muddy river that wound beneath.

'Dis is the yard,' I told Cuba, as we waited at its bourn, 'the one man's marge showed man when man was a young buck.'

The Bath stone house in the area known as Clifton was all original features; sash windows and working shutters. It had a vestibule and behind it a long plot of land that tripped and fell into the woods like the Hanging Gardens of Babylon. It could have been plucked from a fairy tale about two adventurers who had stumbled across the city of God. The front of the house was gated, guarded by statuette men from all nations clothed in white robes and carrying palm fronds. And in the middle of the driveway sat a fountain of living water.

'It's rah massive,' Cuba said. And I understood his astonishment. It was a world away from the one we knew. Even if we owned the yard next to Nanny's and knocked it through, it wouldn't have reached half the size.

We left our push bikes by the fountain and helped each other over the fence and into the back garden. 'Do you know who lives here?' Cuba asked. I shook my head. 'Dey must be up doe, init?'

'Must be.'

My mama used to bring me to this house when I wasn't much older than a toddler. We wouldn't come inside – she wasn't as brazen as Cuba and me – we would only drive to the gate, and she would point up at the windows and tell me how she would imagine herself looking out of them when she was but a child herself.

She would cycle into Clifton and across the Suspension Bridge just to look at the yard. There were other houses on the road, for it was narrow with many mansions, but it was this one that caught her eye. It was the furthest from the street, she explained, as far from the hustle and bustle as one could get.

'You know man's gonna live here someday, cuz,' I announced.

Cuba screwed his face; he didn't mean to doubt me, but he wasn't accustomed to dreams. 'How you gonna buy dis yard, akh? You need White people ps to buy dis – big man ting.'

'Don't watch dat,' I told him. 'Man'll find a way, truss me.'

Cuba put his arms across his little chest and huffed in the manner of a man about to embark upon yet another noble quest. 'Say no more, g, but if you're gonna buy it den man'll help you, init. Dat's what family's for.'

In the back garden the sun caught in the shade and couldn't strike the grass, but its efforts were rewarded with a mellow air that had paid no mind to the weather elsewhere. The grounds were vast, with streams that led from pond to pond, fruit trees and countless flowering shrubs.

'You know deh's horses in the woods, init?' I said, repeating what my mama had told me all those years ago.

'Horses?'

'Yeah, fam. White horses. And my marge told man dat Jesus rides on white horses, blud.'

'I bet dey would sell for ps den, init?' Cuba muttered. We fell silent as we thought about how many packets of sweets we could buy for a white horse that even Jesus would ride. 'You reckon we could sell dem?' he whispered.

I shrugged, and climbed into the low branches of a tree close to a pond. Cuba picked fallen twigs from the base and threw them as far as he could; they broke the surface of the water and floated idly. 'Only if you can catch dem first.' We looked at each other, the fire in our eyes ablaze like jasper stones, then we raced to the bottom of the garden and through the cast-iron gate at its foot.

We spent the entire afternoon chasing the shadows of those white horses, but we didn't catch the swish of a tail, nor the print of a hoof. We returned to the house-atop-the-hill downcast and defeated. I found my place in the tree again, and Cuba took up the twigs.

The water that ran from pond to pond had no foul smell. It was lazy, like a river of clarified honey. I thought if I knelt to taste it I might have refreshed myself after such a disappointing day, but Cuba had other ideas. He pointed toward the house. 'Yo, you wanna see what's inside?'

'How?' I asked.

He took a large stone from a rockery beside the pond and tossed it through the basement window. 'Watch what you're doing, blud!' I yelled. 'Don't break man's yard!'

Ready to run, we waited on tenterhooks for the sound of an alarm, but none came. 'Dis shit's so old,' Cuba said after a minute, 'man knew it wouldn't even have no security, fam.'

'What about my window, blud? Why'd you do dat?'

'Dey'll fix it before you buy it, g, don't worry,' Cuba grinned, 'and if dey don't, I'll send you some ps to cover it. It's calm, bro. We're in dis together, remember? Come, fam.' He swept the broken slivers from the window with his sleeve and we wriggled through a slit wide enough only for ten-year-old boys.

Inside were high ceilings, grand fireplaces, reception halls and drawing rooms. Whoever the owners were, they had spared no expense. Marble floors like sheets of glass. Huge chandeliers in each room. Cushions and carpets from countries outside of any I knew. The kitchen was stocked with an astonishing array of meats, a thousand jars containing every delicacy from marmalades to capers, an assortment of breads and cheeses, a cupboard full of sweet stuffs and an oven bigger than both of us.

And the bedrooms: they could have slept a hundred refugees. It was the first time I saw a pantry and a laundry room. The first time I'd travelled up four flights of stairs not in a block of flats. And that day I realised, more than ever, why my mama had fallen in love with the place; it was perfect – the perfect home.

'What do you reckon dese man do to afford all dis, cuz?' Cuba asked. 'You reckon dey shot?' He appeared in the doorway behind me with two watches hanging from his arm. He'd had to push them up to his elbow to keep them in place. Cuba handed me one as I handed him some food from a cupboard.

The watch was gold like the sofas in the living room and had four faces that ticked at different speeds and pointed to different measures of time. I pocketed it because finders keepers and losers weepers.

We spent the evening exploring the house, eating from the fridge and napping on the beds. We lived like kings until the day grew old and voices came from outside, adult voices. Cuba gripped my arm and we crept to the front door.

Outside, grown-ups were pointing at the house and a fed was crouched over the bikes. The adults told the officer that they were good friends with the owners, who were weekending, and that they had heard a crash out back and nothing since.

Cuba's grip tightened. 'Yo, we need to cut, g,' he whispered. We bolted back through the broken window and lost the law in the woods. From there we ran home, back to Ends. And a decade passed until I reached my twentieth year.

To everything there may have been a season, but some things remained unchanged and I wouldn't rest until I owned that house-atop-the-hill.

2

Enter by the narrow gate; for wide is the gate and broad is the
way that leads to destruction, and there are many who go in
by it. Because narrow is the gate and difficult is the way which
leads to life, and there are few who find it.

– Matthew 7:13–14

There are roads in neighbourhoods like mine all across the
country. Broad roads. Without mansions. In England they have
names like City Road or High Street, except this road was called
Stapleton, and those familiar with her charm might call her Stapes.

They were broad roads because they tracked their way
from one side of Ends to the other. Ends was what we called
our neighbourhood, or any neighbourhood like ours. I wasn't
sure of the reason, whether it was because it was where the
downtrodden saw the light at the end of the tunnel, or because
once you arrived you only left when those in charge wanted to
rebrand. Either way, it was stuffed to the gunwales with people
trying to make ends meet, so the name made sense.

It was a far cry from Clifton.

The moment you left the city's centre you could hear or
smell Ends, whether you took a left after Stapes, or carried

straight through Old Market. The sounds were disorderly. It smelt non-White. It was the other side of Abbey Road and industrial wastebins that were padlocked in other neighbourhoods hung and stank like open stomachs. You could find a million dreams deferred in the torn slips that littered outside the bookie's.

I loved and hated this road.

It would always have a place in my heart, a certain fondness I kept in acknowledgement of how it had shaped the man I had become. I had grown to know Shona right here too, and for that I was truly grateful. Still, I hated it because there was nowhere I was better known, a fact I would soon come to find more troublesome than I'd ever imagined. And nowhere was there a greater example of how much pain we could normalise as human beings.

The road was patrolled by young and old: abtis arranged tables outside cafés, serving tea from pans; they peered into the faces of young hijabis, trying to find a likeness and match daughter to hooyo. Their sons and nephews stood outside corner shops and met at park benches, and together with my cousins, they were watched by the disapproving eyes of our respective elders.

I belonged to the Hughes family. The infamous Hughes family – known to police and hospital staff across the city. Except in truth, I was a Stewart. It was the name written on my birth certificate, and it was my papa's name, but I owed it no allegiance.

Usually, the women in the Hughes family kept their surname if they ever married – which they did, several times – but my mama, Erica, had been all too quick to rid herself of such a burden. That was how my mama viewed any attachment to her maiden name. She twisted the familial bottle cap and poured past relationships down the drain like a wino intent on betterment. She had tried to impart her ideology on to me, but I was Hughes through and through.

A long time ago she had forsaken her desire for the house-atop-the-hill and, as a teen, had wed my papa, then a trainee pastor. And now, much to the mockery of our family, she was a pastor's wife and worship leader and had inherited two names instead of one. Like new shoes, Sister replaced Mrs, and Stewart ousted Hughes.

I had more cousins than rivers had rivulets, and like a doting stepmother, Stapes took us all in. A few of my aunties had council houses on the offshoots, and I think I had a cousin or two in the high-rises that overlooked the toings and froings of the busy road. Those who didn't live nearby could be found on Stapes more often than in their own homes – at Nanny's, in Ladbrokes or one of the yard shops, buying cassava and plantain. My likkle cousins might be found at the blue cage playing ball, and the elders might be at one of the free houses tossing dominoes and talking about things they knew nutun about.

My cousin Winnie called the street itself home. She slept on the baptist church steps and begged cigarette stubs from the gutter. She said she found the gutter more giving than the people passing, but maybe the people passing had nutun left to give.

I sailed the pavements in June as one accustomed to the breaks in the concrete. I swayed clear of battyman poles and touched fists with those who knew me well enough to acknowledge me, but not enough to ask how I was. And even if they had asked, I would've lied and said all was well.

My cousin Bunny spotted me from across the street and touched his hand to his heart, then to the sky. I returned his salute and we kept it pushing.

Bunny was a funny one, unpredictable like the weather. If there was a child in Ends without a father, we said it was Bunny's yute. He was to women what Vybz was to Jamaica's youth – at least that's what he thought.

He called himself the Garfield Sobers of infidelity.

Once, not long before my twentieth summer began, I had seen him sprawled across a bus stop, hair half-cornrowed, tracksuit at his knees, with Winnie asleep on his thigh and a crack pipe in his hand. He'd looked at me through glass eyes but I didn't tarry. The next morning I saw him at the helm of an empty pram, walking through Cabot Circus in a cheap suit with two of his yutes on either side. His arm was linked with a young woman's who wasn't either of their mamas, and he held a brick phone to his ear with his shoulder.

I didn't take more than ten steps before bumping into my next relation. Side-stepping a shrivelled Kurd who shuffled with his head down and his hands held behind his back, I encountered the wide bosom of Aunty Paulette.

Aunty Paulette was my mama's younger sister and she had spent much of her life inside. She wore a fistful of gold rings and one of them chains from Claire's with the letter 'P' in bold italics. Her favourite thing to do was to jam her finger into older men's chests and tell them that she was twice the man they were.

'Wahum, Sayon,' she said, busy picking sup'm from her teeth with her tongue. 'Stand up straight wen mi ahh chat to yuh nuh man, yuh shoulders deh slouch an yuh look miserable, yuh just ahh ruin di day energy man, chuhh. Yuh see Bunny? Mi affi chat to im.'

I told her where I'd seen him.

'Who im deh wid?'

I told her he was alone.

'Good. Mi av ahh bone fi pick wid im, enuh.' She then proceeded to pick the bone with me. Apparently Bunny had borrowed a twenty sheet from her last week and was refusing to pay her back. Aunty Paulette had been forced to borrow the money from Nanny and now Nanny was at her neck because she couldn't play her numbers.

I struggled to appear concerned. I had some change on me, a little less than a grand – my aunty knew that – why else would she complain to her nephew? I took a ball of money from my pocket and unwound the elastic bands keeping the notes together. The house fund wouldn't miss it, so I gave her two twenties and suffered the kiss she planted on my cheek.

'Tenk yuh, Nephew,' she drawled, tucking the money into her brassiere and pushing the words over and around the mint in her mouth. 'Yuh keep outtah trouble now, yuh ear?' And just like that, Aunty Paulette was gone. Gone to inflict an earful upon the next man that eyed her the wrong way or looked at her rear a little longer than she liked.

The end of a dual carriageway split Stapes in two. If the first part was mini-Mogadishu or bantam-Hargesia, the second (top side) was likkle Kingston: more bookies, barbers and chicken shops, more billboards and men sat low in coupés with dark windows.

There was a Pakistani-owned wig shop selling Brazilian hair to West African women. Across the street, their ill-mannered Caribbean competition saw less custom. Further up the road, on the corner of a branching avenue, blue-and-white police tape cordoned off the footpath where I'd taken Cordell's life not two days ago.

The difference between where I lived and where I wanted to

be living was laughable. I wrung my hands as I walked and comforted myself with the knowledge that I would be rid of the filth soon; all I had to do was remain free.

The attending officers who were standing beside the tape scanned the crowds, looking for admissions of guilt in the dark faces of passing strangers, but I made it impossible for them, or anyone else watching, to read my trepidation. As ever, there was bop in my stride and a bounce to my gait, but my mind was split, contorted in a million directions, few of them fruitful.

I'd worked hard these past years, and my boyhood dream was well within sight. If all went to plan, I would be able to offer the homeowners eighty per cent of the house's last valuation. Eighty per cent. Cash. By the end of the year. And with the promise of more to come – surely they couldn't refuse that? But it was just that which bothered me: *if all went to plan*. Because it was only June, and Cordell's death had me scrambling.

I checked the time. I had an appointment to keep and would be late if I dawdled, but as I approached the crime scene I felt I needed something to ease my spirit; and good company, even brief, could do that.

On any other day I would have crossed the carriageway and stopped at the first corner shop for a patty and a bag juice, so in order to maintain the appearance of normalcy that's exactly what I did.

The shop front was painted a deep green and in a high, bright-yellow scrawl the sign read: 'Viv's'.

Viv was an old-timer in Ends. He had come to England with the first ships in the late forties, moved to Bristol for dock work and sekkled a community. Viv's was open from March through October, when he packed up and went back ahh yard fi winter. 'Back to di wife,' he would always say. I would ask, 'Which one?' And he would wink and put a finger to his lips: 'Whichever one nuh baddah mi, star.'

His family was the only one older than mine in the city. We knew each other well and demonstrated our respect through patronage. I gave him an extra tenner each visit and dropped a couple of pounds in the charity box I knew he took a cut from.

Going home wasn't cheap; I didn't blame him.

As I entered the shop I shouted his name, but I needn't have bothered because the tinkle announced my entrance too. 'Viv,' I called. No answer. 'Yo, Viv, yuh cyaan ear mi?' I checked to make sure the officers hadn't followed me inside, then dropped loose change in a box claiming the money went to starving Africans and leant across the counter.

Through a hatch behind the till, a small set of stairs led to a basement that ran beneath two properties. It was where Viv kept his 'hexpensive liquors and hexcess stock'. It was also where he grew marijuana plants in a locked room. He hung the key around his neck next to a beaded chain and a rusted locket with a busted case. The exposed photograph in the locket was of him as a boy sat on his mama's knee. He wore a white frock to match his mama's sweeping hat and gown. Age had stained the picture pink, forcing rose-tinted spectacles on any who caught the young boy's eye.

I assumed the old man was with the greenery and that he wouldn't be long, so I tended the shop to pass the time. It would do well to take my mind from things.

Whilst I waited, two likkle yutes hustled into the store. They wore backpacks bigger than themselves and talked about footballing events from before they were born. They didn't give me a second glance. When I was coming up, an older would have checked us for that. A nod of deference was required, at the very least. I had thought it stupid then, but I understood it now. It was about respect. It was the acknowledgement of something bigger than ourselves. Still, the two yutes were in a world of their own, so I left them to it.

I propped the door ajar and stood in its entrance. In the middle of the road a dread was slowing both sides of the traffic as he shouted sweet nothings at a larger-than-life White woman across the street. A mother took advantage of the temporary tailback and shooed her train of children between the cars. And behind the police tape I could make out the discoloured pavement where Cordell's blood had dried.

Two officers stood beside the tape ready to hurry any gawkers along, but since this wasn't Clifton, the scene was hardly worth much more than a passing glance.

I had never entered the adolescent stage of thinking myself immortal. My mortality was as real to me as the soil I shovelled on to the aunts, uncles and cousins we buried. That was one of the downfalls of having a large family: the funerals outnumbered even the weddings.

A reedy voice came from behind me: 'Yo, scuse me.' The two yutes were waiting to leave. The boy who spoke looked at me through hooded eyes, unsure of what resistance I would provide. The other yute hung at his arm and glared, but didn't offer a word.

'Unuh ain't buy nutun?' I asked. They shared a look.

'Nah,' the spokesman said. They each had their hands stuffed into their pockets, which were fuller than they had been when they arrived. I took my eyes from them and noticed the absence of a handful of sweets and chocolate bars from the counter.

'Say no more,' I nodded, opening the door for them to leave.

As they stepped on to Stapes and shared a triumphant smile, I recalled how close my ear had been to the streets at that age. 'Yo,' I called after them, they half-turned, half-made ready to run, but I beckoned them closer. 'You man heard what happened?' I asked, nodding towards the police tape. They followed my eye and shrugged. The spokesman reached for a Snickers, tore the wrapper, and took a bite.

'I heard it was one Mali yute dat did it,' he said, but his friend was quick to disagree. He ripped a Skittles packet wide open and tipped some into his mouth.

'Nah, I heard it was one ahh dem man from Pauls.'

They shrugged in unison again.

'Could've been anyone, init?' I replied, gladdened that the streets hadn't attached my cousin's name or mine to the hearsay. 'Aight, say no more, enjoy the rest of your day you man; look after yourselves.' They nodded and began to leave. 'An stop teefin,' I called after them. They laughed and skipped away, revelling in the adrenaline rush that being caught allowed.

It was all fun and games in the mind of a child. Consequences were butts of reefers to be flicked into the road and any interference was worthy of prejudice and scorn. But even in my youth I was far removed from a child, and after what had happened, consequences waited for me around the corner like chancers ready to pounce.

It didn't seem like Viv was coming back any time soon, so I paid for the boys' sweets and sought a moment's comfort elsewhere.

3

If someone says, 'I love God,' and hates his brother, he is a
liar; for he who does not love his brother whom he has seen,
how can he love God whom he has not seen?

– 1 John 4:20

St Barnabas Baptist Church was the largest building on Stapleton
Road. It towered two storeys above Viv's, and its spires climbed
higher still. It was built during a time where the regulars would
have covered their noses with handkerchiefs and politely moved
from the pews where the current attendees sat.

Now it watched over the punters, trappers, drug abusers and
mentally ill with the silent disapproval of a wayward father
re-entering his child's life and finding an adult far from whom
he had imagined his child would become. In his children he had
foreseen godly men. Men of the good book. Oh, what disap-
pointments they had become: hypocrites and backsliders.

I found Winnie on the steps.

'Yo cuzzy,' she shouted, quickly moving to block my path.
She wore jeans that stopped way shy of her ankles and hips,
and a brown faux leather jacket with the sleeves rolled to the
elbows. Her lips were cracked and her hair stiff like parched

wool. 'You got anythink for me fam anythink at all money or food I don't mind I seent your girl's dad a minute ago.'

'Is he inside?'

'Nah he just left in a hurry looking like that man that carries the world on his back what's his face some Greek mythology person Antman or sup'm I don't know I seent your girl and her mum last week too Shona's real real pretty pretty like an angel she is ain't she I think that every time I seen her enuh?'

'Did her pops say anyting to you?'

'Nah nah he didn't say nothink to me but he gave me these.' She showed me her palm. He'd given her five pounds in silvers, so I added another five.

'You sure my man didn't say nutun?' I asked again. It was always best to check twice with Winnie. 'Didn't mention he was meetin man? What it was about or nutun?'

'Yeah yeah I'm sure Sayon man I told you I'm sure he ain't say nothink.'

'Say nutun. What you sayin, you ate today?'

'Nah nah you know sometimes I forget init.' She shifted on the balls of her feet and repeatedly re-counted her change. She rarely paused for breath. 'Just been busy you know praying talking to God making sure he know I'm all right cos you know Jesus cares about us init you me Midnight Hakim Shona's parents Erica your daddy Nanny and the rest of our family too Killa Calvin we're sinners all sinners you know but Jesus washed Jesus washed and washed our sins away you know dat init yeah you know that her dad let me inside his church the other day enuh?

'Yeah, I seent him the other day and he axed me to help him move a couple chairs and gave me some food real food not your food that wouldn't make any sense if Pastor gave me dat kind of food den he'd go to Hell not Heaven and dat wouldn't make any sense cos dem guys done the place up nice since I last seent it init lick of paint does wonders init?'

I might have asked Winnie if she'd heard anything about Cordell – after all, bitties were the biggest gossips – but I didn't want to keep the pastor waiting. If I didn't leave, I would end up taking her across the city to collect God knows what from God knows who. I gave her the little food I had left and cut.

Like my papa, Shona's papa was a pastor. The pastor of the baptist church whose steps Winnie called home. And the pastor of the church whose eyes fell hot on my back as I travelled further and further down the road.

The right honourable Pastor Lyle Jennings.

A car sped past, almost hitting the kerb, and it drew me from the intimacy of my thoughts. It didn't slow, but I glimpsed my cousin Cuba in the passenger seat. He saw me too and stuck his head from the window with a grin, signalling that they'd spin back in a second. I waved and crossed the street as the whip disappeared as quickly as it had come.

Cousins were raised as siblings in the Hughes family.

As the oldest living family member, Nanny was the matriarch and everyone did as she said. She bickered with the men in the yard and seasoned food with the women. And she told us to get along, so we did.

That was how Aunty Paulette's second son, Cuba, became my brother.

Cuba and I were born a few months apart. I was in the year above at school, but age ain't nutun but a number and neither of us cared. He was wise beyond his years. We were like twins, though I was red and he was black like treated sugar beets. The rest of our cousins were either red like me or lighter skinned and they used to mock his blackness sup'm fierce; they called him A-Quarter-Past-Midnight, Midnight and The-Dead-of-Night. Nanny too. Cuba was dark like her papa and that didn't sit well in her spirit, but since it got under his skin I never joined them.

Both Cuba and I were around the six-foot mark, with short hair that faded to skin. We could sleep for a matter of minutes and would never get bags under our eyes. Our skin was gloss, with or without lotion. We were smooth criminals and butter wouldn't melt in our mouths.

Every one of my cousins was raised at Nanny's and we all had spent varying degrees of time there as yutes, but none more so than Cuba and me. My parents were never much taken with this world, and by extension their only child. And when Aunty Paulette was free and sober enough to take care of Cuba, her unease with the responsibilities of motherhood made her beat him shades of blue like Black boys in moonlight.

The closeness of our age and the vast amounts of time we had spent together were reflected in our kinship. We walked to school and back together. Ate and bathed together. We liked the same stories and sports teams, the same treats, and were drawn to the same people. We were close with the rest of our cousins, but that was always who they were to us: the rest.

When I was six and Cuba five, the two of us would make a game of climbing Winnie's back and racing through the house like Black cowboys at high noon.

One time, Winnie tripped and knocked Cuba's big brother Jamaal to the floor. Dazed, Jamaal reached for whatever his hand landed on and it landed on me. Whilst he mounted and begun beating me, Winnie took off upstairs and Cuba bolted for the kitchen. He came back with a knife and buried it in his brother's leg.

Even at that young age, riding Winnie's back, playing penny on the wall and pretending to be a grown-up, I knew that I could kill for him. After all, there was no one I loved more on Earth or in Heaven. Except I hadn't thought that my conviction would one day be tested, especially against someone I'd once considered a friend.

4

A Song of Ascents. Of David. Behold, how good and pleasant
it is for brethren to dwell together in unity!

– Psalms 133:1

Across from Viv's was another shop I always made sure to give
custom: a bakery owned by Cuba's and my older cousin, Hakim,
and his Somali wife, Elia, a girl I went to school with and one
of my dearest friends. Theirs was a relationship I took great
pride in, since I had orchestrated it. And since Viv was busy, and
I was still intent on distracting myself, I decided to drop in.

Their shop front was painted misty blue, and their glass door
was marked with a white star. They kept their produce on thick
wooden shelves behind clear plastic lids. On display was a
mixture of East African and Italian sweet and savoury pastries,
giant ribbed loaves of black olive bread and snacks to eat on the
go. They had small vats filled with mahamri or buur – puffy
doughnuts which they served with chai – xalwa, quumbo, plain
doolsho and malawax made with cardamom.

They had trays of torrone – egg whites whipped, sweetened
with honey and mixed with almonds – next to amaretti and
sfogliatella. On the glass counter, above the birthday cakes

and statement pieces, they had a heated cabinet stacked with caanjero. They offered the sourdough pancakes with butter and sugar, or they gave you a Styrofoam cup of stew to take on your way. Pastries and sweet things weren't really Jamaica's speciality, but they sold festivals and bulla cake, as well as pineapple and banana fritters.

The door sang as I pushed it open, and immediately I was hit by two things: the sweetness of the air, and the homeliness of Elia's smile as she poked her head from the back room. 'Sayon,' she beamed, drying her hands on her apron and coming from behind the counter to bundle me in a comfy embosom. She released me after a long while and cupped her hand against my cheek, I smiled despite myself, and allowed her her mothering.

Elia was a tall woman. Tall enough to look me in the eye. She was never without a headscarf, whose colours were a mixture of pinks, blacks and oranges; nor was she ever without a blue-beaded bracelet that spelt her name in white.

She had a sharp jawline with high cheekbones and a pokey nose. We were of opposite complexions since she was clarinet-black like Cuba, but we were often of like mind. She had a disarming loveliness that was difficult to place. It made you feel at ease, even when her upper lip quivered into a smirk and she tenderly mocked you, as she frequently did. Despite life's many hardships, she never failed to greet me with a smile and enough warmth to heat a wintry room.

Aside from Shona and me, Elia was one of the few Black yutes that had always been in the higher sets at school. During break the three of us would rush to one another, our results held high above our heads. We would compare and jockey for the best marks, swapping trash talk and promising to outdo each other the next time.

In many ways and for many years, Elia had been the groyne against the force of my temper. We lived decidedly different lives, and made choices that seemed alien to one another, yet judgement had never clouded her love for me, or mine for her.

Years ago, Elia and Hakim had spent their savings on the renting and licensing of the bakery, so I had offered to help with the apparatus and other equipment, but the way in which I earned my money was a problem for them. It took Hakim weeks to swallow his pride; whereas Elia quickly understood it to be a necessity. She wanted the bakery not only as a business and profession, but as a statement of their new love and life together.

I remembered a time, not long after they'd moved into the bakery, where I tested Elia's morality and our friendship – not through any will of my own; the feds forced my hand. I had one of Cuba's lines for the day and was moving dark when CIDs tried to arrest me.

I was near Stapes and managed to outrun the feds, so I burst in, begging Elia for a place to park the food. Anyone else might have turned me away. The bakery was to be her and her husband's life's work, the driving force that got them out of bed each morning, but Elia was different.

'Give it here,' she said; then she took the heroin and flung it in the fire, its slightly acidic smell lost amongst the breads and pastries.

I was arrested, but not charged. And when I left the station I was filled with more respect for Elia than ever.

My cousin heard our voices and joined us in the front. Hakim was taller than his wife, much paler too. He had a well-built chest and arms, thanks to his time in youth offenders, skinny legs like a true yardman and the recent makings of a stomach.

He had a wide face and short hair. We used to call him 'big head' when we were younger, until the day he forced us all to swallow hot pepper sauce and gave us Chinese burns. Before he reverted he was clean-shaven, unable to grow a beard, now he had enough hair on his face to pass for a Saudi prince, and he tried to convert the beardless amongst the Hugheses with promises of sideburns and bristles.

'Sidee tahay, lil man,' he called, greeting me in Somali. He was the only person I let address me as 'lil man' – anyone else would've been asking for trouble. On his left wrist he wore a beaded bracelet depicting Somalia's flag; a present from Elia. And a silver silhouette of the Jamaican island hung around his neck.

'Waan fiicanahay,' I replied, embracing him warmly. Other than my mama, Hakim was the only other family member to find a way out, and that was thanks, in no small part, to Elia.

When the pair had married both our communities had shown up, and in a city like mine, that had meant reaching deep into their pockets. I helped where they let me but again, since Hakim took issue with my money, I could only do so much.

'What can I get you for today, lil man?' Hakim asked as he returned behind the till and Elia left for the back room. No matter how many years passed it was still a shock seeing him aproned and earning legal money. I still remembered the times when he was as badbruk as the rest of us, worse even, because it was Hakim who showed the youngers how to manoeuvre in the streets, from Jamaal, to his younger brothers Hosea and Killa, right down to Cuba and me.

'Beg you buss man a couple caanjeros and some stew,' I said. 'Man need sup'm warm to calm man down, blud.'

'What's up?' He frowned, ever the protector, but I couldn't tell him. He had his own family now, and this was something I had to handle alone. Besides, since his reversion he had taken to lecturing Cuba and me about our lifestyle whenever the opportunity presented itself. Recently, it had got so bad that Cuba was actively avoiding him.

'Winnie said she hasn't eaten; wagwan, you can't give her nutun?' I said, changing the subject.

Hakim kissed his teeth. 'I feed that girl whenever she stops by. She was only here this morning, init Elia? Was outside the front when we came from home.' There was an often-vacant flat above the bakery, but when Elia and Hakim were first looking for a place to live they decided it was too badly maintained for them, so they moved from their respective parents' homes to the nearby Barton Hill area and rented the bakery alone. 'Winnie don't know what day it is, akh,' said Hakim, and Elia hummed her concurrence from the kitchen.

'Shit's sad,' I said.

'She'll find her feet, insha'Allah,' Hakim said. 'We all have demons we're running from – Winnie more than most.'

Elia appeared behind him and leant an elbow on the counter. 'So, how's my favourite couple?' she said. 'Shona still running rings around you?' Elia never failed to check on us. In fact, whenever anyone asked how I was and what I had been up to, they would ask after Shona too. That's how people knew us: Sayon and Shona.

I couldn't help but smile. It felt good to be asked after as a package, and best when it was Elia asking. 'We're good, enuh. Her artist, Chenaniah, has one concert in Brum, so dey've gone up deh wid her marge. Her pops went too, but he's back now.' My mood darkened. 'Came home early.'

24

'Masha'Allah. That woman can't keep still,' Elia smiled, completely missing my change in tone; I was glad of it. 'She's gonna do big things in this life, insha'Allah. Well, even bigger things than she already is.'

I agreed. There wasn't a more driven individual in the world than my Shona. She had a vision to realise and no one, but no one, could stop her.

When it came to paying for the food we had a routine. They would tell me I didn't need to pay; I wouldn't hear it. They would sneak an extra caanjero or festival into the foil and a ten sheet would accidentally fall from my pocket as I left. Eventually, we agreed upon a foolproof system. They could give me as much food as they saw fit, and in return I could put my money into the charity boxes; they had to empty the coffers every week.

We said our salaams and I continued on, the stew in the Styrofoam singeing the skin on my fingers.

An ostentation of Whites stepped from the number twenty-four bus, probably headed to St Marks Road or one of the few other places where they felt safe. That said, these days you saw them more frequently. Different types of White people too. Seven years ago the only White people you saw in Ends had Black children, dreads or drug addictions. Now there were proper-looking White people who were opening businesses and speaking about the area as if it were their own, as if they didn't come to leech the community and stroke their liberalistic phalluses.

It was strange watching your neighbourhood dilute. You felt helplessness and vexation; at the same time, you told yourself you were being overly emotional and attaching sentiment to an area you neither owned nor were really from. Some days it felt like an invasion, others it felt like an unfortunate inevitability.

25

History would be the first to tell us that when White people saw something they liked, they took it.

My people would say, 'Watch out fi dem; dem nuh like wi.'

Somalis said, 'Cadaanka iska ilaali.'

We all had little sayings warning us from their company.

Lost in my thoughts and my food, I didn't notice a speeding Scirocco pull on to the pavement until Cuba hopped from the passenger seat. He had a bruised eye, a busted lip and thin cuts along his dark cheekbone.

My mouth was full of bread and stew, so I nodded my hello.

'Yo, family,' he grinned, as he leant against the open car door. I smiled back. Cuba and his too-cool-for-school ways amused me no end. He was wearing a puffer jacket and black beanie in June. He looked like a cartoon character about to rob a bank.

'Why you wearin dat, akh?' I laughed, swallowing my mouthful. He checked to see what it was that he was wearing, as if he hadn't dressed himself, then his grin widened.

'Black like man's heart init, you know my ting, cuz.'

Our heads turned in unison as two unmarked police cars swept down the road. Once they were gone Cuba tried to re-ignite our laughter, but just like in the bakery my sobriety returned. I could see the on-duty officers watching us from beside the police tape. And I was certain they knew who we were.

'Yo,' I said, keeping my voice low so as not to be heard. 'I asked a couple yutes whether dey'd heard nutun, but they hadn't. You reckon—'

'Sayon, shut the fuck up, man,' Cuba hissed. 'What's wrong wid you, blud?'

'My bad,' I said, and changed the subject. 'I just seen your marge, fam.'

'Oh yeah?' he said, still irritable and with about as much concern as a city pigeon. 'Where?'

'Bottom of Stapes.'

'She ask you for ps?'

I nodded.

He screwed his face and kissed his teeth. 'What you sayin, you give it to her?'

I nodded again.

'Chuhh. How much?' He reached into his pocket and pulled a roll of money thicker than mine.

'Don't worry bout it, g,' I said, but he ignored my protests and stuffed a handful of notes into my trouser pocket.

'Don't know why she won't ask me for it, cuz,' he said, 'and you need to stop givin ps out like you ain't tryna save.' He took a pre-roll that was tucked into his beanie and put it between his swollen lips. 'More time she knows man'll give it to her if she just asks. Why's she moving dumb for?'

Cuba knew as well as I did why Aunty Paulette would never ask him for money: he intimidated her. When he was a child she was fine punctuating her points with punishment and she would often leave on long absences, whether for prison or fancy; but each time she came back, he was more of a man, and she couldn't punish him any more.

Children often hold their parents to a standard they are unworthy of. They place them upon pedestals and the parents balance precariously until the moment they fall. But Cuba and I were under no illusion. I had left that in Nanny's daycare, and I suspected Cuba had left it in the womb. Childhood and innocence are only synonymous to the privileged.

Cuba barked and slapped the roof of the car. 'Ay, you know Killa's cut his plaits?'

'Which Killa?'

'Killa, our cousin fam; Hakim's brudda, Uncle Marlon's yute, fuck you mean which Killa? Wagwan for you, blud?'

'Say wallahi?' I said, face cracking into a smile. Repeated nicknames were very much a thing in Ends, and there were a number of people around the way who went by the name Killa or some variation; Big Killa, Tiny Killa, Killa Cam, then *our* Killa, who had been growing his hair from birth, probably in an attempt to garner some individuality. 'How come?' I asked. Cuba fetched a lighter from the car seat and lit the reefer.

He took a second before replying. 'Fuckin needs a job,' he explained. 'I told man come work for me but man said he's tryin dis nine-to-five ting now, akh. Got a durag on and everyting, think man's tryna get waves or some shit. Change his whole shit around. Tryna escape Ends, more time. I tried telling man it's impossible, but he wasn't tryna hear it. Once you're fully in dis world only a few can leave fam, and he ain't one of dem.'

'I'm just comin from Hakim's now.'

'Yeah? He try tell you bout Allah again?' Cuba kissed his teeth and laughed. 'I don't know wagwan for my man, come like every time he sees man he's wearin a fuckin thobe and chattin dis Islam shit, big man up doe, changed his life around and dat, but now it come like Killa's tryna do the same ting, blud,' he puffed, 'but like I said it won't work for him, doe.'

Whilst Cuba spoke I leant into the car.

From the stereo Youngs Teflon sang lyrics I knew well. I recognised the driver who nodded at me, but not the three yutes in the back. They looked young, and the boy in the middle youngest of all. He must have been around the same age as the two yutes who were in Viv's store, maybe a bit older. He was black like the seatbelt that ran across his chest and waist. And

28

he had a thin frame and a fat lip to match my cousin's. His eyes met mine and in an instant pleaded for some kind of intervention. I might have ignored him under different circumstances, but my paranoia wouldn't let it rest.

'Wagwan?' I whispered to Cuba, nodding towards the shook yute.

'Nutun,' he said. 'Tyin some loose ends.' He gave me a steely look that said he would flesh out the details later, and that was that. 'What about you, where you goin to?'

'Shona's.'

'Oh rah – is she back?'

'Nah nah, her pops asked man to come round and eat a food still.'

Cuba frowned. 'Sup'm wrong?'

'I don't think so.' But her father's invitation had been playing on my mind too. Both he and his wife had gone with Shona to the concert, and they weren't supposed to be back until tomorrow. But here he was: home, alone.

I had known him for most of my life; like my papa he was the pastor of a church (though my papa's was Pentecostal) and he had known my nanny from when they were yutes. But Shona was out of the city, and never before had her father and I met alone.

Cuba and co. went their way and I mine. By then my caanjeros were limp, so I binned them as I walked the length of Stapes and came to the end of my journey. But as I passed Nanny's, a familiar memory came to mind.

5

For we must all appear before the judgement seat of Christ, that each one may receive the things done in the body, according to what he has done, whether good or bad.

— 2 Corinthians 5:10

'It would be a cold day in hell . . .'

'Hell would freeze over . . .'

It was easy to swear on a place you never believed yourself destined, but there was no way in hell I would ever snitch. That, however, was a difficult thing to prove to someone whose freedom was reliant upon your silence.

I was eleven the first time I saw a man murdered.

A random act of violence, a stone's throw from Stapleton Road, on the night of St Pauls Carnival. Earlier that afternoon our older cousins, who were supposed to have been supervising us, handed Cuba and me a bill each and cut in search of wickedness and women.

The two of us spent the day at the carnival; unchaperoned, gorging ourselves on white rice and oxtail, playing knock-knock-ginger and making general nuisances of ourselves. Despite the money in our pockets, there wasn't a stall we didn't siphon something from; even if it was simply a packet of sugarcane or a goatskin drum.

The carnival was the only time of year when the city's blackness manifested in such magnitude. Small island flags hung from open windows, front yards became shubz, trifling dreads stood upon sound systems bawling raw patois to nobody in particular and basslines swept through the people's hearts, the full moon to their midnight currents.

To a child, it was a riot of colour and fun.

Every now and then we would cross paths with an aunty or an uncle who would busily involve themselves with a lover or their bredrins and pretend they didn't see us. As far as they were concerned, it was their day off from family or any family-related matters.

My cousin Bunny and Uncle Calvin were prime examples: the four times we bumped into them they had their arms slung around different brightly coloured wig-wearing women, and they pushed us aside with ten-pound notes, indifferent to the blood we shared.

As the day grew long the numbers dwindled and the demo-graphic became younger and darker. The Whites retreated to Stokes Croft, the streetlights called children home and the city's Caribbean youth came to the forefront. From the stroke of midnight only dancehall was heard, and love – or lust – became the only agendas.

Cuba and I were sitting on a wall eating sweet plantain chips when we saw Jamaal, Hakim and his brothers Hosea and Killa hustle three yutes into a side street. We followed them and found our family rifling through the yutes' pockets, taking watches from their wrists and comparing shoe sizes. One of the more brazen yutes tried to make a break for it and ended up with Killa's knee in his back and a flicky at his neck.

Cuba stepped from the shadows and his brother's head snapped towards us as if he were a mongrel being caught mounting his neighbour's bitch.

'You man get the fuck out of here!' he said.

'Nah, let Midnight and Sayon eat,' said Hakim, which made Jamaal relent, and he reluctantly handed us some of their newly acquired gains. I took the ps and thought it time well spent, but Cuba had other ideas; he hawked and spat phlegm on to the ground and sneered after Killa.

'Why you usin a shank on civilians for, you pussy?'

'Get the fuck out of here,' Jamaal said again. He took a menacing step towards us so we left, our pockets fatter than they had been before.

'Do you reckon dem man are involved?' Cuba asked as we counted our money.

'Who?'

'Dem man dat deh robbin?'

'Dunno fam, who cares?'

'If dey ain't involved dey shouldn't rob dem like dat, bro – wid shanks and dat.'

'Why not?'

'Dey ain't from dis world init. It ain't right, blud.'

'What world?'

'Dis world, bro. *Our* world. Dey don't understand wagwan.'

'Who would understand gettin jacked, doe? I wouldn't let no one jack man cos man ain't no victim, you get me? I ain't no pussy. If dey robbed man I'd rob dem back, init. If dey shanked man, or done man dirty I'd do dem back, init. Like the Bible says: an eye for an eye, fam.'

'Yeah, dat's what man's sayin, doe. You think like dat cos you're from dis world, akh. Dem man are just gonna go run tell feds, den as soon as dey tell feds deh in our world and we got our own rules, like you said: an eye for an eye. But anyway—' he handed me his share of the money.

'What's dis for?' I asked.

He frowned at me as though it were obvious. 'For the yard, init.'

I had no time to thank him; our cousins came sprinting past with feds hot on their tails. We may not have done the robbing but we had profited from the victims' undoing so we cut short our conversation and ran. As luck dictated, I lost Cuba in the mix and was forced to wait for him beside the bridge that led back to Stapes.

There was a park on the other side of the bridge with a basketball court and goalposts. At night the area became so dark you could hardly see beyond your hand, and earlier that year a young father had hanged himself from one of the beeches that bordered the path.

Finally, after what seemed an age, I saw Cuba wandering up the road and thought it would be funny to lurk in the bushes and surprise him. I crossed the bridge, found a hiding spot and took my place. But it wasn't Cuba who came across the bridge, it was a man and woman, and they were arguing.

I knew the woman's face, she lived not too far from Nanny's, and the man's too, he was a regular at the pubs along Stapleton Road. They were waifs, prone to all manner of degradation, and lived without respect from the neighbourhood they clung to. Their shouting matches in the early hours of the morning were legendary, and once Hakim and Jamaal had to stop him from pummelling her with his push bike.

They spilled on to the path like cornmeal over the side of a pan, slowed by the wine the woman held. Their words were hushed yet rowdy, like only drunkards could manage. The man pulled the woman closer and told her the things he wanted to do to her, the woman pushed away. He pulled her closer, she pushed away. He pushed her to the path so she broke the wine bottle and slit his throat.

I ran from my hiding place, ignoring the woman's wails as a moment of sobriety revealed what merriness had masked. Then a hiccup took her voice as she realised she had been seen.

I didn't stop running until I reached home.

Nanny's was empty aside from Uncle Michael and Winnie; the rest of the family wouldn't be back until morning. I tucked myself into bed and desperately tried to forget the blood spitting from his neck.

Disturbed by my arrival, Winnie intruded to ask why I was home so early but before I could respond there was a knock at the front door. I bade Winnie answer and crept downstairs to watch from a placket in the curtains.

It was the woman, and she still had the broken bottle in hand, dripping with blood or wine, I didn't know which.

Winnie did her best to persuade her that I wasn't home, but she was only capable of so much and the crazed woman pushed her aside. She strode through the kitchen hollering for me to show myself so that she could explain that I hadn't seen what I'd seen. Whilst I hid behind the curtain Uncle Michael stayed behind his music and Winnie watched from the door. I had heard it said that violence was never the answer, but the threat of violence certainly could be: Cuba came bursting through the front door, dripping with sweat and promising death to anyone who had laid a finger on me, and anyone who had allowed another to do so.

He grabbed the same kitchen knife he had stabbed Jamaal with and chased the woman out of the house and back to St Pauls. She was arrested that night for the murder of her partner and, as far as I know, is still in prison.

It was a story that often came to mind whenever I felt uneasy, and one that I'd long ceased trying to be rid of. I clenched my jaw and continued past Nanny's and headed up one of Stapleton Road's tributaries, where Shona lived. Her front garden ran from pavement to door, so I climbed the steps and walked the garden path, anxious to discover why the pastor had returned home early and exactly what our meeting was about.

Her mama kept a tidy home and their front garth was no exception; the hedges were trimmed and the grass mown, flowerbeds sprouted from either side of the path and there wasn't a weed or an empty Magnum bottle in sight. It was prim and proper, but the closer I came to the doorbell the more I could feel the police at my back and the knot in my stomach tighten, and the more I wished that Shona was home.

I would be given twenty-five years if they found me. And since they would certainly deny me parole, I would come out a middle-aged man. Spent and Shona-less. Truthfully, I had only one recourse, and that was to avoid Her Majesty's justice by any means. And in order to do so I had to maintain the perfect façade, at least until the house-atop-the-hill was mine, and Ends was but a fragile memory.

It would be easy to convince acquaintances of my innocence, because they had only my spirit to go by. And it would be an even simpler task to deceive my loved ones, because they would want nothing more than to believe in me. But the pastor was neither of these things; and more than most, I had to keep him in the dark.

6

I have come to my garden, my sister, my spouse; I have
gathered my myrrh with my spice; I have eaten my honeycomb
with my honey; I have drunk my wine with my milk.

– Song of Solomon 5:1

I first met Shona when she was a little girl and I a little boy, five
years before the carnival incident and not long after my mama
first took me to the house-atop-the-hill in Clifton.

My nanny didn't believe in nursery or preschool, and being
a largely uneducated woman who had raised her own siblings
and owned her own home, she had the same contempt for all
levels of education. What could they possibly teach her grandchild that she couldn't? Eventually, however, she let my mama
send me to the reception class at the local primary school.

It was there I first saw her, sitting cross-legged on the scratchy
blue carpet. She turned with the rest of the class as I was introduced by our teacher. Her hair was parted and savagely pulled
into four thick twists and her brown skin shone shinier than her
shoes. She wore red cube-shaped bobbles at the tips of her twists
that rattled as they knocked against one another and she had
multi-coloured bows tied at the tops.

When our teacher asked who wanted to show me around the school her hand shot up. There were other yutes too, boys and girls who wanted the opportunity to exercise some level of freedom and miss an hour of school. Perhaps I was being unfair and they were only trying to be my friend, but when asked I couldn't answer quickly enough. I pointed at Shona and remember the boys huffing and muttering about where my loyalties lay. Shona leapt to her feet, straightened her green-and-white gingham pinafore, and tried her best to appear reserved, but as soon as the door closed her personality let loose.

'Oh thank you for choosing me, Sayon. I thought you were going to choose Maleeka. She's such a liar and a teacher's pet. I told my daddy and he said to just ignore her. Let's go.' She took me by the hand and we dashed along the corridors. 'We'll start in the hall cos that's where we eat food, so that's my favourite place. Are you packed lunch or free school dinners?'

I was enthralled. I didn't know the word then, but that's what I was. Explaining a childhood crush as an adult is a hard thing to do. There was no preoccupation with sex; I had no interest in her body or how she could make me feel.

At the time there were only two things that told me how rare she was. When I wasn't with her but was around her, whether we were across the classroom or at break-time when she was jumping rope and I was kicking ball, I missed her. And when I went home to Nanny's and cycled around the neighbourhood with Cuba, I missed her then too. The idea that I was even thinking about a girl intrigued me. In my youth I concluded the only way I could solve such a mystery was to spend as much time with her as possible.

So that's what I did.

Jamaal was in Year 6 when I was in Year 1, and he was

what street dreams were made of: Ghetts's Ghetto Gospel and Jaheim's Ghetto Love. He and his friends used to stain yutes from other schools on their morning commute, then buy 100 1p sweets and sell them for 10 pence a pop. He began to notice as I spent more and more time with Shona, and every other day he would apportion some of the sweets he bought and give them to me in a white paper bag.

I remember more than one lunchtime when Shona and I sat behind the shed and stuffed our faces. We fed strawberry laces to each other like the scene in *Lady and the Tramp*, nibbled the yolks from jelly eggs, saw who could keep fizzers in their mouths the longest, and put Haribo rings on each other's fingers.

We must have married a thousand times.

She couldn't stand the dusty sherbet on Refreshers and I hated black liquorice, so we sold what we had left. We halved my cousin's asking price and made enough to keep the hustle going.

Shona would run out to the playground and fetch the White boys who were given pocket money and bring them back behind the shed. It was all very hush-hush. I wore Uncle Calvin's old Avirex jacket dem times, and I made the White boys put their money in one pocket and take the sweets from the other. If the teachers caught us, they would see their grubby hands in my jacket. I could either say they were jacking me or that they were planting the sweets and they weren't mine. After they left, Shona and I would celebrate our genius and brazenly dismiss our customers as the suckers they were.

We were Shawn Carter and Beyoncé in ''03 Bonnie and Clyde'. I was André and Shona was on the other side of the game. I went home and watched Curtis Jackson and Meagan Good in *21 Questions* and pictured the two of us. Hosea ripped my favourite songs from LimeWire and I never looked back.

We were the duo I saw in the American music videos and heard about in Kano's 'Brown Eyes'.

I had the love jones.

Cuba joined the primary school the following autumn and we became an inseparable trio, but since he was in the year below, it was only at break-time and after school that we could wreak havoc. We stole Calypso juices from the kitchen and footballs from the younger years. We taxed Penguin bars from the weak yutes and played manhunt with the olders; if they ever took it too far our older cousins would be there to set them straight.

Soon the teachers learnt to curse Cuba's name like his mama did. They had a file full of complaints and report cards a mile thick. They advised me to separate myself from him, or they feared we would suffer the same fate, anchored by the fetters that tied our ankles. When I asked what they meant, they locked their lips and threw away the keys.

When the three of us wanted to be by ourselves we would find the quietest corner of the playground and jump rope. Cuba and I held either end of two cords and sang the same lyrics our parents had when they had been on the playground:

Teddy Bear, Teddy Bear, turn around,
Teddy Bear, Teddy Bear, touch the ground,
Teddy Bear, Teddy Bear, show your shoe,
Teddy Bear, Teddy Bear, that will do.

Teddy Bear, Teddy Bear, go upstairs,
Teddy Bear, Teddy Bear, say your prayers,
Teddy Bear, Teddy Bear, turn out the lights,
Teddy Bear, Teddy Bear, say goodnight.

In the entire school there wasn't anyone with more rhythm than Shona. By the end of the first verse a crowd would have gathered. The dissenters said that she would mess it up when she had to say her prayers, some said the rhyme was too easy and that she couldn't manage a harder one, and a fair few said that they could have done a better job. We invited them each to have a go and they soon realised they couldn't cash the cheques their mouths had written.

Cuba and I whipped those ropes around so fast they burnt the ankles of anyone too slow. The only one who could keep up was Shona, so they left us alone.

In class it was just Shona and me, and we relived the first year we had spent together. We sat at the head table and competed against ourselves. English, maths, science. We had no equals and were often assigned extra work. I had a reading age of sixteen by Year 5, Shona by Year 4.

It was her fierce desire for difference that drove her, and it was she who drove me. I wanted to be forever beside her. She was my rival and confidante. I shared food, secrets and stories with her and she shared herself with me.

I took her to the house-atop-the-hill and promised that one day I would buy it and she could have a room of her own right next to mine. She agreed, on the condition that it was a music room with lots of instruments and album covers on the walls, and it would have to be sound-proof, unless I wanted to hear her playing all the time. I told her I would love to hear her play.

It wasn't until the final year of primary school that I realised my feelings weren't the normal kind you had for a friend. They were the kind of feelings that adults spoke about. The kind that the women in the living room warned the little girls against ever having, whilst prophesying that the little boys would leave a string of broken hearts behind them.

I wasn't afraid of much as a child, but at an early age I became afraid of losing Shona. And in our first year of secondary school, I almost did.

7

Behold, I tell you a mystery: We shall not all sleep, but we shall all be changed.

– 1 Corinthians 15:51

I first met Shona's father on the last day of primary before the summer break – neither of us would be returning, we were both moving to the local academy in September – I remember the whole school on the playground that early summer afternoon. It was sunny. Mothers met their children's friends and shared a word with their favourite teachers. With the teachers for whom their children had only jinxes, they offered strong words of advice on how to better teach and watched them become obsequious and cloying.

Everywhere pickney darted between taller persons' legs and begged to be allowed to sleepovers and parks. Parents, conscious of other parents, smiled and consented to things they would usually never agree to. There was an adult for every child, if not parents then older siblings, friends of the family, aunts and uncles, social workers. Nanny was the family member there for both Cuba and me. She stood outside the gates in her denim trouser suit and chain-smoked pre-rolls.

Across the playground Shona, Cuba and I perched on a wall and watched a footrace between a young dad and his toddler. He had gold in his mouth, a tag around his ankle and a chain around his sable-black neck. The baby girl squealed and stumbled into her mother's arms, the designated finish line, her triumph rewarded with a smothering of motherly kisses. And her father patted her crown.

Cuba looked over to where Nanny was smoking, told Shona he would see her around, and left the two of us alone. Nanny never called to us, just watched and waited for us to come to her. Given her patience, I decided to hang back a little; there was an opportunity here, and I took my chances when they came.

I remember Shona turning and talking before I could say a word. Her eyes were wide and her hands flew from her side as if they were allergic to being still. Whenever she spoke it was as if she couldn't imagine there being anything as important as what she was saying right there and then. If your attention strayed, even a little, she would ask what was so interesting that you didn't have the common decency to listen. So I made sure to nod and smile, I even grunted where I thought it necessary, but in truth I wasn't paying her any mind.

I could hear my heart beating up my throat and pouring from my nose like snot on the lip of a motherless child. So loud I knew she could hear it too. I continued my pretence for as long as she allowed, but once the tips of my ears flushed red she cocked her head to the side and asked what it was that was so distracting.

'Am I boring you, Say? You can tell me if I am. But if I am, you have to tell me nicely, otherwise my feelings will be hurt.' That was her name for me: Say, it rolled from her tongue like fingers across keys.

'You're not boring, Shona, you ain't never—' I didn't finish my sentence, and she never had the chance to force me into doing so, which she surely would have. One minute I was talking to the beautiful Black girl that I had been crushing on for the past five years, the next I was staring up at the towering shadow of her father.

Pastor Lyle Jennings was a man. He could barter the extra nineteen pence from Supermalts, talk philosophy with academics and art with people who made a living looking lengthways down their noses. He was built as though he bent grown men across his knee. His hands could crush cooking apples. He had a father's gut and the sternness of someone well used to command. But even as a yute I could sense that something was off; where some men carried a chip on their shoulder, Pastor Lyle, despite his profession, seemed to bear something far more sinister.

'Who's this, Princess?' he asked. 'One of your likkle friends?' He was softer-spoken than I had expected, but then again I had been expecting a bellow akin to a roll of thunder.

And when Shona spoke to her father, her voice became molasses stirred into a vanilla cake mix. 'Yeah, this is Sayon, Daddy, remember?'

Pastor Lyle's eyebrows raised. I felt my bladder tighten. He knew my name. I was a dead man walking. 'Oh, you're Sayon,' he said. He lifted his hand to strike; he knew I liked his daughter, he knew only a moment ago I had been about to confess. He couldn't have his only child fraternising with the Hughes family. He was a pastor. He had his reputation to think of. I flinched and shut my eyes, preparing myself for whatever punishment he deemed necessary for such an offence.

When none came I opened my eyes to find his hand extended

from one man to another. An offering I gladly took. I swallowed all inappropriate feelings for Shona that day. Swallowed them until I was fit to burst. I promised to find her on the first day of secondary school and hurriedly retreated to where my nanny and cousin waited.

I would have to wait until she was bold enough to step out from under her papa's spires, or I was bold enough to fetch her.

I wished the summer along and so it went. September came faster than a virgin who lied to have his cherry popped. And finally, after what had seemed an age, I enrolled in my first year at the secondary school around the corner from Nanny's.

It was a memorable introduction.

On my very first day I watched two Year 11 girls settle their summer differences in the car park. The evenly matched affair was eventually separated by the on-site policemen, but not before the girls' hoop earrings were lost to the drains and their wigs offed and reduced to prizes in each other's hands.

The buzz after a fight usually causes another, as I heard a yute walking past tell his bredrins. I later learned the yute's name was Cordell. The next time I saw him, he and his friends were stomping on one of my age-mates and emptying his backpack. Cordell lifted his head whilst rummaging through the yute's bag. He saw me and put his finger to his lips, and I kept mine closed, as I always had and always would.

I spent the day searching for Shona. I didn't see her amongst the snapping faces egging the girls on, nor was she in my form. I figured she would be in my lessons but she wasn't there either. Perhaps she was on the other side of the year group? I asked some of the boys if they had seen her, described her as smart, pretty, had her hair twisted into four plaits and could talk for England or Jamaica: they hadn't.

After my impromptu meeting with Pastor Lyle I hadn't spoken to Shona for the whole summer, so perhaps her plans had changed. She was easily smart enough to get a scholarship to a private school; either Clifton College or Bristol Grammar. Perhaps her father had decided to change her first choice after he met me? Perhaps he had shaken my hand and seen right through me? I heard certain pastors could do that. He shook my hand and immediately saw me for the devil that would lead his daughter from the straight and narrow.

Eager to forget Shona's absence I dove headfirst into school life and became the boy in da corner. Fortunately, the rumour mill churned without sleeping. One of the sixth-form boys was pressing a Year 8, and a big-breasted Year 9 girl had been caught giving head in the toilets. There were fights in the canteen, fights on the fields; they even arranged fights at the local park on weekends.

Now that he knew I was trustworthy, Cordell took a shine to me, so he largely exempted me from the bullying and thievery he inflicted on others; but there were still the other olders to contend with, and as the youngest in the school you had to bunch together for protection. Anyone identified as a social pariah was at the mercy of the most vindictive spirits. I saw yutes put in yellow bins and kicked across football pitches. One yute tried to stop my boy Karma stealing his bike and had his head caved in with his own D-lock.

It was a zoo.

With Shona absent and Cuba still in primary school, Karma and a boy called Abdimalik became my two closest bredrins. Karma was a southerner, dark like Cuba with long plaits and censorious eyes. His nose was broad for a Somali and his hair thick with the tightest of curls. On account of his looks some of his countrymen called him 'jareer' and saw him as more Caribbean than their own. It was a misused and hateful word given to them by the ignorance of their parents, and though he would never complain, it pushed him right into our arms.

Where Karma was from Somalia, Abdimalik was a Lander, stocky but quick on his feet and one of the more able athletes in our year. His parents were dead and he didn't concern himself with the opinions of his compatriots. His life was lived to sweet-talk women and woo them with Saturday-night eyes. The three of us were in the same form and rolled with a hotpot of like-minded Caribbeans and East Africans. If one of us got in trouble we all would, and together we would make it from Stapleton Road to Hollywood.

Aside from their rejection of Karma, I had a lot of respect for the way in which the Somalis conducted themselves. For the most part, they weren't fractured like we Jamaicans were on British shores. Where we chose St Pauls or Stapes and would put first cousins in the grave because of it, they banded beneath their flags.

They were as funny as we were, as prone to the silliest of nicknames and loving conversations that would appear to strangers as the bitterest of feuds. Both our foods were interpretations of mostly Indian cuisines and our music had greatly influenced theirs. The way I saw it, the only difference between us was that we called our God Jesus, and they called theirs Allah. That, and we had been living in Babylon far longer than they.

With all the chaos and goings-on, being in the highest sets for the languages, maths and science was a strange duality. The school was more than seventy per cent Black but the higher sets were more Middle-Eastern, Vietnamese and Pakistani, which was an unsettling fact for one of the only cities in the country whose Black population was bigger than its Asian. I never saw any of the yutes in my class on the playground, they just appeared when the lesson began and vanished afterwards, intent on keeping Bristol as segregated as ever.

The only friendly face was Elia's, and she was as cosy then as she is now.

I remember the day I found out she was Muslim; before then I had thought that being a Muslim woman meant wearing a hijab. In primary school each Muslim girl wore the same black, slip-on one-piece with the patterned edges; when they got into arguments it would get sent flying like the Year 11 girls' wigs, but Elia had her edges slicked and her hair styled so I thought her distinct.

Once, in a Religious Studies lesson, the Christian teacher made a comment about the commonality of sexism within Islam. Elia raised her hand and corrected his mistake. She said that in spite of many people's attempts and misinterpretations, religion and culture weren't the same. She attributed the sexism to Arabic culture, and suggested that any non-Arab Muslim who displayed such attitudes had a stolen mind.

'Hating women isn't in my culture or religion, sir,' she said. 'We were taught that by Arabs. How can Islam be a sexist religion when the Quran says: "I never fail to reward any worker among you for any work you do, be you male or female – you are equal to one another." Explain that?'

Rather than acknowledging what she said and applauding her eloquence for one so young, our teacher found fault with her generalisation and suggested she might want to refrain from such inflammatory remarks. She was sent to isolation after expanding upon her point unprompted, but she had made an ally in me.

Elia and I were loved and hated by our teachers. If there was an unsolvable question we had the answers, if no one spoke, we could be relied upon to pipe up. At the same time we didn't mix well with the other races and constantly talked amongst ourselves. Plus every now and then I was inexplicably absent, and more than once I had a group of angry olders waiting for me when the lesson finished.

In Shona's absence, Elia was all that I could have asked for. I tied an orange rope around my waist and dove into the depths, all the while knowing that the gentle and quick-witted Elia was the surface marker to which I could make my return. It was then that I learnt that love and loyalty were birds of a feather to Elia. And that love could take many forms, because in those early months there were times where her insistence that we completed a piece of homework, or that we visited the library, kept me from all manner of trouble.

Still, she could not keep me from everything.

There was a Gypsy yute in our form whose government name was 3G. He was smaller than the rest of us but carried himself as though he were the biggest. No doubt his over-confidence was seated in the lengths his many brothers and sisters would go to protect one another, but we weren't concerned about that because 3G was flashy.

His family lived like crabs in a bucket, and they were known for stealing from Harvey Nichols. And whether it was true or not, it was said that they pilfered clothes from washing lines and back gardens too.

One day 3G came into school with Gucci trainers and a

matching belt, and Karma took interest. He asked 3G where he had bought them, perhaps in order to go out and buy the same fit – who could tell? But 3G took offence and said the unthinkable: he told Karma to suck his mum. The three of us – Karma, Abdi and I – beat him so bad his family waited for us outside the school gates for days. And it cost Abdi and me five pounds each to stop Karma from taking things any further.

After a number of other incidents, one that was entirely Karma's fault and the other Abdimalik's, the school assigned me daily anger management sessions with a Mr Barker.

Mr Barker was a gangly White man, camp, but married to a woman. An adult who blatantly attempted to be down with the youth, but because of his genuine goodwill we let it run. He was there to calm me down in the mornings, and once a week we would write goals for the next. It was long but he had jam, toast, orange juice and stress balls so I kept going. I could bring a friend along too, so I plugged a different bredrin each time.

However, that all became unnecessary two months into Year 7, when I sashayed into my English class, late, and found Elia deep in conversion with Shona.

She was finally here. And yet all I wanted to do was take her away. She was too precious for this place. I needed to wrap her in clingfilm and foil, put her in an empty ice-cream tub and smuggle her out. The teachers were inept and uncaring. They placed low ceilings upon their students and their eyes were bereft of possibility.

The teacher spoke to me, complaining that I had inter-rupted her class. I showed her the middle finger and stayed where I was. It was then Shona noticed me. 'Say!' she shrieked, running from her seat and throwing her arms about my neck.

'Say, I've missed you so much. I've got so much to tell you. How was your holiday? Did you miss me? Don't answer that, I already know you did. Say, I've got so much new music to show you.'

Now it wasn't only the teacher burning a hole into the side of my head, my classmates were confused too. How did I know this girl? I could see from some of their faces that they had already tried to make a move, yet here she was, over the moon about our apparent reunion. I felt a murkiness dye the silver lining of seeing her again.

'Wagwan, Shona,' I replied, coolly.

She flinched a little. 'Wagwan?'

I hated the strangeness in her eye but I was spurred by it. It looked good to be less excited than her. That was how it was supposed to be.

At break a group crowded the new girl, keen to find out where she was from, whether or not she had a phone, and if her parents let her out after dark. There was a number of my bredrins amongst the throng, eyeing her. They asked why she'd started the year so late, and we learnt a relative of hers passed back home and the funeral arrangements had lasted longer than expected.

Elia told her she didn't have much to catch up on, perhaps only on the friend front. The boys took that as their cue to offer their help: the bullies offered protection from any confrontation she might encounter, the sweet-sellers promised her a packet of Chewits every day, and the Bristol City players guaranteed whatever she wanted when they turned pro.

She threw it back at them all.

'I have Say,' she told them. 'Me and him are best friends, and his cousin Cuba who's coming here next year. He's kinda like

Say's younger brother; he's kinda like my brother too. We used spend all day together, init Say?' The group turned to me, the girls prying and primed to tease, and the boys, even my friends, stingy and jealous.

'Nah,' I said, 'we didn't spend dat much time together – me and Cuba, yeah – but we weren't wid you all the time, you're gassin it, still.' And that was that. She excused herself and ran for the bathroom. Elia punched me in the stomach and went after her. My friends laughed and told me I was a jokeman, but at least they didn't call me whipped.

8

Hatred stirs up strife, but love covers all sins.

– Proverbs 10:12

I spent the next four months of my first year in regret. Shona made friends; I kept to mine. We were in the same classes so I watched her and Elia become close, but I was always on the outside. Elia wouldn't ignore me, she was too kind, but she made it clear to whom she was loyal. And despite our closeness, I couldn't blame her. She was disappointed in my immaturity, and probably more than a little scared that I was capable of doing the same to her.

Besides, they got on like bank robbers and getaway drivers, their grades were almost identical and their interests the same. Both of them came from deeply religious homes and despite their differences there was a healthy amount of respect and curiosity. They soon discovered the countless similarities within the two faiths and chose to focus on them instead. Once they navigated the things that polarised them, they simply agreed to disagree.

In fact, they probably found solace in their differences. When Elia left her house and stuffed her hijab in her bag, Shona felt and said nothing. And when Shona swore and used the Lord's name in vain, they remained unchanged. Their conversations were rich and full, their friendship long-lasting and harmonious. And whilst Shona and Elia kept me at arm's length, my circumstances worsened.

Abdimalik had been expelled for stabbing a yute with a scalpel. It made the papers and was quite the hoo-ha. The yute had been badmouthing Islam and being overtly disrespectful, and he was known to press people's buttons, so as far as both Abdi and I were concerned, he had it coming. *Who cyaan ear muss feel*. An age-old saying.

And he certainly felt it.

Abdi chased him from the class and caught him clawing at the pastoral carer's doorknob. He stabbed him thirteen times before he was dragged away. After spending a few months in youth offenders, Abdi was on road shottin for his older brother. He went from backpacks and pocket money to bags and boxes. He used to cycle to the school gates when the day was done and lotion girls with his newfound riches. Six months later he was stabbed to death in Pauls. Wrong place, wrong person.

That didn't make the papers, though.

We were all acting out. The yutes who had been expelled from school were seeing more money than our parents. They had the latest gear whilst we were in school uniform. They smoked and drank, sexed and ate good. They were just like grown-ups.

Where we were cooped up and herded from class to class – overseen by police and teachers who were frequently sent on refresher courses that taught them how to enact citizens' arrests – they could roam free. Those of us who remained pushed the boundaries as far as we could, and when the leadership didn't give a shit, the boundaries could be pushed far.

By now it was February. Another friend of mine had been expelled for having baggies in his locker and, just before the Christmas break, I had been excluded for flooring a teacher. My papa couldn't make the exclusion meeting for church reasons and my mama said it was all too much for her, so my nanny and her fair-skinned lover Mister Sinclair came.

Nanny sat quietly with her purse clutched to her chest and listened to the White people cuss her grandchild. When they'd finished she told them that it wouldn't happen again, then she collected her man and took us home.

At home she told me that she expected more from me and left it at that. With her next breath she asked if Shona and I were still friends. I told her we weren't and she told me to make a change, that Shona was the type of person I needed in my life.

I had been meaning to say something to Shona, to apologise and ask for a return to our past relationship. Our closeness. But she looked happy apart from me, and I didn't want to disturb her peace. Finally Nanny's instruction had given me the reason I needed. And why not go for broke? I waited for February 14th and borrowed enough money from Hakim to buy a box of Thorntons chocolates and some roses; both pink. Her favourite colour.

I tucked the flower stems and chocolate box under the crook of my arm and snuck from Nanny's after school. I could come and go from Nanny's as I pleased, I had no curfew, but if my family saw me with gifts on Valentine's they would easily put two and two together.

They had been teasing me about Shona since my first day of primary school. They poked and pried where they were unwelcome, remembered her name whilst forgoing knowledge of any other friends, and constantly asked after her wellbeing. The women in the living room cleaned fish and said we would be married. The men in the backyard said to wear jimmies less I wanted a yute. When they really wanted to rattle me they would chorus 'Can You Feel the Love Tonight?' from *The Lion King* at mealtimes.

I arrived at Shona's a nervous wreck. Ends was full of yutes from our school and if they saw me I would never hear the end of it. I would be 'Sweetie' or 'Flannel' till the day I died. Jamaican nicknames were simple but jarringly relentless; if you had a stutter you were 'DJ', a limp and you were 'Cyaan-right'. They said what you were and never allowed room for change or growth. You could leave for fifty years, see the world, kill the yeti, but once you returned you would be the same 'Loverboy' you always were.

I caught my breath behind a car wheel across the road from her door. It opened and I heard Shona's voice announce that she would be back in a minute, then she careened down the road.

This was my chance.

I would leave the care package at her door, she would find it and know who it was from. I would stay behind the car to make sure no smackhead stole it. It was perfect. And then it wasn't. The door opened again. Except this time I wasn't behind the car, I was carefully placing the roses atop the chocolates on the Jenningses' step.

'And who are those for?' Shona's father growled.

'No one,' I replied, unthinking.

'No one?' he repeated. 'Marcia, come see this; I think Princess has her first admirer.'

In the background Shona's mother rousted through the corridor, wiping her hands on a blue-and-white checked dishcloth. She was a fiend for a love story.

I wanted to leave before she could make me, but Pastor Lyle read my mind. 'Stay where you are, young man,' he commanded.

As I look back, I think he might have been amused, but in the moment amused was the last thing I thought him, and he certainly would not be amused about it later. In fact, if he had even a glimpse of how it would all turn out, I'm sure he would have flung me and the chocolates up the hill and down the mountain.

'An who wi av yah?' Marcia called. Shona's mother was a good cook, and a heavy sampler of said cooking. No one greater embodied the stereotype of jolliness; it was as if it were a personal goal of hers. She barely reached her husband's chest, but what she lacked in height she made up for in girth; she was like a perfect dumplin.

Marcia smiled as she took me in, the only thing she prayed for Shona, was that she found a man like the one she had, and knew a love like the one she knew. Marcia birthed Shona when she was forty-four. Coming from a family where the elders were now only in their fifties I found it strange, but Marcia made me think I might have been better being raised by parents who had experienced the fullness of life.

'This is Sayon, if I'm not mistaken,' Pastor Lyle replied, answering for me. 'Nanny's grandson.' Anyone who knew my nanny called her that. At the time I didn't know how Shona's father knew her, but I wasn't surprised.

'Sayon,' Marcia cried, 'wi eard so much bout yuh over di years. Aww, isn't dis lovely, wat yuh av deh?'

'No, this isn't lovely,' Pastor Lyle replied, 'it's inappropriate. They're twelve.' He turned to me, 'You've grown since the last time I saw you, haven't you?' I nodded. 'Hmmm. We'll see what Nanny has to say about this.' With that he took the roses and chocolates inside and I never saw them again, and from the look Marcia gave them I doubt Shona ever did.

The three of us sat on their doorstep and waited for Shona to come back. My cheeks burnt as Marcia asked how I was finding school. She said the step from primary to secondary could some-times be too much for young minds. Shona had told them that she had settled in well, that she was enjoying it and that she had made a good friend called Elia. She hadn't told them that we had fallen out.

At mention of Elia, Pastor Lyle kissed his teeth and muttered something about Somalis not being Black and the Quran being nothing but a corruption of the Holy Bible, a distraction wrought by Satan. Luckily, Shona arrived before he could start an explanation. 'Why are you guys outside—?' She paused as she noticed me. 'Say? What are you doing here? Is something wrong?'

'Nah, nutun's wrong.'

'We're just quickly visiting young Sayon's nanny's house,' her father said, rising to his feet.

'Why?' Shona frowned.

'Yuh daddy's being a strop,' Marcia explained.

'You wait here, Marcia, this won't take long,' Pastor said.

Nanny's house wasn't far. And when we were halfway there Shona pulled me a couple of steps behind her papa. 'What's going on, Say? What have you done now?'

'What do you mean, *what have I done now?*'

'Well you're a *badman* now aren't you, always getting into trouble, cussing teachers, fighting. Moving like your family doesn't go church.'

'Dey don't.'

'Well your mum and dad do,' she said. 'Your dad's a pastor. My daddy knows him, so you can't lie to me.' As a young girl Shona was the worst person to argue with, her tongue never tied and her mind somehow managed to keep up with her mouth.

'I just came to say sorry,' I muttered. We could see my nanny's front door. There would be no better time to explain, 'I bought some chocolates for you—'

'Chocolates?' Shona gasped. 'On Saint Valentine's Day? Do you know what everyone at school would say?'

'No one saw,' I promised.

'How do you know?'

'I just know, init.' She took my assurance and sat with it a minute. Nanny's exterior door was always open so Pastor Lyle rapped his knuckles against the frosted glass of the interior.

'Which chocolates did you get me?' Shona whispered.

'Pink ones, and pink flowers too.'

'Pink flowers,' she exclaimed, 'wow!' I didn't know whether it was a good or bad wow and had no time to dwell. Nanny had appeared at the door and was searching to catch my eye, but I found sanctuary in the shingle beneath my feet.

'Hello, Cynthia,' I heard Pastor Lyle say. This caught my attention. It was the first time I heard someone address my nanny as anything other than 'Nanny'. Come to think of it, I wasn't sure why Pastor Lyle had taken me to Nanny's rather than my parents' church.

'Wahum, Lyle,' Nanny purred. 'Who wouldah thought yuh would darken my door after all dese years, was it not yuh who said yuh was done wid di wul ahh di Hughes?' Nanny said, and her eyes sparkled. 'Mi guess yuh just cyaan resist mi, just like back in di days wen.'

Pastor smiled with no warmth. 'And here I was, thinking you might have changed, Cynthia, but no, still the same woman with the same strange morals.'

'Yuh was tinkin?' Nanny said, grin fixed in place. 'Or hopin, Lyle?'

Pastor didn't flinch. 'I'm only here because your grandson is bringing flowers to my door, Cynthia.'

'Fi yuh flowahs dem?'

'She's my daughter, Cynthia. It's inappropriate.' The two of them went back and forth until it was clear they would never agree. Pastor Lyle thought my actions untoward, whereas Nanny thought there was nutun to it.

The whole while Shona stood aside and kept her eyes averted. I kicked gravel through the gate and watched woodlice run from the sun as I broke their world apart. I wanted nothing more than to be inside her head. Nanny and Pastor Lyle were voicing their opinions, and it was obvious where I stood, but Shona hadn't uttered a word since saying wow.

I caught myself staring at her, willing a rise of her head, an absent-minded swivel that brought her to me. I would know then, one look and I would know whether or not I had done the right thing.

Whether or not I was forgiven.

'Sayon,' Nanny called, 'Sayon, listen mi now, chile.'

Pastor Lyle and Shona had closed the garden gate and were back walking along the road. 'Yuh affi walk likkle Shona ome after school every day from now, Sayon. Mek sure she get deh safe. If yuh gonna be bout one another den mi an Lyle agree it's best for unuh to be frens. Yuh undahstan?' I nodded. Nanny put her hand on my head as she turned inside. 'Cheeky bugger, im couldah tek yuh fi yuh mama if im wanted, but no, im want come knock pon mi door talkin bout strange morals an whether or not mi change, im cyaan see imself? Years past, im long married, an still im deh check after mi,' she snorted, whether proudly or indignantly I couldn't tell. 'Come now,' she said, 'wi go find yuh some biscuit or sup'm, mek sure yuh mama nuh ear nutun bout dis.'

Nanny put her arm around my shoulder and drew me inside; still I lingered, sure that Shona would turn at the final second. And she did, though it wasn't as lovers did in Rick Famuyiwa movies; she wasn't pleased by the conversation's outcome, more confused. Her tilted head asked all the questions our distance wouldn't allow. She searched me for an answer and I tried to resist, but found I couldn't – the side of me that had borrowed the money from Hakim and had bought her those flowers wanted her to know. I relaxed. Softened.

And she saw right through me.

9

Quatti buy chubble, hunjed poun cyaan pay farri.

– Jamaican Proverb

I spent the second half of Year 7 in a wonderful haze. A sepia montage with little dialogue and a soundtrack provided by Earth, Wind and Fire. My grades improved. I saw Mr Barker less often, and I walked Shona home every day. We were finally close again, Elia too, but Shona and I were becoming something separate, something adult.

Shortly after the Valentine's Day incident she demanded I explain it all, the chocolates and the pink flowers. So, wilting beneath her chary eye, I spilled it all: how I had been crushing on her from the moment we met. How she knew more about me than anyone. How I remembered everything she had ever told me about herself. I proved it too. Knowing that she would want evidence for such an outlandish claim.

'When's my birthday then?' she asked. It was the first time I had seen her unsure of herself in such a way. We were stood outside her garden gate, facing each other, but her eyes kept darting sideward. She shifted on the balls of her feet, and folded her arms.

'December 14th.'

'Well you should know that, shouldn't you?' she snapped. 'What's my favourite colour?'

'Pink.'

'My favourite song?'

'"God Bless the Child" by Billie Holiday.'

'Favourite album?'

'*Lady in Satin.*' Her eyes glinted.

'What's my favourite drink?' she asked triumphantly. I reached into my blazer and pulled out a strawberry Mirinda. I'd planned on giving it to her anyway. 'Okay, you know me, so what?' she huffed, taking the drink and popping the lid.

'So?'

'What?'

'So do you feel the same? Is it the same for you?'

She hesitated, then leant forward and pecked my cheek, and in the midst of all the passers-by busily playing the protagonist in their own stories, mine paused for a moment, caught like a rest in a piece of music. Then we kissed for the first time, and I've been stuck in the mud ever since.

Elia was quick to come around as well. She told me that she had been waiting for me to man up and apologise to Shona. She admitted that there had been a number of times where Shona had to beg her not to intervene and hurry the process along. She said that it was as obvious as a creation needing a creator that we were hot for each other.

The following year Cuba joined Shona, Elia and me in secondary, but the two of us being in separate schools had changed him. I'd seen signs at Nanny's and when he hung out after school, but seeing him around adults outside of the family again really drove it home. He was rougher around the edges, cared less about strangers' feelings and was quicker to anger.

In secondary Cuba fell into a group similar to the one I'd had. They adopted his family nickname and called him Midnight. On his first day one yute tried to run banter on him but that lasted all of a day. 'Blick' was the go-to insult in secondary school, either that or you were gay. And God forbid you were actually either of those things. But I'm sure the yute who made a comment about Cuba's complexion rued the day they'd ever met.

Cuba beat him until they were the same colour, then when Hosea and Killa found out, he was beaten again, and he should've thanked his lucky stars Hakim and Jamaal didn't hear anything of it.

Cuba was quickly elevated by his peers, and my own friends used him to fill the hole Abdimalik had left; Karma in particular was drawn to him. Cuba had always held a certain sway over people. I could never place exactly what it was about him, but he had a magnetism. He inspired fascination in the same way people were taken by documentaries about serial killers and Mafia movies, they were attracted to his vitality. And where my rebellious phase only lasted the first half of the year, his never ended.

He was gradually moved from the higher sets to the lower as he submitted less and less work. The staff would always mention his potential and obvious intelligence, but refused to put the time into seeing him reach it. It seemed they had received the file a mile thick from our primary school and indeed their minds were made up.

At the same time, Jamaal was gone till November, sent down for a minor bid, and Aunty Paulette went missing for a while

– to this day we don't know where, so Nanny stuffed him in Uncle Michael's room, which he aptly named the madhouse, and spent as little time there as he could. His attendance dropped with his grades. He was always outside. He wasted his schooldays stealing push bikes that were locked in the sheds, then when school was out he would make a nuisance of himself in the community.

One of those many times he said something to me that I would never forget.

Karma and the rest of our friends were playing kerby outside an Irani kebab house, when he looked at me. I remember his expression clearly; it was doleful. His lids were narrowed but they couldn't mask the sadness behind them, nor did his attempt at a smile. We were an arm's length apart but he examined me as if I were in a police lineup. Up and down. Down and back up again. Until he announced, 'You're not like us.'

'Like who?'

'Me and Karma. The rest of our family. I'm like my mum and my brother but more time you're not like anyone, fam.'

I asked him what he meant, because at that age the last thing anyone wanted to be was different.

'You just ain't, init. Everyone wants to be around man but deep down dey hate man, but everyone loves you, g.' Then the football bounced towards us and the conversation was closed.

My mama would always complain about his behaviour. Our neighbours would write to the council with photographic evidence. The council would then send the letters to Nanny who used them to light everyone's spliffs, so they sent them to Sister Erica who deemed it my responsibility. I told her what I thought of her opinion and she washed her hands of the matter.

It wasn't the first time I'd seen her cry in my papa's arms, absolving herself of liability like Pilate did with Jesus.

Our secondary school was primarily home to yutes from Ends, but in each year there were a few kids from other areas around the city, and some of those areas had a history with ours, none more so than St Pauls.

St Pauls was an area that bordered ours. A short walk away from Stapleton Road. It was small and all the more vicious for it. Historically, it was where Bristol's Black population had begun, before we outgrew its confines and spread across the city.

Throughout the mid- to late nineties a war had erupted between the two areas, but it only survived one generation and subsequently quietened in the early 2010s. A number of my uncles had been involved as teenagers, but Cuba and I only witnessed the tail end of the drama. And though it had died down, if you were affiliated with one side, it wasn't advisable to frequent the other.

Unfortunately for them, some of the students at our school had no choice. And Cuba and his bredrins saw a unique opportunity in that and began to tax them every day. If they didn't want any trouble they had to check in. A couple of pounds a day, sometimes he and his friends would settle for paninis or sweets from tuck.

Their behaviour went unnoticed for a month before Cordell took issue. Turned out Cordell was from St Pauls, and I for one didn't fancy our chances against him; he was brawny and threw his weight around. Since I'd joined the school he'd been excluded more than anyone else, but he was never expelled – apparently he achieved good grades in maths and science so the school kept him for their ratings' sake. Cordell confronted Cuba on the playground the morning he discovered Cuba's operation. He had all the yutes Cuba had been taxing at his back and more of the St Pauls lot. I was there with my bredrins and, of course, Cuba had his. It didn't matter that he and I were cool; the ensuing fight went down in school lore.

Outsiders often find it strange that altercations can beget the strongest of friendships, but that's exactly what happened. The next week Cordell and Cuba were rolling with each other after school. The year apart from Cuba had afforded me a certain clarity, so I wasn't surprised when he stopped coming to school altogether. Nor was I surprised when I heard he was running one of Cordell's lines.

He and Cordell became two of those vagabonds who worshipped money above all else. They forsook loyalty to Stapleton Road and to St Pauls, they renounced friendships and pursued ps with reckless abandon.

Back in school, the council sent social workers to Nanny's to chase Cuba's whereabouts, but what was she supposed to tell them? That her twelve-year-old grandchild was selling heroin and sofa-surfing from one dilapidated apartment to the next with crack users and trappers? She may not have been the fondest of Cuba, but she would never turn him in to the police.

Besides, Nanny didn't know where he was most of the time; the only person who did was me. The social workers must have figured this out, because one morning they visited me at school, and with them were two policemen and Mr Barker.

I couldn't tell one fed from the other, they both sported moustaches and held their vest jackets at the chest. I'd heard it said that all police officers either had hero complexes, or they had been bullies or victims in childhood; from the chips on their shoulders I could tell that these men belonged to the victims. Throughout the meeting they scowled their immense disapproval, told me that they too had been in trouble as teenagers and called me 'son'.

Mr Barker pleaded with me to cooperate, but he knew it was a losing battle. I wouldn't give them the name of a man who had grievously wronged me, let alone my own blood. The social workers tried to appeal to my humanity. They said that my cousin was a menace to society. The drugs he sold contributed to thousands of overdoses and drug-related deaths each year. They said that Bristol was suffering a crack epidemic, and if I gave my cousin up they could get him help and make a positive change in the city. I told them I couldn't give a shit about anywhere other than my ends, or about random people dying.

What business was that of mine?

They left empty-handed and Cuba continued doing what he was doing until a year later, when Cordell was sent down for breaking a bottle over a bouncer's head. If he had stopped there he might have been charged with affray, or GBH at the very worst, but he flew off the handle. He rammed the broken glass into the bouncer's neck and got eight years for attempted murder. He gave both his lines to Cuba and told him to find someone he could trust to look after one of them, so of course Cuba came to me.

I remember being hyper-conscious of what Shona, with her fervent Christian views, would think of me trapping. But Cuba knew me well, and reminded me of my dream of owning the palace in Clifton and the music room I had promised her, so I told him I would help until he found someone else.

The line Cuba gave me was for university students, and university students were easy. I barely lifted a finger and sold faster than apples browned in the sun. Weed, pills and cocaine.

A walk in da park. Since lawyers, bankers and business executives supported their children's habits they could hardly complain, and since there was no call to clean up universities the police were happy to turn a blind eye. Boys will be boys. Girls will be girls. I made a healthy profit, all in the name of White yutes living their best lives. And with every wrap, bud and packet I drew a step closer to the honey rivers of Clifton.

10

Ahh nuh everyting come fram above ahh blessin.

— Jamaican Proverb

The money in my trouser pocket weighed heavy as I found some resolution and marched up the Jenningses' garden path, but my nerves were far from serene. Recent circumstances had placed my life's work and aspirations at terrible risk, and when I was only a hair's breadth from it too. And the pastor's invitation to dinner had come at the worst possible time.

I tapped the knocker and waited.

In my mind's eye I could still see the box of chocolates on the steps. The memory brought a wry smile. My pocket buzzed and a message from Shona flashed to the screen; she had sent the fifth single from *African Giant*. Shona was never much of a texter, she would rather travel hours to spend a moment with someone than talk on the phone, so she sent music to let me know I was on her mind.

I heard leaden footsteps on the other side of the door.

The last time I'd seen Shona's father was at a Sunday dinner two weeks earlier. He had been in a good mood then, bussin dad jokes and arguing with Shona about whether gospel influenced soul or soul gospel. But this would be the first time I'd been in his company without Shona or Marcia and I tried to still the abdabs that had taken residency in the pit of my stomach.

Surely the timing of this meeting was coincidental?

Unbidden, a story my mama had told me a long time ago found its way to the forefront of my mind.

One morning service my papa had invited backsliders to the altar as he often did, but this time no one came forward. He asked again, and again there was no response. He looked into the congregation and recognised the majority of the faces that he saw. He thought that perhaps there were no newcomers that morning, that the room was full of good Christians who knew their hearts and knew God.

Then it hit him.

He described it as a fire. A fire that burnt the clothes from his shoulders. He tried frantically to tamp it out, but it wouldn't cease. Next he heard a voice that directed him to certain members of the congregation. Some members he had known for years, others he knew less well. The voice began speaking through him and it called out five of the congregation by name and told them to come to the altar. Frozen with fear, they wouldn't come. The voice warned them once more but still they refused to come of their own accord.

That morning my papa spoke of things he had no reason to know: about members of the church committing adultery with one another, about them stealing from collection and using the church's name to profit from the vulnerable. He knew names and dates, specific times and amounts of money.

The people he exposed left the church that very Sunday.

It was another story I didn't need reminding of, and as the door opened I banished it to the back of my mind.

★ ★ ★

Pastor Lyle Jennings was as large as he had been when I was a child. Perhaps larger, since he'd let himself go. He was olive-skinned and his nose took up half his face. He had the blood-shot eyes of a smoker, but the intensity of a prosecutor. His scalp and cheeks were scraped clean and his black-and-grey goatee cleanly shaped.

The clothes he wore were of a man who didn't care for fashion and wanted the world to know. Unless it was Sunday-wear, in which case he would be dressed immaculately in suits two sizes too big. He sported a watch that he slept with, his reading glasses were kept on a string around his neck, and his wedding ring, which he never removed from his finger.

He answered the door in beige slacks and a pale blue shirt with the top two buttons undone. 'Hey, son,' he said, 'come on in.' He made space for me to squeeze past before checking the road, left then right, then he pushed the door to and followed me inside.

The Jennings household was how I imagined homes should be. Voices were raised only in laughter, there were no badbruk yutes kicking flat footballs through the halls and performing wrestling moves from pieces of furniture they weren't allowed to climb. The guests they hosted were civil, educated; they spoke about politics, world affairs and debated the notion of a biblical book being written by a woman.

There were no glass bottles, ashtrays or grinders on the coffee table. The walls were painted magnolia and stayed magnolia; there were no hand stains. The settees were hoovered and placed according to where the light fell. The Jenningses drank copious amounts of tea like we did, they spoke Patois too, but even that felt different. It was a middle-class Patois that non-Jamaicans could probably understand if they listened intently.

'I saw your cousin Winnie outside the church earlier,' Pastor said, as we stood across from each other in the corridor. 'You spoke to Shona today?'

'Yeah, yeah, she told man still. And yeah, she just sent man a song. Have you?'

'I speak to my princess every day,' he said. I could see that he wasn't entirely present. His red eyes were dimmed by a funny mist, and he kept looking at me as if I were a mirage on an oasis-starved plain.

'How come you're back, by the way?' I asked. I was keen to dispel what I prayed were groundless nerves, but his energy wasn't helping. He was acting as though he knew something, but if the rumours about Cordell's killers didn't involve myself or Cuba, and if he was in Birmingham with Shona, he couldn't know. 'I thought you went with Shona and Marcia.'

'I did,' the pastor said, and I almost collapsed with relief. Perhaps this was a simple dinner between a doting father and his daughter's man. Perhaps my paranoia had needlessly been working overtime. 'But there was something at the church that needed my attention today, and I thought I'd take this opportunity to spend time with you. We've never spent much time alone, have we?' With that he flew back into action and strode towards the kitchen. 'You go wait in the living room, young man, I'm going to finish the food.'

I did as instructed and found myself in the room I knew best. I wasn't allowed upstairs but for the bathroom, and Shona's room was especially off-limits, so I spent most of my time here; with the settees that were large enough to sleep a family, the outdated television, the shelves of Bible translations and studies, and the hundreds upon hundreds of vinyls.

This was the room where you learnt whose company you were in. Even when it was empty you could still feel Pastor Lyle, Marcia and Shona vying for control. On the coffee table the Hebrew Bible rested upon Spike Lee's *Mo' Better Blues*. Marcia's needles and threads lounged over the arm of the settee and Billie Holiday's *Lady in Satin* waited on the turntable, dissuading any who would attempt to dethrone her.

They had family portraits taken or drawn by local photographers and artists hanging on the walls. Fulani figurines that were sculpted from dark wood sat on the mantel, frozen in the complex twists and turns of dancing or lovemaking, or made with a curved vase balanced upon a towelled head halfway along a motionless journey to draw water from a well.

I lifted the needle, switched the record player on and settled the needle down. Once, Shona had explained her love for Lady Day to me. Billie wasn't the best singer, she said, she didn't have the range of Whitney nor the warmth of Erykah. But she knew pain, and articulated vulnerability in a way that could never be taught.

Few had come close since. Etta. Amy. Nina perhaps closest. But no one sang pain like Billie, and in the final years of her life Ray Ellis's forty-piece orchestra and a lifetime of drug misuse had engendered a classic. Shona finished her piece simply: Billie Holiday was Ben E. King's rose in Spanish Harlem. A rose risen from the concrete.

I smiled. You couldn't sit on the fence around Shona. If she thought she was right, by the end of the conversation you would agree.

I burrowed deeper into the sofa. This would be the third night she had been away. My only comfort was that she would be back in the morning; so much had happened, and I hadn't decided how much I could tell her, or if I could tell her anything at all.

11

Therefore I speak to them in parables, because seeing they do not see, and hearing they do not hear, nor do they understand.

– Matthew 13:13

Lost in my thoughts, I didn't hear Pastor Lyle until he put his head around the door. 'Can I borrow you for a minute, son.' It wasn't a question. I followed him into the kitchen and carefully observed his every instruction.

Rub all-purpose into the chicken. Softly, not so fast. Treat it like a woman. Take two seasoning cubes, a little water, get some salt and pepper. There's leftover broth in the fridge, take that and make a stock. Fry garlic in olive oil then mix white rice with coriander, sprigs included (waste not want not), and saffron and coconut milk too. Use the water from the broth. Set it to boil. Preheat the oven. Grease the pan.

Pastor Lyle was a man well used to good food.

We cooked in near silence. An oiled unit: assiduous and trained.

I kept an eye on the pastor whilst we worked. He seemed more relaxed than when he first answered the door, but his serenity made him a difficult man to read. It was true that he was a man of God, but what did that mean? I couldn't shake the feeling that I'd harboured from a yute; he seemed a man who had dragged the darkness from his past, through the baptism pool and out, into the light.

He hummed Nesta Marley as he worked, melting multiple songs into one, then he would hum unintelligibly until he remembered another lyric. This went on for some time until the chicken was browning in the oven and the rice was turned low.

'So how are your parents, Sayon?' Pastor asked. 'Pastor Errol and Sister Erica. They doing well?'

I hadn't spoken to my parents in months, hadn't seen them in longer. 'They're good, still,' I said, 'busy.'

'And your nanny? How's Cynthia?'

'Yeah, she's good as well.'

'That's where you're staying, isn't it? With Cynthia?'

'Yeah yeah.'

'And why's that, may I ask?'

I shrugged. He'd never shown any interest before. 'Me and my parents never really got on, to be honest. Well, there was one time me and my mum were cool, but that was a long time ago.'

'And Pastor Errol?'

'Nah, me and my pops never saw eye to eye like that.'

Pastor Lyle hummed disapprovingly. 'Keep in mind, young man, the Bible tells us that the Lord has chosen each of our fathers that he might command his children and lead his household into righteousness and justice. You would do well to spend time with your father, Sayon, he's a very respectable man.'

My papa was a pastor. I knew scripture. And I'd heard it enough times to know what righteousness meant. If your laundry was aired where the congregation could spy the blotches, you were a sinner in need of revival. If you were fortunate enough to have an office in the church, you could air your laundry in peace and the congregation would be none the wiser.

'The Bible also says turn the other cheek, and we all know that isn't the way to live,' I said. 'That's how you die round here.'

'But shouldn't we aspire to live like that? "Vengeance is mine, sayeth the Lord, and I will repay."'

'So we're supposed to accept our circumstances for what they are?'

'No, I didn't say that.' Pastor Lyle smiled, but his inner darkness was bubbling the baptism pool. Soon, if I didn't accept his offering, he would ram God past my teeth and watch me choke on His Word. 'The Lord our Christ has a plan for each and every one of us. Plans to prosper us, not to harm. Plans for hope and for a future. When we submit our lives to God we're offering ourselves into the plan He's specifically crafted for each of us.'

I refused to shy from the tension in the room. If he was speaking his mind then I would speak mine. 'I don't know about that, sir. A lot of the people in my papa's church are from round here; they blindly put their faith in God and nothing's changed for them.'

Pastor Lyle didn't respond immediately. And when he did it was to change direction. 'I can see why my daughter has so much time for you; you have an inquisitive mind like her, but you're also headstrong and full of conviction. Those things are exactly what you need to succeed in this world, but it isn't this world we're trying to succeed in.'

This time I didn't respond. If he wasn't going to get to the point I wouldn't force him into it. The timing of this conversation wasn't a coincidence, I knew that now, but I still didn't know exactly what it was that Pastor Lyle thought he knew.

'How's your cousin?' he said after a moment.

'Which one?'

He turned with the frying pan in his hand and leant against the cooker. 'Your cousin Cuba,' he said. I tried to keep my face neutral but couldn't. He saw my brow furrow, and I saw the makings of a self-congratulatory smile twist the corner of his mouth.

'He's good, still.'

'He's *good*?' Pastor Lyle echoed, swivelling back to the stove. 'I'm glad,' he quipped, his voice laden with a strange irony. 'He found his way into the church yet?'

'Nah, not yet.'

'All in due time. I came to the Lord late in life as well enuh, Sayon.'

Together we proceeded to the wooden table that stood in the far corner of the kitchen. The rice and fried vegetables were all but finished and the chicken had been wrapped in foil and moved to the lowest shelf in the oven. I slouched and spraddled in my chair, portraying an image of cool that I certainly didn't feel. Pastor Lyle had already laid mats, coasters and cutlery on the table and sat across from me.

He crossed his fingers and leant his elbows on the surface. 'I am living testimony to the Lord's mercy. The Bible tells us that we can come to Him at any time. His arms are open wide and ready to take us in. Only through the blood of Jesus do we come to see Heaven, Sayon. And Jesus takes us in all shapes, colours and sizes.

'One time I remember your great-granddaddy took me aside and he said, "Everywhere yuh go bwoy, yuh skin is yuh only sin." And I listened to him then, I mean why wouldn't I? Nanny's papa, Mister Hughes, was a serious man. But enuh, the Lord tells us differently. Maybe what he said is true of this world, but not of the next. I'm living testimony that the Lord our God is eternally gracious, no matter your background.

'When I was a little younger than you, Sayon, maybe fifteen or sixteen, I was around some bad people. My mama, God rest her soul, thought herself a godly woman, but really she used Christianity as a weapon to wield against my father's wayward-ness, alongside the belt with which she taught discipline.

'My father was a gambler, you see. Took his weekly wage to the bookie's on a Friday and gave my mother the rest of his meagre cash to feed the family and keep the home up and run-ning for the week. She couldn't say nutun to him; he would beat her if she tried. Coming from a home like that, it wasn't difficult to see why I'd be around the wrong sorts. Especially in an area like this – you youngsters call it "Ends" now, don't you? I get it, it's the end of the road if you let it be, but since it was better than what we knew back home, we didn't have no special name for it ourselves.

'Don't get me wrong, I wasn't like any of these regular hoodlums, Sayon, but I've made some bad decisions and I've hurt people. Women especially. I used to spend the night with them and would be gone before they got up in the morning. I used and abused them, never giving them the stability that women need. I was a devil. Even sometimes, when I was at my lowest, I would lose my temper and hit them.'

He paused, as if expecting an involuntary gasp or for me to recoil in disgust. I gave him nothing. I wasn't some naive member of his congregation and my blankness ruffled his feathers. The older the man gets, the faster he was as a child, except in Ends people didn't brag about how fast they could run, they bragged about how close they had come to a life of crime.

Pastor Lyle continued, only with more steel. 'Bad deeds catch up with you. You and your cousin would do well to remember that. And I should know, because my behaviour caught up with me, and when it did I didn't have any wrong-doing family members to protect me. Only the Lord was there to save me.'

His voice ebbed and flowed like a spoken-word performance. He gave time for applause and amens from the back. The less I gave him, the sterner his tone became. This was no longer a man-to-man talk. I was a child. And he was a man.

'Back in my day the whole warring postcode thing wasn't as prominent as it can be now, you see; we were about unity back then, not beef. We were more territorial about our women. And being the evil man I was, I didn't care for the sanctity of relationships. Matter of fact, I specifically hunted women in relationships, I wanted to see if I was good enough to take them away from their partners and sleep with them.

'Growing up, there was this girl in St Pauls, Sayon. Her name was Tracy, and she was real bad, Sayon. I'm talking Lisa Bonet bad. She was a Rasta's daughter, a few years younger than me. Light skin, wavy hair, real pretty. Everyone knew who she was. And Tracy had a man called Badu, and Badu ran with a crew of rude boys that people typically avoided. Hoodlums. So being the man I was, I tried to take Tracy.

'One night me and my friends went to a party she threw. I knew that she liked to drink rum, so I brought a couple bottles to share. I was more of a brandy man myself. I used to drink so much that it very well could have been the death of me.' He snorted and looked at his hands. 'Me and Tracy got drunk and somehow, someway, I suggested we go upstairs and sleep together, and we did.'

At this, Pastor rose to his feet and moved to the back door, its frosted windows reducing the grass in the back garden to lime-green crystals in the changing light.

'To this day I don't know how Badu found out,' he said, 'but a few weeks later I was walking through St Pauls, probably coming from kicking ball or sup'm, and Badu and his people were waiting for me.' He stretched out his hand and jockeyed the door handle, knowing it to already be locked.

'They didn't say a word, just crept up behind me and hit me in the back of the head with a baseball bat or sup'm. I didn't lose consciousness right away. I was tough, so I tried to fight back. I grabbed Badu and kept my arm tight around his neck, but his people hit me until I let go.

'I was floating between Heaven and Earth when they told me to strip to my boxers. When I refused, they took out their knives. They took my clothes and burnt them with their lighters. Badu's bredrins thought the shame of having me walk along Stapleton Road half-naked was enough of a punishment, but Badu disagreed. He was a troubled young man. Came from a troubled home. He took his knife and put it to my face. He told me he was going to kill me there and then. He said that what I'd done was too disrespectful for me to get away lightly. And if he didn't kill me people would talk.

'It was the first time in my adult life that my life had been in another man's hands. It was at that moment I realised that someone far more powerful held my life in His hands: the Lord God Almighty.

'As a young man I was never much taken by Bible stories or God, Sayon. I thought that if God didn't commission the writing of the Bible, my mother wouldn't have hit me so hard. I blamed Him for my poor relationship with my parents: after all, He had made me into what I was and them into who they were. I saw everything as His fault. But with Badu's knife pressed into my cheek, I realised my ignorance.

'Jesus was the whole reason I could draw breath in the first place, and it was His mercy that allowed us to make our own decisions and His blood that bought us an afterlife. Jesus died for our sins you see, Sayon – died for our sins and our free will.

'It was then I realised that I had gotten myself into that situation. That it was me. If I hadn't been chasing inappropriate relations with women I didn't care about, I wouldn't have been there in the first place. I broke down, Sayon. If he's not dead or in jail, find Badu and he'll tell you himself. I was crying, asking the Lord to forgive me, begging Him to give me another chance. I promised that I would give my life to the ministry if He would only extend His hand.

'And as always, Jesus came through, and here I am telling this story to you as right as rain with a lovely wife and a princess for a daughter. Two women I would go to the ends of the earth for,' he let go of the door handle, turned, and the weight of his gaze descended on me, 'two women I would do *anything* for, much like you would do anything for your cousin Cuba, would you not?'

I kept my mouth shut. His attitude was really beginning to irritate me. I could firm the comments about the nature of my family and their need for salvation, because in some ways it was true, many of us were in need of deliverance. But the arrogance that textured his words, the distinctions he made between his family and mine, the implication that Cuba and I were charity cases to be pitied and spoon-fed, it was becoming too much for me to swallow.

The pastor had only to push me too far and he would have a serious problem on his hands, but after the week I'd had, that was the last thing I needed. And the more the pastor drivelled, the more it seemed that my paranoia was justified – that this wasn't a simple dinner, and there was, in fact, an underlying reason beneath his blather. But I wouldn't rush him to it. I would do my best to keep a lid on my frustrations and let the conversation run its course.

12

His winnowing fan is in His hand, and He will thoroughly clean out His threshing floor, and gather His wheat into the barn; but He will burn up the chaff with unquenchable fire.

– Matthew 3:12

Before the pastor could rile me any further, he began administering the final touches to the food and I hurried to collect myself.

Back in school times, in the absence of a stress ball, Mr Barker advised that I pinch the inside of my hand to take my mind from whatever was bothering me, but by the end of the conversation I imagined my palm would be red with marks.

At the stove, Pastor Lyle sat the chicken on the hotplates. The fire beneath the rice pot was off. The dumplins had been fried earlier and placed in a white china bowl to be served alongside the salad. Two plates waited beside the cooker, a dollop of coleslaw already served to one side. Only the plantain was left. Pastor Lyle dropped thick oval slices of the fruit into a film of vegetable oil and presided over them with an eagle eye. If you left them unattended for a second, they burnt.

'Do everything as you would unto the Lord,' he whispered

to himself. 'Come help me dish this food out, yute.'

I took a serving spoon from the drawer and set about dishing the rice, but the pastor stayed my hand. I flinched. And blood rushed to my face. Everything screamed for me to respond to the threat, but when I looked up Pastor wasn't paying me any mind, his attention was still with the plantain. 'Actually, let it wait a while,' he said. 'You can sit back down. I ever tell you how your nanny and me fell out when we were younger?'

'Nah, never,' I said as I returned to my seat, busily pinching my palm.

'But you know we were close once?'

'Nah, not even.'

On the other side of the room Pastor took the carrots and onions that he'd been chopping and swept them into a frying pan. He smiled as he reached for a wooden spoon and tended the vegetables fondly. 'I think we were both around eighteen. Yeah, we must've been, because Cynthia was only just pregnant with your mama. Boy, she was bad back then, your nanny. No one could believe she got pregnant when she did. Everyone in the area wanted her, and no one knew who the fella was – still don't to this day – she'd never say. But that's not a surprise, given how secretive she is.' He paused. 'It was the early eighties, Sayon. A different place to the one you know now. Before any of them Somalians I see you hang around with came here.'

'Somalis,' I corrected him.

'Right, before any of them *Somalis* came here in the nineties and early noughties with their Islam and self-hatred.' I decided not to correct him a second time. I couldn't be bothered to remind him that it was we Caribbeans who had hated them in the first place. We should have welcomed them with open arms as the brothers and sisters they were, instead of with mistrust and severance.

He didn't know what he was talking about, and his chi-chi-misstra-know-it-all tone that rode bareback on a high horse was getting on my last nerve. I switched between drumming the surface and fiddling with my hands like a cat in rehab.

'Viv was still in his shop, though,' Pastor rambled. 'Shop's probably the only thing that's remained unchanged all these years. Back then he would have been about the age I am now, boysah, that's a long time ago, ain't it? Old boy must be about ninety now.' He laughed like adults did, without paying any real attention to whether the joke was funny or not, or whether it was a joke at all. 'Cynthia's a real woman, enuh. She did wonders with her siblings.

'When your great-grandparents passed away Cynthia filled their shoes and then some. Lord knows, she probably did a better job by herself than they ever could have together. I can't remember much about your great-grandmother, to tell the truth, Sayon; the few times I met her she was never really present, always floating in and out of whatever world she was in. But like I said, I do remember your great-grandfather, Mister Hughes.'

He chuckled and like everything else in that moment, it annoyed me greatly; I hadn't known my great-grandfather, but from the little I'd heard he certainly wasn't a saint. Still, it rubbed me the wrong way hearing Pastor Lyle speak about him as if he were one of the family.

'I tell you, I was terrified of Mister Hughes back in the day,' Pastor said, undeterred, 'and I mean terrified. He was an incredibly dark man, your great-granddaddy, figuratively and literally. In fact he wasn't far apart from your cousin, thinking about it now. We used to say if he didn't smile at night you would have missed him. We said it behind his back, of course – no one was fool enough to do otherwise.

'Every day I would bump into Mister Hughes in Viv's or walking home from wherever I was coming from. He used to slap and squeeze Viv's watermelons with his massive hands like they'd done him some personal grievance . . .'

Pastor Lyle continued reminiscing oblivious to whether I was listening. And I got the impression his story was more for himself than me. Whilst he chattered, I studied the cutlery he'd given me; there wasn't a knife.

'How she raised all you mischief-makers by herself, God only knows,' said Pastor Lyle. 'I remember she left school about fifteen, started doing hair in the same living room she raised you in. She forced the rest of them through their education, had your mother Erica and the other two after that. I'm not sure when it was that she met Mister Sinclair exactly, but he seems a good fella. Helped her where he could, not that she needed it. She had practice with children, you see. Raised her brother Michael like she pushed him out herself. Way I see it, Michael's her firstborn, Erica her second.'

My family history lesson seemed unending, but at mention of Uncle Michael the mist returned to Pastor Lyle and the tautness grew tauter.

I could see the mud in him again; the dirt he had dragged through the Jordan River. And the reason for my being there, it felt close.

'See, your uncle Michael was always simple, same how he is now, Sayon. Soft. When we was younger I told Cynthia to take him to the doctor's, find out what was wrong with him, get some help, some support. But she told me to stop making a fuss, said there was nothing wrong with him, that's just how he was, and if I thought differently then it was me with the problem, not him.'

The pastor's energy shifted entirely, he reached into the pan, ignoring the spitting olive oil, and plucked the pieces of fruit from the fire, too engrossed in his own tale to notice the pain.

'She was probably so protective of him because Mister Hughes thought Michael was a bad seed. He used to beat him something terrible, Sayon. Thwack. Thwack. Right up and down Stapleton Road he used to chase him with his slipper or, if he didn't have his slipper, then with those massive watermelon-crushing hands of his. He used to wear these great big ol rings as well so you can imagine Michael's hurt . . .' He tailed off and the mist thickened.

'One time I found your uncle Michael, enuh. Found him in the alley behind my house. I used to live right over there by Fox Road and all sorts of badnesses used to happen in the alleys behind my mother's house. Drugs, stabbings, shootings, you name it. None of them ever bothered me; I always knew the people involved. But this one thing with your uncle Michael has stayed with me for ever.

'It was winter, cold nuh backside. I was walking home late from work when I saw a fox cub lying at the entrance to the alley. The cub had its tail around its mouth and its head was on the ground and it didn't notice me coming, which I remember thinking was strange. It was just staring down the length of the alley, fascinated by something at the far end. I slowed down and tried to see what it was that had the fox's attention without startling it – I know that foxes carry all sorts of diseases, you see – but I wouldn't walk the long way around because it was right outside my yard, and as I said before; nothing comes between me and my home. So I walked right past the fox and I saw your uncle Michael sat in the snow.'

The pastor's back had been turned as he had been frying the plantain, but finally, he faced me, his face fraught with revulsion, words like ashes in his mouth. I quickly halted my distracted fussing, his abhorrence robbing me of all movement.

'Michael had the fox's mother in his arms, Sayon, and he was rocking it back and forth, stroking its mottled fur and making this strange cooing sound. You know your uncle. He's about my size. Big guy. Powerful. He'd snapped the fox's neck, see, snapped it like a chicken wing and was coddling it like me or you might burp a newborn babe.

'I still remember,' he swallowed, 'the fox cub made a God-awful sound when we took the body with us, but we couldn't just leave it there because it would attract rats. So I took Michael straight to your nanny's and we binned the fox on the way. Cynthia cleaned your uncle up. Put him in bed. Then she thanked me for getting him home and that was it. No explanation. No apology.

'So again I told her he needed help, serious help, but again she told me to mind my business. But I was shaken to my core and I couldn't let up, so I asked her what if there was a next time? Or, heaven forbid, what if we found him with one of the neighbourhood children? What if he had snapped one of their necks?

'And do you know what Cynthia said? She told me that if her brother murdered a child, a human child that God had lovingly made in his own image, that she would continue to shelter him, because he didn't mean no harm by it. She said not even God could take Michael, or anyone she loved, away from her.'

Pastor quivered with an ancient rage that made the hairs on

the back of my neck stand. 'Now remember that I knew your great-granddaddy, Sayon. I was familiar with Mister Hughes. And of course, I grew up around all of your uncles and aunties, so I know all the various things they got up to around the city. And even now, I've heard things about Jamaal, and even young Cuba too.

'But it was then, when Cynthia, who I thought to be the most principled of you all, looked me in the face and told me that she would shelter a murderer, not only from the law, but from God, did I truly understand the depravity of the Hughes family. And it was then that I told myself, that me and mine would have nothing to do with any of you, ever. So imagine my pain when Princess introduced you to me on the playground all those years ago, and then later, when you showed up on my doorstep.'

He swallowed. 'But I'm a Christian man, so I took you to Cynthia's anyway, to see if she'd had a change of heart. But my expectations were too high: of course she hadn't.' He snorted, and his blood ran hot, but mine ran hotter. I was no longer pinching my palms, I was gripping the table edge. 'I mean, as soon as she opened the front door she flirted with me,' he said. '*Me*, a *pastor*, a *married man* – still she embarrassed herself, and your entire family, with her shamelessness.'

The final straw.

I leapt from where I sat and flipped the table. Everywhere plates and cutlery crashed as my fists trembled at my side. My shoulders were broad, made broader by the respect I felt I owed the man whose kitchen I was in, whose daughter I loved, but that respect had diminished in the space of a conversation.

He was right not to have laid a knife at the table, because I might have shoved it in his neck. Instead, I collected my things and made to leave, but as I reached for the door I felt him hovering behind me.

'Pastor,' I warned, but I never had the chance to follow through with my threat.

'I saw you, Sayon,' he whispered. The words didn't quite register. 'I saw you,' I heard him say again. 'I saw you kill that boy the other night.'

13

And the dust returns to the earth as it was, and the spirit returns to God who gave it.

– Ecclesiastes 12:7

Two days before my conversation with Pastor Lyle, Cordell made parole and was released from prison.

When Cordell first went down, Cuba had made sure to wire him money, he even wrote him the occasional letter, but he stopped when he became busier and saw less need for Cordell's friendship. So word from inside was that Cordell had switched his allegiances back to St Pauls, and that he would be making a beeline for Cuba as soon as he was free. I warned Cuba that he would follow through but, my cousin being the man he was, he waved it aside.

And lo and behold, Cordell made good on his promise and ran into Cuba the same night he was released. Two days before dem likkle yutes stole from Viv, and two days before I lent Aunty Paulette money.

It was just after 3 a.m. on Stapes. The sky was clear and black. The shop shutters graffitied and locked. The road looked empty but for the foxes in the bins. My day was ending and I was coming to give Cuba his money. He said that he would be waiting on the church steps, where I found him deep in conversation with a hooded figure. I couldn't tell if it was a customer or an employee so I held back a little, waiting for the transaction to finish.

The road might've been empty, but their voices didn't carry across to where I stood beneath the shade of Elia's and Hakim's bakery, they stopped halfway, muffled by a fast-moving wind. Still, I caught the odd word here and there; *nigga . . . no way . . . fam* and *dance*. The words conveyed a sense of urgency, but I didn't think there was anything to it, so across the wide road I put my earphones in.

Earlier in the day Shona had sent me some music that I had been meaning to listen to and she'd want my opinion when I saw her, but half an album later and Cuba and the hood were still in conversation. Now I knew it wasn't a customer – it would never have taken so long, still, from the few glimpses I caught of my cousin, I assumed that the stranger was a friend rather than a foe.

Cuba's face was partially covered by his attire, partially by midnight, but each time the light shifted and I saw him, his face was open, with his usual cool nonchalance. The hooded man, however, was becoming increasingly animated. He flung his arms wide as if to say, 'But why me?' He tapped his chest then Cuba's. I heard more words, questions: *Where were you . . . So wagwan . . . Is dis what you're on?* Still, I couldn't tell if he was recounting a story or if the words were his own.

And still, Cuba was as calm as ever.

I took an earphone out. The wind had died somewhat. The man's voice was displeased and it seemed Cuba's indifference was riling him further. He said something and I heard my cousin laugh. A short barking sound he made when he wanted to ridicule or dismiss something entirely. I took my second earphone out. The man gestured to himself again, then prodded Cuba a second time. And I saw my cousin's shoulders tense, so I started across the road.

I was still certain that it was nothing. At most, an older unhappy with Cuba's success, one who'd come to moan because he was too afraid to approach Jamaal. But as I closed the gap, the glint from the streetlights caught the hood's face, and I saw that it was Cordell.

I picked up the pace. I could hear them clearly now.

'You left man to fuckin rot!' Cordell said. His voice hadn't changed, and it seemed his temper hadn't either; the same temper that had almost killed a bouncer.

'Shut the fuck up, man,' my cousin sang, amused by his former friend's anger, 'deh's bare ways to get your bread up in jail, stop fuckin complainin, akh. Look at you, big Cordell, beggin man for a fuckin handout.'

Cordell stepped backward and took a wild swing.

It grazed Cuba's cheek but was enough to send him reeling. Cordell was a big man, and prison had only made him bigger. He straddled my cousin and threw punch after punch into his cheek and jaw. He missed a couple and hit the pavement, but he wouldn't stop until Cuba was dead.

I was running now.

I took a knife from my trousers. I had carried it ever since Abdimalik was killed. I took the blade and sank it into Cordell's back. Once. Twice. Three times. Four. He was off Cuba now. Stumbling across the road. Bleeding. He leant on the street sign and pleaded for mercy, so I stabbed him again. On the steps of God's house.

14

Therefore whatever you have spoken in the dark will be heard in the light, and what you have spoken in the ear in inner rooms will be proclaimed on the housetops.

– Luke 12:3

I was at Pastor's front door. I could get to Nanny's within minutes.

Of course I would then have to pack and get to the airport, but I could catch a flight to Paris and be on my way to Jamaica by midnight. My cousins would take me in. I knew people that had caught a body, then a flight, and were living their days in the island's countryside, chopping sugarcane and line fishing.

'Sayon,' I heard Pastor Lyle say again. I stuttered some unintelligible response. 'It was you, wasn't it?' he asked.

Those two days since killing Cordell, I hadn't stopped looking over my shoulder. I couldn't remember there being anyone on Stapes besides the three of us, but my paranoia told me there must have been. It was a main road. Still, I had kept my ears to the streets and heard nothing.

With God as my witness I thought I'd got away with it.

My papa's story came to me again. I nodded slowly, and

watched the pastor's face twist into a gargoyle's grimace. 'I thought so,' he said. 'God rest that poor boy's soul.'

The door handle was still within arm's reach.

'Sayon,' I heard Pastor call, 'don't you even think about leaving. I'm not done with you, boy. You better come inside. We've got some things we need to talk about.'

So I followed Pastor Lyle back into the living room and sat – what other choice did I have? I couldn't get to Paris faster than he could call the police. And though he hadn't said he would call them, the threat carried in the air like the smell of food from the kitchen. And a thought occurred to me, one far more terrible than any justice system: 'Pastor,' I whispered, 'you're not gonna tell Shona, are you?'

He snorted. 'You're not concerned with your punishment in this life or the next, eh, son? Wait here.' He left for the kitchen and returned with a bottle of brandy. It was one of those bottles with wide hips and long necks, with room for two hands. I had never seen him drink before but the flask was half-empty.

Still standing, he took a quaff and wiped his lips with the back of his sleeve. 'Life has a funny way of working out, doesn't it?' he said, moving to the window, where he rested the bottle on the sill and leant against the wall. His body faced me but his attention was reserved for the outside world, his expression grim and his head averted as if the punishment for my sin was an airborne contagion.

'Last Judgement aside, it finds ways of making you pay. Of course, most people in this country see the justice system as retribution; prison time and community service or whatever—' Outside, sirens raced past the house and my head snapped towards the living-room door, but they didn't stop. And when I returned my attention to the pastor, I found him studying me.

'—But personally, I think regret is how the world makes you answer for what you've done,' he said, returning to the window with a grunt. 'That, and guilt.' He paused again when more sirens chased after their colleagues. And once more, I didn't know where the conversation was headed.

'Which is the difference between me and Cynthia,' continued the pastor. 'I know my wrongs. I apologise and ask for forgiveness for them. I feel guilt. Remorse. I long for improvement. Strive for change. But your nanny does none of this, she's content with who she is, what she does, and she doesn't give any mind to what God says.

'You know, earlier I didn't tell you the whole story about Tracy and me,' Pastor said, and I noticed him twisting his gold wedding band around his finger. 'I know I said that I've done some things. That I've hurt women. But it's worse than that.

'I was hoping I wouldn't need to tell you really, but here we are, and truth is, I didn't only sleep with Tracy; I put a child in her.'

Pastor stopped fiddling with his ring and took his biggest drink yet. 'After the party, weeks went by and I began to think nothing of our encounter. I was on to the next so to speak. So when Tracy first told me she was with child, I tried denying it. Told her it was Badu's. Whoever's. Anyone's but mine. I'd faced enough violence from Badu and his people. But she insisted, probably figured I would make a better father than Badu or anyone else in her life, either that or she was telling the truth and the child was mine.' His shoulders tensed as he inhaled, then dropped with a sigh. 'But I'll never know, because I made her kill that baby.

'The Catholics have it right about abortion, Sayon: all life is God-given. And like them, I believe it begins at conception.

Now imagine knowing that as the truth, whilst having done what I'd done.' The pastor's scornful eyes flickered towards me. 'It's reprehensible.

'Like I said, that's the difference between your nanny and me. I know the things I've done in the past are wrong, so I've tried to make amends through change and the desire for better. With intent. But Cynthia and the rest of your family flout your sins for all to see.' His lip curled into a grimace, and I was certain that when he looked at me he saw every one of us.

He finished the liquor, down to the dregs, then dried his goatee with his hand. He perched on the window ledge, closed his eyes and rested the back of his head on the wall, letting the bottle slip from his hands to the carpet.

'You were right, you know. I wasn't even meant to be here that night. I was supposed to be with my wife at our daughter's concert, celebrating her passion, her success. But I was called back for some minor emergency at the church two days ago. By the time I finished it was the early hours of the morning, and I told my wife that I would be back up after I'd caught some sleep.

'So I lock up and I stop at the church window like I often do, the one that overlooks Stapleton Road, and I see you stood outside your cousin's bakery. I did think to myself how late it was, but didn't think much of it, really. In face, I thought about leaving right then so I could come and spend a second with you before going home. But the look on your face . . . Then I noticed your cousin, and the boy he was arguing with . . .'

He tailed off. 'You know I looked for you afterwards?' he said. 'I prayed for hours first, asked the Lord for guidance, for the Holy Spirit to fill me with wisdom and lead me down the right path; then I looked for you, late into the morning until the sun rose. And when I couldn't find you I thought maybe I hadn't seen what I thought I had. That perhaps it wasn't you, but another boy, somebody else's responsibility.

'But deep down I knew; because when I asked the Holy Spirit for guidance you know what came to mind? The story about your uncle Michael and the fox cub.' His eyes were still closed but he'd gone back to touching his ring. 'After all these years I'd almost forgotten it. But I believe the Holy Spirit brought it to my mind for a reason; because back then I told Cynthia to get Michael help, and she ignored me. Now years later you've put me in the very circumstance I warned her against. I believe God wants me to take my own advice; so I will try my best.

'After all, does the Bible not say if anyone is caught in a transgression, the spiritual should restore him in a spirit of gentleness? And that if someone brings him back to the truth, he will save his soul from death and cover a multitude of sins?'

His eyes opened and it was obvious the liquor was having its way with him; each of his blinks was becoming lazier, every movement cumbersome. His head listed to one side as he contemplated me, and he spoke like a man who wanted to be rid of the millstone around his neck. 'If my princess hears what you've done, it will be the end of what the two of you have going on; you know that, don't you?'

It was the first time he'd asked a non-rhetorical question, but I said nothing.

I wanted to contest him with everything I had, but I couldn't. Since stabbing Cordell I was far more concerned with how I would explain the situation to Shona than any retribution from Cordell's people in St Pauls or the law. And the pastor knew that.

'You may think that what you have with my princess is stronger than what you've done, that together the two of you can overcome any obstacle you might face, but I'm telling you, Shona will run for the hills if she learns what's happened.'

'She won't,' I heard myself say; it was barely more than a whisper, but it was said with enough hurt to carry across the room.

Pastor grunted. 'Let me ask you a question then. What love is greater than a father's love?' He waited, but again I could provide no answer, and a little malice crept into his tiresomeness. 'You think you know her better than I do? That the love you share is worth more than mine?'

I had no idea what a father's love felt like, but I knew that when Pastor Lyle spoke of fatherly love he imagined his Lord. He imagined the knife that fell from Abraham's hand, the fish that carried Jonah to his calling and the boat that scooped Noah from the flood. He imagined above and beyond. And I realised that I was nothing in the face of such naked certainty.

I would've loved to have beaten him back with assurances of my own. I would've loved to have claimed that Shona would understand that I was protecting Cuba, that there was no other way. I would've loved to have said that Shona would stand by me, no matter the odds, but I couldn't.

'The Lord our God asks much of his servants, and I believe this is my greatest test yet,' Pastor Lyle said. 'These past two days I've sat for hours at a time in conversation with God, telephone within arms' reach, knowing I have two choices; to do what I want to do, which is to call the police and have the law of the land deal with you, to get you as far away from my princess as possible. Protect my family.

'Or to do what God wants me to.

'I would love to curse you, Sayon Hughes. And a part of me wishes now, more than ever, that I turned you from my door as a child. Abandoned you to the corruption of your family name and let you wallow in your worldly punishment, only from afar praying that you would seek repentance before you met your Maker. But I didn't. And now here we are.

'You may be responsible for much of my daughter's happiness, Sayon, that much may be true, but she can do far better than you, we both know that, don't we?' I didn't answer and nor did he expect me to. 'Enuh, have you ever stopped to think about how your relationship with my daughter affects Shona's mama and me? How it looks for Pastor Jennings' only daughter to be with a Hughes?

'If I tell her what I know, it will mark the end for you two. But I'm not stupid, Sayon. She loves you. She may never forgive you if she finds out what you really are. But far worse than that, I know she won't forgive me for being the one to tear you apart, and she's my only child, Sayon. My second chance at being a father. If I lose her, I lose everything. My entire world. And if I allow our relationship to rupture like you and your parents', if I allow bitterness to consume her spirit, then I will be keeping my own flesh and blood from the very kingdom I have strived all these years to enter: the Kingdom of God.

'All sin is the same in the eyes of the Lord, and thus the answer is clear; I can tell Shona, hand you over to the authorities, have you go jail; where you'll become institutionalised and gain allies in sin, further fastening your fate to eternal punishment. Or, I can take you in, as God intends, and have you seek His mercy, as I have. Have you enter the Kingdom of God with my daughter, so that her inheritance is never in jeopardy.

'So, if the condition for eternity is the blood of Christ, and if the Holy Spirit intends to reach you through me; then my goodwill has a condition of its own, because I will restore a spirit of gentleness in you, Sayon, by force if needs be.'

He rose to his feet and prowled the room. 'You have to come out from under the Hughes' influence, young man. You can no longer have anything to do with your relatives. Which means you have to stop associating with your cousin Cuba, cut all ties, because that boy is a lost cause.

'Not only that, you have to move out of Cynthia's house. If that means you move in with us for the time being, then so be it, but you will come into the House of the Lord, Sayon. You will become a disciple of Christ and born again. If you do not feel it already, you will learn remorse, and you will learn to live with your past as I have. To ask for constant forgiveness and continually work to make better.

'And do not think you're getting away with anything, because regardless of whether you go to prison or remain outside; you will face God on the Day of Judgement. And you must be surrounded by His Word in order to find the sincerity needed to repent.'

He stopped his prowling and went again to the window, where seconds became minutes, and neither he nor I spoke a word.

My pocket buzzed. Cuba was outside. And I was desperate to leave. The room had become oppressive. I mumbled that I had to go, and for the second time that evening I headed for the front door.

'Sayon,' Pastor Lyle called after me, 'I will give you some time to think things over, but do not mistake my kindness for weakness and take too long before reaching a decision. I have already waited two days and my patience is wearing thin. And if you do not come back to me with the right answer, then Shona *will* hear about this, and the justice system can deal with you after all.'

I closed the door to without bothering to reply, just as he left his conditions to show me out.

15

You have set our iniquities before You, our secret sins in the light of Your countenance.

– Psalm 90:8

Cuba was sitting on the bonnet of his car at the bottom of the Jenningses' garden. He rested his spliff between his black lips and watched the clouds disperse as the sky tamped the sun's tirade. 'Yo, cuz,' I said, touching his fist. He smiled, and told me that we needed to take a drive.

The people carrier he was pushing had baby seats in the back and a sandalwood air freshener swung from the rear-view. The seats had coffee stains and the amount of dust on the dashboard meant the windows had to be permanently ajar. He passed me the blunt and we took off along Stapes.

'So how'd it go, fam?'

'It was calm, still,' I said, pulling on the weed and praying the colour in my cheeks wouldn't betray the truth.

I wouldn't tell Cuba about my conversation with the pastor, or even that he knew at all. I needed to use the short time that he had given me to reach a decision for myself, a decision that would hurt the least amount of people that I loved as possible.

Besides, I knew the things that my cousin was capable of and doubted such extremes were necessary, for now at least.

'What did her pops want?' he asked.

I shrugged. 'Obviously, my man knows me and Shona are gettin more serious, init, wanted to make sure man knows what man's gettin into.'

Cuba side-eyed me with amusement. 'You let the old man pressure you?'

'Shut yuh mout,' I laughed. It was important for me to appear as normal as I could; you developed an intuition against liars in the life we lived.

'Nah, man's playing, still. My man knows how much you love Shona, fam. You man are for life, you get me? Serious tings man, I respect it. More time I need to find man one light-skinned gyal to breed, have some pretty yutes your colour.'

We laughed, but the smile fell from our faces as we left Ends and drove into Fishponds, up through the north-east of the city.

Whenever we left our area we kept one eye on the mirrors. Unmarked police cars would tail us for miles until we made it home. We knew how to avoid them, though. We knew their registration plates began with WX or EO, gun police drove X5s, and undies were always in BMW estates, and if two White men in a van took the same turns as us, we hit the accelerator.

This time, however, the coast stayed clear and Cuba eased into his seat. 'I got some bad news, blud, but before I tell you just know man's handlin it.'

'Wagwan?'

'You know the little man you seen in the whip earlier?' I nodded. The shook one. Cuba paused, unsure how to package the news. 'He saw you stab my man.'

I sank lower into my seat and kissed my teeth. The more people that knew, the more likely it was that Shona would find out. And the law too. The pastor knew that he couldn't truly threaten me with police, no man could frighten me, but if I was arrested and charged I would be apart from Shona for years.

This was becoming too much of a headache. I held out my hand and Cuba passed the weed.

'But don't stress it,' he said, moving to sponge the water he'd spilt. 'Like man said, man's handlin it.'

'How?' I asked, after taking the longest draw of my life.

'I'm gonna make him come work for man, init. Make man my younger.'

I puffed the blunt and said little for the remainder of the journey.

The yute's name was Junior. He was fifteen and had lived in Ends his whole life. That night he had been going home from his bredrin's when he saw us on Stapes. He knew who we were and thought about taking another route, but by the time I ran across Stapes with my knife swinging it was too late. He could only duck behind a bin and watch the entire spectacle play out.

Apparently, Cuba had seen the little man as he pulled me from Cordell's body. He recognised him from around the way, but he didn't know his name. Still, this was Ends, it wasn't difficult to find out. Cuba asked one of his runners – one of the two yutes who had been in the back of the car – and they had his name within seconds.

The next day Cuba was waiting to pick Junior up from school. He took the little man to a bando on the outskirts of the city. He had people there and introduced the process to Junior. There was a room in the bando with a thick mattress, television and console. After showing him the ropes he told the little man to go into the room and chill for a while. He sent a young girl after him to keep him company. When they came out he handed Junior five bills and welcomed him to the lifestyle.

'Where we goin?' I asked. We were in an area I wasn't familiar with; the houses were either detached or semi-detached, and they all had England flags in their bedroom windows, unkempt hedges and Staffy mutts.

'Pickin up Winnie,' Cuba said.

'What's she doin out here, blud?'

'Tryna get some extra coins, init.'

We pulled into a driveway and waited. Garden gnomes lined the gravel path and rusted BMXs lay abandoned in the over-grown grass. Five minutes passed and Winnie appeared on the doorstep with a saggy White man behind her. He grabbed her face with his fat hands and kissed her on the mouth before slamming the door shut.

She hurried to the car. 'Yo family,' she cried, bundling herself across the baby seats. 'How you man doing you good yeah bless for picking me up Midnight you're a real one big man ting you ain't nowhere near as bad as everyone says you are enuh you're a real one for dat for real and yo Sayon cuzzy what you telling me g bless for dat food earlier dat niced me till just now enuh.'

'Yo, cuz,' Cuba replied. Winnie passed Cuba some money and he gave her a tiny parcel in return.

We had been selling our cousin hard food for the past five years. The way we saw it, if we didn't, somebody else would. The difference being they wouldn't give a toss what it was they were selling her, and truesay most of the stuff on road was watered down and stepped on anyway. The way we did it, we checked the quality, quantity, and made sure she never injected. We regulated her. We didn't really make no money off her either, since it was usually us giving her the money she then used to pay for the drugs.

Together the three of us drove back to Ends and dropped Winnie outside Viv's.

When she hopped out the car Cuba pointed to the houses across from Pastor Lyle's church. They were tall, with stairs that led to basement apartments and had once been enviable; now the brickwork was grey-green instead of beige and the tenants had little respect for anything.

'One more thing, g, you know Winnie sleeps down deh sometimes init?'

'Yeah?'

'Dat's where she was sleeping two nights ago.'

He let his words hang until I grasped his meaning. 'Shit!' I said, banging the dashboard. Dust flew into the air. Could this get any worse? 'Did she tell you she saw?' I asked, but Cuba was already shaking his head.

'She hasn't said nutun to man, but the little man told me he seen her come out after we cut. Said he thought he saw some-one watchin from the church as well. Shona's pops didn't say nutun, nah?'

I promised he hadn't.

'Shit,' I said again. Winnie came out of Viv's and passed us two patties through the window. Viv shipped them from yard. They came fresh and frozen in white boxes, nutun like that cheap, packaged shit non-Blacks sold.

'Yo I'm gonna see you man later just gonna go buck a couple of my peoples in dem yards over deh have a good night yeah love you man take care of yourselves love yeah.' Winnie waved and ran across the road with no mind for the traffic. Cuba honked the horn and we watched her disappear down a flight of stairs. Next to the stairs the police tape had been taken from around the street sign and Cordell's blood had been washed away.

It was like nothing had ever happened.

'It's fucked up, but you know what has to happen init?' Cuba sighed. I stared at him in silence. He couldn't mean what I thought he did. 'We can't deal with whoever was watchin from the church less we find out who dat is, man's already patterned the little man, but Winnie's a fuckin liability, fam, she rah has to go.'

'You're fuckin with me right now, init?'

'You looked after man,' he stated. Slow and careful. The practised words of a certain mind. 'You had my back now man's got yours. Remember what happened last time you left Winnie alone? Dat can't happen again, g, dis is rah serious, blud, it ain't food; dey'll hang you out to dry dis time, truss me. So fuck dat. Dis time just sit back, bake off, and let man cut the losses for you.'

'Dis is man's cousin, fam.'

'Nah.' He shook his head, jarred that I wasn't grasping something so simple. 'Man's talkin bout me and you. You and Shona. The house. The future. Man's talkin about the tings dat matter, g. The fuck has Winnie ever done for our family but caused trouble and brought heat on us? The fuck has she done for you?

'If she wasn't deh dat last time den it wouldn't have gone down like it did. It's simple, blud. If we leave her she'll snitch, whether she means to or not, you get me? Now she's involved and she has to go, cuz. And you best pray dat whoever was in the church keeps deh mouth shut, otherwise dat's another body dat has to be caught.'

'Dis ain't right,' I muttered. This was exactly why I hadn't told him about Pastor Lyle, and I knew I never could. Cuba saw every problem as surmountable, and violence was his pickaxe and rope.

In a way he was right: Winnie was a liability. But above all else, she was our cousin.

Cuba took another pre-roll and lit it with a cupped hand. 'It's shit, but it is what it is man,' he said. 'All we have to do is give her a little more food dan usual. Give her a needle, you know she's been cattin to use a needle again, den she'll take care of herself. After dat you're home and dry, cuz. Home and dry.'

I couldn't hear any more. I pushed the door open and swung from the passenger side. 'Dis convo ain't over, blud,' I told him, then I left Cuba in the car and walked.

There were three witnesses. Some likkle man called Junior. The love of my life's ministering father. And my vagrant cousin.

I had Pastor's threat hanging over me, and now Winnie's life hung in the balance too. The only way I could foresee the situation worsening was if Shona found out the truth of the matter. The last time I'd lied she'd made it abundantly clear that if it happened again she would be done, which was why I had been thinking about telling her in the first place. But there was a thin line between love and hate and Pastor Lyle was right; she wouldn't forgive murder.

16

Behold, the former things have come to pass, and new things
I declare; before they spring forth I tell you of them.

– Isaiah 42:9

The first and last time I had lied to Shona was the same situation
that had caused Cuba to have such little faith in Winnie.

It was the summer after I took my GCSEs. We broke from
school in May and spent the long days as children should:
kicking ball, chasing girls and selling weed. Except I hadn't a girl
to chase. I was glad to settle into the scripted childhood sweet-
heart story with the girl I loved. And aside from keeping the
drugs from Shona and the odd pregnancy scare, life was good.

Shona and I spent our sunny days off Ends, in Bath and
Clifton, where we would check upon the house-atop-the-hill. It
was still owned by the same couple who had been weekending
when Cuba and I had broken in, and it was as charming as ever.

When it rained we stayed inside and watched movies and
played video games. And Shona would curate playlists and sets
for her new radio slot.

To her parents we were best friends, whereas my family put
rubbers in my jeans and the soles of my shoes. Neither side was

wrong, nor was either exactly right. We were somewhere in the middle, happily adrift. Our maturity hadn't extended as far as labels yet, but what did that matter? If I wasn't with Shona I was working or asleep, and since I barely slept, my days were filled with little variation.

Before getting our results we were both happy with how our exams had gone. I cared a little less than Shona so she shouldered the brunt of our concern. At random moments she would sigh and doubt our passing, but of course we passed, and when August came our grades were all As, Bs and Cs.

Shona achieved the highest grades, then Elia, then me. At the time Shona was the only one who had any further aspirations within education. Elia had her mind set upon running her own bakery, whereas I was left to lust after a place I could only hope to attain by selling drugs.

We celebrated our results at Eastville, a family park between my area and Fishponds. Scores of yutes from schools all across the city came to play music, barbecue and swap numbers. A rainbow of black, brown and beige – and White girls who wanted light-skinned yutes. At times such as these tensions were forgotten and enemies could operate in the same space with no passa. When good vibes and sunshine prevailed. I saw yutes arm in arm, laughing at someone else's expense, who on another day had chased one another through estates.

Cordell brought a system and appointed himself the DJ and the sound switched between bashment and home-grown rap.

I had a little pouch full of flavours around my neck and sold them whenever Shona wasn't looking. She chatted away with her friends beneath a crab apple tree and I watched Cuba play football in the distance. The rest of our age-mates fanned about the place, mingling.

Then, from the roots of the tree crawled Winnie with an outstretched hand. 'Yo cuz,' she called. Some of Shona's friends giggled and others openly laughed. Winnie paid them no mind. 'Yo cuz lemme chat to you quick real quick don't worry I ain't tryna get you to take me no place hey Shona how you doing you good yeah?'

'I'm good, Winnie, yeah.' Shona smiled, whilst her friends stood up and went to find somewhere that smelled a little less noxious. 'You looking after yourself?'

'Yeah you know me just getting by by the grace of God you know I don't have to tell you though your daddy's a pastor just like Sayon's daddy both of you got the path laid out for you you guys got the red carpet from Earth to Heaven god bless unuh you know big man ting God bless.'

Shona knew about Winnie's addiction, she knew about Cuba's drugs, but both Cuba and I had threatened Winnie on pain of death that if Shona ever found out about my involvement there would be hell to pay.

'What you need, Winnie?' I asked; the sun would fall and rise if I left her to talk.

'Just a Q cuzzy.'

I couldn't help but laugh. 'You want bud?' I checked, she nodded. 'Where'd you get the money for a Q? You spoke to Cuba about dis?' She shook her head. 'He won't give you dat, Winnie. Not dat much.' I took a draw from the pouch and gave it to her, careful to keep the pouch's content from Shona's attention. 'You can have dis to yourself doe, smoke it here wid us.'

She lit up. 'Wid you two I'm not intruding nah?'

'Of course not, sit down.' Shona smiled, patting the grass. Winnie then took the draw and perched beside us.

'Ay I appreciate you guys so much,' she said, dabbing at her eyes to keep from tearing. She licked the paper and rolled it with a shaky but practised hand. 'I'm so sorry you have to see me like dis in dis way Shona I wasn't always like dis was I Sayon I was fun when you were a yute you remember init I used to carry you on my back and run around the house and outside wid you you remember we used to play cowboys?' I told her I did. 'Yeah dat's what I'm really like dat's the real me not dis,' she paused, and gestured at her brown jeans and stained camo jacket, 'dis mess,' she laughed.

Shona took a bottle of perfume from her bag and put it in Winnie's hand. 'You take this, Winnie; this is yours. I got some face and hand cream for you too.' Before she could protest Shona held up her hand. 'Take it, Winnie, it's fine. Say got it for me and he can get me some more, can't you, Say?'

'Of course,' I replied. My cousin looked between the pair of us and relented.

'You guys are a beautiful couple,' she sighed. I saw Shona fix her mouth to remind Winnie of our label-less relationship, but I interrupted before she could.

'We are,' I agreed.

Shona tipped her head to the side. 'Oh, we are?'

'Yeah,' I shrugged, trying to play it cool, 'don't even deep it too much.' I failed. Shona held my eye until I caved and broke into a massive grin. 'We are,' I said again, this time with more conviction.

'Well then,' Shona said, her own smile competing with mine for the happiest in the city, 'I guess we are.'

The sun fell and the crowd swelled. Bottles of tonic wine and NOS canisters littered the grass and the sound system had spawned another speaker. There were more people now, olders, but the vibe remained unchanged.

Fishponds was a strange area. They had roads like Thingwall Park where houses went for half a million pounds and sold to Asians like sky juice, then there were places like Oldbury Court and Hillfields that were full of Cuba's customers and were about as welcoming as a fist to the face. No doubt it was the former who called the first police cars to the scene.

Like mosquitoes to light, police hovered at Black functions, and one carful was never enough. Soon they had three cars and a bully van. Fifteen police officers strutted through the barbecue like lions at a watering hole. They kept their hands on their cuffs and nodded tight-lipped smiles at our unresponsive faces. They stopped in front of a group of boys I knew and asked what was in their water bottles; they were told in no uncertain terms to fuck off.

Everywhere they strolled they stirred the hotpot, tentatively at first, making sure they didn't break the swede, but when that didn't work they started prodding like a fork to a boiled dumpling. They cornered people into having conversations. One girl began to walk away, so they pulled tasers and headlocked her until she calmed down.

'Say,' Shona whispered, pulling my sleeve. She took my pouch and slid it into her handbag, thinking I might have stowed another blunt, and it was perfect timing because an officer whose face I recognised spotted me.

'Sayon,' the officer called cheerily, 'Sayon Hughes. How are you, son? How's your cousin Jamaal? Haven't seen him in a while. How's he doing with the family business now that your cousin's retired?' I rose to my feet. The officer was joined by three others. 'Whoa, you're getting tall there, ain't you, son?'

'I don't know you, g, don't say man's name like you know

man. Just keep movin,' I replied. Shona rose to her feet and scowled from beside me. And another officer joined the group.

'Don't be like that, Sayon, I know you. I know your whole family, see. I saw Jamaal's younger brother Midnight playing football down there. He's destined for a life behind bars, that one, isn't he? Do you think he knows where Jamaal is? Cos we've been meaning to have a word with him.'

This time I didn't respond, and Karma and Cordell floated to my side. It was a Western stand off, and I knew neither of my bredrins had a problem fighting uniforms. 'Keep movin, g,' I repeated, and they were about to, until they noticed Winnie.

When the police had arrived, the underage drinking and blatant smoking had curbed a little. Not completely, but enough so that the officers felt noticed. Winnie, however, was sitting at my feet, puffing loud without a care in the world.

'What's this?' The officer grunted; he sniffed the air like a character in a children's cartoon. 'Is that ganja I smell? Stand up, young lady.' The officer went to lift Winnie by her shirt, but I pushed his arm aside and barred his path.

'Don't touch my cousin, blud,' I warned him. Another couple of friends appeared at my side. One of the officers held her walkie-talkie to her mouth and whispered for back-up, and all fifteen officers surrounded us. The officer who started it looked from me to Winnie and back again.

'No, no,' he smiled, 'like I said, I know your family, Sayon, but I don't know this one. And she looks like she's taken more than weed, doesn't she? So I'm just gonna have a little search of her person. Then maybe I'll have a search of you, so you stay right there, thank you.'

I was detained. Then, as promised, they searched my person. Afterwards they searched Karma and Cordell but didn't find a thing. Then they searched Shona and found my bag. They didn't waste any time whipping her arms behind her back, nor did they waste time reaching for their cuffs. And I don't know what incensed me more; Shona fearfully calling for me, or the way the arresting officer smiled as I claimed the bag as my own and showed them my line to prove it.

I didn't flinch when they took me away; I didn't flinch when Cuba posted bail; I didn't even flinch when they handed me a ten-month sentence. I served six of those months and was out without a scrape. But I couldn't pretend that Shona's face, as they took the flavours and wraps from the pouch, didn't break my heart.

'Whose drugs are they, Say?' she whispered, with tears in her eyes before they pushed my head into the back of the squad car. 'They're Cuba's, right? I'll go get him, he'll tell them.'

But my silence said it all.

When I came home six months later Shona was at the prison gates with Cuba and Karma. Over the course of my sentence I had written her letters, but she'd only replied to say that we would talk when I was free.

After embracing me, Cuba and Karma went to share a blunt and gave us some privacy. 'Why would you lie, Say?' Shona scowled. 'Did you think I'd judge you or something?'

'You're Christian, init,' I replied, hating the defensiveness in my voice.

'Yes, I am a Christian, Say. And my dad is a pastor. But that doesn't mean that we all have the same views about everything. Your dad's a pastor as well, but that will never be you. We aren't what our parents are, are we? Christianity isn't so black and white.' She prodded her finger into my chest. 'Listen, Say, I'm

119

not gonna be one of those girls whose boyfriends are trappers and they do whatever they're told and never stand up for themselves. And I ain't gonna be one of them girls who waits around while their man sits in jail. I've got too much to do in this life, so you better not go back inside again.'

She stepped into my chest, grabbed ahold of my arms, and put them around her. 'But I won't ever judge you, Say, so just don't lie to me, okay? That's the one thing I can't forgive. You have to promise me.'

And I promised her.

17

What is desired in a man is kindness, and a poor man is better than a liar.

– Proverbs 19:22

Whilst inside I entered a covenant with God that said I would never lie to Shona again, then outside the prison gates Shona impelled herself into the covenant.

Now years later, after killing Cordell, a couple days after my meeting with Pastor Lyle, I was sat inside a breakfast place on Stapes faced with the hardest decision I'd ever had to make.

The place was a full English kind of joint. Black pudding, tomatoes, strong tea and sausages. It didn't shy from suet like the health-nut places in Cabot Circus. It was the designated stop for hardworking people who were up before the sun. They understood that there were some things that shouldn't change, and that grease was one of them.

For all their community work, the church was a bubble, and Shona never told her parents about the time I'd served. In lieu, she told them that we were on a break and Pastor Lyle's delight had quietened any probe he might have voiced. Six months later she told them that we were back together, and he had nothing nice to say so he said nothing at all.

I had arranged to meet Shona at 11 a.m. but arrived early. The café cooked everything fresh so I ordered for the two of us and took the sofas in the corner furthest from the door.

Four builders sat across from me, their arms thick and tattooed, their tongues coarse like sailors', and Bristolian. They hit every 'R' like joyriders hitting speed bumps and spoke with little shame. In fifteen minutes I learnt the names of their women and children, that one of them had the clap and the other owed six grand to a loan shark.

From where I sat, I spotted Junior going about his business (Cuba's business) with some other youngers. My cousin had granted him his life, and he would return the favour with a lifetime of servitude and silence.

The youngers huddled together like penguins, waddling along Stapes as if they owned it, bumping into civilians and slowing traffic with their meandering strides. A stranger might have thought Junior one of them, an evil yute from a dysfunctional family raised into the life he lived, but the discerning eyes of strangers were ignorant and quick to assume. And they would have been far from the truth: Junior was a good yute, from a good home.

Whether I knew him or not, a single glance and I would have picked him from the rest like a prize at an arcade. His new and expensive clothes wouldn't hide him, nor would the company he kept. Our world was alien to him, but it seemed he was intent on passing.

By the time it reached 11 a.m. there was still no sign of Shona.

The next faces I saw outside the window belonged to Winnie and that of her mother, Aunty Winifred. As I knew her, Aunty Winifred was a regretful and corrupt woman. If Pastor

Lyle had sat in his kitchen and told her that vengeance was the Lord's, she would have spat at him, and then taken said vengeance.

I watched her beckon Winnie, and Winnie went to her, head bowed, and suffered the inevitable lecture that followed. Aunty Winifred brought her sermon to a close by whacking Winnie upside her head and giving her twenty pounds. I couldn't hear them, but I knew Aunty Winifred was warning her away from drugs; after all, I'd heard the conversation a thousand times.

Aunty Winifred would make Winnie promise that she would put an end to the 'nonsense', as she called it, then Aunty Winifred would give her some money and leave, satisfied by the warmth that parenthood brought. Winnie would then come running to Cuba or me with the twenty pounds that she was proud not to have borrowed from us.

And so it went on.

'Say!' Shona cried.

She weaved her way through the chairs and tables and crashed opposite me. 'I just saw Winnie and your aunty outside, but you'll never guess what happened this morning. Sorry I'm late by the way.' Her hoody's drawstrings were pulled tight over her hair, her eyes were still a little puffy with sleep and she had thrown on any old thing. 'So, I was in the shower, as you can see—' She tugged at a curl for evidence; it was sopping with water or conditioner, I didn't know which.

'I can see—'

'And Daddy just started using the water from the sink! Like he didn't know I was in the shower!'

'That's terrible!' Our many years together had taught me that she wanted her tendency for drama reciprocated, except she noticed the irony in my voice and gave me a dark look – though it didn't last very long. Her face broke into the same smile she smiled whenever she looked at me, one that alluded to every inside joke we had ever made. Every intimacy. Every affirmation. It was a smile that told me she knew me; she understood. And she couldn't help herself.

The Bible said that partners joined by the hand became one in flesh, but that was already true of Shona and me without the printing of a certificate or the trading of rings. We walked in a coincidence of pitch and sounds, safe in the gentle naivety of youthful love.

Shona was several shades darker than I was. A shade or so darker than a violin. It's funny how complexion is the first thing we notice, as if our other features aren't as prominent. Her mouth was wide and curved in the middle like a violin's waist, her top lip brown, her bottom lip pinkish. She wore her hair in as many styles as Moesha. A shea butter baby. Her nose was broad, close to her face and cute; her teeth were even and white.

When we fell asleep together I used to put my hand to her forehead and counted the fingers it took to cover. She would swat my hand away and laugh. She had a big forehead, like every pretty girl did. Her lids hung low like police helicopters but her eyes were always alive, searching for the next point of inspiration. She had four piercings in her right ear, five in the left. Her parents had started a life-long addiction when they pierced her lobes a few weeks after she was born.

'Tell man wagwan wid dis concert den,' I asked, 'how did it go?'

Shona's dream was to set the music world alight, and she had meticulously planned the steps she needed to take. She subscribed to the ideology that you couldn't be a catalyst for change as a consumer, you had to be in the mix, and in her humble opinion, popular music had taken a turn for the worse.

From birth, Pastor Lyle had her on a strict diet of seventies and eighties reggae: Freddie, Alton, Gregory and Dennis Brown. And hits from the midwestern states of America: Smokey, Stevie and Aretha. She introduced herself to nineties and noughties R&B, she knew rap too and we used to listen to grime through her Walkman earphones.

She studied music. Played a handful of instruments. Read theory. She clung to it like the impoverished clung to moments of power. Shona knew music as freedom, and what better thing to pursue as a career?

She found her first success as a tween writing a blog whose influence reached thousands. Her articles were re-posted by a couple of musicians of some renown and it took her from concert to concert. No matter who came to the city, she was there, dragging me along. Even if she held derisory opinions about the artist prior to seeing them perform, we still went. It wasn't often her mind was changed but there had been the odd occasion where she would gush about how wrong she had been.

Shona was the type of person who wanted not only to understand but also be on everyone's side. She searched for excuses for the artists for whom she had soft spots; she would tell her readers about the pressures of being signed and the incessant call for them to find commercial success rather than their own sound. Her knowledge took her from writing to talking, and when we left school she earned a late-night/early-morning slot on a local radio show.

From there she was able to connect with all sorts of musicians, managers, radio people and videographers. The city's movers and shakers. She met a singer too, Chenaniah, and after writing an EP for her, the pair hit it off. After a year they established a record label and hit the ground running. Their brand was rising and everything was going according to plan.

'Say, it was so good. There were so many good people there. Fans and industry people curious about what we've got going on—'

'You get deh details—?' I said. She was already nodding.

'Of course, of course. I gave them my card and took theirs. Everyone kept saying they were surprised to see someone so young so passionate about the other side of the industry; they were like, "Usually you guys just want to be the singers and rappers," – which I think was shade – but a couple of people recommended some routes to go further in the industry; overall they were really supportive.'

'What routes?'

'Oh, distribution deals and that,' she said, 'nothing I haven't already thought of. Oh and Say, Chenaniah was so good, doesn't she sound like Dinah Washington? You're smiling, I've said that before, init?'

I laughed and motioned for her to continue.

Shona's dreams were as real to me as the house-atop-the-hill. The inroads she had made were already beyond what most people had expected, but I hadn't doubted her for a second.

She used to work her slot on the local radio show, not long after I came out from prison. Her manager entrusted her with the keys, and when she left at 11 p.m. Shona would sneak me inside like a midnight marauder. The room she recorded in was large with tall windows that overlooked the area. It wasn't too far from Stapes and I was still doing my thing in the streets, so I would come after nightfall with my snacks and my weed, and we would smoke and eat and moon dance whilst she played Dwele, Eric Benet and D'Angelo's *Voodoo*.

Oftentimes her conscience won over and she would leave me the weed and her eyes would sparkle and she would tell me everything about the songs she played whilst I lay on the carpet with my eyes closed. I could listen to her talk forever. Fine and mellow. Swinging gently with Nelson. She told me to sit back and *juslisen* to the *luvanmusiq* because I was always welcome in Shona's Urban Hang Suite.

Sometimes she would play the instrumental cuts from *Brown Sugar*'s deluxe, or 9th Wonder, and sing the songs she had written for Chenaniah. Or we would laugh about the times where we had been at our weakest and revel in how tight we were then. On starry nights she would find the brightest and tell me to which constellation it belonged. She would promise me the world and endow it with Jesus' name.

I waited two hours whilst she filled me in, until I could wait no more; I had a decision to make, and she deserved to hear my answer.

'Shona,' I said, interrupting her stream of consciousness, and it was rare that I did, so immediately, she was all ears. I leant forward and took her hands in mine, knocking condiments aside as we rested our arms on the table between us. Her eyes were so miskeen, so innocent and eager as she waited for what was to come.

I was at a crossroads with three avenues: I could ignore the pastor's warning, go on as I was, let him tell Shona and go to trial. I would lose her for sure, but I could find another way to clean my money and if I buss case – still have the house by the end of the year. I could finally leave Ends and breathe life into a boyhood dream, a dream I shared with my brother.

I could adhere to the pastor's conditions and keep Shona,

which meant losing my family and all that I knew.

Or finally, I could tell her about Cordell myself. Take ahold of fate. This is who I was. She knew me, at times better than I knew myself. I could trust her to make the right decision. Couldn't I? But her eyes, so big as she gazed at me from across the table; they were so good. And there was so much I couldn't predict.

I knew then, at that moment holding her hands, that I would do whatever it took to keep her, and if that meant playing Pastor Lyle's game; then so be it.

My choice was made.

So I told her I loved her and she kissed me and carried on.

And once Shona and I had finished our breakfast, she went back home and I went on my way. As I stepped, I took my grinder from my pocket and went about strapping a blunt. I couldn't tell Shona that I'd broken my promise and lied to her, nor could I tell Cuba the entire truth and risk him doing something reckless, but I had to tell someone.

18

Bear one another's burdens, and so fulfil the law of Christ.

– Galatians 6:2

When I was a yute and the school day ended, I would walk from one end of Stapes to the other to darken my nanny's door. I'd walk past Pastor Lyle's baptist church to my mama's worldly family and spend the evening there.

My mama might pick me up some time around nine or ten, or she might not pick me up at all. The times she did, she never stayed longer than a second and my papa never joined her. No two weeks were the same. There was no routine. One week she might be praising the Lord and feeding the flock, and the next she might remember she had a son.

Nanny's was a low-budget motel for the disillusioned and the feet-finders. It was a one-stop shop for supplies and yard food. You came with nutun and you would leave with a couple Tupperwares of oxtail or mutton, a box of Kimberly Clark tissues and the latest hearsay. Nanny had owned the same Victorian terrace since the eighties – when houses in Ends were affordable – before the Asians started buying to rent and Londoners ruined the market.

She had converted the loft and every upstairs room into a bedroom. She herself took the attic, and the bedrooms were divided between whichever family members could afford rent. Nanny had her favourites, and Uncle Michael and I were the only permanent residents. Uncle Michael wasn't righted and rarely left his room but for the bathroom or for one of his daily walks. He was never without his busted headphones and if he met you in the corridor he would whisper 'Ello, son', as he hurried past, his gaze lowered to the carpet, like good Muslim men amongst their women. The other renters varied with the seasons, or more correctly, varied as their employment statuses did.

Nanny's brothers, my uncles and my older male cousins, would sit and smoke in the backyard. They talked women and swapped licks. The dominoes table was always dusted with a little soot and the smell of weed suffocated the air. Red Stripe and Dragon Stout bottles stood beside the flower baskets atop the walls, and baby boys were propped on their fathers' knees.

It was remarkable how many poor decisions had been made in such a cramped space. I wondered how many men had sat and smoked there during the day, before going and getting arrested that night. Or how many men had sat swapping sex stories before sending a soul to Jesus.

I used to sit at the door and listen to the heated debates that occasionally soured into full-blown arguments. Once, one of Bunny's bredrins was pinned against the wall by my cousins Jamaal and Hosea. They beat him until my nanny said it was enough, but by then his face had swollen into a misshapen oval.

Where the backyard was a boys' club, the living room was a hive of feminine energy. A veritable day centre. Young and old, joined at the hip by their complaints about motherhood and men. Young girls' faces twisted as their heads were yanked from left to right with ruthless but deft movements. Younger girls sat between their cousins' thighs in a line of Jamaican nesting dolls and suffered the same fate.

Nanny's three sisters, who had raised enough children for one lifetime, shared a sofa and breaded chicken in metal basins. They clucked and cussed the hairdressing skills of their daughters and nieces.

'Mek sure yuh style it nice.'

'Yuh deh pull di poor pickney dis weh an dat weh, ow she suppose fi do im cousin ead wen yuh ahh do dat, hmm?'

'Yuh roughee!'

The chorus of disapproval was relentless. The elderly always believed the following generation ignorant of the ways of the world, but refused to part with any genuine guidance. They had earned their wisdom through a lifetime of mistakes and ill experiences, and they took a small pleasure in seeing their children falter as they had. The sisters' facial expressions were sentences in themselves and more than enough to spark the flicker of a silver tongue.

'Mind yuh damn business,' young nieces and cousins would retort, defiance quick on their tongues.

'Come yahsuh an finish it, den.'

'Like seh yuh could do ahh better job. Sidung wid yuh likkle chicken an shut up.' Their sentences were always finished with a loud 'Chuhh' and a kiss of their teeth.

Though I called them elderly, Nanny and her siblings were anything but. They were all born in the sixties and only feigned confusion at technological advances, but as soon as they had become grandparents, they'd acted the part. A lifetime of disrespect suffered at the hands of their partners and employers meant they had grasped seniority with two hands, and they would not be letting go for anyone.

The living room was a salon, cookery and courtroom in one. The women passed judgement on any wrongdoers and bade the men of the family mete out the punishment. 'Gwan an see yuh papa,' they would say, sending a backchatting child to fetch the belt.

It was a sickness, making a child bear the tool to the executioner; like Jesus carrying the cross, the child would trudge towards the backyard and inform the relevant man that they needed to be beaten. Their cries would reverberate around the house, but it seemed were only heard by the rest of the yutes who immediately curbed their petty defiances.

I could hear them right now as I stood outside Nanny's front door. It was unlocked, and the second door was fastened by a single latch.

I knocked on the frosted glass. I could still taste the greasy breakfast.

Bunny answered. 'Wagwan, genna,' he said, touching my fist. 'You seen Midnight?' The usual question. I told him that I hadn't seen him since the day before. He took the news with a nod that betrayed his needs like thirty silver pieces. 'Tell the likkle devil, man needs to chat to him when you see him. I got, like, five different numbers for man and none of dem work.'

'Say no more,' I replied, following him along the corridor. Two of Jamaal's yutes, Jaden and Jaylen, pottered across our path into the daycare. They were both three, born three months apart, and if Jamaal was to be believed, three different women were there when they had each been conceived.

'Nanny in?' I asked.

'Yeah, she's in the yard wid Uncle Marlon and Calvin.'

'Cool, tell her I'll be down in a minute.' I took the stairs two at a time and went to my room. Since most stays were temporary Nanny didn't let anyone add many personal touches, thus the rooms had remained the same for years.

The walls were lined with shelves of china cats that wagged their paws, and souvenirs brought from whichever countries the Hugheses had visited: keychains from Anguilla, pottery from South-East Asia and Kool-Aid packets from the States, whose pinkness had long faded.

A giant teddy bear stood next to a dated mahogany wardrobe, the bedsheets bore illustrated flowers and were heavy silk, and the bed had a trove of pillows placed in order from largest to smallest. Nanny inspected the rooms daily, so if a single pillow was misplaced there would be hell to pay. During the few months each year when Nanny and Mister Sinclair were away in Jamaica, standards slipped, but by the time she was back order would have been long restored.

My bedside table kept a pink frilly lamp, a Gideon Bible, my phone chargers and a pile of Polaroids of Shona and me. I kept a pair of trainers beside the door as well as a weekend bag full of Shona's stuff for the nights she stayed over. The rest of my things were in the wardrobe, out of sight. I didn't spend much of the money I earned, instead I kept it in shoeboxes, and each month Shona would mix it with the bread she earned from shows and deposit it into her business account.

We had been doing this for years. But now that I'd made the decision to leave the family and stop dealing, the money in the bottom of my wardrobe felt insecure, and the house-atop-the-hill a fancy at best and a delusion at worst.

I changed and found Nanny in the yard, arguing with her brother Marlon.

I'd never seen a man thwart time with such pizazz as Uncle Marlon; father to Hakim, Hosea and Killa. When the four of them were in a room together he looked more their brother than father.

Nanny was a petite woman, suntan brown, with a small grey afro. When I was younger she covered her hair with red and blond wigs, but now she had back and knee problems to worry about. You outgrew the silly shit, she told me. I had a lot of respect for my nanny, because no matter the troubles in her life, she just went on shuffering and shmiling.

I stood in the doorway and watched her clout the back of her brother's head for some mild disrespect. When she laughed she slapped her thighs and wanted the neighbourhood to know she was laughing. She toped rum and outdrank the men in our family who were twice or three times her size. She peeled plantain faster than anyone and could measure water and rice with her eyes.

She caught me lingering at the door and rose to greet me.

'Ow yuh doin, baby?' she said, stepping inside and closing the doors behind her. Before I could respond she grabbed my face and pulled at the skin beneath my eyes, 'Wahum?' she enquired, she cleared the living room of women and children and shut us inside.

I told her almost everything; about Cordell, Winnie and Junior, Pastor Lyle and his condition, my conversations with Cuba and my secrecy with Shona. The decision I'd made that morning to leave the family for a while. The only thing I kept from her was Cuba's intentions for Winnie, because as far as I was concerned that conversation wasn't finished, and Nanny didn't need any other reasons to disrelish Cuba.

'Don't worry nutun bout Lyle,' she said, 'im know better dan

134

to run im mout to di beastman dem. An Winnie nah go seh nutun to nobody, di likkle yute gon be all right? Wah im name? Junior?' I told her that Cuba was handling him. 'An Shona? Yuh tinkseh Lyle gon tell er?'

'He hates man, Nanny,' I said, 'I rah can't put nutun past him.'

'Well, yuh ahh man now, so mi cyaan tell yuh nutun, but membah wah mi tell yuh before? Dat one deh is ahh keeper, Sayon. Yuh know seh wat yuh ahh do?' I nodded; I would play Pastor Lyle's game. 'Den everyting's all right, baby,' she whispered. She handed me a lemon sherbet, opened a box of tissues and blotted around my eyes.

I wasn't crying.

'Yuh deh tek di poor bwoy life, baby, di least yuh can do is cry ahh likkle,' she said, blotting and stroking my hair. 'Poor baby,' she repeated, over and over, 'poor baby.'

The two of us sat there in each other's arms for some time. 'Yuh mek sure yuh cover it up now, baby. Wat's done is done,' she said. 'Mek sure yuh nuh see di inside ahh dem blasted prison again. Dem nah go do yuh nutun but sadness, yuh ear? Nuh love in deh. Nuh love. Stay yahsuh wid yuh family, now.'

The sound of little hands at the door announced Jaden and Jaylen's re-entrance, but their cherry faces fell when they felt the mood. Jaden offered me his fire engine and Jaylen his bouncy ball. They cast open-eyed glances over their shoulders as Nanny led them from the room and shut the door on them.

'Was I wrong, Nanny? To do what I did?'

She shook her head so hard I thought it might have tipped and rolled from her neck. 'No, baby. No. Listen now. Yuh affi protect yuh breddah. Yuh nuh right, yuh nuh wrong, yuh just all right. Romans 13:8–10 says, word fi word, "Owe no one nutun, cept fi love one another, for di one dat love another as fulfilled di law. For di commandments, Yuh shall not commit adultery, Yuh shall not murder, Yuh shall not steal, Yuh shall not covet, an any other commandment, are summed up in dis one word: Yuh shall love yuh neighbour as yuhself. Love does nuh wrong to ahh neighbour; dehfore love is di fulfilment ahh di law." Yuh know why mi know dat verse suh well?'

I shook my head.

'It's di same ting mi tell Calvin wen im did dem fuckeries an went inside di first time, di same ting mi tell Paulette an Akim wen dem gwan ahh yute offender, di same ting mi tell all ahh unuh wen unuh fuck up.

'Love is di most important ting, yuh ear? Widout love wi cyaan be nutun. Nutun at all. An wat yuh did was di greatest example ahh love, baby. Yuh risk yuh whole life fi save yuh breddah. Fi save yuhself. Kaaz Midnight an yuh see unuhself as one an di same, true? One extension ahh one another.

'Tek ahh life nuh easy, unuh. It weigh pon yuh big time, an yuh tek dat weight an yuh affi carry it fi Midnight fi di rest ahh yuh life. Yuh loved yuh neighbour, an love is di fulfilment of di law. Murder wrong, mi nah go sit yah an seh it isn't, but yuh did ahh right an wrong ahh di same time, suh who can judge yuh?'

I could only nod.

'Only reason mi worry is Midnight nah go want yuh fi carry nutun fi im. An eaven knows seh dat bwoy can rotten like egg – im not stable like mi an yuh. Once di bwoy mind mek up, dat's it. Nobody cyaan stop im. Mi nuh know wahum, Sayon, but mi raise ell innah yuh cousin.'

She unwrapped her own lemon sherbet and held it to the light. It was bright yellow. The white powder in its centre cocaine-white. The edges were rough where the sweet had crumbled, and sharp enough to nick a finger.

'Im tek after im great-grandfather bad, enuh. Black an bad just like di bugger.' She popped the sweet in her mouth, gave my leg a squeeze and helped herself up. 'Well, nutun fi done now,' she said, 'im will only listen after yuh anyway, mi just ope im nah do nutun too stupid. Yuh gonna tell im yuh leavin?'

'Yeah man,' I swallowed, 'today.' It wouldn't be an exaggeration to say that I was dreading it. It wasn't that I feared his anger, only, I had no idea what reaction to expect.

'An den deh's Winnie as well,' Nanny continued.

I hadn't told her what Cuba had suggested, but she knew that we sold Winnie food and that Cuba would do anything for me, and I could tell that she was worried.

'Winnie av fi im problem,' Nanny said, and she hung at the door, half-inside, half-outside, her progress stayed by her thoughts. 'But come di day's end; im family, an family muss look after one another, no matter wahum. Nuh matter ow close dem come to crossin di line, an whether dem cross it or not, family is family.'

She was right.

There were stories in a busy home; secrets unkept. Snippets of big people conversations overheard by children. Shade thrown across the candles at Christmas dinners. Like Pastor said, Nanny raised her siblings, but as far as I understood, she raised some better than others.

Since Uncle Marlon and Aunty Winifred were closest to her in age – and because Uncle Michael was a dud – she had to rely upon them both to help with their younger siblings, but Uncle Marlon had always been a lovable rogue. Some years before either of his boys or I were born, when Uncle Calvin and

Bunny were yutes, he used to take them to burgle houses. He would have them squeeze through bathroom and kitchen windows, before opening the front door for him and his bredrins. He was a loose cannon. And prone to long disappearances. So it was Aunty Winifred who was forced to pick up what Nanny couldn't.

The death of their parents had dashed any hopes of a recognisable adolescence, for any of them, but it had affected none more than Aunty Winifred. She was the one who found my great-grandparents twisted together in a tubful of tepid suds, their naked bodies floating next to the bottle of pills they'd shared.

It seemed children who were denied their childishness always found a way to express it in later life. And Aunty Winifred, a touch broodingly, had followed Nanny's instruction for years, but as she grew in age and into her body, men from around the way began to show more of an interest. And in their interest she found an opportunity to rebel against Nanny's authority, so she soon had Winnie. And though Nanny wasn't best pleased by her sister's debauchery, she didn't kick up too much of a fuss because a child was always a gift from God. And she assumed that with Winnie, Aunty Winifred wouldn't have time to act a fool.

But she was wrong. Winifred fooled around for years without Nanny knowing, right through Winnie's childhood, so of course her reputation grew, as a woman's did. Her name was on everyone's lips at pubs and barbecues. It was spoken over beer bottles and folded plates of jerk chicken. It was called by alley cats, waifs and strays, known to any with a slick mouth and a warm cuddle on offer.

And the man with the slickest mouth was Willroy Williams.

Willroy was broad-shouldered and light-skinned, the usual type for a Hughes woman. He lived in the pubs along Stapleton Road and would drink himself into a drunken stupor every weekend. The saying 'anything with a pulse' was made for men like Willroy, and only desperate women would spend an evening with him. But there were as many desperate women in the world as there were men, and Willroy and Aunty Winifred took a shine to the desperation they found in each other.

Nanny ran a tight ship. She allowed no men inside the house less their name was Hughes, or less two Hugheses could vouch for them. And she didn't rent to couples because she wanted no hanky-panky or goings-on happening beneath her roof. So, given that Willroy had no place of his own, Aunty Winifred was left in a tight spot, one that she solved by sneaking Willroy into her room when the moon was at its highest. But Aunty Winifred shared her room with a five-year-old Winnie. And, as I said, the saying 'anything with a pulse' was made for men like Willroy.

When Nanny found out what had happened she bounced Aunty Winifred from the walls until blood stained the floorboards. She cursed her with her mother's name and forbade her to touch another man or ever to leave her sight.

I caught this all from Nanny's stairs as a young boy listening to Uncle Calvin and Uncle Marlon gossip. They never said what happened to Willroy Williams, but I hadn't seen hide nor hair of him, and it wasn't difficult putting two and two together.

19

So Moses stretched out his hand toward Heaven, and there was thick darkness in all the land of Egypt for three days.

– Exodus 10:22

After Nanny left the room, the daycare resumed. Jamaal's yutes wandered back through the door, sat themselves either side of me and patted my leg. 'It's otay,' Jaden said, 'you can sleep wiv my firetruck if you want.' It would have been rude to do anything other than accept. After five minutes he decided it had been long enough and took it back.

Since Jaylen was the quieter of the pair, we resonated more with each other. I took him into my arms and left Jaden playing with his fire engine. 'What you sayin, lil man? Where's your daddy at?' I asked him. 'He drop you here or your marge?' He leant his head on my shoulder and sucked his thumb. 'Oh say nutun. You gonna do me like dat?' From behind his hand he smiled a gummy grin. 'Let's go see what Nanny's makin in the kitchen, shall we?'

We helped out together. Fetching spices from the high shelves and stirring various pots and pans. The rest of the family milled about and the house filled as the day aged. Everyone knew food was ready at seven and Cuba was one of the last arrivals.

He came through the front door with Karma in tow, and nodded to me before disappearing into the living room, and re-appearing with Jaden. 'Wahum, Nanny,' he sang, going to plant a kiss on her cheek, but the old woman ducked and waved a wooden spoon at her grandchild.

'Now listen to yuh grandmamma, bwoy, mi ope seh yuh aven't done nutun stupid.'

Cuba shook his head. 'Course not, Nanny man, chuhh.'

She hmmed. 'All right den; yuh ungry, Karma?'

'Yes, Nanny,' he said, 'I could eat, still.'

'Mmmh, all right, baby. Cuba?' she asked.

'Yeah, yeah. Just need to chat to Sayon first.' He shot me a look that said to follow him outside but he missed the unease that took Nanny's temper.

'All right well let mi av mi baby dem,' she said, wiping her hands on a dishcloth.

'Nah, nah, it's cool, we got dem,' I said.

So I followed him out, leaving Karma with Nanny. He closed the inner door first, then the exterior. 'Wagwan?' I asked. I thought my news could wait until after his, but I felt Cuba's agitation blowing in the wind before he said a word.

He licked his welt lip and refused to meet my eye. 'It's done,' he said.

'What's done?'

'You know what's done, fam. You're good. I told you I'd take care of it and I have.'

'You chattin bout Winnie?' I said, and he nodded. 'What did you give her?' We were still holding the boys and he didn't respond. 'Cuba. I said what did you give her, blud?' It had only been two days since we'd dropped Winnie on Stapes, and I'd thought the conversation unfinished, but my cousin clearly had another understanding. 'Blud?!'

'Don't worry bout all dat, man,' he said, 'just know it's been taken care of, init. You're home and dry, cuz. Just like man promised.'

He opened the two doors and along the corridor I could see Nanny at the kitchen entrance; she was still wiping her hands on the dishcloth. They must have been bone dry. She craned her neck and our eyes met. I could feel her silence calling out for news I couldn't give her. I couldn't tell her that everything was as it should be, that we had behaved as a family should, so how could I eat from her plate?

Cuba was watching me again. Up and down like a yo-yo, just as he had all those years ago outside the kebab house.

'Jaylen, go see Nanny,' I said, passing him to his uncle. Cuba deposited the two brothers inside. 'What did you give her?' I repeated. Still he refused to meet my eye. He snorted, softly, then checked the doors were shut and his mask cracked.

'You're thinkin what sort of demon would kill his own cousin, init?' he whispered, his back to me. 'Well I did, so I guess it's me init, but you can't change who you are.'

'Nah,' I said, backing towards the gate, 'deh's no way you've done dat, you shouldn't have done dat, fam, dat's man's cousin, dat's *our* cousin.'

Cuba spun around, eyes inflamed. 'I didn't hear you say all dis in the car,' he snapped. 'Now you wanna move all holy? Blud, shut the fuck up, man.'

'I didn't think you'd do it, blud; are you sick?'

'Yeah,' he said, stony-faced, and his hands found his pockets, 'maybe I am.' And he looked at me in the same way I'd seen him look at Nanny when he was a yute, like a cat who'd been rebuked for bringing a dead mouse to his owner's feet.

I didn't eat at Nanny's that night, or for many nights after that.

I strode towards St Barnabas Church as if wading through a waist-high slough. Heavy of foot and short of breath. Stapes opened up beneath me and swallowed me whole. It stank. I saw Junior posted outside the bakery; he nodded at me with a sick grin and shook hands with a cat. Aunty Paulette was getting felt up against the wall, telling the man to stop or she would set her sons on him. On the roof of the church workmen fastened wires that stretched between the spires like grapevines and Aunty Winifred came out of a crack den carrying empty grocery bags.

I stumbled and caught myself on a low-hanging branch. The current carried me home. I climbed the footsteps of Winnie's living room and opened the floodgates. I stepped into the church and left my shoes in the foyer.

Shona greeted me in the corridor, confused, but glad to see me.

'Where's your pops?' I asked. She guessed the kitchens or his office and asked if she could help, but I had no time to waste.

Pastor Lyle wasn't in the kitchens but I found him at his desk. His head was bent to the thick books that scattered the table. He didn't hear me come in. 'Pastor?' I said. He was quick to curb his initial surprise. 'I've made my decision.'

20

Now this I say, brethren, that flesh and blood cannot inherit
the Kingdom of God; nor does corruption inherit incorruption.

– 1 Corinthians 15:50

A week after I was first accepted into Pastor Lyle's home and
St Barnabas Baptist Church, my cousin Winnie was buried.

She had been found days after I left Nanny's, in one of the
yards across from the church. One of her crackhead friends
found her. When he did he hurried to raise Pastor Lyle – who
called me – and we went to Winnie's body together.

When she heard the news Shona broke down. 'She'll go to
Heaven, Say, she's just escaped early, that's all. She's in a better
place. You'll see her again, don't worry. God understands us
better than anyone. Better than ourselves. Winnie knew God
too, she always spoke about Him, didn't she? So don't worry,
we'll see her again.'

I didn't have the heart to tell her I was the last person Winnie
would want to see.

Her bredrin said that he'd fetched us as soon as he'd found
her, but he lied. He would've stashed the rest of Winnie's drugs
and gone through her pockets for change. He knew who I was

too. When Pastor Lyle was outside calling the ambulance he slid across to me, teeth either split or missing. He spoke with a heavy lisp. 'Whatcha give her diss time?'

'Huh?' I replied.

'Whatcha give her, eh? Dat weren't her normal sshit. Sshe wouldah never OD'd on dat sshitty sstuff you was giving her before an I know it wass you dat dealt her dat sstuff coss sshe wouldn't take it from no one elsse. Loads ahh timess me an others tried to get her to come grab gear from other dealerss dat I know, but sshe weren't having none of it sshe weren't, sso I know it wass either you or yer coussin dat did her in. Who'ss dat guy out deh? Ain't he the passtor of dat sstingy church dat kickss us off the sstepss?' I punched him in the mouth to clear my head, but it didn't do anything but dirty my knuckles.

The funeral was held on the last Saturday in June and not a tear was shed because everyone knew it had just been a matter of time.

Shona was with me. Viv came. Hakim and Elia. My parents sent their condolences. Aunty Winifred never took her eye from the incoming rain clouds and herded Winnie's crackhead friends between the gravestones like a faithful sheepdog. Nanny and Uncle Michael led the songs. Jamaal, Killa and Uncle Calvin spent hours shovelling because they refused to let anyone else and Cuba nursed a blunt just like his mama.

Cuba.

He had no words for me and I had none for him, so together we stood in silence, a world apart, watching loam get thrown on to the cousin we put there. And though I hadn't expressly condoned it, I felt as though I had personally strapped the belt

145

around her arm and tapped the needle; because any sin of Cuba's was a transgression of my own.

Throughout the funeral three different pastors said some words. The first recalled Winnie's life alongside her almost non-existent relationship with the church and finished by trying to win souls for Jesus. The second told us that Christians were favoured by God, so if all the Christians prayed hard enough then perhaps God would have mercy on Winnie's deviant soul, then he finished by trying to win souls for Jesus.

The third was Pastor Lyle.

In his own mind I'm sure that Pastor Lyle portrayed himself as a good man. He told us that he would often see to it that Winnie was fed, but what he didn't clarify was that he fed her on the steps of the church to which he refused her entry.

Afterwards, he thanked the other ministers, none of whom knew Winnie, for making their way from whichever corner of the country they came. As if Winnie would be shown mercy because of their presence alone.

I heard Uncle Marlon cuss the church for turning the funeral into a revival, but I didn't pay him, nor any cousin, any mind. Throughout the day's affairs my only concern was Nanny. She must have guessed what Cuba and I had done, yet there was no shout of foul play.

I saw her swab at her eyes with a handkerchief, but it occurred to me that I had never actually seen her cry. After the life she'd lived I figured her ducts were waterless. She hugged me a little tighter than usual and tried her damnedest to ignore Cuba, but that aside, she kept her emotions concealed, that is, until the final wreath had been placed on the freshly filled grave.

As was their custom, the feds were waiting for my cousin Jamaal outside the cemetery. The bastards weren't ones to miss an opportunity, so they clapped him in cuffs and took him to answer some allegations they couldn't prove.

And whilst the family's attention was on Jamaal, Nanny took Cuba aside and banished him from the house. She told him she wouldn't have devilry under her roof, and that is exactly what he was: a devil, just like his great-grandfather.

She pointed at his older brother, who was being stuffed into a squad car, and said that even prison was a punishment unworthy of Cuba's crime. He would burn in Hell for what he had done. She spat at his feet and told him to say hello to Mister Hughes when he saw him.

And I might've intervened, when Pastor Lyle asked to borrow me for a second.

'I've had a terrible thought,' he said. He'd made sure we were away from the milling crowd, away from Cuba and Nanny, so there we stood, between two strangers' graves. 'I'm certain it's groundless, but still I have to ask.' He kept his face impassive, guarded against any who might've glanced at us, and I kept mine the same. 'The timing of Winnie's death,' he continued, 'it's coincidental isn't it?'

I frowned. 'What you mean?'

'She wasn't in any way caught up in what happened?'

I turned so that he could see the disgust written plain on my face, and I spoke softly. 'Are you askin man, at my cousin's funeral, if man had something to do wid dis?'

'No, no, ignore me; it was insensitive,' the pastor said. 'No,' he said a final time, his brow furrowed, his hands clasped behind his back.

I excused myself and later moved the few things I owned from Nanny's into Pastor Lyle's living room, making my move official.

Briefly, I lingered over the shoeboxes in my bedroom, the ones I hadn't yet deposited into Shona's account: if I left them, they might fall mercy to Bunny, or any of my other crackhead cousins. And if I took that much money into the pastor's house, questions would have been unavoidable, and I was balanced on a knife's edge as it was. But ultimately I had little choice, so I took enough to last a couple months, as well as some weed, and hid the rest in Nanny's room.

For a time I would have to back-burner my dreams; see how this all played out before reaching a decision. It wasn't easy, but there was no house without Shona anyway.

A week after the funeral I gave my line back to Cuba. I saw him in the passy of a passing car and flagged him to the kerb. He had Karma and Junior with him, a blunt was in his mouth and he kept a further two tucked behind his ears. Although his injuries from the altercation with Cordell had healed, he looked worse for wear. His hairline was craggy and his skin marked, as if the blunts he smoked were eating him alive. He took the brick phone from me without a word and tossed it into the back seat.

And our relationship went with it.

21

For all have sinned and fall short of the glory of God.

– Romans 3:23

When I told Shona that I was coming to stay with her, that I'd stopped selling drugs and was leaving that life behind, she thought I was joking. She didn't believe me even when I stayed with them for the week between Cuba's admission, finding Winnie and burying her. And she didn't start to until the day she saw her papa carry my luggage into the house.

She was happy. Happier than I'd ever seen her. And it was then I realised just how much she hated the food I sold. She never said so outright, but it was in the little things; she spoke about the future more than before, called to check where and how I was and there was a spring to her step.

And going from living at Nanny's to Pastor Lyle's was an adjustment, to say the least. There was plenty of love at Nanny's, but the Jenningses were unlike anything I had ever seen. There was no cussing in the house, at home Shona played clean R&B cuts and Tamla Motown, Marcia played her gospel in the morning when she bleached the kitchen counters and veneer floors, and Pastor Lyle locked himself in his study for vast periods of time, only appearing to refresh his water or to see a man about a horse.

They had no spare room, so each night Marcia would prepare a makeshift bed in the living room for me. The sofa became my bed and the coffee table my nightstand. Each evening we ate meals around the dinner table. Played board games. Watched quiz shows and put time aside for prayer. And I soon realised that Pastor Lyle wasn't bluffing when he spoke of a father's love.

Each time he left the house he would follow the same routine: he found Shona, wherever she was, kissed her on the forehead and spoke the same words: 'Have a productive day, Princess; I'll see you later.' Then off he went. He collected his briefcase and used a horn to slip into his dress shoes.

Each day was the same, and every day Pastor would pretend to forget about his wife. The front door had rotten hinges that sang the blues when they were forced into action, so Pastor Lyle would whip the door open wide and wait for what always came: 'Lyle yuh don't av no sugar fi mi?' Marcia would shout. Then she would come rustling along the corridor or down the stairs and lips her husband hard and long as if they hadn't shared a bed the night before, or for the past thirty years before that.

When Pastor returned home his woman greeted him at the door with a plate. His place would already be made at the head of the table and his pint glass full with iced orange juice. When the meal was finished Marcia would clean and the good pastor would retire to his study for reading and reflection.

Inside his home Pastor Lyle was a gentle giant, a teddy bear to be cuddled. It was obvious how much he loved his family; Marcia was his rib and Shona his pride and joy; his princess. I saw why Shona had always been so enamoured with him;

he presented the picture of perfection. And between Marcia's tender home cooking and Shona being the Shona I had always known and loved, even I found myself intoxicated.

Pastor would often invite me on his errands and we would tour Ends, buying babygros and prams for new mamas, setting up food stands for the homeless and writing curricula vitae for non-English speakers. We helped single fathers load rental vans and move homes and manned the church nursery if they were understaffed. He called it sowing seeds. And I saw many of the faces we helped in Sunday service.

Pastor Lyle listened to his past sermons on car journeys and would only pause them to ask me for my thoughts. For weeks we had countless debates on life and religion and how the two interplayed. He never conceded to any of my points, and he supported his every opinion with scripture as if it were the only criterion of any substance, which he, of course, believed it to be.

On the most summery days he would open the sunroof and ask me what I wanted to listen to. We didn't run sermons then; I played whatever Shona had sent me. And if Shona ever joined us we relinquished the aux with no complaints.

'You think there's such thing as good and bad music?' she asked one day, Mary Mary playing at full volume. 'Like, do you think there's an objectivity to music, or do you think it's all self-expression and personal preference, so it's all valid?'

'Of course there's good and bad music,' Pastor snorted, and when I agreed, he nodded at me approvingly, glad to have an ally against the force of nature that was his daughter. 'Don't tell me you don't?' he asked, looking at her through the rear-view.

Shona shrugged, and turned to her passenger window as if it were only the two of them who had any sense. 'I don't.'

Pastor Lyle groaned.

'Deh's bare dead tunes,' I said, careful to replace 'shit' with a more harmless adjective. 'Deh's dead genres let alone dead songs, ain't no one tryna listen to no heavy metal, bro.'

'Preach, Brother Sayon,' the pastor echoed. 'Heavy metal is the Devil's music.'

'Neither of you are open-minded enough,' Shona teased. 'It must be nice to walk through life without a critical thought to spare between the two of you.'

'Listen to you, like it wasn't me you inherited your taste from,' Pastor roared, slapping the dashboard, greatly amused by her cheek. 'Not everything is for everyone, and certainly music isn't for everyone who does it, there's wul eap ahh rubbish musicians, popular or not.'

'There's always someone who'll like it, therefore it can't be wholly bad.'

'Like everything else, music has rules,' Pastor Lyle replied, and again, we were united; there were theories and guidelines to separate the good from the bad.

We never reached a conclusion and weren't the type to agree to disagree, so the argument was postponed, certain to be continued another day.

And so the month of July continued. But despite being around each other more than ever, Shona and I could only be intimate when we left the house. And even then, it was only a hand held, or a rested head on a shoulder. Still, after Winnie's loss, I was somewhat glad to not only be surrounded by love, but away from the environment that had made such a terrible thing inevitable.

On the occasions we could steal a moment for ourselves we relived the great summer we'd had after our GCSEs. It seemed she'd found a new love for me ever since I'd moved in, or ever since I'd given up my old ways, I wasn't sure which it was, or whether it was an amalgamation of them both. A love potion poured and delivered to her doorstep sweet-smelling and wholesome.

Whichever it was, she'd finished the lot, and in between the pastor's missions and Marcia's errands we decamped off Ends, to the surrounding counties' National Trust parks and little villages which had never seen Black people. And I have to say, for a time I thought I could get used to a life that wasn't ruled by a telephone and paranoia, but by a routine that kept my head above water.

One day, towards the end of the month, I accompanied Shona to a meeting scheduled in the centre of the city and waited outside until she finished. It was with a distribution label and had the potential to be something big, but sadly it didn't go as she would've liked.

'They wanted a fifty–fifty royalty split, but didn't offer enough in return,' she explained. We were nearing the bottom of Stapleton Road, walking back from Cabot through the estate behind Ropewalk House. Both her hands were wrapped around my arm and passing elders smiled at the young couple in love.

'Would dem man rejig the deal if you asked?'

'Yeah, I think so, but the initial offer was too far from what we're worth. I don't think we're on the same page.' Shona was doing her best to maintain her cool, but her discontent was obvious in her choppy walk, as she continually almost bumped into strangers. She hadn't given the label a firm answer – she needed to talk to Chenaniah (who was in London) first – but it was clear to which side she was leaning. 'We can't just jump at the first offer, you get me?'

'I thought you man wanted to stay independent, anyway?'

'We do, we do,' she said, hurriedly, 'but we're only a small label, init, and if we had someone that could reach a bigger audience, it would be a massive help, you know what I'm saying?'

'I get you.'

'There's bare things they could put on the table as well, if they really wanted us. I mean, some of these companies even give you advances.'

'Advances?'

'Yeah. Smaller than if we signed with another record label, but yeah. And you still own your masters, which is what this is all about.'

'Your masters like your own Clifton yard, ini?'

'*Our* masters, Say,' Shona tutted. 'If I'm having a room in Clifton, then these are as much your masters as mine and Chenaniah's – look at all the money you've put into this.'

'Say nutun,' I laughed, giving her a squeeze, 'but you ain't havin your own room no more. What? I didn't tell you, nah? You're in wid me now, bigman.'

'Nah,' said Shona. We came to a halt, her arm slipped from mine and she used it to shield her eyes from the sun. 'I want my album covers on the wall, remember? And all the instruments; there's no space for you in my room, sorry.'

'Is dat right?'

'Yeah, that's right,' she repeated, breaking into a smile. She took my arm again and propelled us forward. 'Ay, you know back then I thought the yard was just some little boy's dream,' she said, 'but now I can see it so clearly. Me and Chenaniah are doing our thing, we're making a name for ourselves and it's only a matter of time before we get a favourable distribution deal, and now you're off the roads we can focus on funnelling the rest of our savings through the music business and voilà,' she reached to poke my nose, 'one little boy's dream comes true!' She collapsed into my arms. 'Now all we have to do is wait for the owners to move on.'

We smiled as we imagined the future, but Shona was being her typically optimistic self. The only hope we'd ever had of purchasing the Clifton house was privately, with the eighty per cent of the valuation I'd hoped to have saved by the end of the calendar year. But since I'd stopped juggin the money had dried up, and I feared the amount we'd saved wouldn't be enough. And since legal money would never suffice, the stark reality of choosing Shona over both my family and the house was setting in, bit by bit.

We arrived at the Jenningses' to find Pastor and Marcia cooking, except it wasn't Pastor in charge, speaking directions in his soft voice, rather, he was the sous-chef under instruction from the finest cordon bleu this side of the country.

'Hey, babies,' Marcia called, seeing us in the doorway, 'how'd it go?'

'I don't think it was for us enuh, Mama,' Shona complained. She crossed the kitchen, kissed her parents and flung herself into a dining chair, pulling out the adjacent seat as I joined her.

'Don't worry, it'll all come in God's timing, baby,' Marcia promised, and Pastor Lyle was quick to buttress her affirmation with a resonant amen. 'Lyle, go fetch some rice from di cupboard please.' He returned with a big 10 kg bag, carried in his arms like a drunken friend. 'Wat about yuh, Sayon? Wat yuh tink bout it?'

'He didn't come into the meeting with me,' Shona interrupted.

'Oh, yuh didn't go in?'

'Nah,' I said, 'waited outside.'

'Shame, dem might deal wid yuh different if dem knew ahh man was involved.'

'Mama!' Shona groaned.

'It's di way ahh di worl sweetie,' Marcia shrugged, as Lyle held the back end of the bag and she funnelled the rice into a deep-bottomed sieve to be washed, 'it's not mi who mek di rules.'

'Princess can do anything any man can do,' Pastor said.

'An who said she cyaan?' Marcia tutted. 'Lyle juss ush man, yuh confusin tings.'

I smiled at the huge man beaten back by the tiny woman and wondered how the two of them had met. Who'd courted whom? And whether it was before or after Pastor joined the church. I figured it must've been afterwards, because Marcia would never have tolerated an ungodly man.

I imagined him crossing the church floor after listening to the sermon, however many years ago it was, pushing through the congregation, greeting elders by their last names and children by their first. If he was to be believed, he'd been a tall glass of water when he was younger – a man who took women from their men. And a young Marcia would've seen him coming and done her best to pretend otherwise, much like women did in nightclubs.

I tried to picture her younger, fresh-faced and more like Shona, and I understood why Pastor would've crossed the room.

After seeing him coming she might've walked outside, for a breath of fresh air. And he'd have followed and asked for her name. I wasn't certain whether she would've given her first or second, whether she'd have aligned herself with youth or seniority, but whichever she chose, it worked.

Pastor Lyle lifted the lid from a pot on the stove and steam enveloped the room with a warmth and a beautiful aroma of slow-cooked red meat. 'You know what this needs, Marcia?' he said.

'Mmmh?'

'Some red wine.' They both laughed, and Marcia swatted at him, until the pastor left the stove, fetched a carrier bag from atop the fridge and pulled a bottle from inside.

'Lyle,' Marcia gasped, 'enuh wi don't keep drink in di ouse.'

'What? It'll be fine, woman,' he smiled, snapping the lid, 'all the alcohol will burn out and we'll be left with nutun but goodness.' Marcia screwed up her face, unconvinced by her husband's argument. 'What does the Good Book say? Everything in moderation.' He tipped some into the sauce and the smell became richer.

I hadn't paid much attention to his drinking at the time of our first conversation, and I hadn't thought about it since; I had too much on my mind, what with Pastor Lyle's abortion revelation, his subsequent threats and Winnie, but with the pastor openly brandishing wine in the kitchen, the absurdity of it struck me.

The Jenningses had always been teetotal.

I remembered a time in secondary school when Shona found me drinking; immediately she had slapped the Magnum from my hand to the ground and we watched it spill into the drain; the mandem laughed until she threatened to do the same to them.

She'd relented over the years and would let me drink around her, but she would sooner go parched than partake. To her it was the devil's juice. Way worse than weed. And it was none other than her papa who had told her that.

So I studied Marcia's and Shona's reactions; Marcia's tense, with bunched shoulders, and Shona looking nervously between them. That is, until she saw a smirk cross her mama's face and Marcia let loose a loud, barking laugh, dismissing the wine as nothing more than an ingredient, amused by her husband's cheek. Shona's laughter gladly joined hers, and the pastor's too, but I knew differently; his drinking now had a perfect alibi.

Marcia turned to set the table, Shona stood up to help, and I watched the pastor quickly swig at the wine before adding more to the meat. He said that he'd enjoyed a drink as a yute, but now I wondered whether it was enjoyment, or whether he couldn't help himself.

Either way, I understood.

It was like I said – in many ways life with the Jenningses was good, almost a welcome break from the life I'd been living, but no matter how welcome I was made to feel, no matter how secure I felt with Shona, and with Marcia, like the pastor's wine, it was the trees I smoked at the end of each day that gave me sanctuary.

Each evening I waited until the dead of night before stealing into the back garden and smoking under the cover of darkness. Pastor Lyle. The Clifton house. Winnie's life. And Shona was on my mind most often. It was strange, living under the same roof whilst knowing that I was sitting on a secret that would tear our relationship – and quite possibly, the family – apart. So I smoked to numb the incessancy of their voices and allowed myself to be submerged in Jennings family life.

22

Therefore, whatever you want men to do to you, do also to them, for this is the Law and the Prophets.

– Matthew 7:12

The Jenningses attended church every day.

There were two services on Sundays, one in the morning, one in the evening, then another evening service mid-week when the junior ministers preached. On the days there weren't services there would be fellowships or Bible studies. Otherwise, I would be sent to help Marcia in the kitchens or Shona in Sunday school.

Although I had not been in attendance for some time, I was no stranger to St Barnabas Baptist Church; I had been to many Christmas and Easter services with Shona throughout my childhood and teenage years.

And even then I wasn't new to the house of God. When I was very young – no older than five, back when my parents might have spared a thought for my salvation – I was a regular in my papa's church. I would sit in the front pew with my black Oxfords and buttoned shirt. An usher would sit beside me whilst my papa preached and my mama led the choir.

It was an entirely different affair from Pastor Lyle's; his church was more upright, as if the Lord lay heavy in the hearts of the congregation and they knew judgement was a day away. Whereas my papa's church was all swing, soul and merry like Christmas. He began his sermons with 'God is good' and the building caterwauled 'All the time', then off and away the Holy Spirit went and, boy, could that man run.

Where my papa bawled from the pulpit and bullied people into visiting the altar, Pastor Lyle had more finesse. They both patted the damp from their foreheads with flannels, but Pastor Lyle took an intellectual approach and invited people to the altar, always accompanied by big-armed women humming and soft keys to the same effect as murderers riding to drill.

Where my papa used his Bible to strike his enemies at the knees and force submission before Jesus' majesty, Pastor Lyle found the worth of words in the Word of God. Where my papa allowed women into ministry, Pastor Lyle would never deviate from the Scripture in such a flauntingly disrespectful manner. Their differences would be unsettling to any member of either congregation who found themselves in the other.

It was not long after my thirteenth birthday, the first time Shona plucked up the courage to invite me to St Barnabas Church. I knew it wasn't a decision that she'd made lightly. In fact, it took more for her to invite me into her church than into her home. One was simply where she laid her head at night, the other was God's house. It was true my roots were in the church, but by that point she knew how little it meant to me, if anything it probably made asking even more onerous.

By then my Oxfords and buttoned shirt had been reduced to hand-me-downs for my younger cousins, so I had to borrow the clothes Jamaal used for hearings.

I arrived at the Jenningses' house as they were hustling from the door.

'Come get a move on, Brother Sayon, stop dragging your feet,' Pastor Lyle barked, patting my head as he rushed past, 'let's not keep our Lord waiting.' He had been ready from the moment he'd risen. Marcia pinched my cheeks and hurried into the driver's seat.

Behind them Shona trailed in a pink-and-white pinafore, cut in the same style as the school frock she'd worn when I had first met her all those years ago.

If looks could kill she had a knife at my neck.

'Don't say a word, Say, I don't wanna hear nutun,' she said. I kept my laughter behind my lips and buried my face in my sleeve to stop from bursting.

When we arrived Marcia dropped the three of us at the church front before finding somewhere to park. Outside there were ushers waiting for Pastor Lyle like paparazzi at a celebrity's hotel. They handed him sheets of paper and he handed some back. They whispered things like: 'Sister Henry has taken ill,' and 'Brother Tony can't make it today – fever,' bowing and scraping.

Pastor Lyle – literally – took it all in his stride. He shot commands to his right and left and the messengers scurried to do his bidding. He didn't stop until he reached his office door. 'Princess, take Sayon and go save a seat for your mother. I need a moment to talk to God. And make sure you save her that seat, Princess. God's house will be full today.'

And it was.

It may not have been the biggest church in the city, nor was it the smallest, but in the eyes of the Jennings family and the congregation it was the holiest. By the time Pastor Lyle reappeared from his conference with God, the place was teeming like a Black American's concert in Shepherd's Bush.

Ladies couldn't look left without banging the brims of their hats against one another, so choruses of 'Sorry, Sister', and 'God bless you, Sister' interrupted the quiet. Children wedged between their parents found comfort in the stray blasts of cold air they caught from mishitting fans. And brothers with faces like dark moons dabbed their foreheads with kerchiefs and the sleeves of their cotton jumpers.

Where Marcia walked, a flock of children and well-wishers shadowed her footsteps. They told her that Sister Henry had taken ill and the kitchens were running low on olive oil and basmati rice. The little boys asked if she would be teaching their class and the girls took her hand and led her to sit beside us.

She squeezed my thigh and stroked her daughter's hair.

'You're so beautiful, the pair of you,' she said. 'You'll make such handsome babies one day.' Shona, bright with embarrassment, quickly took her hand, which had been resting on my knee, and returned it to her lap, but before she could silly her mother's words Pastor Lyle took to the stage and hush descended.

I didn't know it then, but after living with the pastor for two months, I found that he slept with the Bible. Bathed with it. He tossed it over water and set it in the cradle of a china candle-burner. He inhaled the Word. Became it. If it's true that we are born with a single purpose, then he was born to preach. He took the stage and silence reigned. And he was a sight to behold, a lonesome tree on a grassy plain.

'Good morning, Church.'

'Good morning, Pastor.'

'Please open your Bibles to first Corinthians chapter fifteen, verse thirty-three.'

The quiet was broken by a hundred pages rustling.

Worship followed the initial reading, which was where Shona came to life.

It would've been impossible to count the number of successful secular singers who'd found their voices in the church, and back then you imagined Shona was destined to join their ranks. She sat comfortably between the notes. Eyes closed. Running over and under the other voices around us, wielding sound and silence to wicked effect. She was neither lofty, nor obtrusive, she was just right, like a honeyed dressing to a summer salad.

I saw older sisters smile as they sang, grateful to be close to Shona. The less confident, I'm sure, were glad to hide behind her power, others, adept themselves, saw the glory of their Lord evidenced in the mellifluence they made. There was an undeniable spirituality to music: the world's only universal language. And Shona was the most proficient of speakers.

I was pleased to be beside her, but I was young, and I resented the adoration the Church laid at her feet. Her eyes may've been shut, but mine were wide open. I saw the way they fawned. They knew as well as I did; she was the exemplary pastor's child. And I knew they knew me. Who my papa was. Who my nanny was. That I wasn't a regular in church. Nor did I have an obvious gift from God, one they could recognise as a blessing, proof of either mine or my parents' piousness.

They looked at us as oil and water, and I hated it.

After worship, Pastor encouraged the Church to visit Sister Henry, who was sick. Then the children, both young and old, were sent to Sunday school and the adults unloaded their worries at the altar.

Sunday school was held in a blue, low-ceilinged room in the basement of the church. The younger children had drawn portraits of themselves beside images of Jesus, which we had then Blu-tacked to the wall. The older children had built church buildings out of cardboard and paper and stood them on circle tables in one corner of the room.

The upstairs kitchen sent plastic cups of orange squash and trays of biscuits down in an old dumbwaiter. Quotes from the Gospels were written on yellow stars and stuck to the windows. The whiteboard was stained with ink where some girls had written their crushes' names in permanent marker surrounded by wreathes of hearts and kisses.

Red flames and grotesque demons from the pits of the children's imaginations were drawn around the frame of the door leading from the school back into the world. On the other side white angels floated, each carrying a small harp that one could almost hear in wonderful unison, their euphony greeting the children each service.

The church kept the younger boys and girls together with the older children for refreshments before they were separated into age-appropriate classes.

The youngest children were obsessed with fairness: if one was given juice or allowed to go to the toilet, then everybody's needs had to be catered for. It seemed we were born with an understanding of the Sermon on the Mount's message, if nothing else. We held on to it from the moment we clenched our fists in the womb until the world battered it from our grasp and we fell into adulthood.

But since I had never been a child I set about pocketing more biscuits than could fit in my mouth. If they wanted to point out the differences between Shona and me, then let them; I'd show them oil and water.

I wrapped dark chocolate digestives, custard creams and

malted milk biscuits in paper towels and drank as much juice as a thirteen-year-old body could manage. I could see the injustice in the faces of some of the other yutes, but they wouldn't dare reprimand me. The teachers were on the other side of the room, preoccupied with organising their classes and the whims of the youngest amongst us.

I remember rethinking church; surely nowhere that served endless snacks could be such a pain. Then I felt a tap on my shoulder and a hand snaked into my pocket and took the stolen goods. I didn't even have any spoilt White yutes to blame. I looked past the teachers, who were busily rebuking me, to find the author of my misfortune. The adder in the grass. But everyone in the room was ignoring me. I was the bad seed that didn't uphold churchly values; they didn't care whether or not I condemned myself.

Shona did, though.

She was stood on the other side of the room when the teachers kicked me out. Rooted to the same spot she must've snitched from. She didn't even look at me as I left. And I knew then that I had let her down greatly. I was her dear friend, her charge for the day, whom she had proudly invited to her daddy's church, and I had betrayed her trust by bringing the outside in.

At times my love for the girl made me forget that it was the same Christianity my parents practised where she grounded her sense of right and wrong, and never was I more aware, or afraid, of this difference, than with the pastor's conditions above me, living under the same roof.

I wasn't confronted with my past life at all throughout the first month of living with the Jenningses, mainly because I never left the house without any of their company. And the few times I saw anyone I recognised, I did my best to avoid them seeing me. But on the last Sunday of July, the four of us were walking from church to the Jenningses', where we found Karma posted outside, smoking.

My heart sank.

It wasn't that I was unhappy to see him, I loved Karma like family, but with him leant against the street sign, tracksuit matching, clouds in the air, trauma in the lines on his face and suspicion in the slouch of his back, it wasn't difficult for me to imagine what the Jenningses were thinking. And besides, Shona knew Karma. And putting aside any nostalgic affection she had for him (on account of going to the same school), I imagined he fell firmly on the wrong side of her morality.

'Sayon,' Pastor Lyle said, 'deal wid dis.' He took ahold of Marcia's hand and led her into the house without so much as looking at Karma again.

'Wagwan, killy,' Karma said, his puffer jacket swallowing me whole as he stood and wrapped me in a bear hug. 'Long time. Wagwan, Shona.'

She returned his greeting, kissed my cheek, then went after her parents.

Karma was the friend everyone deserved to have. He was comfortable with silence. Capable of the most passionate debates. We could see each other every day for a summer and I wouldn't tire of his company, or we could not talk for months and pick up right where we'd left. Once he considered you his friend, that was it.

Back home he came from a notorious family; both his father and uncle were ardent members of Al-Shabaab, which, in school, had only served as another reason he was treated differently.

I'd always known, but it'd never bothered me since I was in no position to judge. So when people said that when Karma and his family came to England they brought the rules of Al-Shabaab with them, I didn't care, because I loved him already. Besides it was true enough; Karma was one of the more tapped niggas I knew, something that had come in handy on more than a single occasion.

I'd never been embarrassed by the company I kept before, but with the pastor stomping up the steps to his house, Marcia by his side, and Shona behind them, I felt like the same child rebuked for the stolen biscuits in my pocket. Years had passed since the Sunday school incident, and yet here I was, still bringing the outside in.

'Wagwan?' I asked.

'You ain't spoke to Cuba in a minute, nah?' he asked, licking his lips as he leant back on the street sign.

'Nah.'

'You need to chat to my man, fam; he ain't doin good, wallah. After what happened wid you man and Cordell, shit's been wild, akh. Dem man from Pauls heard wagwan, put two and two together, and shit, dey got four, akh. Since den shit's been peak, wallahi – comin like the old days, blud.'

'What? And Cuba's in the middle of it?'

'Where else would he be? But you not bein wid us is affectin man differently, you get me? You can see it weighin on man. You should chat to him, still.' He drew smoke into his lungs and lifted his head skyward to blow it away. 'Man can deal wid the beef shit, but dat's my nigga, you get me? And I got a bad feelin my man might do sup'm stupid soon, not givin a fuck bout the consequences.'

I swallowed. 'I can't do dat, man.'

'How come? I'm bein serious enuh, akh. Cuba's goin off the rails, blud, doin dumb shit broad day, no bally, no alibi, no nutun, cuz. And wallahi he's gettin worse.'

'Me and him not in a good place right now, cuz.' I shook my head to rid myself of the guilt that was taking over my person. 'Whatever needs to be said would be better comin from you, truss me.'

'Dat's bullshit, wallah,' Karma said, coughing into his hand. 'Enuh my man don't listen to no one cept you.'

'More time he don't even listen to me.'

'Yeah, but he *never* listens to no one else, you get me? Why can't you chat to man, blud? You're movin mad.' He spoke without realising the answer was behind him. The Jenningses' home was a stone's throw from where we were stood, and it was all the reminder I needed.

'I can't, fam,' I said, holding my fist out as goodbye. He dapped me up, but reluctantly, and I sidled past him. And that night even the weed couldn't numb what I felt.

23

Wanti wanti cyaan getti, an getti getti nuh wanti.

– Jamaican Proverb

It was August, a new month. It had been a week since Karma appeared outside the Jenningses' to warn me about Cuba, and my guilt was making me murderous.

What with the hustle and bustle of Jennings' family life, Shona and I hadn't been alone since that day, so we'd taken a trip up to the house-atop-the-hill, because as soon as we were back in Ends, Winnie's death and Cuba's absence were everywhere, following me like weed smoke on clothes.

I'd heard it from other people too, half-friends and acquaintances, who rushed to tell me that the drama between us and Pauls was heating up. But really, I didn't need any more evidence of its severity than Karma showing up on the Jenningses' doorstep. I knew it meant things were worse than they'd ever been.

Once again the area you were from mattered, and Karma and Cuba were loyal to the soil. I felt both responsible and helpless, I should have been by their side to face the coming storm – a storm that I had started by killing Cordell – instead I was unmoored, caught in the very Church bubble I'd scorned for years.

If Shona hadn't been there I might have folded, but she was a constant reminder of what I would be losing if I failed Pastor's conditions. The past week I had been floating constantly between the present reality and the myriad of futures that could unfurl. Karma's warning had robbed me of any peace I'd found the previous month, and Shona could see it written on my face.

'So, how do you feel about everything now, Say?' she asked.

We were sat on a park bench across the road from the house, the same one my mama used to bring me to. It had been recently coated black and had a new dedication notched into its head, celebrating the lives of some dead husband and wife.

'What? How do I feel bout Winnie and dat?' I replied. The suddenness of her question caught me off-guard, but the delicacy of my circumstance had made me into an exceptional liar. I wasn't proud of it, but what was I to do? Either I told her the truth and watched her leave, or I dug deeper into my deceit, all the while knowing she might leave me still. Amidst the madness, the only thing I was certain of was that I did not need Pastor Lyle as an out-and-out enemy, because then he would make sure his daughter was forever lost to me.

'Yeah, Winnie,' Shona said. 'And you must be missing Cuba bad.' She wriggled closer to rest her head upon my shoulder and slipped her arms inside my hoody; she locked her hands around my waist and held me tight. From the bench and past the fountain, we could see the homeowners dithering through the big kitchen window, prepping to host local politicians, niche artists, or whichever minor celebrities they entertained.

'I'm good, still,' I answered.

But Shona wasn't in the mood to be toyed with. She loosened her hold of me and straightened her back until she could look me in the eye. 'I'm serious, Say,' she said. 'You always come up to the house when something's wrong.'

'Not always.'

'Say?'

'I don't know,' I said again, shrugging, as if I was as confused as she was, 'I guess man's just grievin, init.'

Shona frowned. 'You say that, but I haven't seen you cry once, not even at the funeral. You don't have to bury your feelings enuh, Say.'

'Man don't need to cry to be upset,' I replied. Still, I could see that she wasn't buying a word of it. I twisted in my seat to face her. 'You know a while back how you said deh's no such thing as objectively good and bad music? In the car? With your pops?'

Shona nodded warily, unsure where the conversation was headed, but more than a little annoyed I hadn't given her a straight answer.

'Do you think the same about people?' I asked. 'Like, do you look at someone who works for a charity and think *oh, dey're a good person* or like, do you look at a murderer and think dey're a bad person? Every time?'

Shona sighed before she answered. This wasn't the conversation she wanted to have. 'In real life there's good and bad, Say. It may be true that art imitates life, but art presents life as an ideal, init. It's fictional,' she said, as if it were simple. 'It's not the same thing. That's why I said what I said, because art isn't real life; everyone knows in real life there's right and wrong.' She shook her head tersely. 'Why you bringing this up now, Say?'

'Cos now I'm thinkin maybe you were right about the music ting,' I replied. 'What's the sayin? One man's trash is another man's treasure? Why can't that be the same as us, you get me?'

'Sayon,' Shona blurted, 'what are you talking about? I'm asking you how you are cos you've lost your cousin and you're away from Cuba and your family, and all you're doing is changing the subject.'

'I told you man's good, init.'

'You're not good though, are you,' Shona said, 'you think I don't know something's wrong? I'm not an idiot!'

I sucked the air through my teeth. 'Nutun's wrong, Shona man, chuhh!' I said, unable to keep the resentment from my voice, and when Shona recoiled I regretted it instantly.

Outside the prison gates she'd said that Christianity wasn't as black and white as I imagined it, that the Christianity she practised differed from both that of her parents' and mine, but her beliefs about the subjectivity of music didn't carry across to morality. In Shona's mind there were moral absolutes, which was why she had snitched on me in Sunday school.

It really was exactly like Pastor said; Shona would run for the hills if she learnt what I'd done. And if it wasn't that which tipped the scales, my lying surely would.

More than anything, I wanted a way to live with her and Cuba, the both of them harmonious together, but I was coming to realise that it was a pipe dream; truly I was damned if I did, and damned if I didn't.

And it wasn't that I misunderstood her way of thinking. Being raised in a Caribbean home, whether your family practised or not, God was spoken about openly and atheism was never an option. Either you were Christian, Rastafari or Muslim and, at a stretch, God-fearing was a suitable response when the elders asked. He was to Black people what giros were to the unemployed: a crutch.

Even in the Hughes household, God was in the thanks before meals, He was the cure for nightmares and Nanny could hardly finish a sentence without some mention of Jesus' name. So for Shona, who from the womb was taught that God and Christianity were one and the same, He was even more deeply rooted than for most.

So how could she possibly understand me?

It was true that she was the constant reminder of what I stood to lose, but she was also the key with which her papa kept me on lock.

We left Clifton shortly afterwards and made our way back into Ends. And I wondered what had given my thoughts away. But it was my uncle Calvin who told me that women had a sixth sense when it came to their men; they were like bloodhound bitches, he said, one sniff of your ass and they could smell the bullshit.

I caught sight of Hakim and Killa when we arrived at the bottom of Stapleton Road, and they started making their way towards us before I could give much thought to the consequences of failing Pastor Lyle's conditions. To me my cousins were as much a part of the road as the tarmac, the white lines, the double yellows and zigzags.

As much a part of the road as me.

'Wahum, cuzzy? Wahum, darlin?' Killa said, embracing me and Shona, one after the other. We had come to a halt in the middle of the pavement and people, clearly annoyed by the thoughtlessness of the position we'd taken up, looked to barge right through us, but I watched them catch sight of Killa and decide otherwise; instead, they split like river water rounding a jagged rock.

'Assalamualaikum Warahmatullahi Wabarakatuh,' Hakim grinned, bowing his head towards Shona before turning to me. 'What you sayin, lil man?'

I was glad to see the brothers together. Since Hakim had reverted and married they had been somewhat distant, and seeing them gave me some much-needed hope for the possibility of my reconciliation with Cuba.

'What you man on?' I asked, dapping them up. Shona returned their hellos and retreated a shade behind the rest of us, her arms folded, her mind someplace far away.

'Hakim's just chattin shit in my ear man,' Killa said.

'I'm tryna school this eediyat,' Hakim laughed, playfully pushing the back of his little brother's head, 'but you know what he's like, as hard ears as the rest of you.'

'And where'd you think we learnt dat from, bigman?' Killa tutted, and I couldn't help but agree. I glanced at Shona to see if she found the duo as funny as I did, but she was lost, staring down Stapleton Road.

Hakim chuckled, and motioned towards me. 'Why don't you see if Sayon wants that poison you tried givin man?'

'Poison?' I frowned, confused, until Killa reached into his pocket and handed me a packet of sweets. I smiled and took them, déjà vu running amok in my mind. The innocence of the time where Jamaal would apportion Shona and me sweets in the playground felt so far from the tenuousness of the present.

I showed Shona the treats, hoping she'd realise what was in my head and cheer a little, but she only thought I was offering them to her and shook her head.

'Safe, g,' I said, Shona's mood dampening my own.

'You still eat swine, Sayon?' Hakim asked. 'Astaghfirullah, enuh there's gelatine in those.'

174

'Yeah, but Sayon's Christian, akh? Why wouldn't he back gelatine?' Killa asked, triggered by the insinuation in Hakim's question on my behalf.

'Sayon ain't Christian, are you?' Hakim said.

'Nah nah, I ain't,' I said straightaway. I might've been more hesitant if Shona wasn't pissing me off.

'Even some Christians don't eat pork,' Hakim continued, 'init, Shona?'

'What's that?'

'Some Christians don't eat swine?'

'Yeah, that's true,' she said, then she searched her bag for her earphones and promptly removed herself from any further involvement.

'Exactly,' Hakim trumpeted, unbothered by her distance, 'swine's unclean, cuz.'

'Fuckin ell,' Killa said, 'everything's unclean to you niggas.'

'Bro, deep it,' Hakim said. He took hold of his brother's shoulder, imploring him to see sense. 'Swine are the filthiest animals on earth. They eat their own shit, blud. Wallahi, they're the greatest scavengers Allah has ever produced, subhan'Allah. In places where people shit in the streets, they get the swine to clear it up.'

'Why you gotta call dem swine for?' Killa said. 'It's always the non-pork-eatin-niggas dat gotta do dat; dey're called pigs, bro; don't try make dem sound nastier dan dey are, dey're pigs, don't nobody wanna eat nutun called swine.'

'Good,' Hakim laughed.

'Why's it haram in Islam, doe?' I asked.

'To protect us,' Hakim said, thrilled that I had shown any interest at all. 'They carry nuff diseases like ringworm and that, akh, and it don't matter how much you cook it, it don't come out. Once you start readin it you realise everything in the Quran was sent to guide and protect us, wallahi. It's the only reason man could make a change in my life, the whole reason I'm like this now, you get me?'

'Yeah, lucky us,' Killa said, and Hakim swung at him before the two brothers burst into laughter and wrestled in the street, drawing even more disapproving looks from the strangers whose journeys they'd disturbed. And although I was gladdened by their apparent newfound closeness, it was bittersweet, because every time I saw them together I was reminded of their brother's absence.

My cousin Hosea was stabbed and killed when I was fifteen. And though his loss had torn a hole in each of us, it had affected none more so than Hakim.

Before Hosea was killed, Hakim was the baddest of the rotten Hughes bunch. He was the one to boot the licks door open, or to brandish a weapon, or to fashion a scheme. He was the most intelligent and took to his role as an older. He could take the most miskeen of children and turn them into killers overnight. If there was a job that needed doing, illegal or otherwise, Calvin and the rest of the uncles were glad to let Hakim handle it. Hakim was the first of us to make real money in the streets, so the whole ends named him Funds, then he taught what he'd learnt first to Jamaal, then to Hosea and so on.

Which was his biggest regret.

Hosea, as I knew him, was ard bodied. The last of a dying breed. I looked up to him as an example, so when he died I could think of little else, the idea that I was going to follow him overwhelmed my rational mind and I just wanted to be rid of my feelings. I lashed out at school. Lashed out on road. Then when the funeral came I buried my feelings with Hosea's body. But Hakim couldn't. He carried Hosea with him every day still; he crouched beside him when he opened the bakery's shutters in the morning, used his knuckles to knead him into dough, took him to the masjid and knelt beside him in prayer.

Killa too.

Before Hosea passed, Killa was a loose cannon like his papa: you might catch him doing wheelies on the back roads at four in the morning, or waving a flicky around, pressuring other trappers in Ends. He was the fastest to violence and the most unpredictable, but afterwards he became the last to offer his opinion and the first to get sent to the shop. Now he was always plotting how to get rich quick and was shy of a hard day's work.

'Ay, listen, g,' Killa began, clearly intent on continuing some conversation they'd been having before I arrived, and hoping against hope that I might take his side.

Now we were strolling towards the top side of Stapes with no destination in mind, Shona a couple of paces behind, the three of us together. Killa took position in the middle of Hakim and me, and slung his arm around me to share his secret. I couldn't see Hakim, but I could feel him rolling his eyes.

'I'm tryna put you on to sup'm I got goin on,' said Killa, 'one new hustle of mine.' He held a tiny brown brush with thick black bristles and he swept his hair whenever he finished a sentence.

'Killa, man,' Hakim said, 'Sayon don't need to hear this right now, let him and Shona go about their day.'

I told him we had nowhere to be whilst Killa groaned, 'Dead dat Islamic shit, g.'

'I didn't even mention Islam?' Hakim scoffed.

'Yeah, but you was gonna.'

'Tell me bout it, Killa,' I laughed. It felt good to be around my family again, if even for a moment.

'Look, forget my man,' Killa said, brushing Hakim aside. 'Fuckin all you have to do is give man your account details, den I'll pass it to my connect, twenty bags comes into your account, seventeen grand leaves, den boom; you got three grand for doin jack shit. So what you sayin? Easy money, cuz. Easy money.'

'What's all dis?' I frowned. 'I thought you were tryna change, blud?' And Hakim loudly echoed my sentiment.

Killa's face creased with upset and he gestured around him. 'You don't see man robbin no one, do you?' He stopped and lifted his shirt. 'You don't see no nank on man, nah?'

I looked to where he pointed. 'Nah, I guess not.'

'Exactly!' He smiled, letting his shirt fall back over his waist.

'You know fraud is still a crime?' Hakim said.

Killa shook his head and brushed it, 'It's a calm crime, doe – like a legal high. So what you sayin, Sayon? You down?'

'Nah, I'm good, still.'

He kissed his teeth and flashed his brush in my face. 'You prolly think it's some pussyhole ting like Midnight, init? The other week he was tellin man lowe it cos I'm takin from innocent people, but fuck dat. Dem White yutes in suits bang deets all day and call it a nine-to-five so why can't I?'

'Cos you're not White?' Hakim laughed. 'We can't do what they do, walaal.'

'Well dat's fucked up,' Killa said, 'and what's even more fucked up is man's tryna change tings and man can't get no fuckin support from his brudda and his cousin.'

'Anyway,' Hakim laughed. He rested his eyes on me in his typically intense manner. 'When's the last time you spoke to Midnight, lil man?'

My back stiffened. 'Couple months?' I said, and I could feel my skin thin, ready to take umbrage at any insinuation I didn't like.

'You heard he's movin mad doe, init?' Killa said. 'I know you man ain't been speakin since you left.'

'I've heard,' I said.

'You should speak to him,' Hakim said. 'These days I worry about him the most out of all of you man, and we all know no one can get through to him but you.'

In my head I could hear Cuba saying how only some people could make it out of our world, and that neither he nor Killa were one of them, so I put that to Hakim as we crossed the dual carriageway and came to a pause across from the bakery.

'Nah,' my older cousin said, shaking his head vehe-mently. 'Allah leads who he wills, fam. The God of the Quran who performed countless miracles is the same God today. He can draw water from a stone and give life where there is none. Just look at man,' he said, 'if you think about the likkle ginal I used to be, who would've thought man would've turned, akh?'

'Not me,' Killa laughed, louder than perhaps his older brother liked, 'man went from Funds to Hakim, man glowed up and left the family, cuz.'

'Blud, don't call man Funds no more, what did I say, wallahi?' Hakim said. From the moment he'd reverted his former name was taboo. 'And I ain't left the family,' he continued, 'you still see me and Elia at Nanny's every Sunday, nah?'

Killa shrugged, and I hoped they wouldn't make the discussion about me leaving instead; Shona and I hadn't been at one of Nanny's Sunday dinners in forever.

'Exactly,' Hakim said. 'I ain't left, I'm just on different tings now, you get me? I'm a married man. A Muslim. It's still all love, always will be. I just can't get down with what some of you man are on, feel me?' He held up his hands and the atmosphere sobered. 'And there's no judgement, truss me, cos man can't judge you when I was on the same shit.'

His tone grew laboured and his frown lines creased. You could see the guilt that wracked his brain in the way his posture slouched; Hosea lay heavy on his mind. 'More time it was me that showed you man how to do what you're doin,' he said with a lowered voice, 'so I can't say nutun to you man, really and truly, I can only apologise, for real.'

Beside him Killa kissed his teeth, embarrassed by his brother's vulnerability. 'I already told man you don't need to apologise, fam.' He looked at me and rolled his eyes. 'Dis is what my man was on before you came, tryna apologise for us being on road, as if we didn't have a choice. Dis is why no one don't wanna be around you no more Hakim man, pattern up.'

'Nah, big man ting,' Hakim said. His whole body was tense. 'I showed you man the wrong path, wallahi. As an older brother, as an older cousin, it's my job to show you man the right way, which is why man bangs on about this Islam ting so much now. I know it can be jarrin but, alhamdulillah, I've found the right way, you man. The truth. And purpose, wallahi, and I want you man to share in it with me.'

'Who's *you man*, blud?'

'All of us, cuz – you man,' Hakim motioned, 'the whole family.'

Killa smirked at me. 'I don't know bout you, Sayon, but I know Islam ain't for man, init, deh's too many rules, cuz. First day after my Shahadah I'd prolly punch a nigga in the mosque or chop some Muslim ting down.' He roared with laughter and leant on my shoulder, so I laughed with him; but what Hakim said stayed with me.

Other than my mama, Hakim was the only member of the family to find a way out. But the difference between my mama and Hakim was that Hakim understood the importance of family. The bond between us didn't break when he reverted and married Elia; if anything I was closer to him now than ever before.

His devotion might have estranged Killa, but that was more about Killa not being able to confront the loss of Hosea and accept his brother's desire for change. And his relentless preaching might have turned Cuba away, but the rest of us accepted him same as ever, because his love hadn't changed.

We hugged goodbye, and I looked over at Shona to get her attention so that we could leave, but she was already looking at me with an expression I couldn't read. She smiled tightly and we made our way home in silence.

As we walked, my mind wandered back to Hakim. Islam and his love for Elia were Hakim's release, Hosea's loss the catalyst. Killa and the rest of my family were so caught in their own worlds that they didn't spare a thought for how different life could be, whereas Cuba simply didn't believe in another world's attainability, so all my life I had believed in it for him.

In my reflections I realised that I was now the third person to have left the Hughes family, but which was I? Hakim or my mama? Had I left the fold in order to save my family, or to save myself? I didn't have the answers, but I thought a visit to my mama might provide some.

24

Wah di goat do, di kid falla.

– Jamaican Proverb

My mama was a worship leader and a self-proclaimed community activist; she volunteered for numerous projects and decided on which title to adorn herself with depending upon who was addressing her and under which circumstance she was being addressed. If it was a council member she was lobbying on behalf of a neighbourhood issue, she was Sister Erica Stewart. If it was a yute from around the way, she was Mrs Erica Stewart.

I hadn't lied when I told Pastor of our distance; I hadn't spoken to my mama since I got sent down, but I left her home the moment I finished breastfeeding. I had thought the answer as to why I was abandoned in Nanny's daycare would present itself with age, but no matter how many years I had under my belt, I couldn't grasp it.

There was a time where my mama would make some attempt to come back into my life.

I was a toddler and she would collect me from Nanny's and whisk me to the house-atop-the-hill. And there we would spend the day. I loved my mama for those few short hours, but as soon as my papa called she would make her excuses and drop me back at Nanny's.

After one of those times, I remembered asking Nanny what it was about me my mama couldn't love. Nanny wrapped me up and told me that there was nothing that anyone could dislike about me; I was perfect. She explained that my papa was a man who had never wanted children, and that my mama was a woman who had never truly appreciated the worth of family.

I didn't know what it was for sure, but when I compared my mama to Marcia, or to Nanny, she fell woefully short.

What was a mama supposed to do aside from love her son?

A son shouldn't leave his mama's home unless he crossed the doorstep a man already raised. A mama was supposed to feed and love, even mollycoddle. She was supposed to tell you which foot went first, which colour necktie went with which shirt and which stone to cast back at bullies. She was supposed to draw a knife across your palm to show you pain before she dressed and wrapped it with cool binds.

To tell the truth, I wasn't sure what a mama was supposed to do, so I sought her in a café that served the homeless and found her behind a dutchie with a ladle in hand.

As soon as my mama saw me she told me to grab an apron or leave because she was busy. So I spent the better part of my day serving nitties, much like I had in the past – in fact, many of them hailed me and asked after Midnight. They hadn't noticed that I wasn't working with him any more, but I didn't expect them to; it didn't matter whose hand fed them, so long as the hand held their escape.

We finished in the early evening and retired to the courtyard behind the café. My mama perched on the step and wiped her hands on her apron. I took the wall opposite.

Every time I saw her she was looking more and more like Nanny. She had gained weight in her face and flecks of grey in her straightened hair. My mama was one of the few dark-skinned Hugheses, so naturally she'd chosen the lightest Black man she could find and had borne me. As far as I was concerned, I didn't favour her or my papa, which was one of the few things I thanked God for, though I wouldn't be surprised if my papa knelt and thanked Him for the same thing.

Luckily for her, my mama's parenting wasn't reflected in her looks: matter of fact she might have been called pretty in her day, even beautiful. And that wasn't to say that they wouldn't have called her the same now, only she reeked of devotion. Her whole person spoke to the seriousness of her nature, the lack of eyebrows she didn't bother to redraw, the dark lipstick and frown lines – she had her ways and wouldn't change them for anybody.

Once every worker had said their goodbyes and left the building, my mama took a packet of cigarettes from her pocket and set to lighting one, 'Why yuh come look mi for, Sayon?' she asked.

'I went to the yard the other day.'

'Which yard? Yuh papa yard?'

'Nah, the Clifton one.'

She puffed on the cigarette and let the smoke rise into her nostrils and over her head, 'Yuh affi fi stop baddah di people dem Sayon, dat nuh fi yuh yard.'

'But you showed me it—'

'Yuh not ahh pickney no more, Sayon. Yuh affi leave di childish tings behind an grow up.' She sucked on the cigarette.

184

'Hallelujah,' she breathed, 'God is gud. Enuh wi did feed bout fifty omeless people today? Praise God. Opefully tomorrow wi feed another fifty more. Praise God. Yuh nuh mi never undahstan why di omeless don't come yahsuh everyday, but God will guide dem dat deserve it. Praise God.' Her eyes shrunk to slits as she took another puff. 'Really an truly, it might do fi ax yuh why, ini, Sayon? Since yuh seem fi know dem all—'

'Why'd you give up on the yard?'

My mama kissed her teeth and threw the cigarette to the ground. 'Sayon, wat mi juss tell yuh?' She crushed it beneath her heel and strode back into the kitchen. I followed her inside. 'Ow yuh spect mi fi buy ahh yard in Clifton? Yuh tink seh mi Caucasian? It's ahh pretty yard mi did like fi look pon as ahh yute, an mi tek yuh deh ahh couple times, dat's it. Now mi ahh big woman wid ahh usband an nuff responsibility. Praise God, I can't complain. Hallelujah, Jesus.'

The kitchen had already been cleaned by the other workers, but she set about cleaning it again. 'God give mi everyting mi ever ax for, an yuh waan come ax mi bout somebody else yard,' she rounded on me, 'an wahum? Mi ear seh yuh lef Nanny's?'

'Yeah, after Winnie's funeral. The one you and Papa missed.'

'Winnie dead, man, nobody surprised. If God see fit, den mi can see er in di afterlife; if not den suh it guh. Weh yuh deh stay now?'

'Wid Shona,' I replied.

She cut her eyes after me. 'Chuhh, mi ope seh yuh nuh baddah Pastor Lyle an Marcia too much, dem deh good people, better dan di likes ahh yuh an yuh family.'

'*Our* family,' I corrected her.

She barked, and rubbed the counters with as much elbow grease as she could muster. 'Nahsuh, mi name Stewart now.

Mi lef unuh di same time mi lef di yard. Mi ahh child ahh God now, Sayon, tings change. Watch yah now, yuh tell Pastor Lyle an dem bout di time yuh spend innah prison?'

'What about it?'

'Nuh baddah play fool fi ketch wise wid mi, Sayon. Mi ax if yuh tell dem dat yuh spend time innah prison fi sellin illegal drugs?'

'Nah, I ain't told dem. Shona didn't want man to.'

'Boysah, yuh better lef di poor gyal loose, Sayon. Maybe next time mi bump innah Marcia mi could tell er, dem deserve fi know exactly who deh date dem daughter.' She checked to see if she'd gotten under my skin, but I didn't flinch; we both knew she was chatting shit. 'After all,' she continued, intent on winding me up, 'Shona is such ahh lovely, lovely young ooman, Praise God, ahh good Christian ooman. Hallelujah. She deserve better dan di likes ahh yuh. Wen mi first ear yuh deh date mi did tank God dat im finally set yuh on di straight ahh narrow, but mi did speak too soon, enuh.'

I reached for a cloth of my own and set about drying the dishes; it took all I had not to throw them at her head. And by the time we had finished, the entire café smelt of bleach and hard work.

My mama locked the doors behind us, and though she'd been her usual obstinate self, I had my answer; by leaving Nanny's I was abandoning the house-atop-the-hill, thus abandoning Cuba in his hour of need, and he never would have done that to me.

My leaving wasn't similar to Hakim's, whose love for us had never waned; it was more like my mama's, abrupt and uncompromising, and she was the last person I wanted to bear any resemblance to.

'Ay Mama, I'm gonna cut,' I told her, but she didn't reply. 'Yo, Mama?' I said again.

'Mi ear yuh Sayon man, chuhh, nuh baddah bawl mi name like suh.'

I waited until she had finished locking up and faced me; it took some time since she busied herself first with the keys, then with her bag. She was clearly exasperated that I was still there. 'Ay Mama, before I cut I got another question.'

'Speak if yuh muss, Sayon.' She folded her arms across her chest and waited.

'Was leavin me wid Nanny all those years and not havin nutun to do wid man worth it? Like, did you get everyting you wanted from life after you cut?'

Indignation straightened my mama's spine and she drew herself upward. 'Yuh av blasted cheek, enuh yute,' she hissed. 'Mi leave? Nah suh. It was yuh dat lef, Sayon. Yuh lef wen yuh waan run round Stapleton Road wid yuh fool cousin dem an act like yuh nuh av no ome trainin. Yuh lef wen yuh waan go act up innah school,' she took a step with each proclamation, her fingers folded into guns which she jabbed into my chest and her voice rose with her temper, 'yuh lef wen yuh waan go ahh prison.'

Once she'd said her final word she gingerly unfolded her gun fingers, patted her headtop and quickly scanned the pavements, aware that she had her husband's reputation to maintain. Then she drew closer still: 'Yuh tink it was easy fi yuh papa to lead di church wen im son deh in prison?' she hissed. 'Now good evenin to yuh, Sayon. Let dat be di last wi speak ahh it.'

My mama showed me her back and marched away, and in doing so confirmed what I needed her to; I had to make things right with Cuba, or else I would become the very thing I hated.

25

Better is a dinner of herbs where love is, than a fatted calf with hatred.

– Proverbs 15:17

Pastor Lyle wasn't a man to take for a fool, I knew that, but even the warmest of hospitality was a far cry from the comforts of home, and after two months I missed it.

I wanted to sneak over to Nanny's for the day. Grab some love. Eat a dinner. Get my fix before I saw out the rest of my sentence at the Jenningses'. And who knows, maybe Nanny took Cuba back after their argument at Winnie's funeral, and I might bump into him in the kitchen. He would smile at me, and me at him. Then he would hold out his hand, an olive branch, and I would take it gladly. I wanted to know if I was still welcome like Hakim, or would they suffer me like they did my mama?

But I figured visiting Nanny may be a step too far too soon. So I visited Viv's instead.

When his shop wasn't busy Viv sat out front with a metal chair, a bottle of ginger beer and his fisherman's hat tipped over his eyes. The ninety-year-old looked almost too comfortable to disturb in his beige slacks and buttoned cardigan, but the late-August sun was setting and dozing wasn't good for business.

'Yo, Mister Viv,' I said.

He opened an eye, saw it was me and closed it again. 'Wat yuh waan from mi, youngster?' His voice was raspy from years of drug abuse. The skin on his face was smooth but for the liver spots that rose from his shallow cheeks and forehead like gradients on a chestnut plank; perhaps it was better to say his skin still held the colour of its youth and knew the West Indian sun well.

The old man got his kicks from pulling legs, but I was well accustomed to his games. 'Viv? You ain't seen man in how long and dis is how you're treatin man?'

He sucked the air between his teeth. 'Yeah man, mi see yuh deh ahh yuh cousin funeral. But dat's wen mi see yuh, di real question is wen yuh last see mi, star? Yuh don't come by mi shop in ahh while.'

'I been busy, init.'

'Busy doin wat? Mi ear seh yuh tun church-bwoy now.'

'Who told you dat?'

'Yuh tinkseh mi ahh informer?'

'Man's been back in the church for a minute still.' I smiled, leaning up against the side of his shop.

'Move from mi shop bwoy!' Viv snapped. He glanced at me from beneath his hat and broke into a wide grin. The man was a certified mack. He had four gold teeth and the magnetism of a Neo Soul singer on tour in the noughties. His pinky nail was overgrown and his pockets fat. 'Mi just ahh joke wid yuh. Long time, son; come.' He leapt to his feet with the sprightliness of a man fifty years his junior and I followed him into his establishment.

Viv passed me tobacco and some filters from the shelf; along with some Haribos, a packet of biscuits and a Mirinda too. I knew he wouldn't take my money so I waited until his back was turned and snuck some into the till. I snuck the Haribos back as well. After listening to Hakim I'd decided I was done with swine for good.

'Tank yuh fi coverin fi dem likkle devils dat try teef from mi di other mont, yute. Mi catch dem pon di CCTV afterwards,' he said. 'I an I was downstairs wid di tree dem, but really, yuh shouldah shot dem ahh box, enuh? Dem mussi mad, chuhh, tinkseh dem can teef from Viv. Jah nuh seh mi wouldah give dem one serious whoopin if mi did ketch dem.'

'Probably a good ting it was me and not you den, init?'

'Mmmh, probably,' Viv replied. 'Di yutes dem dese days nuh av no ome trainin, enuh. Dem nuh av no mannahs. Dem parents never show dem no love, suh wen dem come innah di worl; dem nah av love fi show, enuh?' He came back from the shelf and leant against his counter, gesturing to the window and to the people passing outside as he ministered.

'Mi membah wen mi first come ahh farrin, back den di yute dem ad mannahs. Kaaz all ahh wi know seh dis life was better dan di life wi ad back ome, so wi work ard innah school, yuh undahstan?' He stroked the grey stubble at the end of his chin. 'Wi study. But now unuh av ahh likkle taste ahh privilege, unuh tun lazy. Just look wahum dehsuh,' he pointed to where I had killed Cordell, 'dat young bwoy stabbed right dehsuh, an mi did hear bout couple other stabbin recently as well. Dis worl tun mad mi tell yuh. Mad. Di yutes dem don't know left from right, right from wrong, an wrong from dem backfoot. All ahh unuh lack discipline.'

He brought his sermon to a close with all the wisdom and

serenity of a Dogon mask. Then he opened the latch that led to the basement and bade me follow. We came back with a carrier bag full of weed.

Every week Viv touted his wares in his local. I would be his security today, he said, but really he just wanted the company; there wasn't a soul in Ends who would trouble him.

In the pub we were met by a trove of familiar faces that hailed us as we came in, and everyone emptied their pockets to buy Viv's produce. He sold plenty and gave the landlord a likkle piece of the action. In the back corner my uncle Calvin and cousin Bunny were playing dominoes for money.

Uncle Calvin was a strapping fellow, tattooed and dapper. I often saw Bunny and Uncle Calvin as indistinguishable. They had been much alike in their teenage years and, as adults, little to nothing had changed. They both had multiple children by different women, had spent long periods inside, moved in dodgy circles and took to absenteeism as if it were an admirable hobby.

Uncle Calvin snapped his fingers when in deep thought and moved his mouth as if he were constantly chewing gum. He called anyone in authority 'guv' and called women 'bitches' but would cut a man's throat for disrespecting his daughters. He still wore the gold watch Cuba and I had stolen from the house-atop-the-hill; we'd given them to him and Bunny, but Bunny had long sold his.

Again, as I greeted my family and helped Viv sell his food, my mind settled on Pastor Lyle. If he knew where I was, who I was with and what I was doing, I was sure it wouldn't have ended peacefully. Given Viv's local and the church were on the same street, my paranoia was justified, but after living with Shona's suspicion and visiting my mama, I needed some normality.

Before either Calvin or Bunny caught sight of me, I wondered whether they would make any snide remarks about my recent absence. And although Killa hadn't made much mention of it (aside from referencing mine and Cuba's distance), I wondered if my uncles would hold it against me; use it as ammunition to put a bullet in me as I ascended, or a rope around my neck with which to catch my descent, because I still wasn't sure which I had taken; a climb or a fall.

I worried, but I was met with nothing of the sort.

'Yo, church-bwoy!' Uncle Calvin called, beckoning me over. 'Wahum, Mister Viv, y'alright? Yuh waan mi fi play yuh ahh and?' My uncle spoke to men and women with the same voice, liberal with both the confrontation and sex that made up his persona.

'Yeah man, deal me in, nuh, mi produce almost done already.'

They made space for Viv at the table and we ordered a couple of drinks.

'Yuh still deh av money church-bwoy? Lend mi ahh couple pound,' Uncle Calvin said, his hand outstretched, and by a couple of pounds he meant twenty. When I handed him the note he immediately put it on the table. 'Watch mi win dis yah round,' he barked. Everyone put their likkle change on the table and the game began.

'Yuh av anyting fi me, guv?' my uncle Calvin asked Viv.

'Yuh av any money fi mi?' Viv shot back. He peeked at his hand and slapped a card on the table.

'Chuhh,' Uncle Calvin rubbed the back of his scalp, 'yuh known mi since ahh yute, guv, an yuh cyaan even spare mi one likkle piece.'

'If mi spare yuh one likkle piece every time, ow many piece yuh tink dat is?' Viv returned. 'Pass,' he said with his next breath, and tapped the table. My uncle kissed his teeth and played his hand. 'Why cyaan yuh follow yuh nephew?' Viv continued, 'Sayon know im stuff an im don't baddah nobody.'

'Sayon don't know nutun, man,' Uncle Calvin said, but I didn't pay him any mind.

Whilst they relentlessly quibbled, Bunny's conversation across the table had caught my interest. Bunny was in his early thirties, a couple of years younger than Uncle Calvin, and over the course of their lives they had been terrible influences on each other.

Like Viv, Bunny had gold teeth, but was equipped with none of his blandishments. He plastered himself with enough cocoa butter to moisturise the city's knees and wore so much cologne it soured your tongue when he walked with any vim. Fortunately, he wasn't prone to walking with purpose, so his company was usually bearable.

'So wat did yuh do next, Bunny?' another man asked him. I didn't know this man. He was fat and unpleasant and spoke to my uncle with so much deference I thought at any moment he might lick his boots.

'What could I do?' Bunny replied, as he checked his dominoes a final time before playing. 'When women reject you, you only have two options, Jimmy, you can either listen to dem mouths or dem bodies.'

The fat man guffawed, and slapped his meaty thighs. 'Yuh right about dat, yuh right enuh, Bunny. Pass.'

'Course I'm right!' Bunny replied. He reclined in his seat and took a swig from his Beck's. I found men who readily accepted sycophantic behaviour, especially from other men, were often-times worse than the sycophants themselves.

'And you know me, Jimmy; Bunny don't listen to no

woman.' Jimmy laughed and slapped his legs again. My uncle continued, spurred by the pig's applause. 'So I took what I wanted. She gave me the pussy dat night, mi tell yuh. She came three times as well. Squirted too. Afterwards, she was beggin for the cocky, I had to tell her to cool off wid all dat. Gyal can be too much sometimes man. It's always feast or famine wid dem.'

I watched for Uncle Calvin's reaction, but he didn't say a word, or even pay attention. Viv was staring at his hand and the rest of the gathered men laughed and spoke of similar experiences.

Uncle Calvin and Bunny were men: their egos were attached to manhood like boyhood was attached to rough play. I was curious how the two men would react if they knew that I'd murdered Cordell. Or that Cuba had killed Winnie. I doubted their response to Cordell would be anything noteworthy; Bunny had just nonchalantly admitted to rape, and I was certain that it was Uncle Calvin who had killed Winnie's rapist.

But the two of them had known Winnie far longer than we had, and if they discovered the truth about Winnie's death there would be violence. Perhaps not directed at me, because Cuba would never willingly reveal my involvement, but towards Cuba, certainly. And no matter how Winnie's death was affecting him, if Cuba hadn't hesitated when putting an end to her, I doubted he would hold back against Uncle Calvin or Bunny, especially if they were the aggressors.

'Yo, nephew,' Uncle Calvin said, and his head didn't rise from his dominoes. 'Pastor Lyle av yuh on ropes like Ali add Liston, yuh basically back innah prison, cept yuh would've turned Muslim, not Christian, in jail. Yuh cyaan even come round Nanny's fi ahh likkle food?'

I felt my cheeks grow hot, but decided to play along. My

uncles were piranhas to blood when they found someone who couldn't take a joke. 'What you sayin, Nanny wouldn't mind, nah?' I asked, certain that she would bear at least a little resentment by now.

My uncle kissed his teeth. 'Mind? Chuhh. Nephew, yuh could kill ahh man right deh in di miggle ahh Nanny's yard an she wouldn't mind, yuh an Uncle Michael er favourites, everybody know dat.'

And he was right; there would always be a place for me around Nanny's table. Finally, I relaxed a little, and the weight I carried lessened.

Across the table Bunny laughed. 'Wasn't it you that turned akh in prison, Calvin?'

'Yeah man, I said some farrin words, every yute-man was doin it back den.'

'So wagwan? You're still Muslim now?'

'I'm only Muslim in prison, darg, outside I'll leave dat to di bwoy Hakim.' He lifted his liquor. 'Yuh tinkseh mi could ever give dis yah beverage up?'

'Weh yuh deh now, yute?' said Viv.

I told him that I was with Shona.

'Follow after Christ fi love,' Uncle Calvin chuckled, 'just like im mama.'

Bunny threw in his two pence before I could tell Calvin to suck himself. 'Doin it for pussy makes sense,' he mused. 'If anyone other dan Shona took you from us den Midnight would've killed dem for sure.'

'Mmmh,' Uncle Calvin said, 'Midnight was ahh bad breed from im born.'

26

And above all things have fervent love for one another, for 'love will cover a multitude of sins.'

– 1 Peter 4:8

Around my family for what was only the second time in months, I knew that part of the reason I had visited Viv's was because I was still jarred about the other day when Shona had treated Hakim and Killa like strangers. Since then we hadn't exchanged more than a greeting in the morning and a 'sleep well' at night. She'd busied herself with her work and helping her mama, and the pastor kept me busy with errands.

It seemed we were both content to wait for the other to close the distance, but neither of us were willing. And I for one didn't plan to; the feeling that I had to choose between my family and her had never felt stronger than that day. I needed her to understand that, but she couldn't. And since I couldn't bring it up to her without baring the rest of my burdens, I had never felt so disconnected from the woman I loved.

So here I was, without her and gladder for it, chatting shit with some old-timers.

No one had been winning consistently, they had all won and

lost a little money, so the mood had sobered and no jokes were shared. Uncle Calvin sat beside Viv and tried to outfox the old man; Viv was preoccupied with Bunny, and Bunny with his sycophantic bredrin, Jimmy.

Partway through, Uncle Calvin asked me to fetch him a drink to whet his mind and by the time I came back he'd finished the game. 'Unuh cyaan match mi,' he smiled, sweeping the money into a pile. Of course, his taunts inspired an encore, and so they continued long into the night.

True to my mama's example, neither Uncle Calvin nor Bunny had been around much when I was growing up, though in their defence, Her Majesty was often to blame.

The last sentence Uncle Calvin had served was for possession of a firearm. He was inside for five of his seven years and managed early release for good behaviour. The night he was arrested would forever be in my mind.

It was two years before Hosea was killed, I was in Year 8, and the firearm that would later lead to Uncle Calvin's incarceration was in Hosea's possession. The pistol belonged to Calvin but he had lent it to Hosea who used it to rob corner shops, bookies and passers-by in idle moments. Back then, Bunny was indebted to a loanshark to the tune of some £10,000. He didn't have the heart to take his fate into his own hands, and since nine-to-fives wouldn't cut it, he'd turned to his older cousin Calvin and pleaded with him to take action.

Uncle Calvin sought to solve Bunny's problem the only way he knew how. Of course, there was no dilemma for Hosea who paid his own debt by returning Calvin's weapon. He even offered assistance, but his offer was refused. Uncle Calvin and Bunny suited up and set out to see the lender.

Their mistake was taking Uncle Calvin's car. It was one of those Lexuses New Yorkers used to rap about, the kind that drew attention, even from people who didn't know anything about cars. Uncle Calvin unloaded the gun and stored it in the glovebox. He put the bullets beneath the handbrake. They wore gloves and black clothes. If they were pulled over Uncle Calvin would face the mandatory minimum five years for possession, but because the gun wasn't loaded they wouldn't be able to prove criminal use or even that Bunny knew there was a weapon in the whip.

Even if they were red, they were Black, and the car was expensive, so of course they were pulled over and of course the police found the weapon.

Absolved of any responsibility, Bunny showed up at Nanny's the following night and the ensuing argument became a part of the Hughes fabric. Bunny wanted Hakim, Jamaal and Hosea to take the problem to the Lexus dealer and have him say the gun was his, so the three of them fetched balaclavas and weapons and had to be persuaded by Uncle Marlon and Aunty Winifred to calm down and see reason.

Nanny was trying to shoo Cuba and me into the front room with the other children and Aunty Paulette phoned my mama to place the fault of Uncle Calvin's waywardness firmly at her absent feet. My mama arrived at Nanny's shortly after, and she was furious.

She strode into the living room and had to be dragged away from Aunty Paulette whom she quickly had in a headlock. Once they had been separated Aunty Paulette tried to retaliate and swung a weighty tump at Aunty Winifred's jaw that spun the fragile woman from her feet and into the sofa. My mama was sent to the backyard and Aunty Paulette was confined to the living room. Not wanting to miss the action, the rest of the family tossed an ice pack to Aunty Winifred and made her administer her own first aid.

In the yard my mama climbed atop the garden table and delivered an off-the-cuff message to the grassroots. 'Calvin deserve jail an wen im get sentence im deserve dat same way, in fact, dem should fling im IPP,' she bawled in front of his mama, cousins and children. 'Why im av ahh gun?' she said. 'Wat person in dem right mind carry gun innah England?' She was met by a chorus of boos. If we had had tomatoes we would have drenched her in their juice. Amidst the noise Bunny's protests rang clearest; he stood beside Uncle Marlon and went word for word with my mama.

'How were we supposed to know they was gonna pull us over, huh Erica?' he bawled. 'If the feds wasn't racist as shit dey never would've pulled us over, den dey never would've found the ting and none of dis would've happened.'

'But why im av ahh bludclart gun innah England?' my mama shouted back, a clap accompanying every syllable. Uncle Marlon and Jamaal barred the path between her and Bunny, otherwise I'm sure my mama would have dragged him through the dust. 'I don't know why unuh pretend after Calvin like seh im ahh saint? Unuh know seh im rotten like egg.' She flailed an arm towards the living room. 'Im was ahh bad seed from im born an everybody know it.'

She turned to the rest of us, spit flying from her mouth. 'Unuh tinkseh kaaz yuh do yuh shit innah di dark it cyaan ketch yuh, but God see all ahh unuh. All ahh unuh!' She levelled her fingers at us all, one by one: 'Im see yuh wickedness, praise be, big ahh small. Hallelujah. An believe mi, Im will come for all ahh unuh, believe dat.'

'Yuh top fi yuh noise now, Erica,' Nanny cried from the door, 'yuh gone far enough.'

It was because of Nanny that I'd never forget that day. The anger in her spirit was as alien to me then as it was at Winnie's funeral. She was a disciplinarian, it's true, but one who never relied upon the strength in her voice more than the firmness in her eye and the fierceness of her reputation. Her hands were clenched white and her fingernails dug so deeply they almost drew blood from her palms. It was the first and last time you might have heard a pin drop in the Hughes' house.

'Don't speak fi God now, Erica,' Nanny whispered. 'God is love,' she said, 'an love forgives.' My mama stared at her mother from the tabletop before climbing down. Without another word, and with her chin held high, she marched through her mother's house to her husband's car.

And that was the last time my mama had set foot in the family home.

At the dominoes table Uncle Calvin had won the last three games and had given me back my twenty with an extra ten. He spent his winnings on the last of Viv's weed.

Tired of losing their money, the rest of them called it a night and went home to their babymamas and children. Outside the pub Viv handed me a Werther's Original and asked if I needed any food. I was a pillar of the community, he said. I would do great things in this life and find reward in the next. He shuffled back to his shop, stiff from sitting so long, and said goodbye with a flick of his hand.

Of course, that was the moment I turned to see Pastor Lyle ushering his late-night study group on to Stapleton Road. He finished shutting the door behind them, and locked eyes with mine; the Devil never slept, so I supposed it was fitting. The next day, halfway through a junior minister's rendition of the Sermon on the Mount, he called me into his office.

27

A righteous man regards the life of his animal, but the tender mercies of the wicked are cruel.

– Proverbs 12:10

Pastor's office was a large room with two entrances, though one was permanently locked. The decorator's vision was dark greens, browns and orange light. The ceilings were high and a row of skylights punctured the gloom. Two leather chairs were arranged beside a bureau that looked made to fit Number 10 Downing Street. A water cooler stood sentry by the door and in the opposite corner a reading area had been constructed beneath mahogany bookshelves.

It was the room of a man in love with order. Everything had its place. The desk was home to his luxe leather-bound King James Version and a photograph of Shona. The plastic cups for the cooler were well stocked. The skylights had blinds that could be drawn from Pastor Lyle's seat. The Bibles were sequenced by the year the translation was scribed and the few empty spaces were festooned with family heirlooms. It was an extension of his house. A reproduction of his study. Pastor Lyle had found structure in the church and made it his own.

Pastor Lyle collapsed into his seat and gestured for me to join him. 'Do you remember our conversation shortly before your cousin Winnie passed, Sayon? About what you did? You remember the conditions to my silence?'

'Yeah yeah, I remember,' I said coolly, though really I was on the edge of my seat. I had taken a risk by visiting Viv and the pub, and I had been caught red-handed. I was very aware that there were ushers gathered outside the pastor's door, I knew that he could send for Shona and ruin everything with a single cry.

'And would you say you've kept to them?' he continued, his voice sweet like the times we ran errands with the sunroof open.

It was throwing me off.

I had expected him to be livid. Frothing at the mouth. I had expected the darkness I'd always sensed in him to be on full display. Two demons either side of his head, their tridents pointed at my heart. Instead he seemed relaxed. So not to be outfoxed, I played along; I told him that I had stuck to his conditions faithfully.

'Good,' Pastor Lyle replied, and the same mist that overtook him when he spoke about my uncle Michael clouded his eyes, then he clapped and shouted 'good' again and it was gone. He lurched to his feet and strode to the water cooler. He fetched two cups and placed them on the desk, one between the KJV Bible and the photograph of Shona, and the other in front of me. Then he reached into his desk and set a bottle of brandy on the table. 'How have you found living with us so far, son?'

'Living with you?' I said, trying my hardest to appear unnerved, but I couldn't take my eyes from the liquor. Since the first time, I'd seen him use wine for cooking and swig at the bottle, but nothing as brazen as this. And certainly not in the church – they didn't even use alcohol for communion, but grape juice.

I quickly concluded that it was a test. Perhaps he hadn't seen me clearly last night and wanted to lull me into a false sense of security before he confirmed his suspicions? Perhaps he was testing my conviction? Or maybe he wanted me drunk in order to find the remaining skeletons hidden in my closet?

'Living with us,' Pastor Lyle said, 'and attending my church. I just wanted to see how you've been finding it? Is there anything I can do to make it more comfortable for you? Anything you feel that you're missing?'

'Missing?'

'*Missing*,' he nodded. 'Shona seems to think that you're unhappy.'

'She said that?'

'Of course!' Pastor said, and his brow furrowed. 'You think I don't talk with my daughter?'

'No, no, of course,' I said, as if I had known all along, but inside I was burning; it only served as further proof we had grown apart.

'Are you thirsty, young man?' Pastor Lyle asked, motioning towards the liquor.

'Nah, I'm good.'

'Are you sure?' He leant forward and began unscrewing the cap, and when the cap eventually came loose he poured himself a little, then did the same for me. He swilled the juice around the cup before quaffing it down. 'I've been feeling real tense lately, and this helps.' He topped up his cup and poured me some more. 'Everything in moderation – drink with me, young man.'

'I'm good,' I said. I wanted to leave, return to the congregation, go anywhere, but the pastor's strange performance left me glued to the seat.

'Over the years I've delivered so many sermons about back-sliders and regression, and you know what I've realised? How easy it is to trip and tumble down a slippery slope with no end in sight.' He poured himself another cup. 'Only Christ is the end.

'I've accepted that to be a parent is to be a hypocrite, young man. To be a pastor too. Should my wife and daughter, and by extension my congregation, follow my teachings or my example?' He drank again. 'They should follow after my teach-ings; follow after Jesus Christ. I am a practitioner of His Word, trying, same as them, same as anyone, to inherit eternal life.' He took another drink. 'Is this as hard for you as it is for me, Sayon?'

'Is what?'

Finally, he raised his head from his chest. 'Aren't you listen-ing?' he said. 'The lying. Doesn't it weigh on your spirit? I suppose it doesn't,' he said, answering for me, and returning to his reflection. 'Sometimes, I wonder whether all this will be worth it in the end, whether you'll bear fruit and enter into the flock, or whether you'll return nothing but empty husks.'

He was all but naked in the chair across from me, his inner-most thoughts laid on the table next to the liquor. And I came to the realisation that he saw me as the answer to his own salvation. I was the devil he hoped to convert, the foremost of his weekly tithes, because if he could bring someone as sinful as me into the church, then he could prove to himself and the world, that he had mastered his past sins.

In his mind he'd swooped low in his sweet chariot and saved me from the barbarity of my family and the roads. Now he would have me embrace the tenets of the one true religion, the only thing that could save a sinner like me; Jesus Christ. And in my condition as an outcast from the 'real world', he would direct my aspirations to heavenly and eternal citizenship, an aspiration over which he had obsessed for years; and now he demanded it of me too, for both Shona's sake and his own.

Thus he would keep me tucked firmly under his wing, and any deviation, any expression of individuality, would be crushed under the weight of the Word and I would be banished to eternal Hell for my sins. And it was because of this power he held over me that I was the one man he could bare himself before.

Late one night, a week after he called me into his office, I was smoking in the garden. I finished and snuck through the back door where I found Pastor Lyle sat in the kitchen, the same wine bottle at his lips, drunk.

'Sayon,' he babbled, and I stopped in my tracks. Immediately I thought the entire ruse over: he may not have directly challenged me about seeing my uncles and Viv, but I knew that I had crossed the line, and that this would do little to help my case.

He used the chair to support himself to his feet and leant against the cooker. 'The lies *have* been affecting you, haven't they?' the bigger man whispered. He sounded almost pleased and took a sip. 'And this is how you've been maintaining; by bringing weed into my house.'

I had nothing.

'Sit down,' Pastor said. And once I had, he sat across from me, much like in June, except now there was a frailty in the way his back bent. 'I know how much you love my daughter,' he began, and he kept his eyes trained on me, even when he drank they didn't leave. 'She thinks it was written between the two of you,' he said, and the ghost of a smile softened his drunken expression. 'And that may be; the Lord works in mysterious ways after all.'

Then the smile vanished as quickly as it came. 'I know my daughter lied to me when she said the two of you took a break a few years back.' I kept my face impassive, but he wasn't watching it for a reaction; he spoke with certainty. 'No one takes a break for that long then carries on as if nothing's changed. She thinks I don't know. You probably think the same. But I know you've already spent time in jail, Sayon. I may not hear everything that goes on around here, but I heard enough to figure that out.'

'That was a long time ago, Pastor,' I hurried. 'I was a yute dem times.'

'You're still a yute,' he said, and briefly his shoulders bunched, fire flitted in his eyes, then a second later it was gone. 'I saw what it did to Princess – your absence. And even though no father wants their daughter to be heartbroken; they would drive a badbruk yute away from her in a heartbeat, if it meant protecting her. Which is what I wanted to do when I first found out about your sentence, but Marcia wouldn't let me.' He raised the bottle to his mouth and drank again.

'She's a special woman, Marcia. She doesn't know anything about what's happened recently, I just told her you needed a place to stay and she opened our home and her heart to you; that's the kind of woman she is, and the kind of woman we've raised our daughter to be. I saw the Lord in action when Marcia stayed my hand those years ago, and again when I watched you and your cousin from the church window and sought His guidance in my office. Both times He reminded me of my past.

Of my transgressions. And the woman I'm lucky enough to have. Who I wasn't worthy of, until I changed.'

He got up from where he sat, came around the table and placed a heavy hand on my shoulder. I felt like I was back in junior school, and I was certain he could feel how ready I was to fight or run. 'You must change, Sayon,' he said, and there was something in his voice I didn't recognise. A softness that made my tension ease. 'Not just for yourself, but for my daughter.'

The wine on his tongue inspired some kind of sympathy in me. My life had made me accustomed to all kinds of substance abuse, and I carried a certain tolerance for it.

'You need a shower,' I said, putting his arm around my shoulders, ready to lead him to the bathroom, 'otherwise they'll smell the drink on you.'

'You're right, you're right,' he nodded, as we tottered down the hallway and took the stairs one at a time. 'You have to change, Sayon,' he said, as he set the shower running, 'it's what God wants.'

I thought it best not to respond; he wasn't in any kind of condition to facilitate a conversation. Instead, I helped him strip. I offered a hand for him to lean upon as he undid his belt and kicked off his trousers. He pulled his shirt over his head and I turned the tap and checked the temperature.

And the second after I shut him inside, Shona appeared in the corridor.

We'd woken her, she explained, as she shuffled to me and rested her head against my chest. It was the first time we had shared any intimacy in a while. And it felt alien. I put my arms around her and felt as though I was embracing a stranger.

'Is something wrong?' she asked.

'Nah, nutun's wrong,' I replied, deception now like second nature, 'I just bumped into your pops at the fridge; said he's taking a shower now.'

She pulled back from me and stared right through me. It was a terrible thing to ask the person you loved what was wrong and watch them lie, so Shona simply returned to bed.

I waited outside the bathroom until the pastor reappeared, and when he did it was without a degree of humility or relation, as I had been expecting; instead he held my eye for some uncomfortable seconds before saying: 'Every man faces God alone,' then turning in for night.

I missed Cuba.

I was lonely, and without a confidant in the world – a feeling I knew Pastor Lyle shared – but where I was newly used to carrying the weight of my transgressions alone, he'd turned to his old friend, and his instability would ruin everything.

28

A man who isolates himself seeks his own desire; he rages against all wise judgement.

– Proverbs 18:1

Despite the close calls, neither Marcia nor Shona noticed the pastor's steady decline; instead, Marcia became aware of the growing distance between Shona and me.

I caught her smiling sadly at our awkward encounters at the fridge, and I overheard her telling Pastor Lyle she'd noticed that when one of us came into a room, it wasn't long before the other made their excuses and left. 'Oh, to be young,' she mused, hugging his huge frame, 'yuh tink dem will work it out?'

'Oh, to be young, indeed,' the pastor echoed.

He never did answer her question. And it made me wonder what he would do if Shona and I never worked it out at all – if we just drifted apart, on good terms perhaps, but intent on separation. Nanny said he wouldn't go to the police, that he was more concerned with eternal punishment than man-made law, but freed from any obligation to protect his daughter, and without me to mould, I wasn't so sure; he was becoming more unpredictable as the days went by.

Early one Saturday morning, Marcia called Shona and me into the kitchen. I arrived first and watched Shona falter at the door when she saw me. 'Wagwan, Mama?' she quizzed, doing her damnedest not to look in my direction.

Marcia was under the kitchen sink, yellow gloves pulled past her wrists, in a grey tracksuit for cleaning. 'Yes, babies,' she hailed, 'mi need unuh to fetch mi some bread, but none ahh dat sliced rubbish from Iceland; gwan ahh yuh cousin shop, Sayon.'

'Hakim's?' I frowned.

'Dat would be di one.'

'Together?' Shona said. 'Surely that don't need both of us.'

'Both ahh unuh are goin,' Marcia answered, speaking without quarrel, nor with any room for negotiation. She held her hand out and I helped her to her feet. 'I don't know wahum to unuh recently, but unuh affi grow out ahh it, especially yuh, Shona. Sayon is our guest.'

'Mama,' she flounced, but Marcia was having none of it.

'Find some money on di table,' she interrupted, simultaneously brushing Shona's rebuttal aside and gesturing at her handbag, which was slung over the back of a dining chair. Shona took her mama's purse then left the room. I sighed, not looking forward to the task at hand, and made to follow until Marcia stopped me: 'Yuh affi talk to er, my love,' she said quietly. 'Whatever it is I don't know, I don't want to know, but she does, so juss ask er, yuh ear? Women need to be listened to.'

'All right,' I nodded, knowing full well that I wouldn't, but it was enough for Marcia to smile and let me go.

'An Sayon,' she said, 'Lyle don't av to know weh yuh get di bread from,' she chuckled. 'No one wants to ear mi chat bout alal dis an alal dat. Im don't even know wat alal means, but dat won't stop im complainin anyhow.'

I laughed, as I was supposed to, and was surprised to see that Shona had waited for me at the door. So together we walked the length of Stapes in silence. I nodded at a few familiar faces and prayed we wouldn't bump into any of my family members. And beside me, Shona kept her earphones in. I could hear the bass and she was nodding her head along to the drums, making it clear that she didn't want to be spoken to.

We made it to the bakery and Shona held out her hands for me to go first, so I pushed inside and joined the back of the queue.

Elia was behind the counter, Hakim darting to and from the back room, gone for a second before reappearing with loaves of bread or sweet things, both too preoccupied with their respective tasks to notice the gloom that had entered the building.

Every time Hakim pushed past Elia, he put a hand on her back or squeezed an arm, or a shoulder. And she didn't pay him any mind. Because he didn't do it for her; it would've been the same as if he'd touched himself; scratched an itch, or stroked his stomach. And she was the same; she pulled him out of the way to reach for high places and held his leg to steady herself on her haunches.

The bakery was busy, so they took two orders at once.

The customers both wanted small things. Cakes or some such. They bagged and tied them. Took the cash and reached for the till. Their hands hit, they smiled, and split. Elia let Hakim get his change, then she took hers; he shut the register and she tapped the numbers; they handed the goods back and both said, 'Who's next?'

It was a marvel seeing how far they'd come, and how in love they still were.

Hakim had once explained it like this: they were souls aligned like soldiers joined previously in the world of spirits, they'd known each other then, then met again in the dunya – the world we now know – so it was always meant to be.

She was his alaf.

The Eve to his Adam; as equal in guilt as glory.

I remembered when they first came across one another: it was a few years back. I was leaving Nanny's to kick ball with Karma and some others, when I overheard Hakim telling Jamaal about this girl he'd seen. He described her as dark, tall, looked like she'd walked straight off a magazine front cover.

This was not long after Hakim had reverted as well so he only had eyes for hijabis.

I interrupted them and asked whether she had any other remarkable features. He shrugged, so I showed him a picture of Elia. 'Yo,' he exclaimed, grabbing my phone, 'dat's her, blud!' He showed her to Jamaal, who approved of her beauty, and Hakim turned to me with wide eyes. 'You know her?' he asked, and I nodded, pleased to be of use.

'She's man's bredrin, fam,' I told him, 'like man's big bredrin from school times.'

I set them up not long after. And I'd never told Hakim how much persuasion Elia needed, but I had to offer financial compensation and promise that she could throw water balloons at me if the first date went badly.

But it didn't; the first led to a second, then to many more.

Growing up, because of the difference in age, Hakim had always been a bit distant from me. He wasn't unloving, only far off, like a top-shelf treat I was rarely allowed. Sure, I saw him all the time at Nanny's, and he would put money in my pocket, but it wasn't until I started juggin that we spent more time together and he began to see me less as his little cousin than as a compeer. And then later, after we lost Hosea and he reverted and married Elia, we became closer than ever.

And when she became a part of the family I grew closer to Elia too. Before, if someone asked me to describe her, I would've said that she was a light. One that everyone wanted for themselves. At times her energy would often be drained brightening those around her, and she would never listen to me or Shona when we told her to take it easy. But when Hakim came into the picture and put her first, it taught her how to do the same for herself, and she flickered brighter than ever. And she in turn helped him manage the pain of losing Hosea; the two hadn't looked back since.

'Lil man,' Hakim boomed, 'why you hiding in the back there?'

'Shona!' Elia exclaimed, our being there brought to her attention by her husband. She left the counter and pulled us both into a hug. I saw Shona smile awkwardly as she returned the embrace, both pleased to see Elia and no doubt embarrassed by the state of our relationship in the face of such naked love.

Hakim's attention was taken by another customer, so Shona explained to Elia that her mum had sent us and what she had sent us for. A second later Elia was presenting us with two loaves of bread and insisting they were on the house.

'If your mum wants it you can't argue with me,' she said, 'it's a gift.'

'Elia,' Shona said, but she was brightening already.

'It's not for you, you can't reject it.' Her eyes glinted and she flashed me a knowing smile. 'And anyway, Sayon can't overpay now he's unemployed.' It was meant to be a joke, and under different circumstances it would've been funny, but Shona was quick to jump at the opportunity.

'Yeah,' she said ironically, 'though I'm not sure he's pleased about that; not everyone is happy to give the life up like Hakim.'

My face screwed tight. 'What?' I spat, and I watched the humour fall from Elia's face as she realised she'd poked the hornet's nest. She checked for Hakim but he was still serving a customer, so she did her best to fade into the background.

Shona turned slowly. She hadn't looked at me since we'd stood in her mother's kitchen, but now she did so brazenly. 'I said, you're not happy about giving everything up,' she repeated, head cocked to the side as she dared me to say otherwise. 'Am I wrong? Or is it something else you're not saying?'

I kissed my teeth loud and long; some customers glanced at us, others openly stared, but I didn't care. 'You're moving mad, blud,' I tutted, 'but if you really wanna go deh, we'll chat bout it later, wallahi.'

'Yeah, but we won't though will we, Sayon?' Shona said. She stepped back to let someone leave the bakery, but her eyes didn't leave mine; they were furious.

'Fuck dis,' I said. 'Yo Elia, tell Hakim I said wagwan.' I wrenched the door open and stormed back to the Jenningses'. I gave the bread to Marcia and told her that talking to Shona didn't work. Nothing would. There was no quick fix for our situation.

It was times like these I felt Cuba's absence most, because in the past I would've gone straight to him. Not for his advice, because, despite the love he had for Shona, he would've told me to do something disastrous.

No, certainly not for his advice, but for his company. There was no fake in him. He didn't try and read between the lines. He took me at face value and would have my back against anyone. It was true we needed people who could give it to us straight, but we also needed people like Cuba, whose companionship was therapeutic.

I hadn't been sleeping well at all since Karma visited me. And if I'd stayed at the bakery long enough for Hakim to greet me, I imagined he would've asked if I'd spoken to Cuba. And I would've had to have told him that I hadn't; making me feel more alone than I could handle.

29

A friend loves at all times, and a brother is born for adversity.

– Proverbs 17:17

Soon it was the first morning service of September, and the pastor and I were emptying the bins when we spied Junior posted outside Hakim and Elia's bakery. I would often see the little man when I accompanied Pastor on his errands, or on a trip to the corner shop. And each time we saw each other he would grin, rubbing Winnie's death and his closeness to Cuba in my face.

He stood with his man-bag slung across his shoulder like a chimp at its mother's neck. He wore two earrings to match his expensive clothes. He had tattoos now, new hair too – waves like Killa's. And he had invested his cash in Turkish jewels. He switched between back-slang and Arabic and had gold in his mouth.

I felt a surge of anger – why was it I had to be constantly reminded of my past and my absence from the family?

Because of recent events feds had become heavy-handed and ever-present, so rumour had it Cuba's runners had taken to selling crack and buj in the early hours and the small stuff at night.

Junior shook hands and nodded nitties in the direction of his bredrin who waited around various corners with wraps and food and anything they needed. Previously, my line had been solely for students, but it seemed Junior had diversified its clientele, and it rubbed me the wrong way.

Cuba assured me that he'd handled Junior, but I couldn't help but feel a corner had been cut. And if cutting corners was necessary, surely Junior was more of a risk than Winnie? His black boat parked outside my cousin's bakery was a constant reminder of my loss; the ease with which he leant against the shutters a slap in the face. When I had first seen him he was a wretch, snivelling in the back of Cuba's car; now he stood with the aplomb of yutes fresh home from short sentences.

With each passing day I wondered more how Cuba was dealing with things. I had bumped into everyone else in my family, or caught a glimpse at least, except the one person I was both desperate and afraid to see.

I was sure it was Winnie's death that had taken root in the centre of his being and its blossom was poison to the spirit. Because it wasn't as if he'd had passa with Winnie. He'd simply chosen me over her. He'd said that he had my best interests at heart, and he'd proven it. And now I was punishing the both of us by rejecting his love.

Pastor and I watched Elia step from inside the shop and open the shutters. She smiled at Junior, who smiled back. Solidarity between workers. She and Hakim would have been baking for hours. Up before the gulls crowed and the crack sold. Now their oven-hot loaves were ready for the early birds to catch.

'Just look at that,' Pastor Lyle said. 'She just lets him be.'

'Who?'

'There, that Somalian girl you and Princess went to school with, your cousin's Muslim wife, she just lets that little yute sell drugs on her doorstep.'

My relationship with the pastor had changed somewhat since the incident the other night. We were almost codees; brought closer by the secrets we shared.

'What's Elia supposed to do about it?' I said, and Pastor Lyle couldn't hide his contempt when he considered me.

'Call the police?' he said. 'Having that young man stood outside her shop makes hardworking people want to shop elsewhere; it's a bad look.' And as if on cue, a squad car pulled slowly along the road. The feds eyeballed Junior, then Pastor Lyle and me, and continued on their way. Pastor Lyle tutted again. 'Though you'd have to personally sell it to them for them to bother making an arrest.'

'You could take him in like you did me,' I said, half-ironically.

Pastor Lyle shook his head. 'You can't save everyone,' he said. 'And Sayon,' he said after a moment, as we watched Elia return to the bakery. 'I may not have said so specifically, but you know your cousin's bakery is off-limits, don't you?'

I supposed it wouldn't do well to tell him that Marcia had sent us there only days earlier. 'I know we've grown closer of late,' he continued, 'but don't think you can start taking liberties with the mercy I'm showing you. I don't need you bringing Islam into my house on top of everything else. And anyway, it wouldn't surprise me if the shop was a front for the rest of your family's activities.'

Across the road a white saloon pulled in front of Junior and out stepped none other than Cuba and Karma.

My cousin looked as though life had finally caught up with him and was primed to overtake. His posture sagged with his

219

trousers and a film of grease dulled his glow. And when his gaze fell upon me he barely reacted. We didn't nod at one another. There was no olive branch. In fact he almost sneered. Karma acknowledged me, but then again there was no gripe between us; we were still all good.

Pastor Lyle seethed beside me, his inner murkiness rapidly bubbling to the surface and I felt him size my cousin up. 'The man of the hour,' he said under his breath.

I was overcome with emotion, but because of Cuba's coldness I sought to hide any feelings behind a well-worn mask of in-difference.

Karma scowled at Pastor Lyle from behind the car whilst Cuba only grinned. Confrontation was the language my cousin spoke best, and if Pastor ever crossed the line he would be in our world; and then even Jesus wouldn't be able to save him.

The air between us grew charged, but we were interrupted when Shona appeared at the church doors, primed to tell her daddy to begin the service. She fell quiet as she took the scene in, and in an instant I knew she saw it for what it was; my old life was on one side of Stapes, whilst her, and her papa, were on the other.

I wondered whether she'd seen the same scene when we had bumped into Hakim and Killa, whether seeing me with my family had confirmed some inner mistrust she held.

Pastor Lyle spun around, wide-eyed and innocent, and I turned as well, tense, with defiance raging in my stance. Shona managed to maintain her composure. She told her papa to start the service as she had been instructed to do, and she waited for me to walk to her side. Across the road Karma and Junior went about their business and Cuba eyed Shona and me, clearly amused by our distance.

We quietly found our seats in the church and Shona made no mention of it.

Thus, the morning service passed without event, but when we returned to the church for evening service hours later, I saw Junior still standing outside the bakery. I stood at the church doors watching him as the congregation filed past me, and something in me snapped. I had finally seen Cuba, but it wasn't enough.

I watched two community support officers walk past Junior. The CSOs nodded at him and he nodded back. He took a call. Leant into the passenger window of a whip. Then climbed into the back. And, as if bade by the fixation of an addict, I hailed a cab and chased after him.

I followed Junior to an area in South Bristol, deprived and White working-class, a place to which trappers did a moonlight flit when Ends was too hot.

There he was met by Karma and Cuba. And again, as I watched from the tinted windows of the cab, I pondered the likelihood of Winnie snitching as compared to the likelihood of Junior doing the same. Cuba handed the little man something and the three of them disappeared into a tower block.

A trapper was easier to control than a nitty. That was a simple fact. One I'm sure Cuba found conclusive. Desperate women sold what they had to support their habits. And prison could either be a last-ditch health service for working women, or an involuntary detox. A detox would have killed Winnie, and she would have said anything, given anyone, to stay free. I understood that much. But Junior was still proving himself a liability, with his high-handed extravagance. And I would have felt a lot more comfortable with Junior in the ground.

The door of the flat swung open and Cuba and Karma stepped

out. Behind them I saw Junior stood over a cat in the stairwell. The nitty was in a wheelchair, his brown hair tousled, his reddish complexion bruised like a berry. The cat's tongue lolled from his mouth, his back arched like a camel's hump and his eyes bulged as he hurried Junior along, and the little man cussed as he pulled the solution into the eye of the needle.

The door slammed shut and I sunk lower in my seat, so as not to be seen, but neither Cuba or Karma seemed concerned with their surroundings. I couldn't help but think why was Cuba partaking in such mundane, bait practices? This was runner/middle management stuff. He didn't need to be here. Karma was right; circumstances were getting to him and he was getting slack.

Behind them Junior jogged from the flats laughing, doing an impression of the cat's rush, then the three of them called another cab and vanished.

Cuba had dismissed Killa's chances of leaving the world that we inhabited; in fact, he dismissed everyone's excluding mine and Hakim's, but what of his own? I had always assumed that I would be the one to drag him from the gutter. The house-atop-the-hill was as much his salvation as it was mine, except now I was left with no house to offer him and no hopes of attaining it either.

Pastor may have banned me from the bakery, but I needed Hakim, and for the first time, the risk of losing Shona couldn't keep me at bay.

When I returned to Ends I was met by Shona at the church.

'I missed you in the service,' she said softly, 'where did you go?'

I still saw the little girl I loved when I looked at her; the little girl on the scratchy blue carpet who had led me around the school, who jumped rope and embraced my family as her own; the girl who'd played me records and told me everything there was to know about music, but now, more than anything else, I saw the good Christian girl.

I hadn't been anywhere, I said. A walk. I needed to clear my head.

30

One finger cyaan kill louse.

– Jamaican Proverb

The next day I found Hakim lounging behind the bakery counter, one leg across his knee, as he completed a broadsheet crossword with a stubby pencil. He unfolded himself when I entered and beamed. 'Iska waran, lil man, you good?' I returned his greeting and he rose to embrace me across the counter.

'The bakery's kinda quiet today, man,' he said. 'Can I get you anything?'

I scoured the glass cabinets for something I fancied and I felt my sweet tooth twang; I bought a couple of buurs and a slice of coconut cake. He served me some saccharine tea from a pan and joined me at the table and chairs.

'Me and Elia started doing crosswords, fam,' Hakim continued, returning to his puzzle. 'We try make them into a competition; whoever finishes first doesn't do the washing-up – serious tings on the line, cuz. I can't lie, it's rah cos of jail that man's so sick at words, enuh? Sometimes it was so boring man used to read the dictionary in there, fam,' he laughed. 'You good, though?'

I told him I was good because I didn't know where to start.

I wanted to lay everything on him. I knew I couldn't, because even Hakim couldn't know about Winnie, but I wanted to. I had a lot on my mind, but most of all I wanted to know how he'd done it. How could someone from the same place as me be sat across the table, in his own bakery, chewing his lip over a crossword? What was it that allowed an escape? That enabled such peace?

For years I had dreamt of attaining such a feeling with the Clifton house, and for years I had thought it far away. But really it wasn't that far at all, because it had always been right here, in front of me.

I supposed much of Hakim's peace was rooted in ownership. This was his place. The customers that pushed through the door came for his produce. The beaded curtain that led into the kitchen was his. The appliances knew his touch and wouldn't respond to anyone else. It was his hand that had painted the walls, tiled the floors and that now served the food.

But before I could find the words, the front door burst open and Elia descended upon us with all the brouhaha I recognised and loved in her. 'Hakim,' she called, her accent full-flavoured like lemon ginger. 'Hakim, Hooyo wants us to make two three-tiered cakes for my cousin Najmo's birthday, but I told her we're too busy. What twelve-year-old needs two three-tiered cakes for their birthday? Hooyo's doing too much, man!' She pushed the top of my head as a greeting and stood before her husband with a hand on her hip. 'You need to tell her we can't do it; we've got Omar's wedding and Husayn Abidi's.'

Hakim flattened his newspaper and beckoned his wife closer. 'I've almost finished the crossword, bro: a feeling or expression of awe, begins with the letter v, ends with n. Ten across?'

'Veneration,' she replied. He scribbled the word and put his pen down with a faint smile. He ripped the crossword from the paper and held it for Elia and me to see.

'I win,' he announced.

Elia held his chin and spoke as if talking to a child. 'I'm so proud of you, my little miskeen,' she cooed. 'Now, talk to Hooyo for me because for some reason she listens to her son-in-law more than her own daughter. And I'm closing the shop,' she announced, 'it's almost the end of the day and people keep coming in and buying stuff, and I don't want to see anyone else's face.'

She flipped the OPEN sign and twisted the blinds on the door before taking her husband's chair opposite me, resting her elbows on the table. 'How are you, Sayon, you lil nacas?' She'd always made use of the few Somali words I knew when in conversation with me, and when she threw in a word I wasn't accustomed to, she would take the opportunity to criticise me for not knowing the language yet. I had little excuse, she told me; I'd grown up in an area where people spoke more Somali than English.

The establishment of a Tower-of-Babel middle ground was becoming more commonsensical as time went by. And now with Black-British culture blossoming, the fruits of our labour were plump and ready to pluck. Where for decades Patois had ridden roughshod over the English we used on the road, now, like the introduction of foreign flora into a Somerset garden, habits from languages such as Somali and Arabic were beginning to ripen.

'Me and the lil man were just talking,' Hakim replied.

'Do you man think trappin is wrong?' I asked.

The husband and wife exchanged looks across the table. 'I do,' Elia answered. She held my eye when she spoke and kept her voice cucumber-cool, keen to avoid any of the judgement that may have accompanied her words, had they been said by anyone else. 'You may not have always been directly contributing to the deaths of your customers, but you do to the deterioration of their mental and physical health at least. Me and Hakim have spoken about it before, we don't fully see eye to eye.'

'Nah we do, still,' Hakim said. He spoke with his hands and patted the table to emphasise his points. 'It is wrong Islamically, I'm just saying, cos of where man's coming from. I understand it, you get me? But nowadays, I don't want nutun to do with it. I've left that life far behind alhamdulillah. Why? What you think, lil man?'

I told them that it wasn't wrong. Not in this world, at least. This world where chicken shops met the demands of the obese and corner shops supplied alcoholics with the means. This world that said that the African dictator was a product of his choices, whereas the Whites that created him were products of their days. This world, where morality and legality were poles apart, pretending some semblance of an acquaintanceship.

To me the answer was obvious.

Hakim asked me if I believed in Allah, at which point Elia rose to her feet, said she had things to do, and left us to talk.

I told Hakim I didn't believe in the Christian God, but in a higher power. Since the belief in a creator had been too deeply ingrained to remove I had long accepted its reality.

And I had been told to not let the people practising taint my perception of religion, but how could I not? I couldn't believe in Jesus Christ because in His bosom He nursed nothing but the memories of my mama's abandonment and my papa's dis-interest. And now He had been further diluted by Pastor Lyle's manipulation.

'But what about Islam?' Hakim asked.

There were certainly things I respected about Islam; the strength of the community, the structure that centred your attention wholly upon Allah.

And although Uncle Calvin was the furthest thing from pious, I knew of people in Ends whose reversions had made marked differences; incubuses and traumatised spirits with no means of expression, mandem who had U-turned to become chaste and wholesome. Perhaps it was true that Christianity had the same effect elsewhere, but that wasn't my reality. And what greater example could I have asked for than Hakim – my beloved cousin? To me his change was the most admirable, because, as he put it: who had foreseen Funds becoming Hakim? He'd had the whole Ends in his palm and had given it up for the sake of Allah.

'It was losin Hosea dat made you revert, init?' I asked, once I'd finished my reasonings.

'Mmmh,' Hakim said, and he smiled in sadness as he did whenever Hosea was mentioned, 'that was my little guy, man.'

Everyone finds different ways to comfort themselves after the death of a loved one. Some people tell themselves that death is inevitable and find respite. Others are soothed by the manner in which their loved one passed. Every loss hurts, and we all find ways of coping, but when a loved one is murdered, the soul can never quite be quietened.

I knew this, and I saw it all on Hakim's face. Disquiet hunched his shoulders and shivered his hands as he reached for his tea. 'I could've done more' were the words that had defined Hakim's life for the past six years, and I knew would continue to for ever.

Hakim drank from his tea and continued. 'I don't even think you know this, fam, but after Hosea died I started moving mad, enuh. And I mean madder than ever, lil man.

'Me and Jamaal must've looked for the niggas that killed Hosea for weeks, cuz. We drove all around the city looking for them, heard they was in Brum so we went up there; heard they was in London so we went down there. I didn't care about money, I was making dumb decisions, being reckless. I was at the lowest point I've ever been at.

'I know you lost a cousin, and I know that hurts, but I lost a little brother, fam. And what makes it worse is it was me that showed him how to move in these streets. How to carry himself. It was me he looked up to. Learnt from. The only way I can think to explain to you how that feels is if Cuba got killed.'

My blood boiled at the thought.

'Yeah,' Hakim nodded – he could see the colour in my face – 'exactly. And that's why I worry about you man the most; because if we lose him, we lose you. And the same the other way round. It's rah you I see myself in the most enuh?' I found this funny, and snorted, which made him laugh too, and the mood lightened. 'Big man ting,' he chuckled. 'I see me in you, and I see Hosea in Cuba. And I know he finds man jarrin since I turned Muslim, but really I did it for you two lil man – Killa as well. Me and Jamaal got a whole generation of Hugheses coming after us, and the last thing I want is for any of you man to live with the regret that I live with.'

Elia called him into the kitchen and he excused himself, returning after a short while to explain that he had to run. He wore a serious expression so I didn't complain. I only stood to hug him and he promised we'd finish the conversation another time.

I wasn't done with their company, so I went to find Elia in

the back, hoping she wouldn't ask about the tiff Shona and I had had the last time we were in the bakery. Thankfully, our conversation took another turn.

'How come you left?' I asked, when I found her. She had something on the stove, something sweet, that smelt heavily of cloves, and she was cleaning a little as she went.

Elia shrugged. 'Sounded like the two of you needed to have time alone. I heard you though.' She left her cleaning for the stove and fixed her hijab as she went. 'Is Islam something you're becoming more interested in, or was Hakim banging on about it again?'

Over the years Elia and I had talked about Islam less than one might have expected; she wasn't one to proselytise.

'Bit of both,' I laughed.

'Oh yeah? Aren't you back in the church, though?'

'Kinda,' I brought a stool into the middle of the room and watched her work, 'but like man was tellin Hakim, it rah don't matter if man's in the church or not; Christianity ain't for man, you get me?'

'Because of your parents?' Elia said.

'More time yeah, man was force-fed dat shit by a bunch of hypocrites, blud. I can't find peace in sup'm I got so much resentment towards, you get me?'

'I'm sure there's some Muslims that feel the same about Islam.'

'Yeah, so let dem go convert to Christianity.'

Elia chuckled. 'Touché. The grass is always greener on the other side.'

'I rah thought you would've been happier dat man's in any way interested in Islam, Elia. What's all dis negative energy you're givin man, chuhh.'

'I am, I am,' Elia said, as she lifted the lid of the pot and stirred its contents with a wooden spoon. 'Urgh, what happened to you, Sayon? Don't be a pussy. If you're serious about Islam then you'll make me the happiest woman on earth, wallahi – I just don't want you to think it'll be the quick fix that Hakim can make it out to be; it's not like going Turkey and getting veneers.'

'What you mean?' I frowned.

'Islam came at the right time and changed Hakim's life, Sayon,' continued Elia, 'and it's been like what? Six years since he reverted? But somehow Hakim's still in the honeymoon phase. I've been Muslim my whole life, Sayon; I know that your imaan goes through seasons. And if you become a Muslim, there will be times your faith is tested, and if you run every time you come across a hypocrite there's no point taking your Shahadah.

'Anything that's wrong with the practice of Christianity you'll find in the practice of Islam is all I'm saying, and if you can accept that, then by all means . . .' She turned and flicked the sauce from a wooden spoon at me to punctuate her sentence.

I wiped my face with a nearby hand towel and threw it at her. I knew that she was right, but I could only go based on what I knew. And I knew Christianity as my mama, my pops and Pastor Lyle. I knew it as sanctimoniousness and gall. As Shona's first love. Whereas I knew Islam as Hakim and Elia.

Elia finished the final touches to what I now recognised as some kind of syrup, and bade me come across the kitchen for tea-making lessons.

She crushed cardamom pods and cloves with a pestle and poured them into a saucepan along with cinnamon sticks, ginger, nutmeg, milk and water. 'You ever speak to Warsame about all this?' she asked; Warsame was Karma's government name.

'Nah, why?'

Elia produced a tray of shushumows from beneath a dish-cloth, and we over-indulged. 'Because Warsame and those other Somalis you hang around with are posted on road all week, but they'll be in mosque for Jummah; isn't that the same as the hypocrisy you're saying you hate?'

She had a point.

I supposed the reason I hadn't deeped it like that was because their lives were the same as mine, and as far as I was concerned, there was a difference between duality and hypo-crisy. We were all walking contradictions, it was human nature; even in love it was said that the thing we loved most about our partner would one day become the thing we most hated. And the niggas I rolled with didn't judge anybody, it was the churchgoers that did.

'Come, Sayon,' Elia said, motioning towards the exit. We'd wasted a better part of the evening stuffing our faces and catch-ing up. 'I'm going home and, unless you wanna stay here, so are you.'

'You ain't cleaning up properly, nah?' I said, looking at the half-filled sink and floured sides.

'Shut up,' she laughed, and she pushed me through the beads that covered the door, 'I'll do the rest in the morning.'

We walked through the front, past the cake counters, shoving and laughing, but as she grabbed her handbag from the table a letter fell from inside. And when I leant to pick it up I saw the words 'eviction notice' stamped in the top corner.

I looked up to find Elia studying my reaction.

'Fuck's dis?' I frowned, the letter held limply in my hand.

'What it says,' Elia said. She took the letter from my hand and tucked it back into her bag. Then she raised her head again, held her bag at her waist, and waited patiently for my questions.

'Since when?'

'A month ago.'

When I pressed further she explained that their landlady was moving them on. Something about the area changing and keeping up with the times. Elia imagined she wanted to convert the bakery, and the run-down flat above, into student accommodation. She clearly didn't want to talk about it, but I still refused to believe what I'd read.

'I can help,' I declared, as Elia locked the front door and we rounded the corner to pull the shutters down.

'You?' Elia said, 'I thought you'd stopped shottin?'

'I have, but it's not like man blew the ps, blud. You man ain't losing money on dis are you?'

'Nah, we earn a nice living, alhamdulillah.'

'Exactly, so if man give you man a little sup'm, den you show your landlord your books, or I dunno, gave her sup'm to hold, she might change her mind?'

'Would that even work?'

'Ay, money talks man. If you give her enough she'll defo lowe it.'

I saw her think about it, before she shook her head. 'No,' she said. 'Damn, I forgot the pole to hook the thingy down.' She pointed to the top of the shutters and I leapt to pull them to the ground, where she slipped a padlock through the holes and locked them shut. 'You know we love you, Sayon, but we can't take your money again.'

'Cos of where it's from? Or cos you don't wanna feel indebted?'

She rose to her feet and held my eye. 'Cos of where it's from.' She put the keys in her pocket and proceeded down the road. I quickened my step to catch up. 'Hakim didn't even want you to know; we didn't want you to know,' she continued. 'We knew you'd offer to help, but we just can't take your money, Sayon.'

'But dat's what family does.'

'Not this time.' She smiled sadly.

'Elia,' I grabbed her by the arms and forced her to stop. 'You're really gonna lose the shop cos of pride?'

'It's principle, not pride.'

'Yeah, whatever, man,' I tutted. 'At end of the day dis is your dream, blud – you not gonna fight for it at least?' My words had the desired effect. I saw hesitance plain on her face, and her eyes fell to the ground.

'It's as Allah wills,' she said, voice low and devoid of hope. She exhaled deeply, her small frame rising and falling with dramatic insistence. 'Whatever Allah wills, will be,' she said again, trying to gather strength in her voice and convince me that she was fine with the way things were. It didn't work.

We stared at each other in silence before I nodded, unhappy with her resolution, and left without saying goodbye.

31

Watch therefore, for you do not know what hour your Lord
is coming.

– Matthew 24:42

Left alone, I had no place to go so I went to the church. I knew
Pastor Lyle and Shona were inside, finishing the evening service,
but I wasn't in the mood for worship, so I sat on the steps.

Both Elia's news and the strength of Hakim's feelings rever-
berated around my head. And I thought that if Hakim could
make changes in his own life, in the hopes that Cuba and I
would in turn follow, then I could too.

What he'd said made sense to me; about how Islam was his
saving grace, his house-atop-the-hill, and the bakery he shared
with the love of his life was the embodiment of his longing
for change. Before, I'd had no idea that the strength of his
conviction was rooted in Cuba and me, but it was a conviction
I knew well, and one I desperately wanted to return to.

I needed a way to make everything right, for everyone I loved.

Sat alone, I was soon joined by a cat. He stumbled across to me,
put his finger to his lips and said, 'Watch dis.' He had a little

foam gathered in the corner of his mouth and he carried a bottle
of White Ace with the casual confidence of a midwife holding
a newborn babe.

He crawled up the steps and tried to enter Pastor Lyle's
church, but the on-duty usher pushed him in the chest and sent
him on his way; he made it as far as where I sat so I went to
the kitchens on his behalf and returned with digestives and a
cup of tea.

'God bless you, my yute,' the tramp purred, pocketing the
biscuits. He poured the tea on to the steps, tucked the saucer
into his jacket and filled the teacup with his tipple.

He wore a patchy mackintosh, a stained hat with a missing
earflap and there were holes in his shoes. He stank, and his
blackness didn't shine, it was dull and unremarkable. It reminded
me of an old piece of liquorice left behind a primary school shed.

'My cousin used to sleep on dese steps,' I said, filling the
silence between us, 'but she died a few months back and we
buried her in St George Cemetery, where my cousin Hosea is
buried as well.'

'Lotsatings appen on dese steps,' the tramp said, coughing
into his fingerless gloves. He hiccupped, and took his hat from
his head. His hair had been shaved in some places and left to
grow in others.

'Enuh, a few years ago my nanny tried to help her, tried get
her off the street and dat; said she could stay in her yard rent-
free, and if you know my nanny you know dat's a mad offer,
but you know what my cousin said? Said she'd rather stay here,
blud. She never explained why, but I think it was partly the
freedom, partly the habit, enuh. If she lived with us she wouldah
had to have got cleaned up, got a job, moved on with her life.
And sometimes dat's rah too much for people.

'A lot of the time it's rah easier to stay where we are, especially when we can't imagine anything else, init. She was too comfortable doing what she did. Living the only way she knew how. More time people don't really change, blud, though to be honest, it was probably my fault she was so comfortable in the first place.'

The drunk stirred and drew nearer; he really did stink to high heaven.

'Half the world don't know whether I'm free or in jail. Whether I'm dead or alive. At least your cousin knows where she is, mate. And you know where she is, so count your blessings, my yute.' He cupped his hand to his mouth and mimed lighting a pipe. 'Ay, you know where I can get sup'm warm?' I pointed him in a younger's direction and watched him stumble across the road.

It would make sense for God to judge us by what we were exposed to, by what we could comprehend and the actions that we took because of it.

The tramp knew dependency like Winnie knew vagrancy, like Cuba knew love as loyalty and how I now knew regret. But the pious would never take to such thinking – *one size fits all*. That's why Pastor Lyle struggled with Nanny's reaction to Uncle Michael killing the mother fox. That's why he had to find a way to separate himself from her.

He needed the concept of good and evil, of right and wrong. It told him that his place was in the sun, and that whilst the evil-doers may prosper in this world, in the next they would crawl on their stomachs.

It catered to his fear and shaped his comfort. He would never accept such thinking because it rendered the worst people innocent in the eyes of God. It suggested that they weren't evil, only broken. Misguided. A just God would never punish those who were not exposed to Him, or those who never stood a chance.

Our ancestors drowned in droves during the Atlantic crossing; for hundreds of years they bled in tall sugarcane fields and on white-sand beaches. A generation passed and our elders landed on Stapleton Road with the sand still in their socks and the ocean caught in their boots. The water dripped from their leather and Stapleton Road became the River Styx.

It took a village to raise a child but our houses were shanties with weak foundations, and the fences that ran the perimeter fought spates and were prone to damp and rust. No one blamed the ocean for the litter on the beach, yet we were held accountable in this world, then told that the Lord our Saviour would hold us accountable in the next.

It was dark when the tramp came back from wherever he'd gotten his food and began shooting up next to me. The evening service had ended, and the usher and the rest of the church had left, leaving only Pastor and Shona inside. I thought about sending him on his way but who was I to interrupt? If that was what he needed to do then he could do it. If God could understand his faults, then I should at least make an effort to.

'Yo, Sayon.'

I looked to the road. Karma was leaning out of a passing car. I saw him tell the driver to pull over, saw him shake the driver's hand, pocket the money he'd exchanged and bop over to where I was sat.

'What you sayin,' he laughed, 'got yourself a new friend?'

He took a seat beside me and I didn't waste any time. Straight away, I asked him about his relationship with Allah, and whether or not he was a Muslim.

'Yeah man, of course, how can you ask me dat, blud?' he said, as he licked the edge of a paper and rolled a blunt with the precision of a tailor stitching a hem. He noticed me staring at the weed and we both burst into laughter. 'Don't watch dat,' he said, 'focus on yourself, g.'

'Nah, but for real,' I said, 'how'd you explain the way man lives compared to what you believe?'

'What, to myself?'

'Yeah, yeah.'

'You know what, g,' he began, 'a lot of niggas think man ain't serious when it comes to Islam, init. Obviously dey see man smokin, dey hear bout the shootings, stabbin niggas, hittin licks, all dat shit, but dey don't see man bowin man's head on the mat in salat, you know what man's sayin, g?

'Man lives a double life, akh, like James Bond or some shit. You know man prays like four times a day, cuz? Minimum. More time man only misses Asr, and dat's only sometimes. I be hittin five a lot. Man's got the five pillars patterned, wallahi; it's just the other shit dat man struggles wid day to day, you know what man's sayin? The real-life shit. But man's done umrah and hajj, enuh? Niggas might not like it, but man have to respect man's deen, you get me?'

'But don't it make you feel like a hypocrite?'

'A hypocrite? Nah,' Karma's braids shook with his head as he lit the weed. He passed it to me before he took a toke. 'I hear what you're sayin, doe. If someone wanted to call man a hypocrite I'd get it, init. People can think whatever dey wanna think about man, init.'

I hid my amusement behind the smoke I pushed from my

lips. If someone called Karma a hypocrite he would've had them on their knees, singing pop songs and begging for his forgiveness as he repeatedly slapped them in the face.

I gave the weed back and he carried on. 'But man's got a plan, g, for all dis, niggas can't be on the road for ever. You know dat, init.'

'Yeah, man knows.'

'Midnight don't know dat, doe,' Karma puffed, 'dat's my nigga, but he thinks dis road shit is gonna last for ever, wallahi. You spoke to him yet?'

I shook my head, but without guilt this time, because I knew that I would soon.

'You ever heard bout the scale of deeds in Islam?' Karma asked.

'Nah.'

'Your deeds on this earth are weighed, init; your bad deeds are weightless, your good deeds are heavy. And since dis life is a test, the aim is to tip the scales in your favour, same as the dunya, you get me?' Karma took a toke, tipped his head and blew the smoke at the early evening stars. 'I can't lie, my scales are hella light right now fam, so if man don't get out dis life, deh's only one place man's goin, wallah, but man ain't goin out like dat.'

The scale of deeds.

It made more sense to me than any doctrine I'd heard in church. Pastor Lyle and my papa often preached about Christ's death, about how he had sacrificed himself so that we might be saved, but if Christ had already done the work for us, then what was the point in Christianity? Islam was clearer. More disciplined. It placed our fate firmly in our own hands. It said: do this, and this will happen.

'I ever tell you why man's on road, fam?' Karma said, after a minute. Beside him the tramp slumped on to his shoulder and Karma shrugged him to the ground. Not that he minded; a strange calm had taken his spirit and he accepted the stone floor as his mattress.

'Cos you was raised in it, init?' I shrugged. 'Same as man.'

'In a way, yeah,' Karma said, 'but it's rah a decision man's made you know? Obviously man knows what man's doin is wrong, init, but dis is man's trade, fam. What the fuck else is man supposed to do? Fuckin, plumbin and shit? Go uni? Nah. True, you can make real money dat way, and for some niggas it works, like my brothers and sisters and dat, but you lose half your ps to the government, fam, and dem man just piss it down the drain more time. End of the day, fuck England, blud. Man don't wanna pay no fuckin cadaan no fuckin taxes.

'Everyting man does is for Hooyo, bro. Man's pops and man's relos back home gave her too much stress, blud, dat's why man moved here in the first place, but now man's givin her stress here. Soon as I make enough ps, ima build her a yard back home, and a school so her and my sisters can teach the yutes dem, den I'm done, wallahi.

'Once I'm back home I'll be proper on deen, cuff one fresh ting, one Barwaaqo or sup'm, raise the pickney dem, make my scales heavy as shit, you get me? But I can't do dat in dis country, wallah. Deep down, if I didn't have Islam, I wouldn't have no aspirations, no direction; den I'd be fucked, you get me?'

'What, would she take your money, doe? Knowing where it came from?'

'She don't have to know,' Karma said, 'if she don't know den the sin's mine not hers, you get me? And more time if man cleans the ps den it's not even haram, feel me?'

241

A couple of youngers hailed us from the pavement, so we climbed down to meet them. They were in an excitable mood, carrying news about some Pauls yutes that had ventured into the area; they were on their way to run them out, they lifted their tops and showed the knives they carried.

'Yeah yeah,' Karma nodded, 'you man do your ting, but don't let it distract you from your money.' They scampered away with Karma's blessing and I thought then that there was little difference between religious discipleship and having youngers on road. Only society condemned one and upheld the other.

I never had olders like that; the only people I'd ever answered to were Hakim and Jamaal. And even then, as I got older, they relinquished their claim over me and largely left me and Cuba to do our thing.

Still, I knew how the system worked.

I knew parents who didn't care and left their yutes to run wild in the streets, then were surprised when they became involved. I knew parents who rode their children hard and barely let them out of their sight, and still because of some coincidence or act of rebellion they ended up on road. I even knew yutes who had no obvious reason to be outside, they didn't live in Ends, nor did they have any bad breed family members – there was just something about it.

Which was how the streets favoured religion. The draw was ancestral. A tug so strong it was transcendent. I had seen the church prey on the mentally ill – I had seen trappers sell to them. I had seen the church rope youngsters into youth clubs – and trappers recruit from them. It was how the world turned.

Karma and I left each other's company and promised to be back in it soon. He was elated I had an interest in Islam, and invited me to the mosque next time he went.

And so I continued to sit on the steps until the early hours of the morning, waiting for Shona and the pastor. And beside me the tramp eventually stirred. He sat upright and stared longingly down the road, and there we remained in a comfortable silence.

I smiled and imagined the two of us made a funny sight to the few stragglers making their way home. They would probably assume I'd sold him the drugs he'd so obviously taken. They definitely wouldn't think that I was waiting for anyone inside the church. The irony broadened my smile, but the pastor failed to see the humour.

I heard him and Shona talking at the church door and fiddling with a bunch of keys, and he noticed the tramp before I could explain. 'What on earth is this?' he bellowed. In an instant he leapt down the steps and slapped the needle from the cat's hands.

'What you doing!' the tramp screamed, and I had to stop him from hysterically attacking Pastor Lyle who crushed the pencil-thin syringe underfoot.

I impelled the crackhead away and told him to leave before he got hurt, but he was still shouting about personal property and having his revenge until he saw the madness that had taken the pastor and decided against it.

'You shouldn't step on syringes,' I told Pastor Lyle, once the cat had left.

'You,' Pastor said, rounding on me, his finger levelled at my chest. 'Did you sell him those drugs?'

'Daddy!?' Shona cried, putting herself between him and me.

'I didn't sell him nutun,' I replied, my face stony. It seemed the change in our relationship meant nothing after all. He thought what he thought about me, and the moment he saw anything that vaguely confirmed his impression, then that was that.

'I can find out if you did, enuh!' Pastor Lyle continued. He didn't appear drunk, but he had the same look in his eye and the same energy grew restless in his spirit.

'You're slippin, Pastor,' I said, doing my best to keep a lid on my own temper, 'don't do sup'm you'll regret.'

'No,' he said. 'No. You don't get to tell me what to do, young man. I'm the adult; you're the child. I tell *you* what to do.'

'Daddy!' Shona said again, and this time she stepped into his chest and pushed him away. Finally, he noticed his princess and remembered himself.

'All right, I'm calm, I'm calm,' he said, holding his hands up, 'but let me ask you again, Sayon, were those drugs yours?' He pointed at the shattered syringe, and his tone might have lightened marginally, but his body language hadn't. 'Tell me the truth, and maybe we can work something out.'

'Dey weren't mine,' I said.

'They better not have been,' he snarled, 'otherwise—'

'Let me talk to Sayon, Daddy,' Shona said, and he let her guide him away from the church, but he held my eye until he turned his back and stalked down Stapes.

Shona came back to me and apologised on her papa's behalf. 'Have you noticed how worked up he's been getting recently? Over the smallest things as well,' she said. 'I don't know what it is; he must be under pressure with the church or sup'm.'

A part of me thought it was amazing how neither Shona nor Marcia had noticed the drinking by now, but I supposed if you weren't looking for something it was difficult to find. Especially considering the fact that Pastor had spent so many years carefully curating exactly how he was perceived. But the stress of the secret and his guilt were eating him from the inside out, and he was losing his grip.

Shona reached to hold my hand, but I instinctively flinched. She brought her hand to her chest. 'They weren't yours though, were they, Say?'

'What?'

'You can tell me, Say. I won't be mad.'

'Are you taking the piss?' I said. I couldn't believe what I was hearing – after all the sacrifices I'd made?

'It's only a question,' she said, uncompromising.

'Yeah, a fuckin dumbass question,' I said. 'Is dat what you're on? You think man would shot outside your pop's church? Am I a fuckin idiot?'

'It was only a question,' she said again, her voice raised, hackles up. 'And I don't know who you think you are, swearing at me, Sayon. You could've just said yes or no, instead you wanna catch an attitude. You've been moving mad weird for long and I haven't said nutun, what do you expect me to think?'

I was about to respond when, across the way, two yutes burst from a tributary.

One scrambled as he turned the corner. He steadied himself on the ground, but barely slowed. The other hurdled the bonnet of a parked car, kicking the wing mirror as he flailed forward.

I quickly pulled Shona up the steps and placed her behind me.

From the street they'd left came another four bodies. Shona clung to the clothes on my back. The pursuers spilled on to Stapes, some with balaclavas and gloves, others barefaced and spitting. Their fingers were curled around the handles of zombie knives.

'Don't run.'

'Tan yuh ground.'

Their voices cracked with youth and vexation, the easy lilt of the Caribbean as plain as day in their speech, and I recognised them as the same yutes Karma and I had seen earlier.

The two boys from Pauls were losing ground as they raced past, and by the time they reached Viv's it was clear there was little breath left in their lungs.

One began to trail the other.

In matters of life and death few had the capacity to think of anyone beside themselves. They put their heads down and pumped towards the dual carriageway. If they could make it across the road and over the bridge into St Pauls, they would be safe. They knew that, and so did their pursuers.

The trailing boy crashed to the road as his legs were swept from beneath him. Shona tightened her hold of me and buried her face in my back. We both knew what was coming next. His pursuers fell upon him, their knives arching high enough for the dim streetlights to catch the edges of their blades before they punctured his chest and stomach. The boy held his hands before him. He managed to deflect some strikes but it was useless. He was fodder for the cattle's trough.

His bredrin stopped in the middle of the road some thirty feet ahead. His chest rose and fell as he caught his breath. With great difficultly he tore his eyes from the scene but there was no way to ignore the breathless cries that assailed the cool air. He knew that if he went to his friend's aid he would never see the sun again.

The attackers lurched in the direction from which they'd come, throwing threats at the boy they hadn't caught, buoyed by the boasts they had buttressed with this assault. They had placed a down payment on bluster for at least a year. In the distance the Pauls boy turned and jogged away, his mind made up; it was too late, there was nothing to be done.

The attackers left Stapleton Road in a hurry.

And as soon as they did Shona left my protection. She ran to the boy and tried to staunch his bleeding with her jacket. She shouted for me to call the ambulance but I wouldn't.

The bridegroom's church loomed over us as Shona loomed over the boy's body, and as she struggled to keep him awake, I couldn't take my eyes from the building.

This was Jesus' house.

His church squatted on the banks of a road once labelled the most dangerous in the country, but it had done nothing for the Ends back then, and it did nothing now.

I bent to touch the steps where I'd stabbed Cordell and snorted softly. They had never been Winnie's; for years she had been trespassing upon His land, and now I stood on His porch a murderer, ignoring the life that ebbed from the dying Pauls yute behind me, and yet there was no vociferation from the great building.

I climbed to the front door and put both hands on the premises. The brickwork didn't crumble and recoil from my hand. The paint didn't chip. The timber didn't moan. If silence was compliance then wasn't that testament to the ruler's guilt?

The do-gooders would argue that we couldn't assess Him by any human measure. That He was outside of our knowledge and understanding. But had He not given us His Word and appeared in the flesh so that we might inherit some basis to live by?

I reached and held my arms towards the spires. They felt further away than they had ever been. Still no lightning struck me. There was a mild wind. Sirens sounded in the distance. Shona must have called them.

The ambulance arrived with police cars and they loaded the yute into the back. Before they left they found a pulse and toasted Shona a hero. If it were my mama in my place, she would have pointed at the same church and given the glory to God. She would have said that if we were not there the boy would have surely died, that God's hand was evident, but hadn't we been there nightly for months?

The churchgoers who claimed that 'the Lord worked in mysterious ways' were the same as the women and men who cast stones; broken keels carried downstream by a tide of nescience they had neither the fortitude nor the will to fight.

The police asked if we had seen the men who had done this. We hadn't. They asked for even the smallest detail: what clothes were they wearing? Did we hear their voices? Could we distinguish their race? We couldn't. If silence was compliance then Shona stepped further into our world that night. Somewhere I had wanted her to be before, as I thought it would make us closer. But somehow in that moment we felt more distant than ever. And I didn't know if I had anything left in me to bridge that gap.

32

There is no fear in love; but perfect love casts out fear, because
fear involves torment. But he who fears has not been made
perfect in love.

– 1 John 4:18

The next morning the church was alive with gossip. Everyone
had heard the news; Shona and young Brother Sayon had saved
a young boy's life.

Praise God.

They reached to touch the cuff of my shirt, the hem of her
dress. They intruded upon our conversations to start another
of their own. They spewed the tired rhetoric of newspapers
and admonished the violence that had taken the minds of
Black youths. They blamed rap, the absence of Jesus Christ,
the ever-growing influence of Islam over the Caribbean community, they swarmed us like flies a glass of lemonade left
poolside at a lido.

Even Pastor Lyle pretended to have forgotten the previous
night's argument. He wrapped us under his wings. Led us from
the lobby to the altar and quietened the crowds with a wave of
his hand and a well-timed, 'Praise God, amen.'

He beamed at us as he relayed the news to the few latecomers and folks who had managed to avoid the good tidings, but like ever, I could still see the gloom in him.

He hated the façade.

It would have been impossible to count the number of 'amens' and 'hallelujahs' in the room. They hung suspended in the air like sweet-cicely incense, their smoky entrails reluctant to decamp for fear of missing another revelation. It was the loudest I had heard the congregation and Pastor Lyle struggled to contain their agitation.

I felt like a gladiator championed for winning a bout against a man who had fallen upon his own sword. When that yute was dying I did nothing. Felt nothing. At first I thought Shona might have explained, stopped to shed some light on the matter, but when I looked to my left I found no resolution; her full lips were clasped tightly together.

The congregation saw it as a great victory. Christ against knife crime. Ever the opportunists the church took it upon themselves to sell salvation and advertise the glory of God, just as they had at Winnie's funeral. Under Pastor Lyle's instruction they prayed for the young man. Prayed that he take the second chance he had been so graciously given, his involuntary baptism in the blood of Christ, and that he'd use it productively, as God intended.

And the church was vociferous in their praise for us, but in reality it was the puppeteer Jesus Christ they worshipped for deftly moving our strings. A sister asked for the microphone and said, quite predictably, that she saw His hand in our being at church that night. In our timing. In our composure and the ambulance's speed.

Coincidence wasn't an explanation, nor was common sense.

Any question of the unknown was fastidiously solved with Jesus Christ.

I wanted to ask the good sister, if Jesus was indeed responsible for saving the yute, where was He when I killed Cordell? Or when we killed Winnie? Or when any of the countless ills went unaffected and unanswered? Was He turning the other cheek? Was He at His curtains? If God's children mistook happy coincidences for divine providence, then how did they explain His absences?

But of course I didn't, and none of these questions were answered by Pastor Lyle, who continued to raise us above his head.

Throughout the sermon he continuously referenced the soul we saved, and afterwards he toasted blackcurrant in our name. He broke the body of Christ and we tasted His blood. The very blood that Jesus spilled in order to save every one of us, especially that poor, poor young man.

The pastor's masquerade continued right up until after the evening service when we were sat around the Jenningses' dinner table ready to eat. With the rice pot as the centrepiece Pastor closed his eyes and outstretched his hands for prayer. The firmness of his sandpaper grip riled the previous night's argument. He finished his prayers and released my hand. In doing so he knocked a glass bottle from the table and it split like a fissure in a skull.

'Look wat yuh mek mi do!' Pastor Lyle said, and Marcia rushed to clean the mess. The pastor's face pulled into a moue, his lips puckered and curled.

'Oh, don't punish di bwoy, Lyle,' Marcia tutted. She tossed a kitchen roll to Shona, who had helped mop the spillage.

'Accidents appen all di time. Ahh nutun. Only man dat never made mistakes was Jesus Christ. And as andsome as yuh ahh, Sayon, mi nuh tinkseh yuh di second comin.'

Pastor Lyle paid his wife's running commentary no mind. 'You've been getting slack, young man,' he hissed, 'you need to get back up to standards and start to pull your weight around here, yuh undahstan?'

Again Marcia interrupted on my behalf. 'Lef im Lyle. Sayon, yuh fine; Shona – another tissue please, darlin.' I went to fetch her one instead, unable to sit still amidst so much tension.

Different environments bred different sensitivities, but we all picked up on certain things. Like the chemistry between young lovers. The quick smiles. The awkwardness. The secrecy. It bred an intuition that could tell a teacher who in the class was dating whom. Or the sensitivity every mother had towards her child. Or that children had towards injustice.

My environment had created in me a unique sensitivity towards tension. The disquiet at a block party that no amount of dancehall could contain. Or the enmity in a barber shop that told you an argument had just been had and two men had come to blows.

Pastor took a drumstick from his plate and bit into its flesh, tearing meat from bone. His attention had not left me, and his attention willed a reaction. 'You must have the shakes,' he declared. 'Cannabis can do that to a man.'

I froze. The looks on Marcia and Shona's faces kept me from feigning ignorance; they both knew about my nightly escapades. But the brandy locked in the church office and the wine came to mind, and embarrassment made my tongue brazen.

'We all got our vices, Pastor,' I said, as Marcia hurried to put the tissues in the bin and Shona headed for the living room. 'But I guess some of us are better at hidin it dan others, init?'

I thought the remark lost amongst Marcia's clamour and Shona calling for me to join her, but when the pastor headed upstairs, I knew that I'd found my mark.

Shona led me into the living room and shut us inside.

'How'd you know?' I asked.

'About the smoking?' she said. She walked over to the record player and stroked the vinyl that sat under the needle, waiting to be played. She sounded worn out. 'I heard you getting up in the night and going into the garden, and if my window was open I could smell it.' The shadow of a smile touched her lips. 'You're not as subtle as you think, enuh.'

I returned the faintness of her smile and sat in the sofa opposite her, some distance away. 'Why didn't you say nutun?' I asked quietly. I didn't know her to often bite her tongue.

'I don't know.' Her hand dropped from the record player to the records kept on the shelves beneath and she flicked through them. 'I guess cos I know you've sacrificed a lot to be here, init. To make a change. And I know it can be a process, init. Well, that's what I tried to tell myself, anyway – you just needed time.' Her volume rose and fell like the tide. One minute her voice was strong; another, vulnerable. She lifted her head and the weak smile was back again. 'And I used to smoke every now and then, remember? At the radio station? So I can't say much, can I?'

She was staggering, clumsily trying to build a bridge across the rift we'd made, but I was too afraid to reciprocate. I knew she so desperately wanted to return to a time where we'd been good, a time far simpler, and those nights in the station were that. But if I went there with her, down memory lane, she'd need me to be completely honest, so when I didn't respond, I saw her smile wane.

A long moment passed. 'Why didn't you try save that yute yesterday?' she asked, and I heard how much it troubled her. Too consumed by my own thoughts, I'd taken the act of violence for granted, and had forgotten that it was probably the first time she'd ever seen something like that.

I thought back to the night after St Pauls Carnival. And remembered how terrified I was; for months I saw the blood that woman spilled wherever I looked.

'Everyone thinks you and me saved him,' Shona continued, in a voice that made me want to hold her, 'but really, if it was just you there, you would've watched him die. Why?' And then she looked at me, her eyes searching for an answer, as if she already knew I wouldn't give her one. And I didn't. I only stared back, my tongue robbed of any language, too accustomed to silence.

'Were you scared?' She prodded. 'Or did you think if you touched him the police would think you'd done it? Or that Daddy would think you'd done it?' She stopped, suddenly aware that none of her questions were being answered. 'I was scared, Say,' she said, 'and when we got home I wanted you to tell me it was all right, even if it wasn't, but then I remembered that things were different now. And I tried to think why they were different, and I didn't have the answer.' Her eyes rooted for a clue. 'Why are they different, Say? What's going on?'

Eventually, I found my voice, and I told her some of the truth; that I was missing Cuba. Missing Nanny. That there was a part of me which regretted my decision to cut them off entirely, and because it was hurting me, I was wrongly taking it out on

254

her; the closest person to me. And I apologised. As sincerely as my half-truths allowed.

That night she snuck me into her room so that we could fall asleep together. She rested her head on my shoulder, kissed my forehead, then we hugged tighter and for the first time in a long time I found heaven between her legs.

Then we slept, sweaty, sex funky. Well, I say we slept; Shona did.

I lay awake for hours, and I came to the conclusion that I couldn't be a child of God; with all the sins I had committed, the lies I had told, it was inconceivable that I could be His son.

I eventually dropped asleep, my limbs entwined with Shona's, but I was woken hours later by a noise. With heavy eyes I looked to find Pastor Lyle sitting in Shona's armchair across the room. His hands were cupped beneath his chin, his eyes dull and trained on me.

I shot up as soon as I noticed him, my tiredness instantly gone. It was still dark out but the sun would soon rise. I was dressed only in my boxer shorts but the pastor didn't pay it any mind. My sudden movement had startled Shona, and his attention switched to her.

She rubbed at her face and surveyed the room. 'Daddy?' She frowned, drawing the covers over her chest. 'What are you doing in here?'

'Princess, I need to tell you the truth,' he slurred. His breath stank, and it was then I noticed the brandy bottle at his feet.

'What the fuck are you doin?' I said.

Shona hit my arm. 'Sayon, what the hell?' she said, but I was too afraid to pay my language any mind, and Shona was too taken aback to truly chastise me. Her head was on a swivel, rocking from me, to the alcohol, to her papa and back.

'I know I have a past,' the pastor said. 'That I have to make amends and be a vessel for the Lord, but this task is too much; you are who you are, Sayon Hughes, you'll never change. And you and your Nanny may live without fear of God, but I can't. We're nothing alike.'

'What the fuck are you doin?' I said again.

'There's something that I need to tell you, Princess,' he said. 'Something that I thought was my trouble to bear, but I can't keep it from you any more.'

'Daddy?'

'Don't listen to him, Shona,' I cried, I stepped in front of the pastor and held her face in my hands, forcing her attention on me, 'don't listen to nutun he says, okay?'

'What's going on, Sayon?' Shona frowned. She was more scared than I was; every suspicion that she had been carrying, that she had only just promised to suppress, came running back, and she was about ready to burst.

'Sayon and I have been keeping something from you,' Pastor continued, and I spun to face him. 'I kept it from you for your sake and God's, him for his own reasons.'

'Is dis what you're on?' I stuttered, turning to face my tormentor. And in his drunkenness Pastor Lyle rose to his full height and dared me to do something about it, and I desperately wanted to, every bone in my body urged me forward, until Shona pulled me by the arm.

'What is it?' she whispered. In her mind she was prepared for the worst, but I knew it wouldn't be enough. Just the mere fact that I had lied was a test, whereas murder, murder was the end.

I couldn't help but crack. 'Please,' I begged, but the pastor's mind was as made as his daughter's was about to be.

The bastard started to speak, so I grabbed what I could and fled from the house, unable to look Shona in the eye, unable to hear the words I had been so afraid of for months; I ran.

33

For Demas has forsaken me, having loved this present world, and has departed for Thessalonica – Crescens for Galatia, Titus for Dalmatia.

– 2 Timothy 4:10

From Pastor Lyle's I ran straight to Nanny's, and there I stayed.

I must've checked my phone a thousand times over the following days and weeks, but there was nary a text and never an album. We were done. Shona and I. I could feel it. I knew it. If Shona felt any differently, if she'd wanted to hash things out, then I would've heard from her, and since I didn't, I had my answer.

Pastor was right; murder was too much for her to bear. And parental love, a love that I couldn't hope to understand, was too great a love to sacrifice for any love I could give.

During the months I'd been gone, Nanny hadn't rented my room or fluffed a pillow; she wanted everything the same for when her baby boy came back. As she knew I would. She'd found my hidden money in her room as well, and returned it without a note missing. And the brick phone I'd given Cuba was waiting for me on top of the Gideon Bible, it was without its sim of course, but the gesture was appreciated.

On the first Sunday of October Nanny served platefuls of plantain and hard dough bread with strips of bacon for the swine-eaters. There were jugs of bitty orange juice and pineapples, plump mangoes and bananas with the perfect yellow-to-brown ratio of ripeness. Dennis Brown sang 'Have You Ever' from Nanny's dusty Sony stereo and I saw my aunty Winifred pour whisky into a glass of milk.

Even Uncle Michael appeared – if only for an instant – removed his battered headphones and patted my shoulder in the manner of someone uncomfortable with intimacy. He said it was good to have me back.

And despite the context; it *was* good to be back.

I kissed the top of Nanny's head and took my plate to the backyard where my uncles Marlon and Calvin and older cousins Killa and Jamaal were sat chasing their daily vitamin D dosage in the October sun.

'Ow was yuh likkle break, Sayon? Lyle brainwash yuh?' Uncle Marlon laughed, as I perched on the doorstep. 'Lyle was always fass, enuh. Always love ahh gyal. Den one day im tun round an start tek dis church ting too serious, star, just like yuh mama an papa. Jah know seh di wul ahh dem mad, Sayon.'

'Yuh mum tinks er farts don't stink like di rest ahh us,' Uncle Calvin added. 'Lyle an yuh papa as well, dem tink kaaz dem find God, dat mek dem better dan di rest ahh wi.'

'Leave dem alone, man,' Jamaal said. Two backpacks lay at his feet whilst he bounced another of his sons on his knee and spoon-fed him baby gunk. Seeing someone so broad feeding someone so tiny always made me smile. 'Aunty Erica probably just got tired of bailin you out, Uncle.'

Uncle Calvin kissed his teeth. 'Wah yuh know bout bail, Jamaal? You didn't even stay in prison long, rudeboy, even Sayon's been prison longer dan yuh. Look, both ahh mi big sister dem aven't done nutun for me, bout bail. Unuh don't know nutun from nutun,' he insisted, much as he had in each of his court appearances.

'Who wants to go jail you jokeman,' Jamaal laughed, 'and true, my marge ain't serious, but she's a better grandma dan mum, I'll give her dat still. She's got Jaden and Jaylen in the front now so big up her ting, init.'

'Well, she can only get better cuh she cyaan get worse,' Uncle Marlon laughed.

Killa stopped brushing his hair for a second to pull a deck of cards from his pocket and my family set about gambling the morning away. I played a couple of hands, won some pounds and sipped a little juice.

When midday struck and it was socially acceptable to start drinking, Jamaal fetched Magnums and Guinnesses from the fridge door and by the late afternoon we were all merry.

Around four o'clock Bunny arrived, and he came bearing dominoes and fruit punch.

'Wat liquor yuh av in yah?' Uncle Marlon demanded, sniffing the wide plastic bowl, whilst Uncle Calvin took the dominoes and began setting up his favourite game. There were glasses and empty bottles on the table but he dealt around them. He wanted as many things on the table as could fit so when he slammed his winning card they would crash to the floor and proclaim his manhood.

'Just drink it nuh man,' Bunny replied.

'Yuh put Wray innah it?' Uncle Calvin said, inhaling deeply. 'Yeah man mi smell it.'

'It don't smell like nutun but fruit,' Jamaal laughed, 'dat's how you know you chat shit.' He took a red cup from Bunny and dipped it into the punch before drinking deeply. 'Yeah man, dat's Wray and his nephew.' He dunked his cup again and let his son have a taste.

The sun dove west, children were returned to their mothers and our blunts lit the evening gloom. Every pastime had been exhausted, the aunties had cooked a storm and we were content to recline in our seats and tend our bloated stomachs.

The itus was warm and welcome so my eyes were slow to open by the time Cuba arrived. He stood in the doorway with a bag on his shoulder and grinned at me. The grease had gone from his face but the weather hadn't. He'd aged in those months we'd spent apart. And I was glad I came back when I did.

'Yo, cuz,' he called, as he and Jamaal swapped goods. 'You back?'

I nodded, mirroring the relief I found in his face.

'For good?'

I nodded again. I had lost one love, but I had regained another. And I was back where I belonged. I could lay tracks elsewhere but my roots were in this house. With my people.

'What you sayin, I thought you was banned from Nanny's?' I asked him.

Cuba's grin stretched from ear to ear. 'Nah man, you can't get rid of me dat easy. You know how Nanny stays, init, the other day she just said the Lord forgives and told man come home for a food.'

The next morning Cuba and I were out the house bright and early. And in my upset I had reached a resolution; if I couldn't love Shona then I would love Cuba to the fullest.

I would take every crumb of violence that I wanted to outlet upon Pastor Lyle, every urge and note of intimacy that I could no longer pour on Shona, and I would offer it to my cousin. I couldn't make up for the time we had lost, but I could do my best to recoup our closeness, and my pursuit of the house-atop-the-hill that I had abandoned in fear of losing Shona, and we could become brothers again.

The morning air was cool and the sky was doing its best to shed its blackness for blue. I drew the strings of my hoody and followed my cousin along Stapes.

These were the hours that made the neighbourhood's nature as plain as broad noses. Early mornings stripped the streets of any farcical disguises and city council ploys like the changing of names, annual street parties or avant-gardist art trails. The pavements were busy with middle-aged Black women contracted to clean law firms and big banks. Kebab houses were serving their last customers on their way home from nights out or long shifts. Cats congregated on kerbs and bus stops, bussin jokes and getting ready for their next fix.

We cut through an alley that led towards the city centre, on the way to fetch my sim card from Junior.

A shirtless blond sat with his legs sprawled beside bags of trash and boxes of fast-food refuse. Chicken bones had been scattered across the alley by rats and foxes scavenging a meal. Pigeons struck at the leftovers. The blond pressed a needle into his arm without a belt or string, or any kind of brace. A little line of blood vamoosed from the cut but I wasn't even sure he'd found a vein. Still, his head sunk on to his chest and he left Earth.

'Your new customer,' Cuba laughed.

'I don't even think donny's finna wake up, fam,' I replied.

His skin was white like smutted milk and marked by acne scars and malnutrition. His thighs were the same size as his calves and his hair hadn't seen water but rain. 'My man'll be dead in a week.'

'Less,' Cuba muttered, kicking the sole of the blond's shoe.

A door swung open into the alley and another man staggered from inside. He swigged from a bottle of Coca-Cola and almost fell whilst reaching to pluck a cigarette stub from the floor. As he saw us coming his eyes widened; it was the tramp from the church steps, the one whose high Pastor had interrupted.

'You,' he slurred, pointing a nicotine-stained finger at me, 'I know you.'

'Who the fuck is dis, Sayon?' said Cuba.

'You said your cousin died,' the tramp said, 'but I know your cousin. Your cousin's Winnie. I know Winnie. Everyone knows Winnie.' He flailed his arms above his head as he gestured to everyone.

'What d'you know bout Winnie, huh?' Cuba asked.

The drunk stumbled over a bin bag as he backed away. 'I know Winnie, init.'

'Why didn't you say nutun on the steps?' I demanded.

He shrugged. Every action was dramatised as if he were auditioning for the final spot in a pantomime. 'I didn't know who you was on about, did I? But I know now. Now I know.' I reared backward and kicked the tramp in his chest. He crashed to the ground and frantically held his hands before him. 'And I know something else too. I do,' he stammered.

'Yeah? What d'you know?' Cuba asked, crouching beside him.

Again the drunk held a finger towards me. 'People are saying you gave her somefink dodgy. Somefink that was meant to mess her up. But when you gave me dat tea you was talking like you cared about her . . .' Cuba took a flicky from the pouch that swung around his neck and let it hang at his side.

I reached for my own knife that waited for me beside my dick.

A line of piss ran from his crotch to his shoes. 'No. No. I didn't mean noffink by what I said, young blood,' he mumbled. 'Honest! I was talking out my ass, ignore me.'

Cuba grabbed a handful of his collar and brought their faces together. 'You're lucky Ends is hot right now, wallahi,' he said, 'otherwise I'd dead you right here, blud. You think I give a fuck about your life? What the fuck does your life mean to me? Winnie was man's cousin, why the fuck would man dead man's own cousin, blud?' He straightened himself out and put the bottom of his shoe on the drunk's chest. 'Use your fuckin brain, you chief.'

Then I hit him hard and we left him with his nose bloody and his lip split.

'What you sayin, how hot is it right now?' I asked, as we left the alleyway behind.

Cuba zipped his blade away and ran a hand across his scalp. 'A couple of the ygs got bagged cos of sup'm dat happened on Stapes the other night, init,' he sighed, 'and dese last couple days dey've got the whole of the Trinity on patrol. And man can't even fuckin sleep cos of all the fuckin helicopters; I know you heard dem as well.'

I told him that Shona and I had witnessed the stabbing on Stapes, hours after Karma and I had seen the same yutes.

'Yeah man, shit's peak right now,' he shrugged, 'I told dem man relax, but you know how you are when you're dat age, you think the world's yours.' I smiled to myself; with Cuba as their role model the youngers didn't have much of an example for cool-headedness. Then again, I couldn't talk. 'Dey got cameras on my man's church now and everyting enuh?' Cuba continued. 'Ends is gonna stay hot for a while, wallahi. Shit's sad.' I thought council cameras atop the church spires seemed an apt addition to the House of God.

Later my sim card was returned by another of Cuba's runners, and it was back to business. My regulars asked where I had been and complained about Junior. They said he was irritable, that they couldn't understand what he said and apparently he'd decked a drunken student for being too touchy-feely. I reassured them that I was back for good and they had nothing to worry about, in fact I would be more available than ever, and encouraged them to pass my number on to their friends.

When I presented their feedback to Cuba he decided to take their grievances to the source. Soon we were back walking along Stapleton Road, Cuba was backing a chicken and chips and I bought a strawberry Mirinda.

I had lost the one thing that anchored me to the other world and my state of mind was rapidly changing because of it. And I resolved that I wouldn't give a fuck any more, about anything.

But where I was fixated on shoving Shona from my mind, money was on Cuba's. 'I been havin too many problems wid my man as well,' he announced.

'Wid who?'

'The little man, fam – Junior.'

'Trouble like what?' I asked, and I couldn't keep the distaste from my tone.

'Nutun like dat,' Cuba smiled, amused at the zeal with which I had replied. 'I told you I patterned my man, init. Dat's man's younger now, he won't say nutun truss me. If my man even thinks about snitchin I'll soak him up. My man knows dat. He ain't dumb, blud. Hear what, I reckon if you gave my man a chance you'd like him enuh.'

He must have seen the disbelief in my face because he tipped back his head and laughed loud. 'Nah, big man ting, donny's got his head screwed on for the most part, just sometimes he fucks up init, like we all do.'

'So wagwan den?'

'He just been movin mad lately. Owes man some ps and he's movin mad slow payin man back and dat.'

'How much he owe you?'

'Like a bag.'

'Shit. How'd you let dat happen?'

'The yute's just shit wid money init. I been giving man ps to hold and he took some of it talkin bout investin it in a wap cos we got passa wid Pauls now. But we got enough guns already blud, and I told you earlier init, it's too hot to be buyin dem tings right now, you get me?'

I knew it; Junior was a risk I wasn't willing to take. I didn't understand the upside to keeping him around, there was a lagoon full of yutes around Ends, enough for the bits and county lines combined. Nor did I understand how Cuba's fondness for him had blossomed. Again, I put it down to our recent distance. If anyone else owed Cuba a grand they would have paid it, or they would be hurt and their relos would have paid instead.

'Dis life's gettin to the little man's head,' Cuba muttered.

'And whose fault is dat?' I asked.

Cuba barked and pushed my shoulder.

It was a funny thing being so close with someone whom others feared. Some days I saw the child I grew up with, and the exterior he had crafted in defence against the world melted like a Flake 99 on a summer's afternoon. I saw the laugh lines that creased with any small sarcasm or cheek. The high-pitched tone that flagged his excitement at the most trivial of things. I recognised his generosity: he was selfless in so many respects (especially with his time), just as he had been as a child. If you needed him he would be there at the drop of a hat, before the hat hit the ground, in fact. Like me he had an uncanny sense for danger and a burning loyalty.

At other times I understood all too clearly why he was feared.

Aunty Paulette sprang from Viv's and crashed slap-bang into my chest, she didn't see her son who was a step ahead of us.

'Watch where yuh deh walk, yute,' she yapped. 'Ay, watch yah now, mi ear seh yuh come back?' Aunty Paulette could hardly be quiet. Her voice was a foghorn made to guide men ashore. 'Weh yuh come from now? Yuh see either ahh mi yute dem?'

Behind her Cuba smacked his lips together and spat at the floor. 'Watch where *you're* goin, bout Sayon, it was you dat bumped into us, blud.' Aunty Paulette shrank an inch. I watched her transition from this great woman who flung open doors, whose walk was a wavy bop, bullish and full of hips, to a rueful shadow of her usual self.

'What you get from Viv?' Cuba asked suspiciously. He took a step towards her and she withdrew further still. 'More time I know you ain't got no ps like dat so why the fuck you in Viv's anyway?' He reached into her jacket and found a packet of cigarettes.

For a second, only snippets of passing conversations could be heard. And in that second I understood how Aunty Paulette and Winnie were related. She became flaccid in front of her second son. Sycophantic. Just as Winnie used to be when she was catting for food. But Cuba didn't care; he didn't take his eyes from the cigarettes.

'Did you steal dese?' he asked, his voice no louder than a hiss.

Aunty Paulette hurried to respond. 'Viv let mi hold dem, im say it's cool.'

'Nah, fuck dat.' He spat again and I thought he might have hit her. We both did, because Aunty Paulette shrank to the size of a thumbnail. 'Sayon, wait wid her, make sure she don't teef nutun else.' He disappeared into the shop.

Through the window we saw him take what was at least a hundred pounds and slap it on the counter. Viv tried to protest but Cuba only apologised on his mother's behalf and came back outside. 'Yo, come let's cut, Sayon.' He handed the cigarettes back to his mother without meeting her pleading eye, and we crossed the road to where Junior and Karma were waiting.

With his mood soured, Cuba had little time for Junior, who saw us coming and held his arms open wide. 'Yo, Midnight,' he called. A stupid grin on his face. Cuba answered him with a fist in his stomach. I embraced Karma who said that he'd made dua that I'd come back, and the three of us rounded on the yute.

We took him down a tributary and Cuba reminded him of the money he owed. Junior was repentant. He gave Cuba what money he had on him. Promised to give him the gun he had bought too. He even offered to go shoeless but Cuba rejected his offer, on account of already owning the same pair.

We gave Junior some food and a deadline for the wap and the money: he had until the end of the week. Then the two of us left with Karma in tow.

I had a hole in my heart, and I would fill it by any means.

34

The backslider in heart will be filled with the fruit of his ways,
and a good man will be filled with the fruit of his ways.

– Proverbs 14:14

The next morning Cuba and I were back at it, except this time we took Jaden and Jaylen along. Both their mothers were arguing with Jamaal, so he was holding them hostage at Nanny's. He had stepped out last night and left them in our charge. We couldn't leave them with Nanny in case their mothers showed up. And since Junior was running errands with Cuba's current car we were left to travel on foot.

The seasons were getting ready to swap shifts. The gloom hadn't completely taken the skies but the grey that characterised the British firmament was arriving at an alarming pace.

The first stop was Viv's. We found the ninety-year-old chatting up some slim ting, talking about had she ever been to the islands? How he was going soon and wanted to fly her out. 'Everyone should come see the Caribbean Sea,' he told her with a golden grin.

Our cousin Bunny was in there too, and he had two women of his own with him.

Bunny's face lit up when we arrived; pleased that there would be another two witnesses to his allure. 'Wahum, nephews,' he purred, 'dese my four likkle nephews,' he explained to his women, 'aren't dey cute?' We ignored him and the soupy voice he'd taken and took a backpack full of weed from Viv, but Bunny wasn't done being Bunny. 'Di bigger two tinkseh dem bad, especially Midnight, the black one, but dey ain't nutun, likkle drug dealer bwoys.'

'Yo, shut the fuck up, Bunny,' I said, 'fore I bad you up in front of everyone.' What we did wasn't a secret, but we had never been the kind of trappers that chased prison sentences to validate our criminality.

The smile on Bunny's face evanesced. He took his arms from his women and a step forward, but neither Cuba nor I worried – Bunny had never crossed a line in his life. There were sellers and takers in our family, and the takers danced to the sellers' tune. We cut with the backpack and Bunny didn't overstep.

The boys' dead weight rendered them cumbersome in our arms. Their cheeks lay fat against our shoulders as we shook people's hands and pocketed the cash they gave us. Occasionally Jaylen stirred and at one point seemed intent on staying awake, but I didn't want the nitties remembering his face, so we shared an earphone each and an old Shona radio show lulled him back to sleep.

By mid-morning the boys were wide awake and curious, and no amount of music would get them back to sleep.

Jaden kept fiddling with the zip on Cuba's pouch and reaching for the handle of his flicky, so Cuba gave him some coins to play with. Jaylen was less disruptive than his brother. Instead he busied himself with my hair, running his podgy hands back and forth.

'Sayon, your hair is funny,' he giggled, patting me like a dog.
'Yeah? What's funny about it?'

'It's just funny,' he said. I rounded on him, my face straight and brow furrowed, doing my best to look threatening.

'Oh, you think I'm a jokeman? You think I'm a joke?' I said, whereupon he slapped my cheeks and lapsed into a fit of giggles. 'Jaden, your brother thinks I'm a joke,' I called. Jaden twisted in Cuba's arms and began chuckling when he saw the fun his brother was having.

'Sayon, you're silly,' he laughed. 'Jaylen thinks you're silly.'
'Yeah? And what do you think?'

'I think you're silly too.'

'We think you're silly,' Jaylen added. I'd had enough of their slander. I took Jaden from Cuba and ran with them to the nearest dustbin. I opened the cover and bunged them on top of the black bags, closing the lid on their protests. By the time I let them out Jaylen was hysterical and Jaden was promising to tell his father. It was then that Cuba intervened.

'Don't snitch,' he said, gently cuffing his nephew round the back of his head. 'Snitches get killed.' He lifted the boys out of the trash and we continued on. Jaden took his admonishment but he wasn't satisfied with his uncle's warning.

'Why'd they get killed?' he asked some time later.

We had left Stapes and were walking to the yard of a customer who lived in the middle of Ends. The sun was warm and the streets were lively. People who knew us touched our fists and nodded as they passed. I felt the boys' pride swell as they bore witness to their uncle's and cousin's popularity; even at their age they understood prestige and social standing.

'Cos dey deserve it,' Cuba replied, 'dem man are the lowest of the low.'

'Who kills the snitches?'

'People like me and your uncle Sayon. People who know deh's a proper way to carry yourself in dis world. People dat get tings done, you get me?' He paused and tickled Jaden's stomach, 'What you sayin, little man? Are you one of us or one of dem?'

'I am, I am—' Jaden gasped.

'Am what?' said Cuba, tickling him pink.

'One of you.'

'I am too,' Jaylen cried. 'Mummy says we're like Daddy.'

'Yeah,' Cuba nodded, 'your pops knows how to carry himself still.'

But Jaylen wasn't finished. 'But Mummy only says it when Mummy's angry.'

Cuba cut in before I could think of a response. 'Fuck your mum,' he said. 'She don't know shit bout shit.'

The customer we were visiting lived in one of the tower blocks that overlooked the dual carriageway. A play area with yellow grass and swings that stank of dog-piss lay abandoned at its foot. A group of teenagers were kicking a punctured football outside the door, but they made way for us as we buzzed in.

The customer was Stacy, one of Cuba's regulars. She sent one of her children to meet us at the lift and another to hold their front door ajar and invite us inside. 'You want anyfink to drink?' the little girl asked, Cuba shook his head and stroked her partially braided hair.

'You want anyting, Jaden? Jaylen?' The boys followed their uncle's suit and shook their heads. 'Nah, we're good, thank you,' Cuba said, smiling down at the little girl. He dropped a few notes in her hand as payment for such a welcome. The girl flashed the gaps in her teeth before dashing to hide her new-found riches from her siblings. And she had lots of them. The flat was smaller than Nanny's downstairs and was made smaller by the clutter and tangle of children.

Stacy lolled on a vast corner sofa, flicking through cartoon channels and breastfeeding her youngest. Her hair was uncombed and bowls of half-eaten cereal littered a skinny coffee table. She ashed her blunt on the table and held her arms out to hug Cuba.

'Ahh, who pickney dem, Cuba? Yuh never tell mi yuh av no yutes?'

'My brudda's yutes still,' Cuba replied, perching on the sofa beside some more of Stacy's kids, who didn't take their eyes from the telly. 'Jaden, Jaylen, say wagwan,' he instructed, and they obliged with the enthusiasm of a doctor passing their patient terrible news.

'Hi, babies,' Stacy returned. 'Wahum, Sayon, y'alright?'

'Yeah yeah, I'm good still, Stace,' I said. I swung my pouch from my neck and handed her the reason we'd come. She took the weed and the hard food, passed me some notes in exchange and slipped pound coins into Jaden and Jaylen's pockets. We heard a loud slap and a wail from one of the bedrooms. When Stacy called for the noise to end and threatened pain, it stopped.

'Sorry bout dat,' she said.

Cuba chuckled to himself. 'Why d'you have more and more yutes every time I come in here, Stace, wagwan? You love a man, init?'

'Dey ain't mine,' Stacy snapped, flicking her head towards the yutes in the bedroom. 'I'm juss lookin after dem fi mi fren dem. I only av six pickney by tree man enuh, star.' She held up three fingers to emphasise her restraint. 'Only tree man did breed mi. An tree man nutun in di grand scheme ahh life.' She took her baby's mouth from her nipple and tucked her breast back into her top. 'Dis one is a real feeder enuh? Love mi titty dem more dan im papa. God rest im soul.'

'Amen,' Cuba replied. He took a pre-roll from his pocket and gestured for me to join him. He lit his and I mine before he leant and lit Stacy's. Together we toasted our reefers and smoked in memory of Stacy's dead babyfather, whom neither Cuba nor I knew.

We stayed for the better part of the morning, watching cartoons with Stacy and her yutes. And Cuba visibly brightened. Whether it was because we were reunited, or we had our nephews with us, who knows? But I was glad to see it. And by the time Junior came to pick us up Stacy had smoked enough weed to buy some more.

'Tek care ahh yuhself, honeys, yuh ear?' she called from her window five storeys up, 'and tek care ahh mi baby dem, di likkle precious syntings.'

We promised we would and the boys waved goodbye.

Junior leapt from the hood of Cuba's car as we drew near. The car was expensive. And Junior's footmarks had stained the paintwork. I could see the shape of a blade by his leg and recognised the awkward limp of someone carrying a long weapon. It seemed the previous day's lesson had done little to bruise his ego.

Cuba had booster seats in the back of the car so we strapped the boys inside and Cuba took the keys to drive.

'Yo, Midnight,' Junior sang, 'why don't you sell dis whip and put the ps on skengs, blud, wallahi dis is worth some mans year's wages, no lie.'

'Where's the ting?' Cuba replied, talking about the gun.

'In the glovebox.'

'And the bread?'

'In the glovebox as well.'

Cuba handed Junior Viv's backpack and sent him on his way, but as I was climbing into the passenger seat the little man stopped me.

'Wagwan?' I said. He didn't have shit to say to me and we both knew it.

He drew closer and kept his voice low. 'It's been a minute so I ain't had the chance to tell you, blud, but I just wanted to say I rate what you did, init. Looking after your brudda like that; that's what family's s'posed to do, you get me? We're s'posed to have each other's backs. Dat Cordell yute had it coming more time—' I couldn't listen to any more waffle.

I grabbed him by the collar, lifted him from the floor and hammered him against the car. 'Shut the fuck up,' I hissed. I felt his body slack and his bravado pour like cognac at a wake. He kept his eyes averted as I pressed my face next to his.

'You don't know what the fuck you're talkin bout, bout he had it comin, dat was man's bredrin, blud. And you didn't know man, same way you don't know me. Same way you don't know nutun bout dis life, cuz. Stop runnin yuh fuckin mout and go work.'

I threw him to the ground and watched him wipe snot and tears from his face with the back of his sleeve. 'Move like you know man again and see if I don't put dis gun on you. Pussy.'

He scampered into the flats with his tail tucked between his hind legs and the hole in my heart filled a little.

That feeling, however, was short-lived.

Cuba and I dropped the boys back to Jamaal, then he gave me the car keys and took off; he had things to do and said I could use the whip to hit whatever sales I needed. That was the plan at least, but as pastors across the country often preached: people planned yet the last word was Jesus', and it seemed He was intent on punishing me.

It wasn't often I happened across Sister Erica Stewart, especially not at Nanny's, or even in Ends for that matter, but as I went back to the car, I found her, waiting for Uncle Michael outside Nanny's front gate.

She was dressed for church with a buttoned blouse that ran to her neck, and sunglasses that weren't worn for the sun, but to avoid recognition. Uncle Michael was the only family member with whom she had maintained any semblance of a relationship, because, according to her, he was the only one with any sense.

'Good evening, Sayon,' she called, amused by the shock on my face, 'so yuh back deh ahh Nanny's? Mi knew yuh couldn't last wid Pastor Lyle an Marcia.'

My mama's hair was twisted into a bun that pinched her features and I could smell the pomade as I brushed past her. She smiled a watermelon smile and Uncle Michael joined us outside. From behind the car I nodded at my uncle, who mumbled a response and kept his face to the clouds. He kissed my mama on the cheek and stood at her side.

'Why you here?' I asked her, there was something about the way her zircon eyes stayed on me, as if she were awaiting a reaction for a revelation she had yet to divulge. I didn't have time for this; I unlocked the whip and hopped into the driver's seat.

My mama tapped a knuckle against the glass till I wound the window down and she rested her bosom on the sill. 'Yuh ear di news?' she asked, her jaw tightening and slackening like a hay-chewing cow.

'What news?' I replied uncaringly, but immediately my mind flew to Shona. Had she found someone else? Some Christian yute? It had been less than a month since I'd left, but there was nothing that would make my mama happier. She probably came to fetch Uncle Michael just so that she could be the one to tell me. And if it was true, I didn't know how I would behave.

'Di yard gone,' she announced.

'Which yard?'

'Di yard deh ahh Clifton,' she said, as her mouth continued to whorl like watercolour on wet plaster.

'What do you mean it's gone?' I said, choosing my words carefully.

'Gone. Sold. Sell up. Wah yuh waan mi fi tell yuh?' I said nothing so she carried on. 'Mi tinkseh dem guh tun dem innah flats, but mi nuh sure,' she flounced her shoulders and continued to chew.

She was lying. She had to be.

35

Or do you not know that your body is the temple of the Holy Spirit who is in you, whom you have from God, and you are not your own? For you were bought at a price; therefore glorify God in your body and in your spirit, which are God's.

– 1 Corinthians 6:19–20

'You're chattin shit,' I spat. 'I'm goin deh now, blud.'

'Mek mi an yuh uncle come,' she said, opening the passenger door and hustling Uncle Michael across the seats before I had a chance to complain.

She parked herself beside me and I pushed the pedal to the floor, eager for her words to be as empty as her love. But when we got to the house-atop-the-hill I found them to be true: the yard was hemmed by tall, Otis-blue boards that announced its new ownership and outlined renovation plans to build apartments.

I watched my future shatter before me.

I left the pair of them in the car and walked across the road. The boards were too high to climb, and I realised I would never see the garden again.

In my desperation I thought if only I could speak to someone in charge, get a quote, a rough idea of the cost, then the dream might still be alive. The company's number was printed beneath the plans but they didn't answer when I called. Their website listed another property in St Pauls so I figured I might find someone there. We may have been in the makings of a full-blown war with the area, but that didn't matter, I would throw caution to the wind because there was far more at stake than my wellbeing.

'Wah mi tell yuh?' Mama said, when I crashed back into the car. 'Yuh travel all dis way fi nutun.' She kissed her teeth when I didn't reply. 'But maybe dis fi di best, eh Sayon? Jesus work in mysterious ways, praise God, hallelujah, so maybe dis will mek yuh catch ahh likkle sense. Yuh never could've afforded dis yah yard, Sayon. No matter ow much drugs yuh sell. Yuh affi live within yuh means. Umble yuhself, enuh? It's all very well yuh av dem dreamin eyes, but dreams nah go tek yuh no place. Praise God. Only ard work ahh Christ can do dat, hallelujah.' She carried on but I drowned her out.

I put my head on the wheel and my hands dropped into my lap.

What was I thinking? There was no such thing as a happy ending.

I'd thought if I worked hard enough, did enough dirt, then there would be a chance at a better life. For me. And for Cuba. And if she ever found room to forgive me; then for Shona too. Now the sliver of hope I'd been carrying had been dashed against the rocks. She'd never have her room with the album covers on the wall, and I'd never hear her play next door. We'd never start a family of our own. Or invest in our future like Hakim and Elia. No. Where I was from, we had to make the best of our circumstances, and that meant simply surviving. And in order to survive, you played by the rules of the world in which you were born.

So what did Clifton matter? Whether I was there or Ends, nothing would change; I was still the same yute who'd killed his former friend and his cousin.

Beside me, my mama spoke of Jesus-sent signs and invited me back to the church, but I wouldn't be manipulated a second time, and certainly not by a woman who took pleasure in my ruin.

'Shut the fuck up,' I said, quietly at first, but when she stuttered, I said it again, with more vim. Enough to provoke a response. But none came. If she thought she could speak into my life whilst remaining apart from it, then she had another think coming. I wasn't a yute no more.

I dropped my mama and uncle back on Stapes, and as Uncle Michael stepped from the passenger seat I stopped him. 'Uncle, you remember killing that fox back in the day?'

He recoiled as if my words were oil spat from a wok, and for a moment I thought he wouldn't reply, 'Mm-mi membah,' he nodded.

'Why'd you do it?'

'Mm-m-mi was pro-pr-tectin im, Sayon,' he eventually said, tripping over his words as was his way. 'Mi didn't mean fi u-urt im like dat, but i-im was mines enuh? Cyn-cyn-cynthia s-say it was like wen God a-ax Abraham fi kill I-isaac cuh im love im.'

I found the house in St Pauls with the same boards, only smaller, small enough to hoist myself over. The yard was a dump; weeds stood taller than the boards and shut out the light, the windows were broken and replaced by wooden slats, and the sound of animals scuttling came from the basement.

There was no one here. And no one picked up the phone again.

All was lost.

I climbed back outside and left the car where I parked it.

We all needed something. A single thing that we could stamp and call our own. A slice of the Devil's pie or a slice of Heaven – it didn't matter which. But what could I say was my own? And what was I to tell Cuba? Or offer Shona if she ever returned? The house-atop-the-hill was to be our future. A testament to what we had, what we had overcome and what we were to be. A haven stowed away from the drama. Far above the noise where the angels struck harps and trumpets blared. And Cuba, since we had first played there, his ambitions had been pinned to the house as much as mine were. Now it was the end of the road and the gates had been closed.

I kept walking until I came to the edge of a labyrinthine estate, one I wouldn't have been caught dead near for most of my life. Now I thought about heading inside. But there was no need, because they found me before I found them.

'Yo, where you from?'

'Ain't he Midnight's cousin?'

I knew what would happen when I came here, it was partly why I came – to kill any hope I had left, and to feel something. And I knew the answer to their questions: I was from the city of men, and yes, I was Midnight's cousin. My home was the gutter. Only those raised here had any hope of acclimatising, and that was exactly what I had done. My company were the jinns and mankind. Jesus' signs couldn't make it here, they were g-checked, torn down and tossed into the back of cars.

And no one could make it out.

Footsteps descended upon me; I felt fists and the soles of

trainers. And I couldn't help but feel as though I deserved it.

The Bible said that I was a child of God, that God was my Father; which is why it was just like Him to abandon me. I could forsake the ways of my family and enter His house, but what purpose did it serve?

The yutes didn't take a thing; it wasn't about the money. I was lucky they didn't have any weapons on them, they said, otherwise they would've deaded me, but maybe that was what I deserved. After all, I'd hurt everyone I'd ever loved, and for what?

Cuba arrived not long after I called him. He helped me from the pavement and we took off past the bridge where I'd seen the drunk woman murder her lover. I told Cuba that the house-atop-the-hill was gone, sold to a company whose trail I had followed into St Pauls. I told him that I had failed him; that our dream was well and truly over.

36

Ungry ungry an full full nuh travel same pass.

– Jamaican Proverb

Without a word Cuba drove me to the bakery, slung my arm around his shoulders, and helped me limp through the door. 'Hakim,' he yelled, 'yo, Hakim.'

But it was Elia who first answered, she pushed through the beads, her hands white with flour and straightaway noticed the blood on my face and lips. 'Warya Sayon, what happened?' she cried, as she ran to my side and helped me on to a seat. 'Cuba what happened? Hakim, bring paper towels and some ice,' she called as she flipped the CLOSED sign and shut the bakery for the night.

Cuba squatted by my side and said that he would be back with reinforcements in a second. 'Catch your breath, g,' he told me. 'We'll sort dis out tonight, wallahi.'

Seconds later I heard his car screeching away and Hakim arrived with the towels and ice. 'What happened, Sayon?' he asked, and for a second he sounded just as he had in the days of old, just like Funds.

'I got rushed,' I winced, 'but don't worry, it's nutun, fam, it's minor.' Nothing felt broken, but everywhere was sore. 'Can you get man a drink?' I asked, and whilst Hakim set about preparing a tea, Elia fussed over blotting the cuts.

She didn't pressure me for the details; in fact she didn't say another word and forbade Hakim from asking too. We weren't friends for nothing: in school when Shona wasn't there, the teachers would send for Elia to help calm me down in isolation, and she'd learnt that I needed time to process things, then when the time was right I would talk, but not this time. I couldn't risk Hakim wanting to do something about it; he had his own life now. Funds was dormant; my cousin had made it as far as anyone could.

In Ends manifold worlds jostled for space like children on the morning bus. There was the world where Elia and Hakim woke with the sun to bake and sell their wares, where Pastor Lyle ran his errands and the congregation put up stalls and ran outreach. Where St Marks Road – voted one of the three greatest streets in Britain – was an offshoot and the Sunni masjid held iftar during the month of Ramadan.

The world where St Barnabas Church stood far from alone, scores of masjids and churches lined the banks, bastions of otherworldliness. Florists, barber shops, halal butchers and yard shops tended the people's needs and the illusion of moral absolutes was sustained. And because of the sun, the world flourished with life, as if the shops were willows and the people animals amongst the shrubbery. But where some loved the sun, the night would always be left for the nocturnal.

For a time Elia stayed opposite me, holding the ice to my brow. She sat where she could shake her head at the customers coming to the door, and point at the CLOSED sign, until I took the icepack from her hands and told her to return to her work.

So custom continued, and strangers did their best not to stare, but I paid them little mind, because all the while my mind raced.

In my world the wares changed in nature. Many of my customers were in the worst of shapes. The stragglers who belonged to the other world hurried along the road. They kept their heads averted and their belongings to their bosoms. They knew they were in a place that wasn't theirs and only through circumstance did they put themselves at risk.

The rules of the road changed when the moon took its place in the sky. The class system was laid bare and practised in its purest form. Government names were shed for nicknames, names earned from savagery or riches. Strangers carried their lives in the way they walked, dressed and spoke. There were no limits. No restrictions on how far one would go in pursuit of success or revenge. It was a world whose simplicity was envied by those who thrived in the day, and when the two worlds collided the nocturnal left with their elastic bands stretched a little wider.

The times I had shared with Shona in the early weeks of moving in, I had tasted what life outside of Ends was like, and I liked it. Wanted it. Yet I wanted Cuba and the rest of my family with me too. Opposing though they were, I wanted the two worlds to blend, have them meet in Clifton, but now with the yard gone; I had lost them both.

The bakery's lights were on and the youngers sold wraps and weed beneath its canopy. I drank my tea, regained my breath, and watched Elia and Hakim work. She ran her hands over and through the dough and, as she kneaded, Hakim wiped dots of sweat from her forehead with his sleeve.

If trappers were given the means they would run rings around the businessmen who committed the same offences as they did.

If fraudsters were given the tools they would inject a new life into banking. Some of the hardest-working people I knew sold drugs. And anyone who sold drugs spent the little time they had spare working to live in the sun. All we had to overcome was generations of trauma passed on by relatives and a system intent on keeping us in place.

'Ay, you man, you reckon I could be a baker?' I asked. The cuts on my face made it painful to talk.

Hakim scoffed and Elia's face broke with playfulness, relieved that I finally had some life left. 'Where?' she laughed, 'here?'

'Anywhere.'

'Why not? You can do anything you want.'

There; the words I had been looking for: there's no life without options.

For Pastor Lyle, who believed that accountability trumped circumstance, me and mine would always be responsible for our own misfortune. In their eyes, we would always be deserving of any ill we suffered, but what choice did we have? It was the madness Winnie lived that brought her to crack, and crack that killed her possibilities. It was Badu's knife at Pastor Lyle's cheek that brought him to God, and God that killed his possibilities. It was the seal set upon Uncle Michael's heart and mind, and for Cuba it was Aunty Paulette, a misspent childhood and an insatiable emptiness. And myself? My possibilities were being broken into flats and sold.

The bakery door burst open.

Cuba was back.

It had only been a couple of hours, and the flotsam to which I clung was torn from my arms and I hurtled along, about ready to accept my reality.

'Sayon,' Elia said. I turned in the open doorway of the bakery and found her bent with worry. Hakim had his arms wrapped around her from behind, but for once he didn't say a word, he could see how futile it would've been. 'You don't have to do anything you don't want to,' she said. 'You can let Allah handle everything, please, you don't have to do anything,' she insisted, her eyes keen and moist. 'Submit.'

I smiled; she was so wonderful, but I wasn't ready.

Cuba lived to see me make it out. More than anything else he wanted to be a crutch I could lean upon in times of need. And as he saw it, I needed him now more than ever. So how could I deny him on the same day that I was denied? We were always saving each other, it was what we did best. So I left Elia, Hakim and the lights of the bakery and went to deal a blow to the men who would have me drown beside them.

Outside, Cuba and Karma waited in the car and together the three of us sped from Stapes. Karma was wearing a balaclava that he had rolled up like a beanie. His hair swung with the car as he hit the tightest of turns at forty miles per hour. Cuba had changed; both of them were wearing black gloves and black tracksuits. Dark clothes for a dark deed, black like our hearts.

'Dis shit ends tonight, wallahi,' Cuba spat, 'are dem man mad? Think dey can touch my nigga? Dese fuckin neeks, didn't even get man properly. Man's a big fuckin man. Cuz, man don't ramp, man got fuckin guns. Watch. Dem man are done, fam. Fuckin done.' He spoke largely to himself, his emotions a visible mass that clouded his vision like a hotboxed whip.

His hands shook as he pressed weed into his grinder. 'Yo did you bell Junior?' he asked Karma, who nodded. 'Good. Tell dem man to come ready, if dey ain't ready tell dem man don't fuckin

287

come. Dey tried dead man's brudda, blud. Are dey sick? Say nutun. Watch.'

He finished rolling and shakily put the reefer to his lips. He took the gun that Junior had bought from the glovebox and checked it was loaded. 'We need to go test dis, fam. I don't know where dat likkle fassyole got dis, so we're gonna test it den we're goin Pauls and someone's gettin blammed, wallahi. Same day. I don't give a fuck. If dey look like dey was involved, dey was involved yuh get me.'

Karma echoed his intention and we whipped ourselves into a frenzy.

We drove to some fields in the outskirts of Bristol. An area the police would never associate us with. The car didn't matter either, it was a dinger and would be burnt by the end of the night. By the time we arrived my blood was white-hot, and the self-pity I'd been harbouring over losing my house and my injuries had been replaced with a burning anger.

'Who's shootin?' I said. Cuba strode ahead of us and aimed at a nearby tree. The bark twisted and tore open. A car pulled up behind us and Junior and some other yutes stepped from it. They all wore masks and gloves; it was like a surgeons' convention. And in many ways it was; everyone had blood on their hands.

One of the yutes passed Karma an old shotgun and the others stood by, ready for orders. Junior stood there too, bone idle, just as he did outside the bakery. And no matter how Cuba spun it, he didn't belong in our world.

'Yo, lil man,' I called to him, 'let me chat to you a second.' I took him aside as Karma and Cuba piled into the cars with the guns and yutes in tow.

'Wagwan?' Junior asked. I took the change I had from my

pocket, a little less than a grand, I told him there would be more coming, as much as it would take; he only needed to get the fuck out of the city. 'What?' he laughed. But it was hollow, he was unsure of himself, he didn't know where he stood with me and I was glad of it. He wasn't built for nocturnal life. He was a civilian. And this would be the one mercy I showed him.

'Take dis bread, and get the fuck out the city, blud,' I said again, but his eyes dulled with a childlike sullenness.

He shook his head and began to walk to the cars. 'Nah, g; keep your money.'

Since he didn't want my mercy I drove my fist into his face and laid into him as he fell. Here was a boy who I could apportion some blame. If he wanted to insist that he and I were the same then he could share in my misfortune, but I refused to have him alongside us any longer. If I was to be a villain, if my life was to end in Ends, then so be it. And maybe it made me a demon, but I didn't care. I had lost the house, lost Shona, lost hope. And now someone would feel my pain.

I didn't stop when Junior curled into a ball, I stopped when there was blood on my shoes. And I made him kiss it off. He could barely lift his head but he pursed his lips and put them on the soles of my feet. I stamped his head into the ground a final time and jogged to catch up with the others.

'Wagwan?' Cuba said, too hyped up to make a fuss. I told him that if we were going to do this we couldn't afford to make the same mistakes: this time there would be no loose ends.

St Pauls was almost empty by the time we got there. The bookies were closed, the pubs vacant. There were a few drunks and a handful of nitties but that was it. We drove through the estates over and over again until we gave up and parked in the middle of their block.

There was no one about.

'What we supposed to do now?' one of the yutes asked. Cuba hit him in the mouth and sent him home. No one spoke another word until midway through the early hours of the morning we got a phone call from the other whip; there was a hooded figure sat outside a house to our right.

'Who's dat?' Karma whispered. Everyone ducked lower in the car and tried to make them out, but we couldn't. 'You recognise man, Sayon? Shall we check?'

'Nah, fuck dat,' Cuba said, 'if dey're outside at dis time dey're involved. Yo, Sayon, swap wid me.'

I took the wheel and he climbed into the back. We spun round the block and pulled alongside the yute. I wound the windows down and Cuba and Karma pushed their guns outside the car. A second later a body dropped from the wall and the crime rate rose. We didn't wait to see whether he had left this world or not. We cut, burnt the car and were back in Ends before the sun rose.

37

And so we have the prophetic word confirmed, which you do
well to heed as a light that shines in a dark place, until the
day dawns and the morning star rises in your hearts; knowing
this first, that no prophecy of Scripture is of any private inter-
pretation.

– 2 Peter 1:19–20

A week later it was November, and I was perched on a Stapleton
Road bollard with Karma and Cuba across from me, leaning on
the wall like Mecca and the soul brothers.

'How much you need?'

I shook a cat's hand and another's, and another's. The skies
were grey like the knuckles of the men and women I served. In
this part of the world there weren't four seasons, maybe three,
more likely two. The much-romanticised transitional seasons of
the year were found more in literature than reality.

It had been a week since the shooting and there hadn't been
any repercussions. Not from St Pauls. Nor from the police.
Once again I had got away scot-free. And I was beginning to
worry for our city's law enforcement. The cuts and marks on
my face had either scabbed or become bruises, Ends was eerily

calm, and once the gossip died down, it would be as if nothing had ever happened.

Cuba and Karma were of course unaffected, they were lighting up and chatting shit. And every now and then a yg would come skidding up to us on a push bike carrying news, questions or a man-bag.

Junior was nowhere to be seen, so it seemed he'd gotten my message.

'Enuh what Karma, shut the fuck up,' Cuba laughed, and the weak winter sun shone against the silver in his mouth. 'Man can say what man wants, cuz, cos man knows if you brought a yard gyal to hooyo, she'd have a panic attack, cuz.'

Karma made a 'keke' noise when he laughed and he shuddered like leaves in the wind. 'She rah wouldn't, you know,' he said, 'as long as she's Muslim it's all good, bro.'

Cuba inhaled deeply. 'Ain't no yard gyal turnin Muslim, fam, not for no one; end of the day only yardman turn akh, more time you don't see no gyal revertin do you?'

'You think I couldn't make her, doe?' Karma replied, hurt by his bredrin's vote of no confidence. 'Don't disrespect my ting, fam; man could make any gyal tun Muslim for me, akh – big man ting. Yo, ain't dat Hakim?' he said, and our heads swivelled to find our cousin striding towards us with his typically intimidating gait. He might have left the life, but its effects were long-lasting and the way he carried himself meant he would often frighten people unwittingly.

'What you saying, you man?' Hakim said, once he arrived and he dapped us up. 'Assalamualaikum, brother,' he said to Karma, who returned his salaam. These days it was rare to see him outside of the bakery and rarer to see him without Elia, but as ever I was glad to be in his company. 'What you man on?' he asked.

'Makin money, g,' Cuba grinned, 'what else is there to do?'

'I hear that,' Hakim smiled, but I could see that he was here for reasons other than banter. The last time I'd seen him we were rushing out of the bakery, and it clearly hadn't left his mind. He turned to Karma. 'Yo, before I say anyting, you were in the whip the other night, init?'

'When?' Karma frowned, not one to incriminate himself.

'Last week, after Sayon got beat up.'

'Oh oh yeah,' Karma nodded warily, 'man was deh still, how come?'

Hakim looked at each of us before replying, 'I heard someone got shot in Pauls that night, heard they died.'

I felt like the yutes I'd caught stealing from Viv's, and I saw Karma look away, but when I glanced at Cuba he was still smoking and holding Hakim's eye. 'Yeah, I heard dat still,' he said, as innocent as you like.

'Look,' Hakim said, 'I don't want the ins and outs, but you man know how this ends init?'

Cuba couldn't help but sigh. 'We ain't yutes no more Hakim, blud.'

'I know, I know,' Hakim said, 'that's why I'm coming to you man on a level. If this was back in the day it wouldn't have gone like this, truss me. You know what man was on, but times change. I have to respect you man's ting now, so this is why I'm here now tryna tell you man that it don't end well.'

'Yeah, whatever, man, we know; it either ends in prison or six feet in the ground,' Cuba said, 'you think what you're sayin is new to man, cuz?'

'Cuba, blud,' I tutted, 'hear him out.'

Cuba kissed his teeth and went back to his weed, but he'd already drawn out Hakim. 'You're rah ignorant, blud,' our older cousin said, 'you think cos you got everythin on smash you're winnin in life? Legal money is winning, blud. Not havin to look over your shoulder every two seconds is winnin. Being around niggas dat actually have your back, instead of some opportunist niggas dat would take ps over you every day of the week. You ain't livin, blud.'

'Legal money, yeah?' Cuba smiled. 'If legal money's so sick why you gettin kicked out your bakery, cuz? Dat's what happens when you work for someone else.'

Shit. I knew telling him would backfire.

Hakim visibly darkened, but he wouldn't be deterred. 'Man knows where it ends, cuz,' he said, but he was getting more and more worked up and I didn't see the conversation ending well. I stepped between Hakim and Cuba and steered him away. 'Wasn't losin Hosea enough for you man?' Hakim demanded. 'Sayon,' he said, rounding on me, no doubt pissed that I had told Cuba about the bakery, and embarrassed that I even knew at all, 'wasn't losin Hosea enough, blud? And you as well, Warsame, I know you lost niggas to this street shit.'

Karma nodded, and I knew his thoughts immediately went to Abdimalik.

'Exactly,' Hakim said, 'and don't think man don't know dat from where you're standin deh's no other options, but deh is blud, deh rah is, you man can do anything, wallahi.'

'Bullshit,' Cuba laughed. The only way he knew how to respond to confrontation was with aggression, and though he was doing well and keeping it beneath the surface, I could see how irate he was becoming. 'Every nigga says dat shit, but it's bullshit, wallahi. Deh's bare shit man can't do, cuz. Man can't go uni can I? Don't got the grades. So what? I'm supposed to make ps wid a trade? Become a fuckin baker, like you?'

294

It was the same argument Karma had made to me and, despite trying to keep the peace, I was interested in how Hakim would respond.

'You're already a businessman, Midnight, a fuckin good one as well,' said Hakim, 'so how bout you apply some of dat fuckin energy, dat creativity, to figurin it out. Or what? You want man to hold your hand and show you the way like a fuckin yute?'

'Get dis jokeman out of here, man, wallahi,' Cuba said, flicking his hand in Hakim's direction. 'You made it out, fam; so speak for yourself init, but don't think every man can do what you did just cos you done it, you're one example out of a million, blud.'

I put my arms around Hakim and led him away, but he wasn't quite finished. 'You need to watch yourself, lil man,' he called to Cuba, 'cos you're gonna take a lot of niggas with you when you go down, you're moving xaasid, wallahi.'

Once Hakim and I were at a suitable distance he shrugged me away from him. 'And wagwan for you Sayon, blud? It's like you're tryna disappoint man or sup'm? What the fuck you thinkin ridin out like dat? And you're runnin round tellin everyone me and Elia's private business? Dat shit's got nutun to do wid you, blud. Nutun.'

'You man need to let me help, cuz,' I said. 'I tried tellin Elia dat's what family's for, but unuh tryna keep secrets, cuz.'

'Nah, move wid all dat man, we don't need your fuckin help,' Hakim said. 'You need to focus on yourself and pattern up, Sayon. You're throwin your life away for dis shit? And what about Shona?'

'Me and Shona are done, bro,' I said, 'been done for months.'

'Oh yeah? Is that why she came to man's shop lookin for you today?'

My heart leapt into my mouth.

'Yeah,' he nodded, 'she was deh dis mornin, askin for you, I told her you'd buck her at Nanny's, I should've told her you was posted on the block wid Midnight and Karma like a fuckin idiot.'

'When did you tell her I'd meet her at Nanny's?'

He checked the time. 'Like now-ish.'

I left him where he was and ran down Stapleton Road.

Nanny's door was open, but Shona was nowhere to be found.

I found Nanny juggling Jaden and Jaylen and trying to knead dumplings for the night's giblet gravy. The little boys were covered in more flour than was in the bowl and were looking immensely pleased with themselves. 'Look, go baddah yuh uncle,' Nanny said, when I arrived in the kitchen. The boys faithfully lifted their arms to be held and I hoisted them up into my arms.

'Has Shona been here?' I asked, out of breath and holding my ribs tenderly.

'Nah suh,' Nanny replied.

I supposed I'd gotten here first. I kissed the top of Nanny's head whilst she tended the stove, and resigned myself to waiting.

'Yuh spoke to Lyle since yuh lef?' Nanny asked after a second.

'Nah,' I replied. Now that he'd used his trump card there was no reason to spare the man any mind. He was nothing to me. And if he decided to go the police there was nothing I could do about it, but by now I didn't think he would. He'd already punished me enough.

Shona was on my mind more than anything else. I had spent the past several months convincing myself that she was out of my life. That there was no possibility of a future between us.

Never fully believing it myself. And now she was back. And once again I felt that there was light on the horizon.

'Lyle all right, man,' Nanny mused, 'im juss too concerned wid im God an not di people im share di worl wid, enuh?'

'You say "im God" like say he ain't yours as well, Nanny.'

Jaden wriggled free of my arms and ran to the living room but Jaylen was comfy where he was. Nanny ripped a piece of a fried dumpling and made Jaylen blow on it before popping it into his mouth.

'Im everybody God,' she shrugged, 'Muslim, Christian, Indi. All ahh wi pray to di same God, no matter wat wi call im. Dat's why wen Akim did tell mi im waan call God, Allah, I didn't mind enuh? Not one bit. Nah suh. Kaaz ahh di end ahh di day, wi all in di same boat. An wahum wid Shona? Yuh seh yuh spectin er?' The doorbell rang and was answered. 'But wait,' Nanny smiled, 'speak of an angel, come in lovely, come in.'

I followed her eye and saw that Shona had arrived.

Nanny took Jaylen from my arms and rested a hand on my cheek as she shuffled past. 'Membah wat mi tell yuh bout dis one, Sayon, yuh affi old on tight.'

I met Shona's eye and without a word she turned and walked outside. There was no room for negotiation so I followed her into the front yard, but Shona didn't stop there, she led me from my nanny's all the way to the cycle path that ran behind the house.

There she rounded on me, her eyes wet and her hand stinging as it slapped across my face. She told me to talk, so I did. My heart wasn't on my sleeve; I cut it from my chest and offered it at her altar.

I told her about Cordell, about Junior and his involvement. I told her how her papa had witnessed it all and had used it to manoeuvre me into the church. I told her about the tension between us and how we had tried to hide it from her.

She began crying in earnest halfway through, but when I went to comfort her she pushed me away and motioned for me to continue. So I told her about losing the house-atop-the-hill, the St Pauls shooting and the argument with Hakim. Finally I told her about Winnie, about Cuba, and about the overdose we induced. And then I broke down too, because, as Nanny said: after all I had done, it was the least I could do.

When I was a yute I cried often; I cried when Killa took my toys, when Hosea and Jamaal forced me to be a dummy for their wrestling moves. And I bawled most when my mama promised to collect me from Nanny's and forgot.

A combination of beating and relentless mocking had long sucked it from me, and the last time I had cried was as a young boy, but standing in front of the woman who I had lost and loved brought the weight of it all crashing down upon my shoulders.

'You lied to me, Say,' she said, caught somewhere between vexation and upset. 'I distinctly told you not to lie to me, but you did anyway. And Winnie? *Winnie*, Sayon? That's your cousin! You loved her. How the hell could you let Cuba do that?'

I had no words left to defend myself.

Shona squeezed her eyes shut and ummed and erred, searching for a way to articulate her feelings without any more waterworks. 'I'm sorry about the yard, Say. I know how much that meant to you, but you can't go around deciding what I can and can't know about you, either. I want it all or I don't want any of it, and that's for me to decide. Not you, my dad, not anyone else.'

It was all too much for her. Not only had her father fallen from the pedestal that she had him upon her entire life; I had disappointed her too.

And what a strange emotion disappointment was to circum-navigate. It wasn't a mountain to climb, or a valley to trek. It didn't share the emotional highs that anger brought, nor was it low enough to wallow in depression. It was slow and stagnant, like a marsh on a moor. It sapped your will and made your legs tired. I knew it well. It was where I imagined Winnie.

'What made you come back today?' I pried gently.

'I wasn't going to,' she replied, her voice grittier than before, 'you know how many times I've cried over you, Say? How many nights? It had to stop somewhere, and I needed the answers, so here I am.'

She told me that her and Pastor Lyle's relationship was shot to pieces. That after I'd run from the house she'd confronted him about it all, about the alcohol too, which brought Marcia running. Once she'd calmed down, she'd made him promise not to go to the police, and the three of them had argued for the rest of the week until Marcia took her to spend the weekend away. She said she needed some time apart and didn't know when next they'd speak.

'You know what pisses me off the most? You both treated me like some little girl,' she said, 'like some naive little princess, like I didn't grow up in the exact same place you guys did, like I haven't been next to you forever, Say. I don't get it.' She laughed without any mirth. 'How could you not come to me with this? You think I'm too precious or sup'm? You think I would've gone to the police?'

'I think you would've left me.'

'Did I leave you when you went jail?' she said. 'No. I told you back then that Christianity isn't black and white, that I'm not black and white, but you couldn't trust me to love you and did the one thing I told you not to do. I could've left a million times, Sayon – you're not exactly a fuckin saint – but I didn't, and that should've been enough for you. The two people I thought knew me best don't know me at all.

'Whatever, it's over now,' she said, wiping tears from her face with the back of her hand. 'Me and Chen got a distribution offer from a major label by the way, so I'm moving to London, cos that's where they are and it'll just make things easier. I don't know how long I'll be there, Sayon, maybe for ever. That's why I came today.'

And although I didn't deserve to feel heartbroken, I did.

'This could spark my whole career,' she continued, speaking as if to a stranger, 'get me everything I've ever wanted. Everything I've ever worked for. I don't know why I'm telling you this to be honest, but you know what's mad? I'm so used to you, Say, you've been right there next to me forever, so in spite of everything, you're still the first person that comes to mind whenever anything happens, whenever I have any news.'

'Shona—' I tried, but she held a hand up and stopped me again.

'No, don't tell me anything right now, Say. I don't need to hear it right now.' She swallowed and drew determination from the pit of her stomach. 'I'm gonna go London, and you're gonna stay here and think about what you want from your life, because no one else can live it for you. I need actions, Say. Your words just don't cut it any more.'

It was strange, but with both of us wiping tears from our faces, I felt the best I had in months. I needed hope to survive, and finally I felt a glimmer. It may have been a goodbye, but it didn't feel final. And she may have been off to London, but if I could change my life around whilst she was away maybe, just maybe, we could try things again. She stood on her tip-toes and I crouched to let her plant a kiss on my forehead.

And then she was gone.

I promised myself that for the time being I wouldn't chase her, because if she needed some time, then I would finally put her happiness first.

As I walked back to Nanny's I recalled how Pastor Lyle had said that Shona wouldn't be able to forgive murder and, frozen by fear, I hadn't once considered the fact that Nanny had.

Pastor Lyle might have thought her a far cry from Christianity, but she had done her best to raise every single member of the Hughes family to love one another as they loved themselves. And no matter the foolishness we brought into her home, she loved us. For all the theorisation and ceremony of Pastor Lyle, my papa and mama, they didn't come close to the praxis of their religion's core belief; God – Allah – is love.

And like Nanny, Shona was too.

38

In the name of Allah, the most Compassionate and Merciful.

– al-Quran

The following week, I handed my line back to Cuba, for good this time, because if actions spoke louder than words, then I prayed they would reach London before I did. Once I had my life together I'd decided that I wouldn't wait; I would run to Shona. I would show her exactly how serious I was about her, and about the future we could build.

It was time for the turning of a new leaf.

I may not have been able to get one of those well-paid nine-to-fives that Karma spoke about on account of my record, and the house-atop-the-hill was still being broken into flats, but I had my savings, and there was the bakery.

Hakim and I hadn't made up since our disagreement, but I planned to hash things out over the coming days, and I would speak to him about it then.

Cuba was more understanding this time around. I saw him the day after Shona and I spoke and he took the brick phone with an expectant smile. 'You sure bout dis? Dis the last bludclart time we do dis, wallahi.'

I was sure, but when I went to explain my reasonings he stopped me.

'I get it man, you're special.' He spoke as if he had known this day was coming all along. He may have dismissed it the first time, but that was because I had dismissed him. This time it was different; this time the love hadn't changed. 'You might be the one don other dan Hakim dat can make it out dis shit,' he said, 'so go for it big bro.' We embraced but I couldn't let what he'd said pass. I asked him what it was he saw in me, what he had always seen in me.

'How many GCSEs you got?' he responded, tossing the phone from one hand to the other like it was a satsuma.

'All the ones I took.'

'So what like eight? Nine?'

'Sup'm like dat, yeah.'

'And you and Hakim's gyal are still close init? What's dem man's name again?'

'Elia.'

'Yeah, see you got the grades to do sup'm in life, sup'm real. And you got peoples outside of dis, you get me? Even the church took you in, blud. You think dey would've done dat for man?' He laughed like lifers discussing redemption over a game of cards. 'No way, fam. Even back in school times the teachers would always tell man how well you were doin when man was doin shit; I don't know if dey was tryna motivate man or what but it didn't work, wallahi.

'Same way at Nanny's every man had higher expectations for you from the jump. Nanny would've never let you drop out of school, fam, but she let me. Everyone just looks at man like one devil yute. And what? Cos I favour some old relo? What a shit reason, blud. But it's calm doe, cos man never felt dat from you.

You always thought man was the same and treated man like your brother, your real brother, so I'll always love you for dat, cuzzy.'

His face grew sombre and his words gravelled. 'I'd do anything for you because of dat, wallahi. Truss me. But we ain't the same, man. All the shit I've done is unforgivable, remember it was me dat dragged you into dis in the first place. Man was built for dis. I'm stuck in dis shit, g. No God can love a nigga like me. Don't matter if it's Jesus or Allah, blud. It's sup'm man came to terms wid a long time ago, you get me, but you? Hakim was wrong about me, but he was right about you. So go grab your girl and don't make the dumb mistake of thinkin you only got one path to take.'

I told him that he was wrong, on most accounts, but one in particular: it was I who had always needed him, and it was I who should have been thanking him, not the other way round. I wasn't special. It was because of Elia and Shona that I had done well in school. And it was because of Shona that I was still afloat. Which is why I now had to make real changes.

Days later I sought Hakim.

I asked him to step outside the bakery for a second and he followed me, sceptical though he was. 'Wagwan?' he asked. 'Everything good with you and Shona?'

I relayed to him all that had transpired between us and he brightened. Then I told him that I planned to revert to Islam and all the angst in his spirit fell like dew from a waymark. He threw himself around me and dragged me into the bakery. 'Elia, Elia,' he screeched, 'the lil man's revertin, alhamdulillah, I prayed this day would come, what did I tell you?'

Elia's face shone with a peaceful twinkle. 'Masha'Allah,' she grinned.

I gave them my reasons. Islam would fill that which I had always lacked; discipline. Its structure would be the ruler to my newfound growth, a tangible change.

Then I heaped any praise that I hadn't saved for Cuba and Shona on the couple. They were the example I needed. Elia's, whose precious love was cut from the same cloth as Nanny's and Cuba's. And Hakim's example: where for years I had been looking for a shred of evidence that I could exist as my most honest self, balanced between the two worlds I inhabited, Hakim was all the proof I had ever needed.

'When are you taking your Shahadah?' Elia asked.

'The imam's ready now,' I replied, then I turned to Hakim, 'I want you to be there as witness, family, Karma's here too, he's waitin round the corner.'

'Then let's go,' Hakim shouted, he rushed to grab his coat, kissed his wife and we were out the door in a flash. 'Now you've done this Cuba won't be far behind.' He beamed as the three of us strode for the masjid, but I didn't share in his optimism.

Still, I knew that every time I touched my head to the mat, every rakat, and at the end of every salat, Cuba would be in my duas. And whether Allah interfered or not, perhaps as Hakim had been my example, I could one day be Cuba's.

lā 'ilāha 'illā-llāh, muḥammadun rasūlu-llāh.

There is no god but Allah, and Muhammad is the messenger of Allah.

Alhamdulillah.

★ ★ ★

After I spoke those fateful words, Hakim, Karma and I strolled from the mosque accompanied by more Black Muslims than a Tory could shake a stick at.

Old friends walked and talked with their hands clasped behind their backs and the younger men went off to play football in their white khamiis and Nikes. The imam lent me a thobe in order to feel the part, and amongst the wave of black and brown faces that flooded the streets I certainly did.

The mosque lay beside a community centre and eyeballed a freehouse across the street. Through no volition of their own, the community centre wasn't good for much. It hosted a couple of weekly exercise classes for the elderly and was the home of Shona's old radio station, but beyond that it was closed more often than open.

The proximity of the pub was clearly a point of frustration for the Muslims. Not long after prayer had finished an inebriated cadaan stumbled from the establishment and started pissing against the wall, chorusing 'You'll Never Walk Alone' in full spirit. Karma kissed his teeth. Another nigga muttered, 'White people are so tapped, wallahi,' as he passed.

There were a few Pakistanis and Arabs, but most of the attendees were Somali and Djiboutian. I saw some Caribbeans amongst the crowds but we were noticeably absent. If this had been a Hausa mosque we might have been difficult to spot, but amongst East Africans we stuck out like sore thumbs.

It occurred to me as I people-watched, that if it were not for his people's own self-hatred, Karma may not have been as close with Cuba and me. And perhaps he might have lived a different life if the bullies hadn't forced him into our company. Perhaps as the Patois and Somali languages were poured into the Black-British pot our cultures would grow in love for one another, but there was an equal chance they would mix like oil and water and refuse to be branded by the disingenuous stamp of race.

Karma's line called him away, leaving Hakim and me to wander back to the bakery.

'Have you decided on a name?'

'A name?'

'Yeah, your Muslim name,' Hakim said excitedly. 'You're starting afresh, init.'

'I hear you,' I laughed. And I had landed upon a name; a lapel pin to wear with pride. 'Abanus,' I announced. It meant ebony.

'So what? You man are Midnight and Ebony now?'

I was glad my cousin had caught on so quickly. 'One and the same,' I smiled.

The faraway sun left the air mild, and the day was pleasant enough to delve into an uncomfortable tête-à-tête. 'So, man's been thinkin bout dis bakery situation, Hakim.'

'Ah lowe it, lil man,' Hakim said. It seemed Abanus would take a while to catch on. 'Don't ruin this blessed day, akh.'

'Nah we need to talk about it,' I insisted. I refused to let them squander the bakery because of Hakim's pride. As far as I was concerned it was something he'd have to swallow, otherwise I'd go over him and fix it myself.

'I can't have any more haram money in our bakery,' he explained, 'I know you helped man when man was under it before, but you're a Muslim now, you get me? You have to understand.'

I held a hand in front of him and paused him in the middle of the road. 'Hakim,' I began, 'you rah have to let me do dis, blud, I got all dis cash just lying around, g—'

'Give it to charity,' Hakim interrupted, 'that's zakat.'

'Nah, fam, I worked hard for dis shit, I ain't giving it to no stranger. I'd rather give it to the people I love, you get me? You have to let me do dis,' I said again. 'Wallahi, man needs dis, blud. If man can do dis for you den man can start makin dat legal money you was on about. Den man can be proper on deen. And man can show Shona dat man's changed, fam, dat man's serious now, do you understand? Dis is man's way out.'

He promised he would think about it, which was all I could ask for, so I dropped it.

Days became weeks until a month had passed since I'd seen Shona last. It was nearing the last month of the year, and I was ready to run to her. I woke early on the day I was due to leave for London. I packed my belongings, walked around Ends, and ate a meal with Karma in the greasy café.

By mid-morning I returned to Nanny's to say goodbye. I hadn't spoken to Shona yet, but I knew where she was staying and looked forward to presenting her with the new me. I was slightly nervous about how she'd take my reversion, and Cuba called me an optimist, but I had faith that she would see it for the progress it was.

But saying goodbye proved more difficult than I imagined. When I arrived I saw leng-man swarming Nanny's front yard like Black yutes outside high-rises, and I could see some rifling through the house itself. Armed police, with guns on their hips or slung around their shoulders, were everywhere.

Two officers had my uncle Michael pinned to the tarmac with their knees dug into the small of his back and their rifles pointed at the rest of my family. Uncle Michael was singing at the top of his lungs. Beside him Cuba's head was being pressed against the pavement. His face was cut where they had struck him and he was swearing blind, threatening the families of every officer present.

Aunty Paulette was pinned to the wall and Jamaal was engaged in a shouting match with several senior-looking feds. Uncle Marlon held Aunty Winifred in his arms. Killa was fixing a durag over his waves, looking shifty. Uncle Calvin and Bunny were nowhere to be seen.

The air above my family was thick with smoke like a half-full rubble bag: everyone who had a hand free was puffing on something. Nanny stood in the doorway with Mister Sinclair massaging her shoulders. Her eyes found me amongst the small crowd that gathered on the other side of the road and begged me to run. I wasn't sure whether the feds were there for Cuba, Jamaal, Calvin, Bunny, me or anyone else; nor was she, but neither of us wanted to find out the hard way.

She blew a kiss and I pocketed it for safekeeping.

I made it as far as the coach station before three squad cars pulled my taxi and arrested me on suspicion of murder.

39

The repayment of a bad action is one equivalent to it, but if someone pardons and puts things right, his reward is with Allah.

– Ash-Ṣhūrā 42:40

The feds said they had a witness that tied me to the St Pauls shooting.

And though the witness remained unnamed, I knew it was the little man, without a shadow of doubt. He was the only person who knew enough, and had reason enough to tie me to the scene of the crime. Junior was our very own Judas. And like Cuba had told Jaden and Jaylen: snitches got killed. The rule was age-old and set in stone.

The little man's possibilities diminished the day he witnessed Cordell's murder. It was sad, but Ends was like that sometimes. Anyone could catch a foot on the roots protruding from the bank and land face-first in the deep end. And he might have been a product of his days, but we would hold him accountable for his choices.

* * *

I was held for twenty-four hours in Horfield Prison and faced multiple counts including possession of a firearm, criminal use of a firearm and first-degree murder. Junior hadn't given up Cuba or Karma but the feds knew there were other people involved because two different guns had been used. So the very same day they arrested me they asked which of my cousins was there.

'Was it the big fucker' – Jamaal – 'or the little devil?' – Cuba. 'Or how about Funds?' they asked. 'Is he back in business?'

I only opened my mouth to repeat for the thousandth time, 'No comment.'

Overnight, I prayed for salvation in my cell. Not because I deserved it – on the contrary, I thought, if anything, Winnie's death warranted my sentencing. It would fulfil some sort of poetic justice. Still, I put my head on the mat because if I spent any more time inside I wouldn't be allowed to leave the world in which I lived and, given my recent change of heart, the timing would have been too cruel.

It was exactly as Nanny said. Her Majesty was an expert at the promotion of retrogression. And I think it fair to consider her prisons the ultimate death of possibility. Even more so than a six-foot grave, bearing in mind the chance of Jannah.

On account of the nature of my alleged crimes I was kept in custody and attended the magistrates' court for pre-trial the next day.

My entire family showed out. Nanny fiddled with her cross. Viv couldn't make it because he was in Jamaica. Hakim and Karma appeared the most concerned. Uncle Calvin kept his eyes closed throughout, no doubt to combat the flashbacks. Bunny chewed his nails, Uncle Marlon and Aunty Winifred held hands, the rest of the aunties held the children and Jamaal calmly

311

avoided the police officers' glares. And Cuba – Cuba was the angriest I'd ever seen him. It seemed that he too had realised that Junior was at fault, and I worried for the guilt it made him feel.

And just before the proceedings began, I saw Shona arrive with Elia. Actions were indeed louder than words, and my actions had brought her all the way from London.

She refused to meet my eye, just like she had outside Nanny's on Valentine's. And I didn't blame her. She, just like me, would have been harbouring hope, a desperate, almost laughable desire that she would one day return and find a changed man. And from where she was sitting in the courtroom, I had failed her. I wanted nothing more than to break free from my cuffs and convince her otherwise, but since she refused my eye, all I could do was leave it in the hands of Allah.

Three cadaans sat across from me when I pleaded 'not guilty'. With or without a witness, the prosecutor had little to go by. The police loved fearmongering as much as the church, and a part of me believed they were only trying to get to Cuba or Jamaal through me. Still, the magistrates were White like baby sick, so they accepted the limited evidence and established the case, moving me to the Crown Court.

On the bright side, Crown Court was held within a couple of weeks and the next judge waived the relevance of my prior offence, because I'd been a minor at the time. And since the only evidence was eyewitness testimony, I was allowed to go home and await my next court appearance, provided I gave them notice about any changes of address, surrendered my passport and reported to the nearest police station every day at five. But anything was better than a cell.

Everyone was waiting for me at Nanny's. They cheered as I

stepped from my taxi. Immediately Cuba tried to apologise for not handling Junior as he said he would, and begged me to let him make it right, but I had more pressing matters; Shona was nowhere to be seen, but she was still in the city, so I hurried to find her.

I caught Shona as she was leaving her parents' house, two suitcases hot at her heels, on her way to the train station.

'Shona!' I yelled.

When she saw me she slowed but didn't stop, she would've played our reunion a hundred times over, with a hundred faces, a hundred opening words and a hundred different tones with which to say them, but I doubted she envisioned it like this. 'It's like Daddy said, you don't want to change, Say,' she said.

'How is this my fault?' I said. 'I told you what happened in Pauls.'

'Yeah,' Shona snorted. 'Well at least you didn't lie to me about it this time,' she said with as much sarcasm as she could muster. 'Is the little man the witness? What was his name again?' she continued, but I was tired and had reached the end of my tether.

I wanted a chance to revel in my present freedom, in my unfortunate arrest that had brought about our timely reunion. And, more than anything, I wanted to tell her about the changes I had made, how ready I was for love.

'Can we talk about something else?' I asked. 'How've you been? How's London? What's dis music ting sayin?' But my pleasantries were gobbledygook, gibberish to set aside like an apple pie on a fairy-tale windowsill.

'Who's the witness?' she demanded.

'The little man.'

She humphed like her papa. 'So what? Cuba's gonna sort him out for you and then you'll get away with this one too? What's that gonna be then, Say? Three bodies you and Cuba got? Four? You two are basically the grim reapers now, aren't you?' She shuddered and her fury became upset. 'This wasn't how this was supposed to go, Say. You were supposed to get your act together so we could sort this out. You were supposed to have changed.'

'I have changed, Shona,' I shouted. I grabbed her by the shoulders and her suitcases fell to the ground. I would do anything, give anything, to convince her. 'Look at me,' I begged, and she did. 'I've stopped juggin, I've given my line back to Cuba, for real dis time, I don't deal nutun no more, wallahi billahi, I don't.

'I've become Muslim too, Shona. I took my Shahadah with Hakim and Karma the other day. And I know it's not Christianity, but you know how man feels bout Christianity; it never could've been for man. But I got a good feelin about dis Islam shit, wallahi. I'm finally on the right path, you know? The path you always wanted me on. And I'm doin it for myself, Shona, for real. Dis ain't sup'm you'll have to force me to do, you know? I'm serious about dis. And I'll prove it, cos with all the ps man was gonna use for the Clifton house, I'm gonna buy the bakery – Elia and Hakim's bakery, Shona. Serious shit. The owner's lookin to move dem out.

'At first man was thinkin man would just help dem out, but den I thought I may as well just cop the whole ting you get me? Kill two birds with one stone. Dat way we got your music ting and we got property now. We could build it up, start a chain. Fuck the yard in Clifton. I don't need dat shit when I have you. You have to truss me, Shona, I had everyting patterned before dem man arrested me over dis bullshit. Believe me, I've been making changes, Shona, I promise I have.'

She waited until I tailed off and gently shook herself loose. 'But it's not bullshit, is it, Say?' she said. 'You might go away for this, for a long time, and I told you I'm not waiting for you again—'

'Do you trust me?'

'Say—'

'Shona,' I said, 'do you trust me?'

'I do,' she said after a second, and it hurt me seeing how difficult it was for her to say. 'It makes me feel like an idiot,' she admitted, 'but you know I trust you, Say.' I promised her that everything would be fine; if the feds had had any further evidence I would have been denied bail and held in Horfield much longer. 'But if you go back—'

'I won't,' I swore, and I thought my conviction might comfort her.

'Say,' she stuttered, 'I've got something to tell you, Say, but first you have to promise that you love me.'

Immediately, I promised.

She was ten weeks pregnant – with twins. And her baby-daddy was a murderer. She had known a few weeks after I'd left their home.

She had planned on telling me outside of Nanny's, but became too overwhelmed. Instead she told herself she'd wait for me to pattern up, and when I was good and ready and came to fetch her, she would tell me then, but my arrest had ruined it.

Shona left her suitcases on the kerb and I drew her into my arms, whispering assurances like the genius sang the blues. She only repeated, 'If you go back I'm stuck, Say, I'm stuck,' over and over. But her fears wouldn't come true. I wouldn't answer to any man-made law. I had stacks of shoebox savings, enough to make our life comfortable. I would buy the bakery and stay where I was. Her music would buss and she could move between cities. And life would be as we made it.

I wouldn't be like my papa and mama. Nothing would come between my children and me. If something reared its head I would tear it clean off.

I was happy. Before she left I told her I wanted girls: Mecca and Medina. Two innocent offerings to make amends, because for the rest of my life I would swap good deeds for bad until I had burdened the scales in my favour.

Unfortunately, the price of a future with the love of my life and my children was a final transgression.

40

We decreed upon the Children of Israel that whoever kills a soul unless for a soul or for corruption in the land – it is as if he had slain mankind entirely. And whoever saves one – it is as if he had saved mankind entirely.

– Surah al-Mā'idah 5:32

It was damson dark by the time Cuba came to me. I found him perched on Nanny's wall, wrapped in his black clothes and gloves, he fingered the trigger of a gun hidden in his trousers, and his inner chaos was back. I asked him if the deed was done. And he responded by looking down the length of Stapes.

I wondered what he found when he looked at it: Stapleton Road. Whether he bought into the colonial lies and saw gold in its concrete slabs; whether he looked up at the billboards and lusted over the life they sold. I wondered if he remembered the days when we treated it as our playground: the rails and fences our swings, and the benches our climbing frame. I wondered whether he saw it as a broad road at all, or whether he saw a muddy river like I did.

'It's done,' he said at last, 'for real dis time.'

He told me how it went down. How he and Karma had

hunkered low in a dinger just outside Junior's parents' house, waiting for the moment the little man showed his face. They were draped in black again. A colour the West knew well as a plague. A colour of bad omens and ignorance. One that spoke ill of the same people who claimed allegiance to its name and invited mockery from every corner. A colour that carved fate into stones and cast them into the sea.

But Junior's parents were wise in their caution, they knew the trouble their son had found himself in, so they drew their curtains and left them drawn.

Cuba told me how he had no idea whether Junior was hiding with them or not. In fact, if he wasn't maddened by the idea of losing me to the system, he was sure their wisdom might have prevailed, but a mind maddened is a mind lost, and in his insanity Cuba told me that he wasn't concerned about this world or the hereafter.

He was back to being the lost soul who had murdered one cousin to save another, so both he and Karma rolled any thought of repercussions into the blunts they strapped, and smoked away their disquiet. Once they'd had their fill, they donned their ski masks, took their weapons and kicked Junior's door in; they put shots through him and retreated into the night.

Shona would work out what had happened when she heard the news. She might even ask me if I had anything to do with it. And if she did, I would tell her the truth. I would never lie to her again. And I knew that she would believe it to be wrong; but by killing Junior, Cuba had removed the one thing still fastening me to that old world of ours, and he had given my family and me a future.

And now here he was.

But there was something about the way he was relaying

what had gone down, whether it was the finality or the rasp with which he enunciated his words – it should have given me an inkling that something was wrong, but it didn't. He'd kept his eyes on Stapes whilst he retold the story, but once he was finished his attention returned to me. A lack of sleep and his addiction to trees had rendered his eyes two carmine pools, full of urgency. 'You got anyting else dat needs handlin?' he asked.

'Nah,' I said. 'Nah, long as everything's good on your side den we're all good, g.'

'Good,' he nodded. 'The yard?'

'Still being broken into flats,' I answered.

We fell quiet. There were too many words to say, too many directions to take and neither of us wanted to lay ourselves bare.

Junior's betrayal weighed on him. I could see it in his slouch and in the paranoia with which he gripped the gun. Allah's fondness for irony meant that he had found himself in the same fenland where Shona was, caught in the same soft mud that had become Winnie's home; except that he was disappointed with himself, a fate often worse.

'You gonna cut till dis dies down?' I asked.

'Yeah, man.'

'When you gonna be back?'

'Dunno, cuz.' He was despondent and downcast, so I tried perhaps the only way to get through to him and told him about Shona and the twins.

He snorted and smiled in disbelief, then he laughed from his belly and leapt to hug me. 'You're gonna be a pops?'

'You're gonna be an uncle again, g.' I laughed.

He hurdled the wall and ran into the middle of the road, blasting his troubles aside. 'No way!' he screamed at the top of his lungs. 'You're gonna be a pops? Dis is mad. What the fuck? What did Shona say, blud? Is she happy?'

'She's in shock, fam. She's happy, doe.'

'Yeah, fuckin hell, man's in shock too,' he laughed. 'Ay, I'm proud of you, killy. And I love you, big man ting; I love you. You're gonna be a sick pops. Know dat. For real.' He came back to the wall and sat there smiling at me until it almost became uncomfortable. He clapped his hands. 'Calm,' he announced, some decision of his made.

'Wagwan?'

'When dey being born?'

'Just over six months.'

'Say nutun, I'll be back dem times,' he promised; but again, something seemed off. Then he twisted from the wall and set off down the river banks.

'Blud, where you going?' I yelled after him.

He waved over his shoulder and I could see the expression on his face; it was resolute, like junkies shopping for spoons. 'You got responsibilities now, akh,' he said. 'Tell Shona if the yutes come out dark dey'll end up like me and nobody wants dat.'

And that was the last I saw him: walking down Stapes, waving at me as he went.

Some of the family were confused about his disappearance, especially when Karma came back from his own extended hiatus six months later, but I wasn't. Because Cuba didn't agree that Junior was the final thing tying me to our past; he believed that he was.

Once, Hakim had explained the depravity that Hosea's loss had pushed him into, what losing a little brother was like, and back then I thought I understood, because to Cuba and me, death was a playmate. The girl next-door who we invited outside. He had flirted with her and I had too. But it wasn't until Cuba left that I finally understood why Hakim centred his day around Allah. Why he preached so often and worked so hard. Because 'cousin' wasn't a word that could explain our bond. Even 'brother' couldn't fully. A piece of my soul walked down Stapleton Road that night, and it was a piece that never came back.

It was December, almost the New Year and the troubles of June seemed a lifetime away.

Hakim and Elia came around as I knew they would; they knew my money was haram, but they couldn't pass an opportunity to help set me on the right path.

In recent weeks I had learnt that we, as Muslims, begin most things with the recitation of 'Bismillah ar-Rahman ar-Rahim': in the name of Allah the most Compassionate and the most Merciful. We do not invoke Allah's other names nearly as often as we invoke Him as Merciful and Compassionate, which tells us everything we should know about how to carry ourselves. And one day I prayed Elia and Hakim would be able to forgive themselves and recognise what they had done for me as un-sullied mercy and compassion, as I already knew it to be.

In the meantime, I promised them that Shona and I would treat their bakery as our perpetual residence. Our haven that ignored the slush from the madness outside. To the previous landlady it may've been a liability, but she didn't love the area like we did. She didn't know Stapes.

I bought the flat above the bakery too, planning to do as much of the work that needed doing myself, in time for the babies, who were due in the summer. And it gave Shona a place to stay now she'd moved out of her parents' house, whilst she was bouncing between Bristol and London.

She'd left on amicable terms and, using Marcia as the mediator, had tentatively begun to repair her relationship with Pastor Lyle.

Eventually, she wanted for our yutes to have a strong connection with him, and now that he had no hold over me, I didn't mind. I vowed I wouldn't become the man that he was, I would allow him his weaknesses in the same manner Allah allowed me mine. So I supported the mending of their relationship and we largely stayed out of each other's way. And when the twins were good and ready Shona and I would settle down and infuse the flat and bakery with new life.

Given time, the cabinets would be gold, and we would wear green aprons of fine silk and brocade, and recline on adorned couches. Excellent was the reward for our patience, for our change, and good was the resting place we owned.

The arrangement made Elia happy, and she was made happier because of the twins, although she and Shona were refusing to name them Mecca and Medina. Shona wanted to call them Ari (short for Aretha) and Billie (as in Holiday). Elia wanted to call them Maya and Amina. And for some reason we all imagined them girls, perhaps because we all wanted them to live decidedly different lives from the ones their pops and uncle had.

I informed the police and courts that I'd changed address, and my court date was set for the spring of the following year. Of course Junior's death was treated with incredible suspicion; I was placed under surveillance and Cuba on the Most Wanted list, but I knew they wouldn't find him, and with Junior gone I felt confident about the outcome of the trial.

Thus I spent my days leading up to the twins' arrival planning to expand my business. I'd decided I would turn the bakery into a chain and take it to other ends around the country, areas whose identities were being threatened, where I could instill a sense of community. Real community. Because Shona and I had decided that we would stay in Ends whether the house-atop-the-hill ever became available or not. I figured if we wanted to make a change in my world it wouldn't make sense to leave it. And besides, if I left our world the same as when Cuba left it, then what sort of brother was I?

'I'll see you later, Nanny,' I called. I held Jaylen and Jaden either side of me and was taking them to see my shop.

I smiled as we stepped on to Stapes and hoped my little nephews would come to love it as much as I did, because there weren't any roads like mine anywhere in the world.

Roads whose houses were like lofty mansions, with roofs made from the hollow of a single pearl. Whose dwellers were like brilliant stars, far away in the east or in the west of the horizon. Roads that tracked their way from one side of Ends to the other, without a single tree, except that whose trunk was made of gold.

The shop fronts were the finest souks and the north wind blew and scattered fragrances on faces and clothes. Anyone who came went back to their families with their faces shining. The street was a river of clarified honey, and its banks were musk. There was no sun and moon, no day or night; passers-by knew morning and evening from the light that shone from the open door of my bakery.

Together with Jaylen and Jaden we sailed over the pavements in December as the natives we were; accustomed to the breaks in the concrete.

'Dis is the place,' I told them, 'the place man's bought. I

know you man been here before, but it's mine now, you get me?' The boys looked up in amazement. 'By the way,' I continued, lowering my voice and drawing them near, 'Hakim told man whoever gets to the kitchen first, eats whatever he wants.' The boys looked at one another, fire like jasper stones ablaze in their eyes, then they turned and raced into my little slice of Heaven. Inside I heard Elia shriek for them to slow down and Hakim roar with laughter.

I paused at the entrance before following them in. 'What do you reckon dese man do to afford all dis, cuz?' I heard little Cuba ask. A smile played at my lips and there were tears in my eyes; I would carry him with me for ever, just like he had carried me.

All in all, it was an end of sorts. The end of lives. The end of life as I knew it. I was born to one tributary and cast from the other, still fated to follow the river to its mouth. But they say that an end is often a beginning, and this was one of those times.

Ends was what we called my world. I only hoped it would be known as such; a world without end.

Acknowledgements

First and foremost, alhamdulillah. Eternal gratitude to my parents for providing a haven and their endless love. Love to my brothers and my sister, some of only a few people I care about more than myself. Big up my peoples, who are too many to name, but whose turns of phrase, jokes and lives appear throughout the novel, and who have helped shape me into who I am today, and who I will become tomorrow. Love to my part of the city for being home and showing me the richness of life. To my agent, Anne-Marie Doulton, for taking a chance. And a final thanks to my editor at Wildfire, Ella Gordon, and her assistant, Serena Arthur, for their wisdom and passion.

Everyone I love can find themselves in here in some way.

About the Author

Moses McKenzie is of Caribbean descent and grew up in Bristol, where he still lives and writes full-time. He is twenty-four years old. *An Olive Grove in Ends* is his first novel.